An Assembly Such as This

A NOVEL OF

Fitzwilliam Darcy,

GENTLEMAN

PAMELA AIDAN

A TOUCHSTONE BOOK
Published by Simon & Schuster
New York   London   Toronto   Sydney

TOUCHSTONE
Rockefeller Center
1230 Avenue of the Americas
New York, NY 10020

TOUCHSTONE and colophon are registered trademarks
of Simon & Schuster Inc.

First Touchstone Edition 2006

For information regarding special discounts for bulk purchases,
please contact Simon & Schuster Special Sales at 1-800-456-6798
or business@simonandschuster.com.

Designed by Jan Pisciotta

Manufactured in the United States of America

10   9   8   7   6   5   4

Library of Congress Cataloging-in-Publication Data

Aidan, Pamela
    An assembly such as this : a novel of Fitzwilliam Darcy , gentleman /
    Pamela Aidan. —1st Touchstone ed.
        p. cm
    1. Darcy, Fitzwilliam (Fictitious character)—Fiction. 2. Bennet, Elizabeth
    (Fictitious character)—Fiction. 3. England—Fiction. I. Title.
PS3601.I33A94 2006
813'.6—dc22

                                                2006041801

ISBN-13: 978-0-7432-9134-7 (pbk.)
ISBN-10:   0-7432-9134-4 (pbk.)

To my father and mother,
Eugene and Elaine Stanley,
who gave me the freedom
to try

Contents

An Assembly Such as This

CHAPTER 1

At Such an Assembly as This

*F*itzwilliam George Alexander Darcy rose from his seat in the Bingley carriage and reluctantly descended to earth before the assembly hall above the only inn to which the small market town of Meryton could lay claim. A window from the hall above opened, allowing the lively but poorly executed music of a country dance to invade the serenity of the night air. Grimacing, he looked down at the hat in his hands and then, with a sigh, positioned it at precisely the correct angle on his head. *How, exactly, did you allow Bingley to maneuver you into this ill-conceived foray into country society?* he berated himself. But before he could begin a review of the events that had deposited him there, a hound perched on a nearby carriage sent up a mournful howl.

"Precisely," Darcy commiserated aloud as he turned to the rest of his party. Immediately, he saw that his friend's sisters held the same expectation for an enjoyable evening as himself. The expression that passed between them as they shook out their skirts was at once equal parts elegant disdain and long-suffering. His gaze then traveled to his young friend, whose face, in contrast, was alive with excitement and curiosity. Not for the first time Darcy wondered how Charles Bingley and his sisters could possibly be related. The Bingley women were properly reserved, but Charles was invariably and indiscriminately gregarious. Mrs. Hurst and Miss Bingley were elegant in their dress and manners. Charles was . . . Well, he was now quietly fashionable in his dress—Darcy had at least taken him in hand in that regard—but he still retained an unfortunate propensity to treat anyone merely introduced to him as an intimate friend. The Bingley sisters were not easily impressed and radiated a studied boredom in regard to all but the most exclusive of entertainments; their brother took pleasure in everything.

It was just this exuberance of character that had made Charles the object of several cruel jokes among the more sophisticated young gentlemen in Town and had been the means of bringing him to Darcy's notice. Unwillingly privy to the planning of one such humiliation conducted during a game of cards at his club, he had heard enough to disgust him and form the resolve to seek out the unfortunate youth and warn him away from those he had thought his friends. To Darcy's surprise, what had started as Christian duty became a satisfying friendship. Charles had come far since his first visit to Town, but there were still moments, like the present, when Darcy despaired of ever cultivating in him a proper reserve.

"Shall we go in, then?" asked Charles, appearing at his side. "The music sounds delightful, and I expect the ladies shall be equally so." He turned and extended an arm to his unmarried sister. "Come, Caroline, let us meet our new neighbors."

Darcy took up a position in the rear as the Bingley party moved into the small hall and ascended the stairs to the assembly room floor. Having disposed of their hats and the ladies' wraps, Bingley; his brother-in-law, Mr. Hurst; and Darcy ushered the ladies to the entrance, where they paused to assess the features of the room and its rustic occupants. At that unfortunate moment the music came to a halt, and the dancers made their final turn in the pattern, causing most of the room to face the door. For a few breathless heartbeats, Town and Country took stock of each other and rushed to a dizzying variety of conclusions.

Darcy nudged Bingley forward into the room as the dancers quit the floor in search of refreshment and gossip. He could feel the eyes of the entire room upon him and wondered that he had ever doubted the rudeness of country manners. It was as bad as he had feared. The room was abuzz with speculation as he and the rest of Bingley's party were exclaimed over and weighed to the last guinea. He could almost hear the clink of coins as they counted his fortune. In the space of a few moments, the man to whom Darcy guessed he might lay the blame for their invitation to the evening's entertainment came hurrying toward them. Bowing a degree more than was necessary, he took Bingley's hand in a vigorous clasp.

"Welcome, welcome, Mr. Bingley, and all your fine party, too, I am quite sure," exclaimed Sir William Lucas as he encompassed them all in a great smile. "We are so very honored that you have come to our small assembly. Of course we are all anxious to make the acquaintance of your estimable guests . . ." Sir William's voice trailed off as he turned an expectant countenance upon Darcy and then Bingley's sisters.

With great enthusiasm, Bingley made the proper introductions. Darcy's own bow to the obsequious little man was one of the merest civility. To Darcy's pained annoyance, instead of depressing Sir William's deference, it had the unfortunate effect of increasing that gentleman's regard and secured the man's continued efforts to engage him. Finally, after the ladies and Mr. Hurst were introduced, Sir William ushered them all to the refreshment table where Miss Lucas, his eldest daughter, stood with her mother and family. There, the Bingley party was introduced to the rest of the Lucas family, and Bingley, knowing his duty when it presented itself to him, offered himself to Miss Lucas for the next dance. Sir William presented his arm to Miss Bingley, and the Hursts followed the two couples out onto the dance floor.

As the music began and the other dancers took their places,

Darcy positioned himself against the wall, away from the table and the knots of neighbors and relatives that framed the room. Everywhere he turned, eyes narrowed on him in frank appraisal or fluttered in a mock of modesty. His countenance hardening, he withdrew into a stance of studied indifference, masking the cool disdain that vied with hot annoyance in his chest as he watched the ebb and flow of country society before him.

Why had he agreed to this waste of an evening? There was no beauty, conversation, or fashion to be found in the entire room save among those with whom he had arrived. Rather, he was surrounded by the common, the dull, and the trite, that class of the barely gentrified whose idea of conversation was no more than gossip—and that of the vulgar sort of which he was the current object. Darcy could not help but compare his present circumstance with the last time he had been to Tattersall's in search of a suitable new Thoroughbred stallion for his brood mares. Then and there, he privately vowed to purchase no more horseflesh at auction.

Hoping for relief from his solitary disquiet, he looked about for Bingley as the dance came to an end, finally locating him across the room in the process of being introduced to a matron surrounded by several young women. Darcy watched in resignation as Bingley bowed to each of them during the introductions and then offered his arm to the handsomest girl, securing her for the next dance. Bingley's ease in any society in which he found himself always amazed Darcy. How did one converse with perfect strangers across the boundaries of class or station and in such a setting? A score of cautions and strictures acquired over a lifetime loomed darkly in Darcy's mind, adding to his discomposure and deepening further still his withdrawal from social intercourse. His eyes followed Bingley and his partner through the first patterns of the dance and then returned to the matron and her entourage. What he saw there caused him to groan, startling a passing young gentleman who, after a brief glance into Darcy's stony visage, hurried on.

The object of Darcy's displeasure wore the expression of a plump, old tabby that had just been presented with a bowl of rich cream. Her satisfaction and avarice were almost palpable as she kept close watch on Bingley and the girl. *Her daughter? Likely,* he determined, *although there is little resemblance.* There was no doubt in his mind as to where her thoughts were leading; he had seen that look too many times to be mistaken. Bingley must be warned against showing any particular attention in *that* direction. The slightest sense of partiality and the woman would be en-camped upon the doorstep of Bingley's home, Netherfield.

Darcy made his way to the refreshment table, his back stiff with displeasure at the duty to his friend that lay before him. Accepting a cup of punch from the girl behind the table, he suffered her smiles and giggles with a show of composure he was far from feeling.

At that moment, Bingley appeared next to him, secured a cup from the girl with a smile and a wink, and turned to his friend. "I say, Darcy, have you ever seen so many lovely young ladies in one place in your life? What do you think of country manners now?"

"I think of them as I have always thought, having certainly been given no cause this evening to do otherwise."

"But, Darcy, surely you cannot have been offended by Sir William's attentions." Bingley smiled ruefully. "He is a good sort, a trifle officious, but—"

"Sir William's attentions were not uppermost in my mind as I considered your question. You cannot be unaware of the vulgar gossip we are figuring in even at this moment." Darcy's jaw clenched in agitation as a rapid review of the room confirmed the truth of his observation.

"They probably wonder, as do I, why you have not danced as yet tonight. Come, Darcy, I must have you dance. I hate to see you standing about by yourself in this stupid manner. You had much better dance. There are many pretty girls who would, no doubt—"

"I certainly shall not! You know how I detest it, unless I am particularly acquainted with my partner. At such an assembly as this"—Darcy's eyes swept the room disdainfully—"it would be insupportable. Your sisters are engaged, and there is not another woman in the room whom it would not be a punishment to me to stand up with."

"I would not be as fastidious as you are for a kingdom!" exclaimed Bingley. "I cannot stand seeing you so! Upon my honor, I never met with so many pleasant girls in my life as I have this evening; and there are several of them, you see, uncommonly pretty."

"*You* are dancing with the only handsome girl in the room," Darcy replied, looking at Bingley's partner from the last dance.

"Oh! She is the most beautiful creature I ever beheld! But come, she has a very charming sister who would, I believe, suit even your taste, at least for an evening. Let me procure an introduction. She sits out the dancing just over there."

"Which do you mean?" replied Darcy, turning in the direction of Bingley's gaze. A few chairs distant from where they stood sat a young woman of about twenty who, in contrast to himself, was obviously enjoying the evening. Although she was sitting out the dance for a lack of available gentlemen, her small feet would not accept their banishment from the dancing and tapped discreetly beneath her gown. Her eyes bright with amusement in the scene before her, she seemed a favorite with many, being saluted by both ladies and gentlemen as they passed by her. She was near enough that a slight change in the direction of her gaze caused Darcy to wonder if she had been listening to their conversation. His suspicions were confirmed when her smile seemed to take on a more quizzical appearance.

What was she thinking? Intrigued, he allowed himself to examine her. At that moment, his object turned toward him, the smile still gracing her face, but now with one delicate brow arched in question at his blatant scrutiny. He hastily turned away, his discomposure with her discovery of him setting him further at odds with his companion. If Bingley imagined he would be content with what other men overlooked while he enjoyed the company of the only passable young woman present, he must think again!

"She is tolerable, but not handsome enough to tempt *me*; and I am in no humor at present to give consequence to young ladies who are slighted by other men," he objected sharply. "You had better return to your partner and enjoy her smiles, for you are wasting your time with me." Leaving Bingley to make of his advice what he would, Darcy turned abruptly and walked as far from the vicinity of the disturbing female as he could. For the rest of the evening he occupied himself dancing with his friend's two sisters and, when not engaged with them, discouraging any who attempted to draw him in conversation. His indignation with the utter waste of an entire evening among undistinguished strangers was reflected in a countenance which assumed such a forbidding cast that he was soon left to himself. He could only sigh with relief when the assembly finally came to an end and Bingley's carriage pulled forward to receive them.

While Bingley extolled the pleasures of the evening, Darcy settled back into the squabs, observing his companions. As he had suspected, Miss Bingley and Mrs. Hurst would not concur with their brother's raptures and were in nowise hesitant to express their complete dissatisfaction. As the Bingley family discussed their differences, Darcy turned his gaze out the open carriage window into the night. Some small commotion at the inn's entrance attracted his attention, and leaning forward, he espied several of the local militia playing the gallant to a group of young women emerging into the night. With great flourishes and exaggerated bows, they competed to escort the ladies to their carriage. A low, delightful laugh escaped from one of the ladies, drawing Darcy forward to seek out its source. There, beneath the crackling torch, he found it and, with a tingling jolt, saw that it was the young woman of the enigmatic smile who had so discomposed him earlier. He watched as she gently refused the arm of the young officer and motioned him off to assist one of her sisters. Then, with a sigh of pleasure, she gracefully adjusted her wrap and lifted her face to the beauty of the night sky. The simplicity of her joy caught him, and as the carriage lurched forward, Darcy found that he could not take his eyes from her. With an inexplicable fascination, he watched her until a turn in the street took her from his view.

"Ahem."

Darcy settled back into his seat and faced Bingley, whose cough and raised eyebrow asked a question he was not willing to answer. With a shrug, Darcy again turned his gaze out the window and into the night, steadfastly dismissing all thoughts of country misses, especially those with amusing secrets lighting their eyes.

The morning following the Meryton assembly found Darcy alone at table in Netherfield's sunny breakfast room nursing a cup of black coffee as he perused a letter from his sister. The Bingleys and Hursts were not yet down, recovering, as it were, from the previous evening's events. Discerning no reason to break his habit of rising early, he had come down to find he had the breakfast room to himself and an eagerly anticipated letter from his sister, Georgiana, awaiting his attention on the sideboard. He had poured a cup of the steaming brew, tucked the letter under his arm, and looked about him for a comfortable place to enjoy both. If he had been at either his London home or his estate, Pemberley, he would have headed for his library. This, however, was not Pemberley but Netherfield. And as the house was lately rented by his friend, its library was sadly neglected and quite the most uncomfortable room in the place. He would have to settle for the more public breakfast room and hope that his hosts would indulge in enough sleep to allow him the privacy his letter deserved.

As the rich coffee aroma wafted around him, Darcy broke the seal on a more substantial letter than he was used to receiving from his sister. Lately, since the incident with George Wickham, her letters had consisted of a few lines merely: reports on her lessons, her progress at the pianoforte, names of visitors, and the like. The gentle glow that had heretofore characterized Georgiana had receded to gray ash in her heart—wrenching retreat from the world. Darcy prayed that the glow was banked only for the moment and that her exposure to such evil had not permanently damaged her ability to take her place in Society. He unfolded the fine pressed sheets and read:

18 October

Dearest Brother,

I pray this letter finds you well and happy in your sojourn with Mr. Bingley and his family. How do you find Netherfield? Does it please, as Mr. Bingley promised?

How did he find Netherfield? The manor was pleasant enough, except for the library. It was certainly enough for Bingley to handle at this point in his life. Yes, it would do . . . if only the society . . . He returned to the letter.

I received your letter of the ——th on Wednesday last and meant to respond immediately to your kind solicitude but found that, at the time, I had too little to warrant the trouble of sending a letter to Hertfordshire. That has now materially changed, and I doubt that I can express myself in a way that will adequately convey my present feelings.

Darcy sat up a little straighter as a tingle of concern sped down his back. He reached for his coffee and took a large sip.

I know that you have been greatly concerned about me since the events of last summer and, frankly, dearest brother, I have been very uneasy. I could not find it possible to trust anyone, excepting yourself, or accept the merest commonplace without suspicion. I desired no social intercourse and took no joy in anything save my music, which, I must confess, also took on a melancholy air. This did not go unnoticed by the new companion you sent me. Mrs. Annesley, wise woman that she is, forbore to tease me with it or offer bracing reproofs. She did, however, insist on taking extended walks about Pemberley, claiming that only I could truly show her its beauties and, of course, my favorite views. She also encouraged me to take up what Mother had to lay aside so long ago: visiting the families of our tenants. After considering her proposal, I found that I desired to make these visits; indeed, that I should have done so long ago.

I know not how, precisely, it came about, Brother, but I find myself no longer cast down about the past. It will always affect me, but now I know it will not rule me. Mrs. Annesley's gentle counsel and quiet self-possession have been a soothing balm and a worthy model. You have chosen well, dear brother, and I am mending under her care into a stronger vessel.

The letter fell gently onto the table as Darcy's tension evaporated with a sigh he could not repress. The remainder contained the usual reports of educational and musical progress, albeit with a more lively tone than he had received from Georgiana in some months. He closed his eyes briefly. *She will be well,* he silently assured himself.

Hearing footsteps, Darcy quickly folded the letter, slid it into his coat pocket, and rose from his chair. Miss Bingley swept into the breakfast room, checking only for a moment upon seeing that he was alone at the table. Motioning to a servant to abandon his post at the door to serve as waiter, she nodded in response to Darcy's bow and allowed him to select a chair for her.

"Mr. Darcy, you are a model for us all." Miss Bingley looked up at him as he assisted her in sitting down. "Up so early—before dawn, I daresay—after such a fatiguing evening in such fatiguing company. I wonder at your fortitude, sir!"

Darcy retrieved his coffee and resumed his seat at the far end of the table. "I cannot lay claim to such merit, Miss Bingley. Merely habit, I assure you."

"A well-considered habit, Mr. Darcy, I am convinced. But your coffee must have gone cold! Let Stevenson pour you fresh. There can be little more disagreeable than cold coffee! I cannot abide it." Miss Bingley shuddered prettily. Darcy hid the twitch of an incipient grimace behind his cup as he took another sip. It had gone tepid, but he would not give Caroline Bingley encouragement to play out the cozy domestic scene she was creating in yet another unwelcome bid for his personal interest. Snapping his cup down upon the saucer, he began to rise when she surprised him with a question about his letter.

"Pray, tell me what your dear sister writes. I long to know how she gets on with her new companion. Does she complain of her, or is it too soon for that? I do wish she could have come with us to Netherfield." She sighed pettishly. "What a relief her company would be from the local country squires and their 'worthy' dames." Miss Bingley rearranged the food on her plate as she contemplated her new neighbors. "Charles insists that we make calls. I am sure, Mr. Darcy, you will agree that it will hardly be a pleasure. No more so than last night's assembly. I ask you, sir, was last night not trying to your sensibilities?"

Darcy cast about for remembrances of the previous evening. Trying to his sensibilities? An echo of the distaste he had felt reverberated through his body. Yes, most trying. Officious bores, simpering young women, and forward older ones. All of them measuring, weighing, their eyes following every move . . . Suddenly he remembered eyes with expressive brows arched in challenge at him, intriguing eyes alight with secrets and amusement. He must have dwelt on the memory for some little time, for the loud clink of a spoon vigorously stirred against the sides of a cup recalled him to the presence of his questioner. Miss Bingley's smile barely covered the pique she was obviously feeling at his inattention, for her eyes were narrowed as she waited for him to answer her question.

"Trying, Miss Bingley? Perhaps to those gentlemen like myself who find no great pleasure in dancing. But surely you were the recipient of much kind attention and admiration?" Darcy's smile was smug. She could not deny the obvious solicitude that had enveloped her at the assembly. Disdain of that solicitude would be unbecoming while acknowledgment of success in such restricted society was nothing with which to feather her cap, especially in his company.

"You will excuse me, Miss Bingley," he continued, claiming rather than requesting his release. With an uncertain smile, she could do no more than nod as he rose to take his leave. As he strode toward the door and the stables beyond, the picture of a quite different young woman, her eyes lifted to the night sky, formed in his mind, catching him in midstride. Shaking his head, he resumed his way to the stables. *To horse, sir! It is the fields and fences you've come to explore, not the local nurseries!*

He entered the stable yard, gratified to see Nelson ready at the mounting block and eager for a good run. Swinging into the saddle, he brought his thoughts into line with the desires of his mount and made for a beckoning countryside awash in the rays of a glorious autumn morning.

CHAPTER 2

A Man of Property

*D*arcy returned to Netherfield from his morning ride with an increased admiration for the countryside in which it nestled. The farms were neat and, with the recent harvest, appeared prosperous. The fields were bordered by wall, fence, or wood in a manner pleasing both to the eye and to the palate of even an avid hunter or horseman. The lands attached to Netherfield itself were in need of attention, but Darcy had found nothing drastically wrong that careful management and an infusion of capital could not correct in due course. All in all, a tidy estate with a minimum of problems but those that would teach Bingley what it was to be a man of property. Dismounting, he gave Nelson a hearty, affectionate pat on his great neck, ending with a gentle pass down his broad forehead and a lump of sugar pressed against his soft muzzle. Neatly extracting the treat from Darcy's hand, Nelson nickered back his esteem. With a laugh, Darcy handed him over to a lad emerging from the stables.

A man of property. A soft, barely perceptible smile flitted across Darcy's face as he heard the words echo in his head, but in his father's voice. Under the careful tutelage of his father, Darcy had begun at an early age to learn what those words meant. He swore that his earliest memory was sitting astride a saddle, securely anchored in his father's lap, his fingers twisted in the horse's mane as the elder Darcy rode spring inspection of the farms and holdings of Pemberley. He could have only just been out of leading strings, perhaps three years old, but the memory was vivid enough to convince even his parents that it was a true one. That ride had served as his introduction to his station in life and its attendant responsibilities, both of which he now shouldered alone and with a just satisfaction that acknowledged, without hesitation, the excellent preparation given him by his father. Often and often, Darcy had occasion to thank Heaven for his father's daily example of attention to duty and the practical experience he had gained under his guidance. It had made Pemberley the jewel that it was. He hoped he could serve his friend Bingley as well.

"Aha, there you are!" Bingley's voice boomed as Darcy entered Netherfield's hall. "I suppose I dare not hope that you have waited to allow me the pleasure of taking you on a tour of Netherfield's lands?" Bingley stood in mock sternness in the doorway of the morning room, his arms crossed and his brow lowered, glowering at his friend.

"No hope at all, Bingley," he responded without contrition. "It's this deuced autumn weather! It just pulls one out-of-doors."

"Indeed?" queried Bingley imperiously, in obvious delight at the unusual experience of having the upper hand with his friend. "I rather thought it was the prospect of having to provide amusement for Caroline this morning that pushed you out! Lord knows, I would be off in a shot!" The hauteur Bingley had assumed was then replaced with a genuine frown as he continued. "But really, Darcy, I was very much looking forward to riding over the estate with you."

"And you shall," Darcy hastened to assure him. "I apologize for anticipating you, but I needed to encounter Netherfield for itself without seeing it through your eyes, as would happen on a joint tour. Well you know that you would be filling my ear with rhapsodies about this stream or that wood." Darcy paused briefly at Bingley's strangled objection to his scenario. "You know I am right! Such distractions would give me no opportunity truly to be of service to you."

With a crooked smile, Bingley ruefully acknowledged the reasonableness of his friend's excuse. "I know it is not, nor will it ever be, a Pemberley. But even I know it can be more than it is," he responded. "The thing of it is, I have not the slightest idea where to begin."

"You may begin with allowing me to change out of my riding clothes and joining me over some refreshment in the"—Darcy glanced about the hall for a room into which the ladies or Mr. Hurst were unlikely to wander—"library." Seizing the opportunity, he added, "Would it be possible, Charles, to have some comfortable chairs moved there? It is really quite spartan."

"Of course, Darcy, immediately. I can't tell you—"

"Then don't, old man. Hold your gratitude until after you've heard me out." Darcy could not help but grin at the enthusiasm on Bingley's face. "After you've found yourself up to your waistcoat buttons in paper, broken quills, agricultural reports, and bills, and feel that you still feel a compunction to thank me, I'll be glad to entertain it." He began moving toward the stairs, then checked and turned a serious countenance upon his friend. "I warn you, Bingley, earning a Cambridge fellowship is nothing to becoming a complete man of property. I have that on the greatest authority."

"And who, pray, might that be, O my master," quipped Bingley.

"My father," replied Darcy quietly as he turned and started up the stairs. "He did both."

Gaining his room, Darcy carefully removed his sister's letter from his coat pocket and read again the first part, his eyes lingering on the first page's last line, "I am mending under her care into a stronger vessel." Tenderly, he refolded the letter and pressed it to his lips. "Please God, it is so," he murmured, placing it in his secretary, then pulled the bell that would summon Fletcher, his valet, and what he required for a day spent at the country estate of his friend.

❦

Ensconced as they were companionably in the library amid the threatened blizzard of papers and broken pens, the remainder of the morning passed quickly for Darcy and Bingley. When Stevenson tapped at the door to announce that an afternoon repast was available and that the ladies desired their company, the two rose from their labors well satisfied with the progress that had been made and ready for a diversion.

"Whatever have you been doing all morning, Charles? Caroline and I could find you nowhere about!" complained Mrs. Hurst as she poured tea for the gentlemen and her sister. "Mr. Hurst particularly desired to see the coveys and discuss plans for a shooting party this morning, did you not, my dear?" She paused for an instant to look vaguely over at her husband, who at that moment appeared interested more in hunting the victuals set before him than those less sure ones out-of-doors. Darcy and Bingley accepted their cups, quickly setting them down at the opposite end of the dining table.

"I spent the morning most satisfactorily, Louisa. Darcy has consented to offer suggestions on how I might improve Netherfield, make it more—"

"More like Pemberley!" cried Miss Bingley as she fixed on Darcy a look of entreaty. "Oh, Mr. Darcy, can it be done?"

"Caroline, you mistake me." Bingley looked at her with annoyance. "You must see that Netherfield can never be Pemberley, for Hertfordshire cannot be Derbyshire! Nevertheless, I believe, and Darcy agrees, that Netherfield possesses interesting possibilities that time and patience will reveal. Now," he continued hurriedly, "what communication have we received from our neighbors? I would expect quite a few cards to have been sent after last night."

"Yes, I suppose one could say a few." Miss Bingley sniffed as she flicked her fingers at the pile of correspondence in the tray before her. "There are one dozen letters of welcome, seven invitations to dinner, four for tea, and three notices of assemblies or private evenings of musical entertainments. Really, Charles, what does one do for society in such a place?"

"Society?" Bingley responded. "Enjoy it, I say! The assembly last night, for example. I am sure I have rarely had a more pleasant evening. Yes, it is true! Do not frown so, Caroline! The music was lively, the people received us most warmly, and the young ladies—"

"Charles, you are too undiscriminating," interrupted Miss Bingley. "I have never met people with less conversation and fashion or more conceit. As for the young ladies, they were certainly young but—"

"Come, Caroline, I cannot allow you to speak so of at least one young lady," Bingley interrupted. He turned to Darcy, who had just risen from the table, cup and saucer in hand. "Darcy, support me in this! Was not Jane Bennet as lovely a girl as could be dreamt of?"

Darcy strolled over to a window while sipping at his tea and looked out onto a greensward hedged by boxwood and a gravel walk. The lack of accord between Bingley and his sisters was of long standing and had manifested itself in innumerable ways since his acquaintance with the family. Generally, Darcy's sympathy lay with Bingley in these unpleasant exchanges, but today the turn of the conversation reminded him of the resolve he had formed the previous evening to caution his friend.

Without turning he replied, "Lovely? I believe I called her handsome. If she is lovely, I bow to your superior judgment, as you danced with her. I did not."

"But you do have eyes, man!" Bingley responded energetically.

"Which I employed, at your insistence, you may recall." Darcy shifted his stance, his focus remaining on the scenery beyond the window. He sipped again at his tea. "She smiles too much."

"Smiles too much," Bingley repeated in disbelief.

"A man must wonder at such a profusion of smiles. What may be their cause?" Darcy turned then and fixed Bingley with a penetrating look, as if to infuse him with the force of his disapprobation. " 'Favor is deceitful, and beauty is vain,' if I may be so bold as to quote. Think, man! Do these smiles indicate a happy, even disposition, or are they a practiced pose, a charade of good nature designed to entrap or to cover an absence of real intellect?" Darcy paused, his words stirring up violent memories within him of George Wickham, whose smiles and flattery, both man and boy, had masked a vile, corrupted nature. Unable to trust that his emotions would not betray him, he turned abruptly back to the window.

Bingley regarded his friend with some astonishment while his sisters sagely nodded their heads in agreement with Darcy's opinion. "Mr. Darcy is quite perceptive, as always, Charles," Miss Bingley concurred. "Miss Bennet seems to be a sweet girl, but what can she mean with a smile continually about her? I must say, I could never find so much to amuse or please me to keep me forever smiling. It is undignified and shows a want of good breeding. What say you, Louisa?"

"I quite agree, Caroline. Miss Bennet appears a sweet, charming thing, and I wish her every bit of good fortune she deserves. I cannot like the rest of her family, though. It is a wonder that they are received, except for Miss Bennet's smiles."

Darcy only half-attended as the sisters proceeded to shred the characters of their new neighbors. The sudden surge of anger he had experienced while dissuading his friend had surprised him, and he hardly knew how to settle his emotions in drawing room company. He walked down the room to the far window, as if intent on a different perspective of the greensward. What he needed was exercise—violent physical exercise—to banish his personal demons.

Wickham! Had he not vowed to put Wickham and his infamy behind him, promised himself not to allow the man's actions, his betrayal, to intrude on his composure? Yet the innocent smiles of a pretty stranger had again excited the rage and helplessness he felt—still felt. Darcy leaned one arm against the window's frame, his face a grim, white mask reflected back to him in the glass. *Enough!* Wickham's poisonous sway had to stop. It must stop, or every time Georgiana looked at him she would see it, and he would not have her crushed again, especially now that she had found strength to face the world.

Darcy let a slow, measured sigh escape him as he set his mind to calm his thoughts. His body, he found, was not as obliging. What he would not give for a good sword and a worthy opponent at this moment! He almost laughed. Instead, he recalled himself to his purpose, which had been to rein in Bingley's galloping admiration of Miss Bennet, not to encourage him into a disgust of his neighbors. He acknowledged that he may have been harsh, but it was for the best. It would not do for Bingley to leg-shackle himself so young and to a mere local miss. Nevertheless, the neighbors should be rescued from the tender attentions of Bingley's sisters.

" . . . her sisters, all four of them!" Miss Bingley's disdainful laugh abruptly reinstated him into the conversation. "Mr. Darcy, you cannot be amused by the immodest behavior of Miss Bennet's sisters? You would not wish your sister to act so." Darcy favored Miss Bingley with a bow in silent agreement. "But the local militia do not seem to take such antics into aversion," she continued. "They are in agreement with you on that head, Charles. The Bennet girls all are favorites. Not only Miss Bennet but the next younger, Miss Elizabeth Bennet, was also accounted a beauty! Mr. Darcy, what say you to that? Is Miss Elizabeth Bennet a beauty?"

Darcy's hand involuntarily convulsed around the delicate china cup. Elizabeth! Yes, that would be her name, the name of a queen—so directly did she regard him! A beauty? An intriguing woman, a maddening woman, likely, with such a bold air. But a beauty? His emotions now engaged on an altogether different object, he maintained his gaze out the window, his back to the room, even when Bingley addressed him with more than a hint of exasperation in his voice. "Well, Darcy?"

Without turning, Darcy gathered himself to deflect Miss Bingley's barb and discipline his own unruly thoughts. "She, a beauty?" he replied, his diction precise and clipped. "I would as soon call her mother a wit."

The light mists of an autumn morning rose gracefully around Netherfield, whispering invitations to field and wood that Darcy was hard-pressed to decline. This was especially so as he did not anticipate the morning's activities with any expectation of enjoyment. Reluctantly, he turned from the library window and his contemplation of the enticements that creation was unveiling to consider the ordeal before him. That it would be an ordeal rather than a pleasure, he was in no doubt. Indeed, Morning In was that sort of social ritual which he could very well do without, but the present circumstance and its very nature made it a necessary evil.

Darcy picked up the book he had been intent upon reading before being drawn to the beauty of the morning and sank into one of the large wingback chairs that now graced the library. In this next step in Bingley's venture into the life of the landed gentry, Darcy knew himself to be of little help and questionable ability. There was no question but that Bingley must establish himself in his new neighborhood, and that meant receiving its prominent residents. Although they were not in the first circle of London Society, the Bingley family was of considerable social stature and would certainly assume leadership in the society of Meryton and its environs. Such expectations required a Morning In. It could not be avoided. His brow furrowed, Darcy fingered the pages of his book, absently turning them as he contemplated the morning in front of him.

"So, here you are!" Bingley's voice pierced the silence before the sound of his steps reached Darcy's ears. "I'll warrant you've been here since before breakfast." He quickly surveyed the room. "Yes, I see your coffee on the desk, so I am sure I am right. I knew you were either here or gone ariding." He cocked an eye at Darcy as he took the other chair. "Fortifying yourself for the onslaught?" He leaned forward and lowered his voice. "Or planning a strategic retreat?"

"The former, tiresome whelp," Darcy replied with reluctant

humor. "Although the latter would be more to my liking, as you well know."

"Oh, it will not be so very bad, Darcy," Bingley replied, leaning back into his chair and stretching out his legs to inspect briefly the shine on his boots. "We will have met most of them before, either at the assembly last Friday or at church yesterday. I am quite looking forward to receiving." He glanced at Darcy's face and then returned to a study of his boots. "That is, some of them. Looking forward, I mean, to seeing . . ." His voice trailed off.

Darcy rued the breach that had opened between them since his warning concerning Miss Bennet and hated that Bingley felt uncomfortable talking about her with him. He knew he had better repair it before time made it a chasm. "I imagine there will be some members of certain families who will make an appearance this morning, Charles." He was rewarded with a cautious smile, so he continued quietly. "I hope, for your sake, Mrs. Bennet does not bring all her daughters with her, else you will have to divide your attentions as thinly as you did yesterday."

Bingley laughed aloud. "I accept your well wishes, however difficult it was for you to extend them, and heartily concur. I had no idea what a sensation we would cause merely by attending church." He shook his head in disbelief. "You saw how it was! I could not finish one sentence before being inundated with five more questions or invitations."

"Miss Bennet, as I recall, was not one of the throng," Darcy pointed out.

"No, nor her sister Miss Elizabeth Bennet" came Bingley's pensive reply. Darcy elected to ignore this last observation. "They, both of them, were engaged the entire time in a protracted conversation with the vicar and his wife."

"No smiles?" asked Darcy, then wished he had refrained from the jibe.

"As a matter of record, yes," replied Bingley evenly, not entirely sure of the intent of his question but, evidently, determined not to be intimidated. "I was able to catch her eye before Caroline hurried us into the carriage." He paused and assumed a dramatic pose with one hand pressed to his heart. "I was rewarded with a smile that has nourished my hopes for almost—can it be?—twenty-four hours." He and Darcy both laughed then, as much at Bingley's drama as with relief to be again on intimate terms.

When they had regained control, Bingley rose. "It is almost time, you know. I was coming to tell you that a lad from the stable had run up with news of a carriage about a mile from the gate." He paused, took a deep breath, and looking Darcy straight on, continued, "I know how you dislike these things and count myself well blessed that you have consented to stand by me through it. I cannot think how I would—"

"There is no need, Bingley," Darcy interrupted, turning slightly away. "Your friendship is reason and reward enough for whatever service I can render you." He strode quickly over to a small table supporting a decanter. "Now, let us complete our preparation for the morning. What say you to a small glass of fortitude before we face the dragons of Meryton?" Anticipating a positive response, he removed the crystal stopper and poured the amber liquid into the awaiting glasses. Bingley appropriated one and, lifting it, saluted him. Darcy solemnly returned the gesture.

Moments after they had replaced their glasses, a sharp rap was heard on the library door, which opened to admit Miss Bingley. Almost before she rose from her curtsy, she extended her hand to her brother and fixed both gentlemen with a determinedly bright smile. "Charles, Mr. Darcy, our first guests are even now descending from their carriage, and I am told another has been sighted not far behind. We shall have a full morning, I am in no doubt."

"And you will preside over it beautifully, Caroline," Bingley said, looking down into his sister's face. "You will be reigning over Meryton society in no time."

Miss Bingley acknowledged her brother's compliment with a tightening of her smile. "We shall see, Brother," she said, and then turned toward Darcy with an altogether different expression. "Mr. Darcy, I must thank you again for sharing your prayer book with me yesterday. I cannot imagine how I came to lose mine. It is so vexing! I am sure I will find it soon. I am never without it, you know." During this extraordinary speech, Bingley had looked questioningly at his sister, but at her last statement, he started visibly, then looked to Darcy for his reaction to Caroline's newest cast for his approval.

It took all Darcy's self-control to prevent the telltale twitch of his lips as, with a solemnity worthy of a bishop, he assured Miss Bingley of his confidence in the success of her search. "Although," he concluded, "such constancy in the perusal of its lines must make its loss almost immaterial, for you will surely know much of it by heart." Miss Bingley was saved the necessity of a reply by the announcement of the arrival of guests. With a deep curtsy and swish of skirts, she quickly left the library.

Bingley was able to contain himself only long enough for his sister to be safely away. "What," he managed between gasps for breath, "is all this about her prayer book?" Darcy's look of innocence did not deter him for an instant. "Come, you must tell me! Caroline never looked at her prayer book since she left finishing school nor paid attention to a sermon. When you came down to breakfast yesterday prepared to attend services, I thought my sisters' eyes would drop out of their heads! I'm sure I should slip their maids a guinea each for the uproar they endured waiting upon Caroline and Louisa a second time in one morning."

"Why should they be astonished at my attending church?" Darcy replied. "They have seen me do so regularly in Derbyshire and surely are aware that I have a pew in St. ———'s in London that Georgiana and I rarely fail to attend."

"I am not sure. Perhaps because we are not in Derbyshire or London." At Darcy's puzzled expression, Bingley plunged on. "I believe they think you do so only to be seen." He hastened to explain. "They attend only if they hear that some influential person-

age is planning to be there. Your more frequent attendance is excused, I gather, on the grounds that you must feel obliged to set an
example to your tenants and sister and that your position requires
you to put in an appearance to maintain certain connections."
Bingley lapsed into an embarrassed silence.

Darcy's left eyebrow had risen quite decidedly during Bingley's
recital, and at its end, he took a step backward and slowly circled
the chair, drawing his friend's attention to the book he had intended to begin, the first volume of *The Works of the Reverend
George Whitefield*. Bingley colored and then laughed shakily. "Of
course, did they know you as I do. Such silly ideas . . ."

Darcy leaned over the chair back, picked up the volume, and
with a wry smile tossed it to Bingley, whose face immediately
flooded with relief. "They may not be that far off in their estimation, Charles. I cannot deny that duty has been more often my
motivation than anything approaching real devotion." He nodded
toward the book in Bingley's hands. "At least, that would be Reverend Whitefield's assessment." Bingley quickly put the book on
the desk, as if it had suddenly become too hot to hold.

"But you wish to discover the meaning of her prayer book."
Darcy gave a short laugh. "It is quite simple, really. You remember,
of course, that we were late arriving at Meryton Church due to your
sisters' change of costume. When we had finally found seats and
opened our hymnbooks, my attention was most decidedly caught
by a feminine voice coming from behind us. Such a sure, rich soprano I had never heard outside of a London choir, and against my
better judgment, I turned slightly to see who it might be."

"Miss Elizabeth Bennet, was it not, Darcy?" At his friend's nod,
Bingley continued, "Yes, I heard her also and was vastly pleased to
listen to her. Her voice drowned out the caterwauling that Louisa
calls singing."

"I will not comment on your sister's ability, but about Miss
Elizabeth Bennet's, I do concur." Darcy paused, attempting to recall the moment. "It was an unexpected pleasure to hear hymns

sung with such feeling and beauty. I confess, they are what inspired me to attempt Whitefield again after avoiding him for some time now." He gave himself a slight shake. "Regardless, Miss Bingley noticed my distraction and its source. Shortly thereafter, she discovered the loss of her prayer book, and, as was only correct, I offered to share mine. I hardly needed it, as I *do* know the most common ones by heart. This fact, I believe, she noticed as well, and putting the incidents of the morning together, we arrive at the reason for the conversation of a few moments ago."

Bingley shook his head, a show of consternation on his face as he opened the library door. "You bear up under it very well, Darcy, I must say." He then peered down the hall outside and, turning with a twinkle in his rarely clouded eyes, exclaimed, "All clear!" and started down the corridor to the drawing room.

CHAPTER 3

En Garde!

$\mathcal{D}$arcy allowed a few heartbeats to pass before following Bingley. Slowly he closed the library door behind him, waiting another few moments for the solid click of the heavy oak door to cease its echoing in the empty corridor. Measuring his stride, he made his way, pausing at a pier glass to check his cravat and straighten his waistcoat. *Malingerer!* he accused the reflection in the glass. *Just slip in quietly, secure an easily defended position, and wait the blasted, tedious thing out!* The face in the mirror looked askance at him, seemingly dubious about this tactic. *Advise me on a better course then, sir, and it shall be done!* The mirror figure eyed him steadily for a few moments, but as it had no alternative to offer, its regard crumbled. *I thought as much!* growled Darcy as he pulled at his waistcoat.

The sounds of conversation and light laughter began to impress themselves upon his consciousness, and with a final look of derision at his hapless reflection, he squared his shoulders and presented himself to Stevenson, who deftly opened the drawing room doors and prepared to announce his arrival. As the footman drew a deep breath, Darcy placed several fingers on his arm, shaking his head and motioning him to keep silent. Quickly stepping aside, Stevenson allowed him to pass by and closed the doors.

Darcy stiffly observed the room. It was not yet full, it still being early. Bingley had been right that most of the visitors were people he had already met. Caroline Bingley was performing her duties of hostess to perfection, although, Darcy thought, her smile did not reflect a correspondingly perfect sincerity. He cautiously examined her court, composed of an assortment of wives of landowners and prominent merchants. Bingley was already nursing a cup of tea and involved in conversation with the vicar and his wife while a bevy of young ladies hovered within earshot, waiting anxiously, no doubt, for the vicar to leave. Darcy turned to observe the young gentlemen and militia officers who had gathered in a semicircle around the great bow window that looked out onto the carriage-way approaching Netherfield.

"Sir," murmured a serving maid. Darcy looked down at the tray she held for his inspection. "With Miss Bingley's compliments, sir." The aroma of his favorite coffee, prepared as he preferred, arose from a cup that lay next to a choice selection of biscuits. He glanced over to Miss Bingley, bowed slightly as she inclined her head in acknowledgment of his notice, and availed himself of the refreshment. At that moment a frisson of excitement arose among the cluster of men at the window. Several of the young men broke from the group and began to disperse about the room, principally moving closer to the doors. Curiosity overcoming his reserve, Darcy moved into one of the abandoned places at the window to view the cause of such expectant behavior.

A carriage of common style drawn by only one horse swept up the carriageway. It had barely stopped when the door was flung open and a flurry of petticoats descended onto the graveled drive. "Miss Lydia." One of the men near him laughed. "Now we shall have some fun!" said another, and both turned to join their fellows at the door. Darcy vaguely recalled the face beneath the bonnet from the assembly but could not place her within a family. He sipped his coffee, curious to see what would come out of the carriage next. What he saw caused him to halt in midsip. *The tabby!* He gulped down the scalding brew. *That meant . . . !*

Outside, Mrs. Edward Bennet was busy shaking out her dress and shawls in preparation for ascending the steps of Netherfield. Behind her were Miss Jane Bennet and another sister, helping their mother in those preparations and, with her head only just poking out of the carriage door, Miss Elizabeth Bennet. Mrs. Bennet turned, addressing some remark to that daughter as she stood on the carriage step. Miss Elizabeth replied and then flashed a good-humored, rueful smile to her elder sister as their mother proceeded up the stairs. Darcy's unwitting interception of that intimate message caused him to flush with embarrassment, and he pulled back from the window with alacrity. Turning, he spied an empty chair with an excellent view of the door and took possession of it.

The disturbance at the window could not, of course, have been unnoticed by the Bingleys, brother or sister. Miss Bingley turned a frowning countenance upon her brother, who excused himself from the vicar and strode hastily to the window. Seeing only an empty carriage pulling away, he had just turned to inquire of Darcy when the drawing room doors opened. Stevenson appeared and, in a voice choked with suppressed amusement, announced, "Mrs. Edward Bennet, Miss Bennet, Miss Elizabeth, Mary, Catherine, and Lydia Bennet." For a moment, the silence in the room was complete, as portentous as at the anticipation of the first sight of a new bride. Oblivious to the entrance she was making, Mrs. Bennet clucked to a daughter behind her to stop fidgeting and advanced into the room to make her curtsy to her hostess. When the Bennet girls finally appeared in the doorway, the entire room seemed to let out its breath. Miss Bennet, a becoming blush coloring her features, softly smiled at the ladies and gentlemen who greeted her as she made her way over to Miss Bingley. The youngest Bennet sister entered so closely behind the eldest that she almost tripped over the train of her dress, affording her an excuse to latch onto the nearest male arm for support. Giggling and tossing her curls, she greeted the young man by name and was soon surrounded by several of the young gentlemen and officers, entirely forgetting the necessity of making her curtsy to the ladies of the house.

Darcy watched apprehensively as Bingley pushed through the knot of persons surrounding his sisters and stood next to the divan so as to greet the newcomers properly. With some relief, Darcy noted that the manner of Bingley's greeting to Miss Bennet was formal and correct in all respects save, perhaps, the intensity of his regard. A shriek, followed by a giggle, brought Darcy's attention sharply back to the officers, where he identified its origin in the anticipated "Miss Lydia."

Despite his resolve, Darcy's gaze was drawn again to the doorway, which now framed the last of the newcomers. Miss Elizabeth Bennet. Her arrival provoked more than one young officer to abandon his place and advance toward the door. These movements soon obscured her from Darcy's view, but not before he had seen an expression on her face that had been replaced with a smile in response to the warm greetings of her friends. Indeed, its nature quite surprised him. Unconsciously, he rose from his chair in search of a more advantageous angle from which to observe the lady until he found himself, much to his chagrin, standing next to Charles behind the divan just as she sank into her curtsy to Miss Bingley. Watching her intently, he hoped to discern a trace of that ironic expression which, even now, he was beginning to discount as his own imagination.

Miss Elizabeth Bennet's head was still inclined as she rose, but Darcy could see that she held her lower lip captive, biting it in a futile attempt to prevent a dimple from appearing. Her eyes flashed upward briefly before being cast down again in the proper manner. *There! Yes, I was not mistaken! The impudent little piece!* Darcy drew up straighter, congratulating himself on not being deceived by the bland expression now on Miss Bennet's face as she regarded her hostess.

"Miss Elizabeth," drawled Miss Bingley. "You already have been introduced to my brother, Mr. Bingley?" Without pausing for an assent to her question, Miss Bingley indicated her brother standing just behind her. "Charles," she began as she shifted her gaze over her shoulder, "Miss Elizabeth Ben——" Whatever she had been about to say stuck suddenly in her throat as she beheld not only her brother but Darcy as well eagerly awaiting the introduction. "Miss Elizabeth Bennet," she repeated, her smile tightening slightly.

Their guest sank into another curtsy as Charles bowed. When she arose this time, Darcy noted, it was with a decidedly softer complexion.

"Miss Elizabeth, I believe we met briefly at the assembly Friday last, and for three days since I have owed you an apology." Bingley's smile belied the seriousness of his words.

"An apology, Mr. Bingley?" she responded in the same spirit. "I would readily accept any apology you have to offer, but I insist on first being made aware of its occasion. Pray enlighten me, sir, if you please."

"You insist, then, on a confession as well as an apology?" Bingley's pretense of horror elicited a low, charming laugh from his inquisitor.

"Most assuredly! Quickly now, or your penance will be that much more severe."

"Heaven forbid, I shall confess all! Here it is: I neglected to claim the dance you had so graciously promised me. Shameful, is it not, Miss Elizabeth?"

"Yes, indeed, sir. I should be mortally offended at such a slight."

"There were extenuating circumstances, I assure you," Bingley hastened to explain. "Immediately before the dance was to begin, I discovered Miss Bennet in need of some refreshment, which, believing there was sufficient time before the set formed, I offered to procure. On my journey to the table I was accosted by two—no, three gentlemen—"

"Of the road, no doubt?" Elizabeth interrupted him. "I warn

you, Mr. Bingley, nothing less than three highwaymen will satisfy my pique."

"Three highwaymen it was, I am certain of it," agreed Bingley, affecting such a look of desperation that Elizabeth dissolved into laughter, which he immediately seconded.

"You are forgiven, Mr. Bingley, but only because your desertion was in the assistance of my sister. Such gallantry must always be encouraged."

"Thank you. You are very kind, Miss Bennet." He glanced beside him, meeting Darcy's guarded visage. "But I am remiss and will soon be required to extend another apology, for which I will not be so easily forgiven." Bingley drew himself up. "Miss Elizabeth Bennet, may I introduce my friend, Mr. Darcy?"

Darcy had not found himself able to enter into the banter between Bingley and Miss Bennet, excusing his reticence with the fact that they had not yet been properly introduced. Her ability at amusing repartee surprised him. He had become absorbed in the little farce in which they had engaged, but Bingley's return to the formalities and subsequent introduction recalled him to his surroundings. Miss Bennet's assent to the introduction was, he thought, unusually subdued given her good humor with Bingley. He felt himself stiffen into his usual pose of indifference.

"Darcy, I have the great pleasure of introducing Miss Elizabeth Bennet, and if you will both excuse me, I see that your sister is in need of something or other; and I am the only one who knows where it is." With a wink at the flash of alarm on his friend's face, Bingley bowed himself away and hurried toward Miss Bennet.

"Mr. Darcy," Elizabeth murmured. As she made him her curtsy and he returned his bow, Darcy cast about for something to say, silently castigating himself for getting into the middle of exactly what he had resolved to avoid. Still bereft of an opening gambit, he fell back on the usual social inanities he so detested, looking steadily past her ear as he mouthed them.

"Your servant, Miss Bennet. You have lived long in Meryton?"

"All my life, Mr. Darcy."

"You have not been to London, then?" he responded with surprise.

"I have had occasion to visit London, sir, but not during the Season, if that is what you mean by having 'been to London.'" The archness of her tone caused Darcy to frown slightly at its meaning, and involuntarily, he looked her full in the face. She appeared all innocence, but something told him it was not so. Perhaps it was the almost imperceptible lift of one shapely brow or the tendency of her dimple to peep out. Regardless, he knew himself to be an object of amusement. He was not pleased to be such a figure.

"I should not consider time spent in London merely to visit dressmakers' shops as having been to the city at all," he replied coldly.

"Mr. Darcy, you are too kind!" Her simper was such that he knew he was not meant to receive it as anything but false and that his attempt at depressing this young woman's impudence had utterly failed. His eyes narrowed. Why on earth should she pretend to thank him? He had certainly meant no compliment! His suspicion at her purpose was shortly to be confirmed.

"That a gentleman of your discrimination should regard my gown as a *London* creation! But I must disabuse you, I fear. It is a *local* concoction only, but be assured, I shall certainly repeat your pretty compliment to my dressmaker." She sketched another quick curtsy before his astonished mind could form a coherent reply. "Please excuse me, Mr. Darcy. My mother is in need of me."

Pretty compliment? Compliment, indeed! Sputtering silently, Darcy stared after her as she made her way through the now crowded drawing room. True to her word, she went to her mother's side, pausing only briefly to exchange a greeting with friend or neighbor as she glided gracefully past them. He forced his mind to stop reeling in circles and cast it back to the beginning, the moment when she had entered the doorway and her face had betrayed her opinion of her hosts. *Or, more correctly, her hostess,* Darcy amended, recalling her lively exchange with and genuine smiles for Charles. He looked about the room for Miss Bingley, easily discovering her surrounded by a ring of guests who, it appeared, were attending her every word. At the moment, she was holding forth on the "terrible crush" at Lord and Lady ———'s, what she had said to Lady ———, and what her reply had been to Sir ———'s little witticism, punctuating it all with a haughty sniff and an elegant shrug of her shoulders. The group tittered appreciatively, and Darcy noticed several young women attempting to imitate Caroline's air as a wave of shoulders lifted and fell. Elizabeth Bennet was not among them, being occupied with a smaller circle of admirers and close female friends.

No, Miss Elizabeth Bennet was not impressed with the London sophistication of Miss Bingley or Mrs. Hurst, nor did she appear to feel the necessity of inveigling her way into Caroline's good graces, as most of her neighbors were doing this very moment. Instead, thought Darcy with dawning comprehension, she found Miss Bingley's manner objectionable! Far from cultivating her, she had, by the drollery in her eyes, assigned her a place among the ridiculous, as one might do with an amusing but slightly mad relation. Having satisfied himself on what Miss Elizabeth Bennet was about, Darcy found the discovery to have engendered two equal and opposite emotions, which struggled manfully in his breast. The first was to stiffen in indignation at the impertinence of the lady in judging her betters. The second was an impulse to laugh in agreement with her assessment. A twinkle had almost reached Darcy's eye when he was struck with the remembrance that Miss Bingley was not the only resident of Netherfield who amused Miss Elizabeth Bennet. The twinkle was ruthlessly suppressed as he considered again her manner toward himself.

She had delivered him a facer; he acknowledged it without hesitation and, now, with some detachment. Her turning of his thinly veiled setdown into a supposed compliment had been masterfully done. But what had possessed him to speak to her so in the first place? He reviewed the events of their meeting in his mind. Had it been her archness in reply to his desultory attempts at small talk, or had he been put off at the very beginning by the obvious change in her demeanor after Bingley's introduction? Bingley, she liked, but what did she think of him?

Do I cut the same sort of figure in her mind as Miss Bingley, he asked himself, *or is her manner a pretense, a game of flirtation she hopes will capture my attention?* Absentmindedly, he twisted the ruby-crowned ring on his smallest left finger. Or could it be altogether something else? He recalled her repartee with Bingley over his slighting of her at the assembly and her threat to exact penance. Suddenly the muscles in his stomach tightened, the events at the assembly replaying clearly in his mind. That was it! It had to be! She had overheard his graceless, ill-considered comment.

"Idiot!" the self-appellation escaped his lips. *Having received no apology, she thinks to exact her due by force of wit.* Darcy pondered his theory as he gazed at its object, who was, at the moment, tête-a-tête with Miss Lucas. *What should I do, if anything?* he asked himself guiltily. He owed her an apology, without a doubt, but what would he say? "Forgive me, Miss Bennet, I was a perfect ass last Friday?" And if he did, what would be her reply? Would she forgive him with a pretty speech or use the opportunity to deliver him a setdown before the entire neighborhood?

He paused in his consideration of the possibilities to close his eyes, putting several fingers to work on his temple. No, no matter that he had hurt her pride, he would not lay himself open to the vituperation of a country nobody for the amusement of herself or her friends. If she had chosen to sulk, he would be bound, but as it was, she had elected to draw swords. Darcy looked up again and found Elizabeth Bennet at the side of her elder sister, both of them looking at a portfolio of Miss Bingley's latest sketches. *A bold move!* He smiled to himself. *I understand you now, but I fear you are not up to weight if you think to play that game with me!* The smile was now accompanied by a satirical eye as he bent to the task of discovering more fully his adversary's qualities.

Circling the room, exchanging a word here, a nod there with Bingley's new neighbors, Darcy observed her without notice. Her voice, he noted, was well modulated and pleasing to the ear, but that was to be expected given her singing in church the day before. Her manner among her friends bespoke an openness and sincerity that was charming but certainly not reflective of the deportment expected in the level of society to which he was accustomed. Her face, he decided, was of the "milkmaid" variety: full, clear, and healthy but lacking the distinction required to be considered fashionably classical. She moved gracefully enough, he acknowledged, but the flutter of her gown betrayed a lack of symmetry about her person that would not please the purist.

Unusual in her manners, to be sure, he pronounced to his waiting sensibilities, *but lacking the physical and social graces that bespeak a truly genteel upbringing. It is well for her the officers are enchanted, for that is all the further she may look.* Darcy waited in vain for his emotions to second his verdict, but they were frustratingly unwilling to accede to his judgment, urging instead that more information was called for and a final decision on the lady should be postponed to a later date. Turning his attention to the lady's family, Darcy knew no such reluctance. No one with ears or eyes could fail to note the shrill, nakedly calculating manner of her mother and the immodest forwardness of her youngest daughters, whose only recommendation was their youth. He exhaled sharply, expressing his disgust with them.

"Come, come, Darcy, such a negative view. I am sure that tomorrow's shooting will be most enjoyable." Absorbed in his internal debate, he had barely noticed that he had drawn near Bingley and the group of gentlemen with him. Evidently a shooting party was being planned, and his snort had been taken as distaste for the idea. Nothing, he suddenly realized, could be further from the truth. A day out-of-doors with dogs and guns, far from the intricacies of a country drawing room, was exactly what he needed.

"On the contrary, Bingley, an excellent idea." Darcy clapped him on the shoulder, the relief engendered by the prospect of a day so spent rendering him more voluble than usual among strangers. "Gentlemen, has Bingley told you of his newest acquisition? It is the sweetest fowling piece you have ever seen . . ."

Later, over dinner, Miss Bingley recounted the events of the morning to those gathered at table. Mr. Hurst had pled a thunderous headache before the meal had been announced and was happily entertaining a decanter of brandy in his room, leaving his fellow men and his wife as audience for Miss Bingley's recital. Bingley settled comfortably in his chair at the table's head, giving all the attention to his sister, as his good nature allowed. Miss Bingley's façade of self-possession during the departure of their guests had not fooled Darcy for an instant; she fairly crackled with the compulsion to recount, analyze, shred, and preen. Bingley had warned him of the futility of any attempt to check her while they had awaited the summons for dinner in the gun room. He had told him he would give his sister free rein—as if he could do otherwise—and Darcy should prepare himself for an evening of cattiness and gloating.

"And no, you may not plead a headache, as that excuse has already been proffered by Mr. Hurst. And if you think for one moment that you can escape what her brother cannot, you are knocked in your cockloft! It is part of being brother to a woman whose chief concern is attaining the first circles of Society." He sighed to Darcy as he squinted one eye and looked again down the barrel of the fowling piece, checking his latest adjustment to the sight. "She must thoroughly examine today's campaign. What do you think"—he handed the rifle to Darcy—"is it right?"

"Wanting to be in the first circles, or her method of rising to them?" Darcy responded, bringing the weapon up to his cheek and settling the stock into his shoulder.

"Neither, sir! I refer to the sighting." Bingley rejoined sharply and then fell silent while Darcy, in some regret for his flippancy, checked the alignment. When he finished, he snapped it down and placed it firmly into Bingley's hands.

"Charles," he began.

"You are most fortunate in your sister, Darcy," Bingley interrupted him quietly. "Miss Darcy does not plague *you* so. Has she ever given you a moment's worry?" Darcy went very still at his words, waiting. "But she is so much younger than you and will be in the first circles immediately she comes out," Bingley continued without noticing his lack of reply. He started to chuckle to himself. "Imagine if Caroline were my younger sister!" He invited Darcy to join in his amusement at the thought. "Oh, it is too delicious." A knock at the door ended the absurdity as Stevenson announced dinner. "Ah, duty calls; and you, my friend, are required to be in attendance, if only to help pick up the pieces of what is left of our neighbors when she is finished," Bingley said.

As promised, Bingley did not attempt to govern the dinner conversation, except for an occasional "Tsk, tsk, Caroline!" and shake of his head. Meeting with such little opposition to her comments seemed to encourage Miss Bingley to think that her observations and opinions were shared by the company about the table. Mrs. Hurst, of course, echoed or embellished her sister's sentiments, each inspiring the other to new heights of criticism and ridicule.

"Now, Louisa, that is too cruel!" Miss Bingley gave her sister's hand a small slap. Mrs. Hurst protested contrition until her sister continued slyly, "I counted only *two* chins on the lady, but then I did not have the felicity of seeing her sitting down, as you did." Mrs. Hurst let out a small shriek, covering her mouth with her hand while Miss Bingley settled back in her chair with an ill-concealed smirk. "Really, these country folk are not very entertaining." She glanced covertly at Darcy. "It was all horses and hunting with the gentlemen. And the ladies! Not a one could speak of current fashion or had even the slightest acquaintance with the theater! Poetry is likely as unknown a language here as is Italian," she concluded with an arch smile in Darcy's direction. Mrs. Hurst giggled obligingly, but his lack of response appeared to decide her upon a more sober course.

"Charles, I have chosen to accept three particular invitations to dine and one afternoon social during this next week. Please oblige me by making room in your schedule for them."

"May I ask, dear sister, where we are engaged?" Bingley templed his fingers and rested his chin on his thumbs as he turned and winked at Darcy.

"Wednesday night with Squire Justin, Thursday with Mr. and Mrs. King. They are accounted quite prominent and are said to be worth three thousand a year, if you can imagine! Friday we dine with Colonel Forster and his wife. Do you suppose the woman laughs so on purpose, Louisa, or am I the only one put in mind of a donkey?" At each name Bingley sank a little lower in his chair, and when the colonel's name was mentioned, he looked to have given up hope. ". . . and Saturday evening at Sir William Lucas's." Miss Bingley ticked off the last name on her list and looked up to see her brother brighten considerably. "Is this acceptable, Charles?"

"I leave the social aspect of the campaign in your capable hands, Caroline. I request only that you leave me some time for more gentlemanly pursuits and that you plan on attending services while we are here. Regularly," he added, with a look which communicated that he would brook no objections.

Miss Bingley's eyes flew involuntarily to Darcy, whose return of her regard was the picture of blandness. "Of course, Charles. That goes without question, as you well know."

"Now," said Bingley, capitalizing on the success of his demand and the disorder into which it had cast his sister, "I wish to observe that the morning went splendidly. Caroline, you are to be congratulated." Miss Bingley demurred sweetly. "I have no doubt that our Morning In will be the subject of much conversation and that we are well launched into Hertfordshire society." He allowed his sister her opportunity to disclaim her achievement, however briefly, and proceeded with determination. "You must know that I have proposed a shooting party for tomorrow morning and expect that six or more gentlemen will come. If you will arrange the breakfast and notify the household staff, I will endeavor to alert the stablemaster, groundsman, and gamekeeper of our plans." Bingley's fingers tapped the arms of his chair at each detail, his face flushed with the delight of having his own estate to order as he wished. "It will be my turn tomorrow, my dear sisters, to advance beyond the ground you have taken today."

During the ensuing rush of questions, admonitions, and assurances between Bingley and his sisters, Darcy withdrew into himself. He had noted his friend's despair at not hearing a particular name in his sister's list of social engagements and, subsequently, his elation at the mention of Sir William. Having personally observed the close relationship of Miss Lucas with one of the Bennet sisters, it was not difficult for him to deduce the reason for Bingley's revival. *He hopes that Miss Bennet will also be one of the party. It is entirely probable. Which means . . .* He let the thought go unfinished and forcibly brought himself back to the problem of his friend and Miss Bennet.

He reached for his wineglass and, cupping the bowl gently in his hand, swirled its contents as he stared unseeing down into the deep red vintage. Perhaps he was reading more into Bingley's regard for her than was or ever would be there. His friend would be the first to admit to a propensity for falling in and out of love faster than a hare has kits. There was no reason to suppose this attraction was any different. Darcy brought the glass to his lips and held the wine momentarily at the back of his palate before allowing it to slide down his throat, feeling its warm and heady glow spread. *Let it take its course. Offer other inducements to distract his attention. Keep him busy with Netherfield.* He carefully replaced the glass on the table before him. *Surely, it will pass.*

As Darcy replaced his wineglass on the table, his hostess motioned for the footman to refill it, but he covered the bowl with his hand and shook his head.

"Is the wine not to your taste, Mr. Darcy?" she asked assiduously. "I would gladly send for another."

"No, do not trouble yourself," Darcy replied. "The wine is excellent." He began to rise from his place but was forestalled by Miss Bingley's request.

"Mr. Darcy, you cannot be leaving so soon. We have yet to hear *your* impression of Hertfordshire society." She looked round the table to garner support for her request. "I am sure it will be most amusing."

Darcy looked to Bingley, covertly seeking deliverance, but his friend could only grimace and shrug his shoulders. Shooting him a ferocious frown, Darcy resumed his chair and turned a countenance of hastily assumed indifference to the ladies. "As you say, Miss Bingley, the country people here are 'not very entertaining.' They are, though, the sort commonly referred to as the 'backbone of the Empire,' and as we must look to them to supply much-needed brawn, it is, perhaps, unreasonable to expect a surfeit of wit."

Of the two ladies, Miss Bingley regained her composure first, but not before she had resorted to her napkin, wiping the tears of laughter from her eyes. "But what of the ladies, Mr. Darcy?" A cruel gleam of anticipation illuminated her eye. "Surely you do not include the local females in the supply of brawn?"

"Not at all, Miss Bingley. I would not be so ungracious."

"But, sir," she pressed on, "you have acceded to their lack of brawn and have discounted their wit. On what basis, then, may we discriminate among the ladies of Hertfordshire?"

"You hint at the most obvious where females are concerned, Miss Bingley. You wish me to comment on their physical attributes, their beauty, if you will." Vastly uncomfortable with the turn of the conversation, he motioned to Bingley. "It is your brother rather than myself to whom you should apply for that judgment."

"We know what Charles thinks," she replied, a note of peevishness in her voice. "To him they are all diamonds of the first water. It is your opinion we would hear; is it not, Sister?"

"Yes, Mr. Darcy, do tell us," Mrs. Hurst requested brightly, then glancing at her sister, added mischievously, "I would especially enjoy your further views on the Bennet girls."

"Darcy," intoned Bingley with a pretense of menace, "I will not countenance a comment on Miss Jane Bennet save of the highest order. You may confine your assessment to her sisters . . . to Miss Elizabeth, perhaps? Now, she would be *my* idea of beauty if it were not for her elder sister."

Silence fell as all three of Darcy's dinner companions awaited his reply. It passed through his mind as he wiped his hands with the napkin on his lap that in some mysterious way Miss Elizabeth Bennet was continuing to exact her penance for his stupid blunder. So, with as much insouciance as he could summon, he made it clear as he criticized her face, her form, and her manners that Miss Elizabeth Bennet was not *his* idea of perfection in a woman.

CHAPTER 4

Intermezzo

The morning of the shooting party dawned crisp and clear, affording the gentlemen an excellent day's sport. Armed with advice gained from Darcy's experience in arranging these matters, his own engaging nature, and his new fowling piece, Bingley handily established himself among the prominent sporting men of the district. His weapon was exclaimed upon, his kills congratulated, and his company so required at future hunts that he could hardly be blamed for considering himself the most fortunate of men.

Despite repeated attempts by the other gentlemen to draw him out, Darcy stayed obdurately in the background, concentrating on the further training of the young hound he had brought with him rather than the conversation of the party. He reasoned that it likely would be as Caroline Bingley had complained, "all horses and hunting," and therefore something to which he need only half attend. Even that was merely for Charles's sake, to help him sort everyone out later when they discussed the events of the day over a glass of port in the library. This was Bingley's time to make his mark, and Darcy had no wish to divert the attention of the neighborhood away from his friend.

Darcy took a deep draught of the cool, fresh air, holding and savoring it as he had the wine at dinner the night before, then exhaled slowly, causing the field and wood before him to waver in the vapor of his breath. The party had continued across the field without him, their voices fading into a quietness that nourished peace in his soul. The peace was soon broken, however, by an urgent appeal for recognition from the region of his knee. He stooped down, balancing on the balls of his feet as he scratched the hound behind its ears.

The animal was just out of puppyhood, all legs and big feet, with a passion to please his master that verged on the comical. The look of unabashed adoration he lifted to Darcy plainly battled with the sheer joy he was experiencing to be, at last, out in the fields. Darcy laughed softly as he watched the struggle between obedience and impulse cause the dog to quiver with suppressed excitement. The bundle of confliction finally cast him a look filled with such pleading that he would have had to have been made of stone to resist it even if he had not suddenly felt an echo of the same struggle within himself. He gave the beast a brisk caress and, snatching a good-sized stick from the ground, stood up again to his full height and looked down on the animal in stern command. Hound and master eyed each other, each watching closely for any blink of movement on the other's part that would indicate a weakening of resolve. Darcy allowed the tension between them to mount until, with a great heave, he flung the stick and shouted out the most beautiful word for which a dog might hope. "Fetch!"

Like a tightly coiled spring suddenly released, the hound leapt forward in silent, total concentration on its quarry. In a matter of seconds, sounds of scuffling indicated that he was searching for his prize in the high, dry grass. Darcy sauntered in the direction the hunting party had taken, confident that the dog's enthusiasm for the game would shortly bring him to heel. He was not disappointed. Wresting the stick from him, he flung it again but gave no command. The hound sat directly before him, blocking his way, a question in his large, young eyes. Darcy waited. A small, impatient whine escaped his muzzle and ended with a sharp bark.

"Fetch!" The command almost caught the hound unprepared. Off he bounded, and Darcy continued on his way, quickening his pace. He caught up with the others just as the hound returned, proudly bearing his treasure securely in his jaws.

"I say, Darcy, your dog must be of extraordinary use to you. Mine will retrieve only game, while yours provides for the fire to cook it as well!" quipped one of the gentlemen standing with Bingley. The group laughed genially, Darcy joining them.

"Gentlemen, this has been a most agreeable morning's work," said Bingley, pausing with pleasure as he was interrupted by several hear, hears. "Thank you . . . my pleasure." He nodded back, acknowledging their accolades. "I, for one, have found it to have worked up a considerable appetite. Shall we turn back and see what my cook has deemed appropriate provender for gentlemen returned from a successful morning's hunt?"

Hefting his weapon over his shoulder, Darcy recalled his dog from his intense perusal of the prized stick and turned back toward Netherfield. A clap on his other shoulder brought his head around sharply, but he relaxed immediately when he realized it was Bingley coming up behind him.

"What do you think?" his friend asked in a whisper as they tarried behind the others. "May I report my mission accomplished to my sisters?"

"Without question," Darcy assured him, and added with a wry smile, "Take care you do not stand for a seat in Parliament next election, for you will surely win if you continue as you have begun!"

Bingley laughed heartily, then leaned toward Darcy conspiratorially. "I have it on reliable authority that the family of a certain young woman has also accepted an invitation to dine at the squire's tomorrow evening. And," he continued, blind to the martial light that appeared in Darcy's eyes in response to his news, "while it is *likely* that we may find them at the Kings', it is *certain* that they will be at the colonel's, for the youngest daughter, I have learned, is a particular friend of the colonel's wife."

"You have neglected to mention the assembly at Sir William's. Why is that, I wonder?" Darcy decided that Bingley's ballooning exuberance could stand a judiciously delivered pricking.

"Oh, I knew that they would be included at the assembly," Bingley replied, oblivious to the intent of the question. "*I* wonder you did not notice that Miss Elizabeth Bennet and Miss Lucas are fast friends! They are often in each other's company." Bingley shook his head incredulously at Darcy. "Really, Darcy, you are usually more observant!"

Darcy snorted at Bingley's naïveté but forbore to correct his misapprehension. *So, Miss Elizabeth, we are to be continually thrown into each other's society?* he thought. *What will be your next tack, I wonder.* Bingley moved away to rejoin the other gentlemen, leaving Darcy to contemplate what forces he would need to marshal for tomorrow night's engagement.

By the end of the evening at Squire Justin's, Darcy knew himself to be thoroughly routed. Nothing had gone as he expected. Eschewing any form of strong drink that day to ensure himself a clear head, he had come prepared to parry wit and grace with his disturbing adversary. If the opportunity arose and all went well, he also intended to offer her his apology. Neither was to be.

Looking back, he realized he should have known that an evening beginning as inauspiciously as this one had could never, once in motion, be recouped. They had arrived at the squire's more than fashionably late due to some detail of Miss Bingley's dress that displeased her at the very last moment. They were further encumbered by the unfortunate throwing of a horseshoe by the carriage's team leader, necessitating a slower than usual passage through the countryside. The muskiness of Mrs. Hurst's perfume, which seemed to pervade the carriage, was nigh on giving him a headache, so that by the time they had finally gained their host's drawing room, Darcy was hard-pressed to maintain an even temper.

Insisting that he be the last of the party to make his bow to their host, Darcy paused a moment just within the door to clear his head and regain his equilibrium. Miss Bingley was heartily welcomed by the squire and then handed ceremoniously on to his wife, who, with the daughters of the house, returned her curtsy in awed silence. Visibly pleased with the effect of her entrance, Miss Bingley condescended to inquire after their health and soon thereafter was gratified to be the center of attention, consisting of clothes envy on the part of most of the ladies and appreciation for the drape of those clothes on the part of the gentlemen. The Hursts followed, and then Bingley made his bow, receiving also a great shaking of his hand as the squire apologized for the pressing nature of his duties, the urgency of which had denied him the pleasure of joining the previous day's hunting at Netherfield. "You must tell me how you like your new weapon, Mr. Bingley. I have been considering the purchase of just such a model."

"I would be delighted, sir, to tell you all, but would not a demonstration be worth a thousand words? You must come to Netherfield at your earliest convenience and try it for yourself," Bingley generously proposed, the invitation further cementing his approval among the denizens of Hertfordshire. He moved on to make his bow to the squire's lady and was received with much apparent pleasure by the good woman and her daughters.

Darcy then presented himself to his host. "Mr. Darcy, sir," began the squire, "I hear you have a most accomplished hound. The word is that after it has presented you with your trophy, it gathers wood for a fire, unpacks your hunt bag, and prepares the game in the Italian style for your dinner!" The small group of gentlemen in their vicinity laughed appreciatively. "Sir, name your price! I must have this wonder."

"My apologies, Squire, for you have been seriously misled,"

Darcy replied. His lower lip twitched slightly but he did not cease his sober regard of his host. "The hound is but young and still in much need of training. I regret to say that the Italian style is quite beyond its capabilities, but as the hound insists on putting garlic in everything, your informant's mistake is understandable." Darcy's understated humor was greeted with dead silence for a moment, then the squire roared with laughter and the others joined him.

"Well done, Mr. Darcy! I see more goes on in that brain-box than your face betrays. May I present my wife?" The squire did the necessary, and Darcy soon found himself free to join whatever knot of fellow guests he might choose. Miss Bingley and Mrs. Hurst were well occupied with admirers. Mr. Hurst was arguing the merits of Gentleman's Pride against Gray Shadow in their last race. Bingley was ensnared in a hunting conversation that Darcy could plainly see he wished to escape, as every few sentences he craned his head around, looking about the long room.

Yes, where are the Bennet sisters? Darcy began to search himself. Dismissing the group around Miss Bingley, he began a perambulation of the room. He was about to move past some people gathered around a settee when the gentleman in front of him stepped back, nearly colliding with him. Sidestepping in time not to be trod upon, he suddenly found himself face-to-face with Miss Elizabeth Bennet.

"May I wish you good evening, Miss Bennet?" he began quickly, his bow to her as elegantly correct as if he were under the eyes of the queens of London Society. Her curtsy was his equal in correctness.

"You may, sir," she said, paused, and then added somewhat distractedly as she looked up at him, "though whether it be good will depend upon ourselves, will it not?" Her lips curved into a perfunctory smile that appeared and then vanished in a moment, but not before Darcy was captivated by the sparkle that even such a slight smile could not help but put into her eyes. His confusion increased as she stepped to one side and peered around him, a slight frown creasing what he was forced to concede was a lovely brow.

"If you would please excuse me, Mr. Darcy, there is something that needs my immediate attention."

"Certainly, Miss Bennet," he managed to say, if only to her back, as she hurried away. Taken somewhat aback by this treatment, Darcy first thought that she was continuing to pay him out his punishment for his ill-considered words on both of their last meetings and that her seeming avoidance of himself was part of her game. But as he watched her engaged in soothing the flutterings of her mother and "having a word" with a younger sister, he saw that her abrupt leave-taking had some legitimacy and that his suspicion was unfounded.

At dinner Darcy experienced some regret that he was not strictly within Elizabeth Bennet's sphere of polite interchange, being seated across the table and two chairs down; but he was close enough to witness her easy and engaging manner with those fortunate enough to share her end of the table. With grudging admiration, he could not help but note her delightful way of teasing gruff, old Major ——— into good humor on the one hand and, later, assuring a shy, young country dandy that the knot of his neckcloth was "bang up to the mark" on the other. Whether she was exchanging wit or listening in sympathy, he marked the uncommon intelligence displayed in her beautiful, dark eyes and wondered that he had dismissed her so thoughtlessly at the assembly.

His opinion sought on a matter by a fellow guest to his other side, Darcy was a few moments before he could return his attention down the table. It happened that the conversation around Elizabeth Bennet had ebbed, affording her an opportunity to partake of some refreshment. She extended a slender, dimpled arm and grasped the stem of the wineglass between delicately formed fingers. Darcy watched, inexplicably fascinated, as with unconscious grace she slowly brought it to her lips. She sipped the wine, ever so slightly, and gently returned the glass to its place. As she released it and returned her hand to her lap, Darcy released the breath he had not realized that he had been holding. He quickly averted his eyes before she could notice his inappropriate behavior, directing them instead to his own glass of wine. His pulse somewhat elevated, his grip on his glass was not as sure as hers had been, and the wine sloshed dangerously in the bowl as he raised it. *What is the matter with you?* he scolded himself, then swallowed the contents without tasting anything.

The squire pushed back his chair from the dinner table and suggested, with a broad wink, that the gentlemen might enjoy a bit of something that his business agent had acquired for those of discriminating taste. It awaited them in his card room; would they be pleased to accompany him? Darcy rose along with the other gentlemen, at the same time anxious and loath to leave for reasons he preferred not to explore.

After accepting his glass of very illegal French brandy, he turned to discover himself being observed by an older man on whose countenance there played a look of interest. At Darcy's involuntary stiffening, the look transformed into one of bemusement, and Darcy received, to his astonishment, a salute from the man. In puzzlement, he returned the salute, lifting his glass in like manner, and tipped a few drops down his throat. The brandy was excellent, and Darcy closed his eyes momentarily, the better to appreciate its warming glow. When he opened them, he beheld the beaming face of his host.

"Mr. Darcy, I venture to claim that even you have not often partaken of such a fine example of the distiller's art!" The squire barely paused for Darcy's assent before continuing, "I only wish that we could get American tobacco as easily as French brandy."

"We could, if it were British tobacco again," bellowed the major, coming across the room to join them. "I say, be done with all the palavering. Show them the business ends of our cannon in their capital's streets and put an end to this nonsense! United States! Phaugh! Mark me, sir. They'll be marching on Canada colony if someone at St. James's does not mind more than the cut of his waistcoat. When I was there in 'seventy-nine ..." Thereupon ensued a heated discussion of the impending war, from which Darcy happily excused himself.

He found a comfortable chair in a quiet corner and settled back into its depths with no more purpose than to enjoy the truly fine brandy. Holding up his glass to catch the light from the lamp at his side, he noted with approval its delicate amber color and how it glittered deliciously, scattering the reflected light. Before the thought could be stopped, he was comparing its display with what he had observed in Miss Bennet's eyes. He swiftly brought the glass down on the table. *Fool!* he admonished himself under his breath as he shifted uneasily in the chair.

Wondering what had become of Bingley, he looked about, locating him near the fireplace conversing with the man who had saluted him and who thanks to his host he now knew to be Mr. Bennet. Darcy could well imagine how intensely Bingley was trying to gain the older man's good opinion, for the earnestness on his face was almost painful to behold. Although Mr. Bennet appeared to be giving Bingley his equally earnest attention, Darcy thought he detected a glitter of sardonic amusement in his eye and was not entirely pleased. His sense of duty to his friend argued that he go to his rescue but, given his own curious exchange with the gentleman, Darcy felt a decided reluctance to intervene. He was only too thankful when the squire suggested that they rejoin the ladies.

The short distance down the hall from the room the gentlemen were quitting to the one they were entering seemed deceptive to Darcy, for the contrast between the two spoke of a journey between worlds. The card room had exuded the familiar atmosphere of masculine society: the aroma of brandy and pipe smoke, the creak and sigh of leather chairs, and the noble regard of hunting trophies from years past bending their gazes down from the walls upon a domain of men. Conversation swirled in the low-lit, wood-paneled room from horses and the hunt to the price of corn and talk of war. Understandings were reached, bargains struck, and connections made that would assure the peace and prosperity of the region for some time to come.

The world into which they were entering glowed in a myriad of candles, flowered wallpaper, and the sweet scent of tea and sherry. All bespoke a female society, whose unwritten rules and unpredictable behavior had never ceased to cause Darcy consternation. The exceeding amiability of his parents' marriage and the good sense and excellent understanding of those whose company they had enjoyed had ill-prepared Darcy for the nuances of the drawing room or assembly hall. Prevarication and pretty, insincere speeches had not been part of his education. Such behavior had been uniformly regarded as unmanly and insulting. Yet upon his entrance into the wider world of his peers, he had discovered that their habitual use was expected and even praised, especially when the two sexes met in society.

Unwilling to engage in the banality or intrigue that passed for drawing room conversation, Darcy attempted to retrieve his poise for the expected joust with Elizabeth Bennet. The anticipated matching of wits had not occurred and had left him curiously dispirited. Thinking to catch Bingley before they were plunged into the drawing room, he moved in his direction, but his friend seemed quite intent upon gaining the room and did not notice him. Proceeding then on his own, Darcy stepped inside and moved to a table set with assorted sweets and sherry. He studied it briefly and selected one of the sugary concoctions. As he savored it, he looked up to discover Bingley encouraging Miss Bennet to sit upon a small couch and then gesturing toward the table of sweets. She gracefully nodded her assent, and flushed with pleasure, he strode purposefully toward Darcy and the refreshments.

"Ah, Darcy," Bingley addressed him, a grin spread from ear to ear. "Step aside, man. I am commissioned on an errand for a lovely lady and must needs return quickly, or I fear I will be supplanted."

Darcy looked over Bingley's shoulder as he bent to his task. "No, you need not fear, Bingley. The lady's mother is saving your place. If I am not mistaken, she will harry anyone who would dare try to sit next to her daughter until your return."

Bingley paused just long enough to ascertain the truth of

Darcy's words and then chuckled quietly. "Mrs. Bennet has her uses, Darcy."

"And what of Mr. Bennet?" asked Darcy in a low voice. "Were you satisfied with your interview?"

"A most interesting man and very acute! Not like his wife at all." Bingley straightened, balancing his burden of a plate of biscuits in one hand and two glasses of sherry in the other. "I believe we have reached an excellent understanding." Darcy rolled his eyes. "Cynic!" responded Bingley. "But I have no time to waste on you, Darcy. Miss Bennet awaits, and mother or no, I do not intend to lose my chance now that I have finally engaged her." With that, Bingley departed in haste.

And where is the other Miss Bennet? Darcy searched the room while he reached for another biscuit and a cup of tea. A slender female hand claimed the cup before him. He looked up to find it in the possession of Miss Bingley.

"Mr. Darcy, permit me to prepare you a cup. It *is* one lump, is it not?" Darcy tried valiantly to twist the grimace he felt surfacing into something that resembled appreciation. "There . . . just as you like it." Miss Bingley offered him the tea with an air of intimacy that Darcy could not like.

"Thank you, Miss Bingley." He accepted the cup and stepped back a pace. "Please, do not let me detain you. I believe the gentlemen over there anxiously await your return." He motioned generally in the direction of one of the groups of guests.

Miss Bingley made to move past him but checked at his shoulder to whisper, "It is all *so* tedious, is it not, Mr. Darcy?" The tickle of her breath on his ear was unwelcome, and it took all of Darcy's years of training to rock smoothly back on his heels away from her. He covered his move by snatching another sweet. "You must be bored to distraction in such undistinguished company!" she continued. "Why, the squire is a veritable caricature."

"Not the kind of society to which we are accustomed, I grant you," Darcy admitted, "but, Miss Bingley, you must admit *some* utility to the evening. Your brother is well regarded among these people already, and this evening's end will see him more so. You, as his chatelaine, will undoubtedly assume a leading role in the community as well. You are, in point of fact, nicely begun. Your reception tonight was most gracious, and it would seem that you are universally admired. That cannot help but advance your brother's influence."

Miss Bingley's eyes flashed, and her lips took on a pout. "Not quite *universally* admired, Mr. Darcy."

"Miss Bingley, surely you are mistaken! I am astonished," rejoined Darcy, though himself quite certain of the source of her discontent. "Of whom do you speak?"

"Miss Elizabeth Bennet," she confessed. "I detected her insincerity at Netherfield, and her behavior here tonight only confirms the truth." Miss Bingley shook her head sorrowfully. Then, with her shot delivered, she excused herself, latched onto a young man dressed in what was locally considered the height of fashion, and requested his escort across the room. As they left, Darcy heard her exclaim upon his neckcloth, advising him to speak to her brother's valet about its proper arrangement.

The moment Miss Bingley's back was to him, the frown on Darcy's face disappeared. He lifted the cup to his lips to disguise the sardonic smile that the frown had masked and that he could no longer prevent appearing. *Elizabeth Bennet—jealous! How rich!* Darcy shook his head and, following through with his pretense, sipped the now tepid brew. Immediately he wished he had not. Looking about him in desperation for a napkin, he found none to hand so was forced to swallow the wretched stuff. By way of remedy, he quickly bit into another sweet and abandoned his cup at the nearest table.

A touch on his arm brought Darcy round to behold his host with a glass of sherry extended toward him and a look of sympathy on his face. "Not partial to tea, are you, Mr. Darcy?" Darcy took the sherry and bowed his thanks and agreement. "Don't touch it myself, unless it has got plenty of sugar and milk. Otherwise . . . vile stuff! When I heard about the Americans throwing a shipload of it into their harbor many long years ago, I knew that we had lost the colonies. Any group of people with *that* much sense would be the devil to stop in *whatever* they decided to do!"

Darcy could not but smile in the face of such good nature as the squire's. It occurred to him that his condescending opinion concerning such men and their function in the Empire might profit from some refining.

"Speaking of those with sense, here comes one now." The squire gestured with his wineglass. "Have you been introduced to Miss Bennet? Miss Elizabeth Bennet, I mean."

Darcy followed the squire's gesture in time to see the lady in question pass by them, her arm linked with that of the youngest of the squire's daughters. Miss Elizabeth's companion was clutching what appeared to be a small piece of needlework, a sampler perhaps. Her head was hung in shyness as Elizabeth gently seated her, assured her it was "perfectly lovely," and called to some of those nearby, "Do come and see Fannie's entry in Meryton's needlework exhibition." Suitably appreciative sounds of admiration rose from the group as the sampler was examined and praised. Darcy watched as Elizabeth called their attention to the subtlety of its creator's design and then quietly withdrew from the group while the young girl blushed and beamed at its center. She stopped a small distance away, and Darcy could see her judging her handiwork. With a small, quick grin of satisfaction she turned and joined Miss Lucas directly across the room from where Darcy and the squire stood.

The picture Elizabeth Bennet unconsciously presented as she bent toward the squire's daughter, lending her encouragement and support, had been loveliness itself, and Darcy had caught his breath in the delight of it. The natural grace of her figure, inclined in sweet concern for a shy child, tugged at something within him that had easily resisted the officious attention and elaborate blandishments of those with a fourfold Miss Bennet's consequence. She had struck no attitude, as was so wearisomely *en vogue* among females in London. Her subsequent charming actions had shown that her sole intent had been to give pleasure to the child and, perhaps, to her parents.

"Mr. Darcy? Pardon me, Mr. Darcy?" The squire's voice, solicitous yet amused, broke upon Darcy's consciousness. He blinked a few times and released his breath in a way that could easily have been taken for a sigh. "Perhaps a little of the sherry, Mr. Darcy? Ah, yes." He paused as Darcy nearly emptied the entire glass. "Lizzy Bennet is as true as she appears. No artifice there and, as I said, uncommon good sense, all wrapped up in as neat a little package as could be desired, eh?"

As the squire rambled, Darcy could feel the mortification of what had happened course through his body. His own sense of confusion over the increasing fascination he felt for her was burden enough, but that it should be so easily apparent to the world was intolerable. When he had first entered Society, his natural reserve had earned him a reputation as proud, and in those earlier days, he had allowed this to serve as a shield. Lately, according to Bingley, it had become transformed into armor. Shield or armor, it was not serving him well now. With great effort he drew on his past habits and answered the squire in a chill, quelling voice. "I could have no opinion on that, sir. If you will excuse me?" Bowing quickly, he walked away, the squire staring after him, his eyebrows raised in surprise.

Darcy's stony countenance dissuaded any he passed from attempting to engage him. He found a single chair with an unobstructed view of the greater part of the room and, sitting down, attempted to regain his equilibrium. He was attracted to her, that was indisputable. It was certain, though, that Elizabeth Bennet had taken no opportunity to come in his way again after dinner. For a few troubling moments, he entertained the disconcerting possibility that he simply was not of interest to her. If this were so, it would be a singular experience. Ever since his uncle had introduced him to the hallowed halls of Almack's, he had found himself courted by haughty, matchmaking mamas and deferred to by their husbands in the hopes that he would toss his handkerchief in their daughters' ways. Indeed, until this expedition to Hertfordshire, he could not recall a single female of marriageable age who had not couched her syllables in terms designed to elicit his approbation or entrap him into matrimony. The fantastic notion of Miss Elizabeth Bennet's disinterest was quickly discounted. Her short and dissatisfying exchange with him before dinner had encouraged him to believe that he had escaped the category into which Miss Bingley had been placed. That he no longer was an object of amusement he received with equanimity, but that he now seemed to rank among the furniture nettled his pride.

A few officers gathered around a couch near Darcy who had been engaged in an increasingly loud disagreement suddenly erupted with a noisy call for a lady to come and arbitrate a most vexatious matter. From under hooded eyes, Darcy watched as the opinion of the drawing room on the most suitable arbiter among the ladies wavered and then swelled to a chorus that named Miss Elizabeth Bennet. With a fine mixture of amused tolerance and modesty, she passed by Darcy on her way to the judgment seat the officers had cleared for her. A hint of her perfume drifted to him as she passed, and he found himself riveted by the gentle swishing of her gown. At that moment, without being entirely clear as to why her regard of him should matter or what was his ultimate goal, he set about devising a plan to obtain her particular attention. Reason briefly protested, but the gate was opened, the path beckoned irresistibly, and Darcy's imagination slipped past the posterns and on to the mysteries of a woman whose charms he found increasingly disturbing to his composure.

CHAPTER 5

To Know More of Her

*S*everal mornings after the squire's dinner, Darcy sauntered down the corridor to his friend's chamber and delivered a brisk knock on the door. A stumbling sound issued from behind the great oak portal, followed by the sound of a fob or watch hitting the floor. "It is no use," he heard Bingley groan to his valet. "Open the door; let him in, and be done with it!"

The door swung wide on its hinges, assisted by the tip of Darcy's riding crop. "Dare I hope you have at least *eaten*, Bingley?" Darcy sighed as he surveyed the turmoil of the room and its occupant. "You did say 'in the saddle, nine o'clock, sharp,' or did I mistake you?"

Bingley sniffed wistfully at the tidy breakfast of ham, rasher of bacon, eggs, and assorted delicacies that awaited his attention on a tray in his dressing room. The smell wafting through the open door looked to drive him mad. "I cannot think what possessed me to make our appointment for such an early hour," he groused as the chamber clock chimed a merry nine o'clock. "You know how I dislike the morning air. Too damp by half!" He continued dressing, glancing the while at Darcy, who still stood in the doorway but was now tapping his riding crop repeatedly into the gloved palm of his hand.

"If you have come to ring a peal over me, I promise you leisure to do a thorough job of it," he offered desperately, "for I must have something to eat!" So saying, he dashed for the dressing room and the breakfast tray. Following Bingley into the next room, Darcy grabbed a chair and brought it up to the small table, which groaned under the weight of silver serving bowls. His own fast broken over an hour ago, he shook his head at Bingley's offer to share the bounty and began to remove his gloves.

"Ring a peal over you? Did I really appear that grim?" At Bingley's nod, Darcy slapped his gloves on his knee as he dropped into the chair.

"I fully expected a royal jaw-me-dead about lapses in punctuality, the dangers of keeping good horseflesh waiting, failure to fulfill promises, and whatever other defect of my character you could lay your hands upon!" ventured Bingley between bites of ham and gulps of tea. "Are you sure you do not want something?" he offered again.

"No, nothing," Darcy murmured, and fell to studying his gloves. "Although everything you just now mentioned is true." He looked reprovingly at Bingley from under gathered brows and was promptly rewarded with a sugar lump cast at his head.

"There, I knew you could not resist a lecture, though it was a mercifully brief one. Tell me, is your father your model in this as in all else, or have you perfected that towering frown on your own?"

"It is my own creation, Bingley, part and parcel of that armor you say I have donned, and by the by, it is extremely useful. Now, are you finished, and may we begin this tour of the countryside you were so mad for last night?"

Bingley nodded vigorously, his mouth being stuffed with toast and jam. Wiping sticky fingers on a cream-colored linen napkin, he rose from the table. "Your obedient servant, sir," he intoned, bowing to Darcy in his best servile manner.

"May that day come quickly! Get your gear; the morning is

beautiful, and I am on edge for a good gallop." With that, he strode out of the room, leaving Bingley to follow as he might.

The groom brought Nelson to the mounting block as soon as Darcy appeared in the stable yard but had a difficult task keeping him there when the great black became aware of his master's approach. His ears pricked forward, and swinging his massive forequarters around to face the entry arch, he pulled the groom with him as he surged toward the sound of Darcy's boots on the cobble.

"Nelson, you brute! Leave off dragging that poor fellow around!" Darcy tried without success to look sternly at his horse, who was too occupied in nickering a greeting to be concerned with the welfare of his groom. Darcy reached out his hand for the reins. "Here, give them to me. You will never get him back round, I fear." Only too happy to relinquish them, the groom placed them into Darcy's hand and backed away to watch.

Under his master's direction, Nelson allowed himself to be led back to the mounting block, and Darcy neatly swung up, gathering the reins into his expert grip. He was almost tempted to ride on and leave Bingley to catch him up. Instead, he nudged Nelson into a trot, then a restrained canter, directing him into a tight figure eight that circumscribed the stable yard, thus demanding the animal's full attention to his commands.

"On edge," he repeated to himself as he signaled Nelson to change lead at the crossing of the eight. He had described himself so to Bingley, and the phrase limned him perfectly. Ever since the evening at the squire's, his entire being, body and soul, seemed in the grip of distraction. The cause of his disquiet was no mystery. The object herself, though, was nothing *but* a mystery, whose lure he found difficult to ignore.

The last two evenings had been spent in Miss Elizabeth Bennet's presence, though not strictly in her company. Bingley's information had been correct, and Darcy recalled the unexpected exhilaration he had felt upon confirming her attendance on both occasions. It had taken prodigious concentration on his part to position himself close enough to overlisten her conversations and fulfill his own social obligations without attracting her notice or the curiosity of others.

Darcy felt Nelson tense, awaiting his signal as they again approached the crossing of the figure. He leaned slightly to the left, applying pressure with his knee as a toss of Nelson's head communicated his displeasure with such disciplined exercise. Once, not long after the horse had been broken to bit and bridle, Darcy had taken him out into the wilder grounds of Pemberley, eager to see what the animal could do. The vista before them had excited both horse and rider, and before he knew it, Nelson had the bit between his teeth and they were careening over field, ditch, and fence in a manner that had both thrilled and terrified his rider. Both had survived the neck-or-nothing ride with only a few bruises, and Darcy had taken care in Nelson's training that the like should not happen again; but the emotions that had overwhelmed him then had not been forgotten.

Thrilling . . . yet terrifying! Darcy mused as he brought the powerful beast beneath him to a neat, precise halt at the center of the eight. Those emotions seemed to have resurrected recently in his breast, but this time their cause did not threaten danger to his body. He leaned over Nelson's neck and stroked the powerfully muscled arch with approval and affection. *No, the danger the young woman presents is to your heart . . . your very soul,* he acknowledged to himself. *No less thrilling*—he paused and stared hard across the fields toward Longbourn—*and certainly no less terrifying. Miss Elizabeth Bennet, what have you wrought?*

His friend's "Hallo" broke Darcy's reverie, and he turned, waving his crop in greeting. "More than past time you should have appeared, Bingley! Waylaid by a vicious poached egg?"

"Waylaid by an insistent sister, more like! Caroline wanted to be assured of our intention to dine with Colonel Forster and his officers on Monday next. Said she was obligated to invite someone for dinner and wanted to spare us the inconvenience of entertaining them."

Darcy answered Bingley's shrug with one of his own and commanded him to mount quickly and join him at the front of the manor house. Nudging Nelson into a brisk trot, he left the stable yard behind, reining the horse in when he had gained the carriage drive. *It is beyond the time for excuses,* he told himself. *I require that you speak to her at Sir William's this very evening.* Darcy squared his shoulders but then bit his lower lip and looked up into the bright morning sky. *And God help you!*

"Your coat, sir." Fletcher carefully eased the form-fitting garment up onto his shoulders, then tugged the front down and into place. Stepping back, he surveyed his master's appearance with a critical eye that had brooked no imperfection in his dress for the last seven years. Darcy awaited the verdict with a mixture of impatience and apprehension. He might not have brought his most fashionable clothes to the country, he thought while his valet circled him as if he were an objet d'art, but what he had, he desired to wear to the Lucases' gathering with some distinction. "Very good, sir. 'Every inch a king'" came the judgment. Darcy nodded.

Bingley met him in the hall, his eyes fairly crackling with anticipation. "Good, you are down and ready! I have warned my sisters they may dally all they wish, but *we* are to leave in ten minutes." He flung a dismissive hand toward the stairs. "They may all ride in Hurst's carriage if they want to arrive late!" He began to draw on his gloves as he sent the footman for their greatcoats. Darcy stepped to the door as the sounds of hooves on gravel and rattling harness grew louder and then came to a halt.

"Your carriage, Bingley. Do you wish to leave—"

"Immediately, Darcy. What good fortune, not a sister in sight. Hurry, man!" With a conspiratorial grin, Darcy quickly shrugged into his greatcoat and grabbed his hat and gloves.

Bingley raced down the stairs and leapt into the carriage with Darcy on his heels. "Drive on!" Bingley shouted, pulling the carriage door out of the servant's grip. He shut it with a bang and then collapsed on the seat opposite his friend.

"Miss Bingley will not thank you for leaving her to travel with the Hursts," observed Darcy as the carriage pulled smartly away.

"True," responded Bingley, settling back into the cushions. "Just as I shall not thank her for inviting Miss Bennet to dine at Netherfield on a night when I was sure to be absent! You remember why I was late to the stable this morning? Well, Miss Bennet was the guest my sister did not want to 'inconvenience' me with entertaining. Had I not discovered the truth by pure chance, Miss Bennet would have come and gone leaving *me* none the wiser!"

"Perhaps your sister merely wishes to strike up a friendship with Miss Bennet independent of your regard," offered Darcy, schooling his face so as not to betray his doubt of any such purpose. Bingley merely returned him a skeptical eye.

The remainder of the drive passed pleasantly in recollection of their tour of Netherfield that morning. They talked of plans, with fields planted and harvested, ditches cleared, ponds stocked, fences mended, and livestock added until the estate had fair become Paradise by the time they reached the gates of Lucas Lodge. As the carriage swept past the stone pillars, their conversation dwindled, and both men felt descend upon them an awkward silence, which deepened the closer they drew to their destination.

Sir William's effusive welcome was accepted by the two gentlemen with aplomb. Darcy allowed Bingley to say all that was correct for both of them while he covertly surveyed the drawing room. Their formal greeting delivered, he accompanied Bingley into the room but abruptly changed course when he saw his friend's destination was a table in an alcove adjoining the drawing room. There the two eldest Bennet sisters and a number of other young ladies were gathered around Miss Lucas as she demonstrated techniques in the painting of china, a rage that had swept higher Society a year ago, Darcy recalled, but was now considered passé in London. Before Bingley could make his bow to them, he was enveloped in a rainbow of muslin. Darcy looked away, cringing at his near escape from the crowd of females who were now demanding Bingley's opinion of Miss Lucas's art. He availed himself, for some minutes, of a nearby window offering an excellent view of the lodge's park before conscience prodded him to look back at his beleaguered friend, only to behold Bingley wearing a beatific smile and with the situation well in hand.

A rustling among the ladies put a period to his meditation on Bingley's remarkable ability and drew his attention to one particular lady. Her eyes crinkled in merry good nature, Miss Elizabeth had taken a seat at her friend's elbow. Captivated, Darcy watched as she chose a small piece of china, lifted it appraisingly, and then, with a mischievous grin, dipped her brush into paint and applied several bold strokes. The first brush was summarily abandoned for another. Down it was plunged into another color and applied as boldly as the first. Gasps and laughter erupted all round as she set down the piece for the group's inspection.

"There, Charlotte, I have exhausted my talent at china painting. You may fire it or dispose of it as you wish. Who is next?" Elizabeth handed her brush to an eager young gentleman, vacated her chair, and sketched a quick curtsy to the group. "If you will please excuse me." She smiled at them and faced in Darcy's direction. Immediately, he turned his head away from her, feigning indifference to her approach.

Darcy sensed rather than beheld her step past him. A curious but delicious tingling sensation swept through him in response to her brief closeness, the warmth of her seeming to drift around him caressingly as she passed. Mesmerized, he looked after her, his stomach knotting as she paused only a few feet away in contemplation of the company scattered before her.

He must have moved, however involuntarily, for Elizabeth suddenly turned back to him, her countenance exhibiting a startled air, which told him that she had not noticed him.

Before he could adequately appreciate the blush that colored her cheeks, she curtsied deeply to him. "Mr. Darcy! Pray, pardon me."

"Miss Bennet." He favored her with a clipped bow and hastily moved away, almost treading on Miss Bingley as she entered the room.

"Mr. Darcy!" she purred. "Pray, tell me you are not leaving! I depend upon you, sir, to rescue me from the stifling boredom that is sure to descend any moment, if it has not done so already." She took possession of his unoffered arm and demanded a promenade about the perimeter of the room. "How wicked of you and my brother to hie off by yourselves! I was quite desolate." She pouted prettily as they made their way.

Miss Bingley set a leisurely pace, but all too soon they drew near to the group in the alcove. "Oh, look, Darcy, they are painting china! How gauche!" She sniggered, not bothering to lower her voice. "No one paints china anymore. No one in *London* would admit to such a thing!" Darcy found that, although he was forced to acknowledge the truth of her observation, he could not join in her amusement and wished his companion had not exhibited her disdain in such a public manner.

Thankful that they had at last completed the circuit of the room, Darcy handed Miss Bingley over to the solicitude of their host. Seeing that a pot of strong, hot coffee had been added to the tables, he accepted a cup and took himself to the large fireplace whose finely carved mantel dominated the room. Leaning against it, he attempted to ameliorate the tension he felt by putting names to the faces around him but found that he was unable to prevent his eyes from searching out Elizabeth Bennet.

There! Surrounded by a group of officers. Darcy felt the tension in his chest ratchet upward. *Now, she has broken away and goes in search of? . . . Ah, yes, the invaluable Miss Lucas.* He had cause to think well of Miss Lucas, Elizabeth's friend and confidante. Her conversations with Miss Bennet had naturally been the most instructive as to the latter's character and interests, making them the most worth overhearing. He had gathered every bit with growing interest as accumulating pieces of the mystery of his fascination for her.

The ladies were engaged in a lively conversation with Colonel Forster, who seemed quite at ease with them both. Darcy put down his cup and set himself unobtrusively in the way of catching their discourse. Its content this time was of a disappointing sort, a campaign for a military ball that any female in the room might be capable of launching. The colonel graciously capitulated, the ladies curtsied their thanks and moved on, their heads quite close in shared confidences.

Suddenly, Elizabeth laid a hand on her friend's arm and, with a pleased manner, directed her attention across the room. Darcy followed their gaze and with much less pleasure saw Bingley and the eldest Miss Bennet conversing in low tones in a secluded alcove. They were not unobserved by still others. Darcy could see Miss Bingley watching her brother with displeasure and then cast at himself a look that demanded he do something. With great reluctance, Darcy started across the room.

"Did not you think, Mr. Darcy, that I expressed myself uncommonly well just now, when I was teasing Colonel Forster to give us a ball at Meryton?" Darcy stopped short in astonishment as Elizabeth Bennet turned and tossed him a saucy smile with her impertinent question.

For a few eternal seconds, he despaired of retrieving the use of his faculties. He stood transfixed, his mind desperate to form the sort of riposte that such a query required but failing him utterly. "With great energy; but it is a subject which always makes a lady energetic," he replied with a coolness that was the antithesis of the riot of emotions in his breast.

Elizabeth's eyes flashed at his answer, and her chin lifted slightly. "You are severe on us." The accusation hung in the air, electrifying the distance between them in a manner that was at once alarming and intoxicating. Darcy knew immediately that she was referring to more than his innocuous observation. His words at their first meeting had not been forgotten. It was time to apologize. He took a quick, steadying breath.

"It will be *her* turn soon to be teased," intervened Miss Lucas apprehensively, attempting to dispel the antagonism between her friend and her father's distinguished guest. "I am going to open the instrument, Eliza, and you know what follows." The light of challenge in Elizabeth's eyes dimmed into that of a genuine chagrin in which she seemed to invite Darcy to participate as she acceded to her friend's unspoken warning.

"You are a very strange creature by way of a friend! Always wanting me to play and sing before anybody and everybody! If my vanity had taken a musical turn, you would have been invaluable." She paused and turned to Darcy. "But as it is, I would really rather not sit down before those who must be in the habit of hearing the very best performers."

"Lizzy!" exclaimed Miss Lucas, her voice edged with agitation. "Do oblige me!"

"Very well." Elizabeth sighed with charming reticence. "If it must be so, it must." She lifted a grave aspect to Darcy's intense regard. "There is a very fine old saying, which everybody here is of course familiar with—'Keep your breath to cool your porridge'— and I shall keep mine to swell my song."

She turned away in the company of her much-relieved friend, who as threatened, opened up the pianoforte that stood before the great window. The instrument glowed in candlelight as Elizabeth took her place before it. The other guests crowded toward the instrument, but Darcy stepped behind them, seeking some privacy in which to compose himself and evaluate what had passed between himself and the bewitching Elizabeth Bennet.

Undoubtedly, there had been some tension, he admitted, *but surely her words at the last had been provocative.* He warmed to the thought. She desired an apology, that was certain. But was he deceived in believing that she would be open to more once it was offered?

The first notes of a popular air interrupted his thoughts, vibrating delicately through the drawing room. Darcy recognized it at once as a piece that his sister had been working on before the fateful incident of the summer past. His familiarity with it excited his curiosity and drew him forward to seek a place from which to observe the lady without notice. Discovering a suitable vantage point that gave him an unobstructed view of her profile, he quietly sat down.

Technically, her performance was not the finest, but the lightness and emotion her fingering conveyed were arresting. Then, when she joined voice to music, Darcy learned enchantment. With growing pleasure, he surrendered to her rich timbre as it washed over his senses. The plaintive entreaty of the song and the tender expression that graced Elizabeth's features as she sang gave rise to a resonance in unexplored depths within him that spread rapidly throughout his being. Darcy leaned forward, unwilling to miss any nuance, and tightly gripped the armrests of his chair. It was all he could do to stay in his seat, so strong was the urge to draw closer. He imagined leaning over her, reaching past her to turn the score's pages . . . her warmth, the scent of lavender.

He could not say when she struck the air's last note, lost as he was in the spell her song and his fancy had conspired to weave. Applause circled the room, recalling him, but it quieted before he could add his own. Cries of "Another, Miss Eliza!" were insistent enough to give the lady pause as she rose from the instrument. A beguiling smile revealed a sweetly positioned dimple as she graciously acceded to the general demand and resumed her place. Darcy could not prevent his sigh of satisfaction when she placed her fingers once more upon the keys.

Her second selection was as the first—elegant in its simplicity—but possessed of a joy of life and love that contrasted happily with its predecessor. Darcy felt a smile spread across his face that he would not have wished to account for had he been observed, its origin so private that he himself was not sure of its meaning. This time he kept his wits about him and joined in the appreciative applause at the end. Elizabeth rose again from the pianoforte and would not be persuaded to return. Swiftly, she made way for another to take her place and stepped lightly through the audience, accepting the praise of her friends and neighbors with what seemed to Darcy a most becoming absence of self-consciousness.

A concerto followed Elizabeth's performance, played flawlessly by another Bennet girl but lacking the ease or inspiration found in her sister's simpler offering. Darcy rose from his place in the middle of it in the hope of seeing more of Miss Elizabeth Bennet or catching Bingley before his sisters found him. Before either object was attained, the concerto ended, and a Scotch air set a number of the younger set to dancing at one end of the room. The loudness of the tune and the noise of pounding boots made it quite impossible to hold a conversation. Darcy stood in silent indignation, his anticipation of further intercourse with Miss Bennet, or anyone else for that matter, now dashed beneath the feet of a country reel.

"What a charming amusement for young people this is, Mr. Darcy!" Darcy turned to his host, who had suddenly appeared at his elbow, and regarded Sir William with a world-weary fixity. Sir William waxed eloquent on his subject, taking no notice of his guest's lack of accord. "There is nothing like dancing, after all. I consider it as one of the first refinements of polished societies."

"Certainly, sir," Darcy replied, provoked into sarcasm, "and it has the advantage also of being in vogue amongst the less polished societies of the world. Every savage can dance."

If he noticed Darcy's manner, Sir William took no offense but merely smiled. "Your friend Mr. Bingley performs delightfully, and I doubt not that you are an adept in the science yourself, Mr. Darcy."

"You saw me dance at Meryton, I believe, sir," Darcy answered him, unwilling to comment on his proficiency at an activity that held little appeal for him.

"Yes, indeed, and received no inconsiderable pleasure from the sight." Sir William's praise of his dancing gave Darcy to wonder whether the man had need of spectacles as well as common sense. "Do you often dance at St. James's?"

Darcy almost shuddered at the thought. "Never, sir."

"Do you not think it would be a proper compliment to the place?" Sir William inquired in all seriousness. Darcy's years of training enabled him to remain still while every nerve in his body screamed to be removed from participation in one of the most inane conversations of his experience.

"It is a compliment which I never pay to any place if I can avoid it." There, he could be no plainer than that!

Evidently, Sir William had exhausted his opinions on dancing, for he now embarked on a new tack in his bid to continue the engagement of his distinguished guest in his most protracted public exchange to date. "You have a house in Town, I conclude."

Darcy bowed his acknowledgment of being in possession of a domicile in London and prayed that his silence would encourage Sir William to entertain his other guests with his opinions.

"I had once some thoughts of fixing in Town myself, for I am fond of superior society," he confided, "but I did not feel quite certain that the air of London would agree with Lady Lucas."

Darcy elected to offer no sentiments on London's air or its suitability for Lady Lucas, hoping thereby to bring the interminable conversation to an end. Instead, a beneficent smile appeared on Sir William's face. "My dear Miss Eliza, why are not you dancing?"

Darcy swung around sharply, in time to surprise the look of total confusion and not a little alarm on the lady's face. Both emotions were quickly subsumed and replaced, when she dared to look him in the face, with an appearance of indifferent politeness.

"Mr. Darcy, you must allow me to present this young lady to you as a very desirable partner. You cannot refuse to dance, I am sure, when so much beauty is before you." With the ease that came with long acquaintance, Sir William possessed himself of Elizabeth's hand and turned to present it gallantly to Darcy. The opportunity to hold her hand in his and repeat that contact throughout a form was a serious temptation, which Darcy, though surprised by this good fortune, was well inclined to entertain. He stepped forward, but before he could assure her of his willingness, she drew back.

"Indeed, sir, I have not the least intention of dancing," she hastened to inform Sir William. "I entreat you not to suppose that I moved this way in order to beg for a partner." Darcy sensed her fear at once again being presented to his notice only to be dismissed.

"Miss Bennet," he interrupted, gravely summoning up every ounce of propriety he possessed, "I would be most gratified if you would allow me the honor of your hand." Her expression told him plainly that she believed no such thing.

"You excel so much in the dance, Miss Eliza, that it is cruel to deny me the happiness of seeing you," Sir William wheedled. "And though this gentleman dislikes the amusement in general, he can have no objection, I am sure, to oblige us for one half hour."

No objection in the least, thought Darcy, suddenly in more charity with Sir William than he would have thought possible only moments ago.

"Mr. Darcy is all politeness," said Elizabeth, smiling in anticipation of emerging from this encounter the winner.

"He is, indeed: but considering the inducement, my dear Miss Eliza, we cannot wonder at his complaisance; for who would object to such a partner?"

It was a question for which neither party was prepared to venture an answer. Elizabeth looked at Darcy archly, eyes sparkling in triumph and, murmuring her regrets to Sir William, turned away. Although disappointed, Darcy could not help but admire her poise and amusement in the awkward situation into which they had been drawn. Miss Elizabeth Bennet was so much more than he had expected to encounter in the savage hinterlands of Hertfordshire. His admiration deepened as the picture she had earlier presented at the pianoforte flashed through his mind. A touch on his arm awoke him from these pleasant thoughts.

"I can guess the subject of your reverie." Miss Bingley's bored tone assured Darcy that his thoughts had not been read on his face.

"I should imagine not," he replied.

"You are considering how insupportable it would be to pass many evenings in this manner—in such society." She sighed a commiserating sigh. "And, indeed, I am quite of your opinion. I was never more annoyed! The insipidity, and yet the noise—the nothingness, and yet the self-importance of all these people! What would I give to hear your strictures on them!" She tucked one hand inside the crook of his arm and with the other smoothed away imaginary wrinkles in his coat sleeve.

"Your conjecture is totally wrong, I assure you. My mind was more agreeably engaged." Darcy politely but firmly removed her hand. "I have been meditating on the very great pleasure which a pair of fine eyes in the face of a pretty woman can bestow."

"Indeed, sir!" she returned with a careful indifference. "And which lady may be awarded the credit of inspiring such reflections in one so inured to flirtation?"

"Miss Elizabeth Bennet," came Darcy's unguarded reply, and in such a straightforward manner as to give her no clue concerning the seriousness of his regard.

"Miss Elizabeth Bennet! I am all astonishment. How long has she been such a favorite? And pray when am I to wish you joy?"

Refusing to be drawn into saying anything that might fuel her suspicions, Darcy replied vaguely and ignored her continuing drollery. He wished only for the evening to end. A desire for a glass of brandy, a crackling fire in the hearth, and a comfortable chair from which to enjoy both while he contemplated the new pieces of the puzzle of Miss Elizabeth Bennet occupied his thoughts to such a degree that Charles could get no more than a few syllables out of him. Whether out of gratitude for Darcy's forbearance with his preoccupation with the eldest Miss Bennet that evening or out of a sense for Darcy's need of solitude, he arranged for the rest of their party to return to Netherfield as they had come.

As they settled in for the journey, Bingley cleared his throat a few times, only to be ignored. "Darcy, is there something the matter? I've never seen you so." He laughed nervously.

"The matter? No, Charles, nothing is wrong. At least, I do not think so." His voice trailed off as he looked out the carriage window into the cool, starry night. After a few moments he gathered himself together and turned back to his friend. "Your little foray into the country has brought more than we expected, I daresay. That is all."

CHAPTER 6

Feint and Parry

The evening with Colonel Forster and his officers had been, in Darcy's opinion, a welcome one. Although not of a military bent himself, he appreciated the company of gentlemen whose ideas of honor and service, king and country, were not unlike his own. He listened with more than polite attention to the colonel's stories of his campaigns against Napoleon and even more so when the man recounted a meeting with Admiral Nelson himself, a hero of Darcy's from his youth. Even Charles had allowed himself to enjoy the evening once he arrived and downed a glass of good port toasting the ladies of Meryton along with the younger officers. Their journey to the rented rooms that served as the officers' club had been punctuated with vituperation at the perfidy of his sister in inviting Miss Jane Bennet to Netherfield on a night she knew him to be engaged elsewhere. The evening's dreary, wet weather had mirrored Bingley's mood, tempting Darcy to come short with him. But knowing Bingley's rare bad tempers to be mercurial, he had held his tongue and merely cocked an eyebrow at his more extreme vows of revenge.

They were now on their way back to Netherfield in a rather mellowed state of mind and quite ready to seek the quiet comfort of their beds. Thus, the degree of noise and activity among the servants that greeted their arrival home was beyond what either gentleman expected or desired. Catching Stevenson flying through the hall, Bingley demanded of him the reason for the unsettled state of his home.

"Begging your pardon, sir, but Miss Bingley's guest was taken very ill and—"

"Miss Bennet! Do you refer to Miss Bennet?" cried Bingley.

"The very same, sir."

"What has happened? What is being done? Good heavens, man, do not keep me in suspense!"

"The apothecary is sent for, sir, and we await his arrival at any moment. We thought you were he." In light of his master's agitation, Stevenson unbent and continued in a sympathetic tone, "I do not know any of the particulars, sir. If you applied to your sister . . . ?"

Without a backward glance Bingley bounded up the stairs in search of Caroline, leaving his friend to fend for himself. Darcy followed him up the stairs but at a more sedate pace and with the object of seeking his own rooms. He laid his hat, gloves, and stick on a table in his sitting room while acknowledging his valet's greeting.

"It seems there has been some excitement here tonight, Fletcher."

"Yes, sir. A young lady became ill at dinner, sir."

"A problem in the kitchen?"

"Oh, no, sir."

Darcy waited a few seconds before raising his brows, signaling his desire to know more. Fletcher, betraying no surprise at his master's interest in the health of a country miss, supplied more detail.

"I had heard that she arrived at Netherfield quite damp, sir. A result, no doubt, of traveling on horseback for three miles in the most appalling downpour."

"On horseback!" Darcy's incredulity encouraged his valet to continue.

"Yes, quite, sir! Mr. Bingley's sisters were astonished as well. The young lady was supplied with dry apparel immediately but fell seriously ill in the midst of supper. I understand they are awaiting the apothecary, or what passes for one in this place, sir."

His face grave, Darcy nodded his comprehension. "Fletcher, there is no question that the lady is indeed ill?"

"I would not know, sir."

Darcy snorted his disbelief. "Come, come, Fletcher!"

His valet evidenced some hesitation but then confessed, "I have heard talk among the upstairs maids which would indicate genuine concern that the lady has become feverish, sir."

As Fletcher helped him out of his clothes, Darcy puzzled over such strange behavior. To set out on a journey of three miles on horseback in threatening weather did not seem, to him, a course of action that the gentle Miss Jane Bennet would undertake. The inducement of an evening at Netherfield he acknowledged to be great for a country-bred girl. But a country-bred girl would be equally aware of the folly of chancing a soaking. Why had she not taken her father's carriage? Surely he would supply her any means in his power for furthering her acquaintance with the Bingleys. Mr. Bennet was, without a doubt, a curious fellow but not one to disregard the welfare of his daughter. Therefore, to what purpose or by whose design had she come in this manner?

Now dressed in his nightclothes, Darcy dismissed his valet and carried the candle into his bedchamber. Setting it down, he dropped gratefully onto the welcoming bed and slid beneath the downy coverlet. He reached over and cupped the candle's flame, blowing it out with a sigh. As he stretched out his long limbs and plumped his pillow, a new aspect of the matter struck him. If Miss Bennet became so ill she might not be moved, would her next eldest sister not come to see her? He was certain of it, and that prospect he reflected upon with some satisfaction until sleep claimed him.

The next morning dawned with the bright sun and gusty winds that usually follow a storm. The breezes had licked up much of the rain from the evening before but not enough by the early hour at which he rose to tempt Darcy to a morning ride. He knew he ought to work out the fidgets to which Nelson was undoubtedly treating his groom, but the mud they would kick up would be horrendous, and the horse's hooves would cut up the turf dreadfully. No, as much as he would relish an hour on horseback, he did not relish cleaning up the dirt in which he would return. Nelson and his groom would have to work out an understanding on their own.

Coffee awaited him on the sideboard, and cup in hand, he sought out the library and the letters from his steward and house-keeper at Pemberley that required his attention. An hour later, noises from the hall alerted him to the presence of the rest of the household, and folding his letters, he went to join them in the breakfast room.

"Mr. Darcy, up before us as usual, I see." Miss Bingley greeted him with a smile and a nod at the empty cup and saucer he laid on the sideboard. As Darcy helped himself from the platters arrayed before him, a servant entered and bent to speak privately to Miss Bingley. When he had left, she turned to her family at table with a sigh. "Miss Bennet is no better, I fear. It seems she must remain our guest a little longer."

"Can anything more be done for her, Caroline?" Concern flooded through Bingley's voice. "Perhaps a physician from London should be summoned."

"Surely, Charles, that is her family's decision! It would not do to act so precipitously. Mr. Darcy, you concur in this, do you not?" Miss Bingley looked to Darcy, confident of his support. In consideration of his friend's anxiety, Darcy would not reply at once. With reluctance he seconded Miss Bingley's opinion of the matter but took care to couch it in terms he hoped would soothe Bingley's concern. The meal progressed in silence for a time but was interrupted when the door suddenly opened, revealing an extraordinary sight.

Framed in the doorway was Miss Elizabeth Bennet, her cheeks a becoming rosy hue but the rest of her person in a pronounced state of dishevelment. From the condition of her boots and petticoat, it was obvious that she had been some time out-of-doors, most probably walking across fields. Her hair was windblown despite her bonnet, its ribbons in a hopeless tangle, and the hems of her dress and pelisse were spattered with mud. Darcy's lips twitched in delight at the charming picture she made, her eyes brilliant from exertion yet guardedly defiant of any censure that might be accorded her unannounced and untidy appearance.

Bingley was the first to move toward her. "Miss Elizabeth! Welcome, welcome . . . Please come in and sit down! You have walked all the way from Longbourn?" At her nod he shook his head. "You must be very tired." Pulling out a chair, he gently pushed her into it. "Please, do sit. There now, you have come for news of your sister."

Darcy knew a moment of unreasonable jealousy when Elizabeth raised a grateful face to Bingley as she accepted the seat. "Thank you, sir. You are very kind." She paused briefly, tugging at the ribbons of her bonnet. "What can you tell me of Jane, Mr. Bingley? Is she very ill?"

"I regret to say my sisters tell me Miss Bennet did not sleep well. She continues to be feverish and is unable to leave her chamber."

Elizabeth rose quickly from the chair and begged that she be taken to her sister immediately. "Come, Miss Eliza," drawled Miss Bingley in soothing tones, "Louisa and I will take you up. We were just about to visit your sister ourselves, were we not, Louisa?" Between them, the two women quickly swept their new guest out of the room.

Darcy was careful not to watch as the ladies departed but instead finished his breakfast, a pensive Bingley keeping him silent company. Finally, he laid aside his napkin and regarded his friend with compassion tinged with some exasperation. "Bingley, no one will be served by the two of us keeping vigil outside Miss Bennet's door. I have some letters to post. What do you say we take them into Meryton ourselves? We shall have to stay on the roadsides and no mad gallops . . ." He left the question unfinished. During his discourse Bingley had stirred and, by its end, evidenced some interest.

"I would be sorely tempted if you were to, say, . . . allow me a go on your Nelson?" he replied with an impish grin.

"I would be writing your death warrant should I allow something so harebrained! You are not so disconsolate that I would tempt fate merely to cheer you." Darcy tried to look severe in the face of Bingley's attempts to look inconsolable. "Come now"—he abandoned his pose—"do we ride for Meryton or shall we wander the halls of Netherfield, waylaying everyone who comes out of Miss Bennet's chamber?"

"Meryton it is, Darcy!" Bingley joined him in laughter but then paused and continued in a more serious manner. "I am glad that Miss Elizabeth has come. She will know her sister's health better than the servants or, Heaven forbid, my sisters. I think Miss Bennet would want her sister by her rather than strangers." He was silent for a moment, then seemed to come to a decision. "If Miss Bennet is not better when we return, I shall invite Miss Elizabeth to stay at Netherfield until her sister can safely be removed to her home. There is nothing objectionable in that, is there, Darcy?"

"Nothing at all, Bingley. All the demands of propriety are met. It is an excellent idea."

"Good! Then, I shall meet you in the stable in twenty minutes, no . . . one half hour, and we will be off to Meryton to post your oh-so-important letters." Bingley's lightened mood lent a spring to his step as he made for his chambers to change into riding clothes. Needing far less time to change, Darcy poured himself another cup of coffee and took it to the window, leaning one shoulder against the frame.

Was Elizabeth's presence at Netherfield truly an excellent idea, as he had just told Bingley? To be so often in her company, here, where he had achieved a certain level of easiness, threatened his comfort; yet it was the perfect place to deepen his acquaintance with her. Here, *she* would be the guest, the outsider, and *he* would have the advantage that familiarity bestowed.

He shifted his stance, lifting the cup to his lips as he contemplated what the next few days might hold. No society of strangers to placate or play to, no competition for her attention, no clever, meaningless chitchat to invent or maintain. He could fence with her—that their interaction would resemble that activity, he had no doubt—at leisure. Regardless of the excellence of the idea, the real question confronted him: Which did he desire more, his continued comfort or the thrumming excitement of verbal swordplay with Miss Elizabeth Bennet?

"Mr. Darcy, can you inform me of my brother's whereabouts? Miss Eliza has entrusted me with a request."

Miss Bingley's habit of interrupting his thoughts was growing wearisome, but he turned to her with a polite reply. "He has gone to change into riding clothes. We thought it best to leave you to your nursing in peace so you will not feel obliged to entertain us as well as your patient." He laid aside his cup and bowed, adding just before he left, "Do not let Bingley leave before you have spoken with him. He has come upon an excellent idea."

Miss Elizabeth Bennet was not to be found in any of the public rooms of Netherfield on the two gentlemen's return from their ride. Nor did she appear in the course of the afternoon. Darcy had kept an ear attuned for any strains of music from the drawing room or a low, pleasing voice issuing from the ladies' parlor, but the house was silent save for the noise of servants about their duties. By supper, he began to feel disgruntled and at short ends. Having arduously come to the conclusion that he desired her presence despite the havoc it would wreak upon his composure, he found her absence now grated upon him.

It was not until six-thirty, when dinner was announced, that she finally joined them, dressed in a clean frock lately sent from Longbourn. Her hair had been brushed back into order in a simple but becoming style and bound with a plain ribbon. Darcy's resentment of her absence for the whole of the day melted somewhat in the pleasure he received from seeing her at last. His pleasure was, however, short-lived.

"Miss Eliza, how have you left our poor Jane?" cried Miss Bingley, cutting off Darcy as he stepped in their guest's direction. He checked his movement and retired, unwilling to become part of a charade of Caroline's contrivance. Miss Bingley possessed herself of her guest's arm, patting it solicitously as Elizabeth informed the party that she was distressed that she could not make a favorable answer to their kind inquiry. The gravity of her demeanor and the concern in her eyes gave Darcy to be ashamed of his earlier impatience with what he had deduced to be coyness on her part. She was clearly troubled, and her vigilance over her sister was evidenced by the weariness in her face.

"We are truly grieved, are we not, Louisa? Jane is such a sweet girl to be suffering so." Miss Bingley eased Elizabeth toward the dining table and seated her at the end opposite Darcy's chair. Darcy frowned in displeasure at the seating arrangements. Perhaps he could take Hurst's seat for the evening? "It is so shocking to have a bad cold," continued Miss Bingley.

"So shocking," echoed Mrs. Hurst. "Mr. Hurst, your chair." She motioned her husband to the place beside Elizabeth. Hurst, to Darcy's consternation, lowered his bulk into the seat with uncharacteristic speed. "I dislike being ill, excessively."

"As do I, Sister." Miss Bingley shuddered. "Excessively! Therefore, I never indulge in it. Why, my constitution will not allow it. There now, Miss Eliza. I hope you are settled in."

Darcy took his accustomed seat at the table at Bingley's left and resigned himself to entertaining Miss Bingley and Mrs. Hurst, who made persistent demands for his attention or opinion. Occasionally he was able to steal glances down the table to observe how Elizabeth was managing with Bingley's brother-in-law as her only companion. Her conversation and behavior were, to say the least, subdued, and he could not catch anything of what she was saying. Once, he heard a disdainful outburst from Hurst, but the only words that he could distinguish were "not like ragout," which made no sense to him whatsoever.

As soon as the last course was removed, Elizabeth excused herself and returned abovestairs to resume the care of her sister. At her withdrawal, Darcy was only too glad to accommodate Bingley and consent to retire, along with Hurst, to the gun room for a brandy. But before he rose from his seat, Miss Bingley called them all to attention.

"Well"—she sniffed in a dramatic fashion—"I daresay I have never met with such intolerable manners in my life! Indeed, if we were not favored with insufferable pride one moment and with impertinence the next, I know nothing of the matter!"

"Of whom do you speak, Caroline?" asked Bingley, a thundercloud gathering upon his brow. Darcy also stared at her in silent incomprehension. He leaned back in his chair, crossing his legs, and absentmindedly began twisting his napkin.

"The chit who just walked out the door, Bingley," came the answer from a most surprising quarter. Hurst threw down his napkin. "Can you imagine? Preferring a plain dish to a ragout! No style at all, or conversation either, for that matter. Silent as a nun until you press her, then out comes the most opinionated nonsense."

"What! Mr. Hurst"—Miss Bingley laughed—"does her 'beauty' not make up for these defects? I have heard her eyes rated as quite fine." Hurst's only reply was a disparaging grunt, causing Darcy to wring another twist in his napkin.

"You are quite right, Mr. Hurst," said his wife. "She has nothing, in short, to recommend her, but being an excellent walker. I shall never forget her appearance this morning. She really looked almost wild!"

"She did, indeed, Louisa. I could hardly keep my countenance." Miss Bingley dropped her gaze to her plate, then looked up at Darcy from beneath slyly lowered eyelids. "Very nonsensical to come at all! Why must *she* be scampering about the country, because her sister had a cold? Her hair, so untidy, so blowsy!"

"Yes, and her petticoat; I hope you saw her petticoat, six inches deep in mud, I am absolutely certain." Mrs. Hurst laughed.

Although Darcy had become inured to the Bingley sisters' habit of shredding the characters of their acquaintances, their unprovoked attacks on Elizabeth he could no longer tolerate. This presented him with a quandary. Should he object to their malicious gossip? Doing so would probably result in more stealthy attacks on her and a never-ending stream of innuendo toward himself. Should he hold his peace? He was, after all, their guest. There must be some way . . .

"Your picture may be very exact, Louisa," said Bingley sharply, "but this was all lost upon me. I thought Miss Elizabeth Bennet looked remarkably well when she came into the room this morning. Her dirty petticoat quite escaped my notice!"

Well done, thought Darcy. Perhaps Bingley would prove up to weight and quash his sisters' intractable habit without any interference on his part.

Undeterred, and with her attention still upon Darcy, Miss Bingley drove her point home. "*You* observed it, Mr. Darcy, I am sure, and I am inclined to think that you would not wish to see *your sister* make such an exhibition."

"Certainly not," he replied, a slight tremor shaking him at the remembrance of the exhibition of his family that had so narrowly been averted.

A smirk upon Miss Bingley's lips warned him that his reaction had not gone unnoticed. She leaned toward him confidently. "I am afraid, Mr. Darcy," she observed in a half whisper, "that this adventure has rather affected your admiration of her fine eyes."

Darcy's piercing, dark gaze leveled on her, and an enigmatic smile played upon his lips. "Not at all," he replied, "they were brightened by the exercise."

Fletcher had taken his leave, firmly closing the chamber door behind him, but Darcy remained seated before his dressing table, staring unseeing into his mirror. It had been true when he had said it, he ruminated silently, and upon further reflection, it retained its veracity.

"It must very materially lessen their chance of marrying men of any consideration in the world."

The subject had been the barely respectable London relations of their guests and that connection's influence upon the prospects of the young women abovestairs. Bingley had evidenced an alarming willingness to dispute their status with his sisters until Darcy had stepped into the conversation with his dampening observation. Charles had not been pleased with it and had lapsed into a silence on the subject that Darcy had hoped his sisters would emulate. Rather than take his cue, they proceeded to entertain each other with further witticisms at the expense of those they had lately professed to pity. Darcy could not imagine what prompted them to repair to Miss Bennet's room for a consoling visit after such a display, but so they did until coffee was announced.

Alone now in his chambers, Darcy shook his head, his disquiet with the evening driving sleep away. *Caroline Bingley.* With her face, figure, and fortune, she moved easily among the first circles of the gentry and could well aspire to attain those of the nobility, despite the fact that her fortune was acquired through trade. Society's approval of her family was only lately given, yet she behaved as rudely as a duchess and as heartlessly as a jade. Darcy shuddered at the thought of such a woman as his life's companion and mistress to his estate and its dependents. His thoughts then turned to the more pleasing but troubling person of Elizabeth Bennet. She was the daughter of a gentleman from a long line of gentlemen who, despite her ridiculous mother and lamentable younger sisters, had inherited that gentility in full measure. But because her family had fallen upon straitened times, their status, though secure in the environs of Hertfordshire, had declined in larger society from welcome to bare acknowledgment.

She may reign in Meryton—Darcy sighed—*but in London, she would be disdained while altogether less worthy women are courted and praised to the skies.* He rose, then, and made his way to his bed. But sleep still eluded him as the exchanges of the evening replayed in his brain. How had it started? Ah, yes, with books. She had elected to read rather than play cards . . .

"Miss Eliza Bennet despises cards. She is a great reader, and has no pleasure in anything else." Miss Bingley's praise was elegantly edged with scorn. Darcy looked at her in surprise, her attack coming so immediately upon the lady's appearance among them. Elizabeth had been taken aback as well, or perhaps her few moments of silence were due to weariness, Darcy could not be sure. Her eyes widened at Miss Bingley's remark and then returned to the tome in her hands before she ventured a reply.

"I deserve neither such praise nor such censure," she cried. "I am *not* a great reader, and I have pleasure in many things."

Bingley, whom Darcy knew to possess the romantic soul of a knight-errant, came to Elizabeth's rescue with a sincere compliment followed by a self-deprecating description of his own reading habits.

"I am astonished that my father should have left so small a collection of books," interjected Miss Bingley. "What a delightful library you have at Pemberley, Mr. Darcy!"

Darcy very much doubted that the contents of his library excited quite the degree of delight in Miss Bingley's bosom that her tone implied. It was much more likely that the wealth to which the sheer number of volumes attested was what excited her admiration.

"It ought to be good," he replied, but eschewed any credit for it by adding, "It has been the work of many generations."

Miss Bingley could not admit his modesty. "And then you have added so much to it yourself." With an air of intimacy she continued, "You are always buying books."

Darcy almost ground his teeth in annoyance at her persistent flattery and, equally, at the amused light that was appearing in Elizabeth's eyes at his discomfiture. "I cannot comprehend the neglect of a family library in such days as these," he maintained as he tossed the cards in his hand into the play on the table.

Miss Bingley proceeded in her raptures from the library at Pemberley to the house in general and on to the surrounding gardens and countryside, ending with an admonishment to her brother to take it for a model and to build for himself nothing less than its equal. Her brother good-naturedly agreed to her scheme and offered to buy Pemberley should Darcy decide to part with it. That possibility was of so absurd a nature that the group laughed genially.

With that topic exhausted, Miss Bingley cast out another with which to secure his attention. "Is Miss Darcy much grown since the spring? How I long to see her again! Such a countenance, such manners, and so extremely accomplished for her age."

Bingley looked sharply at his sister, trying, Darcy supposed, to dampen her fulsome compliments. Failing, he again attempted to direct the conversation into more neutral courses. "It is amazing to me how young ladies can have patience to be so very accomplished as they all are. They all paint tables, cover screens, and net purses . . ."

"My dear Charles," Darcy remonstrated as he forced his eyes away from Elizabeth to regard his friend, "your list of the common extent of accomplishments has too much truth." Seizing upon the opportunity afforded him to excite Elizabeth's opinions, he forwarded his own. "I am very far from agreeing with you in your estimation of ladies in general. I cannot boast of knowing more than half a dozen in the whole range of my acquaintance that are really accomplished."

"Nor I, I am sure," seconded Miss Bingley. Darcy ignored her, turning his gaze expectantly upon Elizabeth. She did not disappoint him.

"Then you must comprehend a great deal in your idea of an accomplished woman."

"Yes; I do comprehend a great deal in it."

"Oh, certainly," Miss Bingley hastened to intervene. "No one can be really esteemed accomplished, who does not greatly surpass what is usually met with." She proceeded then to catalog an array of knowledge and talents that only the best education could afford and the most enlightened parent would deem appropriate for his female progeny. ". . . or the word will be but half deserved," she concluded with a pitying smile at her guest.

Elizabeth returned her regard with some consternation, her lips pressed together and a martial light in her eye. Greatly desiring to know her mind, Darcy pressed her further, adding, "All this she must possess, and to all this she must yet add something more substantial"—he nodded at the book in her hands—"in the improvement of her mind by extensive reading."

"I am no longer surprised at your knowing *only* six accomplished women," she threw back at him, fairly bristling. "I rather wonder now at your knowing *any*."

Darcy nearly threw back his head and laughed at her delightful indignation, but he confined himself to raising an eyebrow at her protest. "Are you so severe upon your own sex, as to doubt the possibility of all this?" he goaded her.

"*I* never saw such a woman," Elizabeth blustered, her confidence seeming to falter. "*I* never saw such capacity, and taste, and application, and elegance, as you describe, united."

The other two ladies present, Darcy recalled, had immediately cried out against her expressions of doubt but were soon brought to order by Mr. Hurst's complaints of their inattention to the game at hand. A few minutes later Elizabeth had retired and taken with her all the sparkle the evening had provided. Satisfied with the beginning he had made, Darcy had excused himself from playing another game and, sending a summons to his man, had left the Bingleys to their own devices.

She is certainly not a toadeater! Darcy chuckled quietly to himself as he shifted around in the bed for a more comfortable arrangement of limbs and pillows. She would not swallow absurdity with a smile in order to please, nor bow to it in the face of mounted opposition. "Miss Elizabeth Bennet"—he spoke as if addressing her—"regardless of your unfortunate connections, you are a singular young woman. I wonder what weapons you will bring to the fray tomorrow."

The following morning found Miss Bennet a little improved under the loving care of her sister; therefore, a note was dispatched to Longbourn. The answering of that note with the persons of Mrs. Edward Bennet and her various daughters on Netherfield's doorstep occurred, to Darcy's mind, all too quickly. Presently, they attended Jane Bennet, and he and the Bingleys lingered in the breakfast room, awaiting the ladies' descent. Bingley passed the time pacing, now sitting down to gulp at a cup of tea, then bounding up and pacing again, only to throw himself, moments later, into a chair against the wall and fiddle nervously with the porcelain shepherdess who reigned on the pretty little table that matched the much-abused chair.

"Charles, *do* put the Dresden back on the table before it is broken," hissed Miss Bingley, her small reserve of patience with the intrusion of the Bennet family quite at an end. "And *please* do not pace so!" she added when Bingley once again thrust himself out of the chair. "Mrs. Bennet can have nothing upon which to object. Jane has been afforded every attention, and she is surely regaining her health. Country-bred girls are notoriously hearty creatures, are they not, Louisa?"

"So it must be, Caroline. How else can they be such excellent walkers!" Mrs. Hurst's snigger was interrupted by the sound of the turning latch of the door.

Mrs. Bennet, in the lead of her daughters, entered the room all aflutter with expressions of concern for Jane's condition and a horror at the idea of removing her to Longbourn that took no one but Bingley by surprise. By the end of her extended recital of fears and of Jane's merits, Darcy was certain he had resolved the mystery of Miss Bennet's remarkably unwise journey to Netherfield two nights previous. The only question that remained and had nagged at him since the note to Longbourn was sent was: Who would be called upon to continue nursing Miss Bennet? It was entirely possible the lady would require Elizabeth at home and send *another* daughter to try her luck at Netherfield. Or a servant . . . or, Heaven forbid, he swore silently, his jaw tightening, the mother might intend to stay! He studied Elizabeth's face as she crossed the room in her mother's wake and was puzzled at the anxiety he saw in every line. *This does not bode well . . . Could there be some truth in Mrs. Bennet's protestations? No, if she is anxious, it is for her mother!* He continued to watch them all from his vantage point at the window, the sun shining over his shoulders, as if he were attending a play. Mrs. Bennet simpered and smiled while the younger girls ogled the richness of the room and the ladies' dresses, giggling and whispering to one another in the most uncircumspect manner. Elizabeth had found refuge from the antics of her relations in a light repartee with Bingley. She held herself less stiffly now, he noticed.

"Lizzy"—Mrs. Bennet's voice cut through the brightness of her daughter's conversation—"remember where you are, and do not run on in the wild manner that you are suffered to do at home."

Darcy's musings were swiftly brought to heel as the shrill voice caused all conversation in the room to a stop. His back stiffened. He glanced at Elizabeth's face, noting the briefest appearance of pain in her guarded countenance before she turned back to her mother. The woman was impossible! Seething in displeasure, he quickly turned his back upon the room before he overstepped propriety himself. Was she so lost to proper feelings that she could scold her daughter in their presence!

Bingley stepped into the breach of shocked silence. "I did not know before," he said, continuing the thread of his conversation with Elizabeth, "that you were a studier of character. It must be an amusing study."

"Yes," she replied. Her voice sounded quite small at first but steadied as she spoke. "But intricate characters are the *most* amusing. They have at least that advantage."

Darcy turned back at her words, determined to encourage Elizabeth and disoblige her mother. "The country can in general supply but few subjects for such a study." Elizabeth looked up at him questioningly. "In a country neighborhood," he explained, "you move in a very confined and unvarying society."

"But people themselves alter so much," she replied, a merry twinkle giving testimony that a diverting example lay behind her words. "There is something new to be observed in them forever."

"Yes, indeed," cried Mrs. Bennet stridently, evidently offended by his estimation of a country neighborhood. "I assure you there is quite as much of *that* going on in the country as in Town."

Darcy stared at her, incredulous that he should be the object of such a person's insupportable manners and open animosity. His glance flickered to Elizabeth. The look of apprehension mixed with mortification was returning to her face. He swallowed the stinging setdown that clamored to be set loose, clamped his lips together in a grim line, and turned silently away.

Conversation resumed as he slowly walked about the room. Although he gave the appearance of disinterest—now gazing out the window, then withdrawing into the perusal of a book—he was careful to remain within hearing of Elizabeth. His subterfuge was little rewarded; Mrs. Bennet, once in command of the conversation, would not relinquish its control. She waxed eloquent now on the attention Jane had received from a London gentleman when she was but fifteen years old. "He wrote some verses on her, and very pretty they were," she concluded grandly.

"And so ended his affection," Elizabeth hurried to interject. Darcy stopped his perambulations and looked at her curiously. "There has been many a one, I fancy, overcome in the same way," she continued in a strained voice. "I wonder who first discovered the efficacy of poetry in driving away love!"

"Driving love away, Miss Elizabeth? Curious! I have been used to consider poetry as the *food* of love, not its executioner!" Her head came up at his contradiction, and he saw with complacence the gleam his words of challenge had returned to her eyes.

"Of a fine, stout, healthy love it may," she shot back at him. "Everything nourishes what is strong already. But if it be only a slight, thin sort of inclination, I am convinced that one good sonnet will starve it entirely away."

Truly, he could not prevent the answering smile that o'erspread his face, even if the whole room *was* looking at them. A few moments of silence passed. Then Mrs. Bennet turned to offer her thanks for the kind attention Netherfield had extended to her poor, sick Jane, and she rose to take her leave. Darcy observed her with some trepidation, wondering anew what had been decided about Jane's nursing.

"Mr. Bingley," spoke up the fidgety one, "you promised us a ball at Netherfield, if you will remember, sir. Everyone is expecting it! It would be the most shameful thing in the world if you do not keep your promise!"

"I am perfectly ready, I assure you, to keep my engagement," responded Bingley, to Darcy's complete despair. "And when your sister is recovered, you shall, if you please, name the very day of the ball. But you would not wish to be dancing while she is ill."

"Some of us would not wish to be dancing whether she is ill or no," Darcy murmured to Bingley as Lydia Bennet went into transports over his friend's amiability. Bingley shot him a quelling look, which he received with resignation. The very last thing he desired was society on the scale of a ball, be it in the country or in Town. His peace would be cut up entirely in the hustle-bustle of preparations, not to mention the daunting prospect of doing his duty by the ladies of Hertfordshire during the event itself. His only consolation, and bright it did suddenly appear, was the opportunity it would afford him to claim the dance he had been denied at Sir William's.

Mrs. Bennet clucked at her chicks and brought them into line as she made her curtsy to the Bingleys and lastly to himself. He inclined his head at her salute but straightened to see only the back of her bonnet as she hurried all the girls through the door. The desire to know whether Elizabeth would remain overcame Darcy's caution. He stepped into the doorway in time to witness her place a dutiful kiss upon her mama's cheek and see the lady turn away with a last admonition before the door was firmly shut behind her.

Elizabeth stood perfectly still there in the light of the entry hall, looking out at the retreating figures of her mother and sisters. Darcy could not guess her emotions, as she faced away from him, but the slow, determined manner in which she squared her small shoulders told him that his delightful antagonist was not quitting Netherfield or their battle of wits. As she turned and walked slowly toward the stairs, Darcy stepped back into the breakfast room and shut the door. His thoughts on the morning's events so thoroughly commanded his attention that the sly remarks of Miss Bingley concerning the shocking behavior of their visitors were quite lost on him.

11 November 1811
Netherfield Hall
Meryton, Hertfordshire

Dearest Georgiana,
    I received your letter of the ——th with great pleasure, perusing its lines sufficient times to allow me to quote it at length whenever I wish to assure myself once again of your

newfound contentment. Since you have done me the honor of writing so particularly, I will reply in the same vein and confess that I have been greatly concerned for you since we returned from Ramsgate and for these several months thereafter. That you have recognized the evils of the melancholy under which you had sunk and suffer their afflictions no longer, I thank God. You write that they have made you a "stronger vessel," and I should like to know more of this, but I can only regret the circumstance that precipitated such a lesson and that you should have been so cast down these last months. For the fault was never yours. If there is fault to be laid at anyone's door for what happened last summer, the greater weight of it falls to me. Do not protest, dearest, for it is so, as I have told you before. I should have taken more care. The pain my negligence has caused you hangs heavily on my heart.

Do you remember—it is a vast number of years ago!—when you were very little and I had the totty-headed notion that leaping upon you unawares was great sport? After I had resisted all our estimable father's appeals to my sense of justice, you will recall that with great sorrow he made short work of me with his cane. But it was your tears at my well-deserved strokes that reduced my proud boy's heart to rubble. And so it has ever been, even to the present day.

(I pause here to execute a request pressed upon me by Miss Caroline Bingley, in whose company I am attempting to compose this missive. It is her earnest desire that I recall her to your remembrance and apprise you of her intense longing to see you once more. My duty in this is now discharged, and you may receive her sentiments as you wish.)

To continue: If I have done well in sending Mrs. Annesley to you, it is a balm to my conscience, and I receive your assurances with a heart of gratitude to the mercy of God. She seemed a quite worthy woman, coming to me with the most

excellent references and testimonies I have ever seen. That her
influence has been instrumental in your recovery and has
encouraged a maturation of your spirit confirm her in my
estimation. She must, indeed, be a remarkable person, and I
look forward to knowing her better when I join you at
Pemberley for Christmas.

(I beg your forgiveness for the disjointed nature of this
letter. Miss Bingley has again importuned me with
compliments. Suffice it to say that she regards all that the
Darcys do as done to perfection.)

Miss Bingley is not the only person present as I write.
Charles, of course, is here, as well as his other sister, Mrs.
Hurst, and her husband. Two others are temporarily part of
our small party: Miss Jane Bennet and her sister Miss
Elizabeth. Miss Bennet came for dinner with Charles's sisters
several evenings ago but fell very ill. Her sister Miss Elizabeth
has come to nurse her until she is well enough to return home.

Pray, excuse me again, as I take up this letter once more
after an interruption. I was drawn into a discussion, quite
against my better judgment, with Charles and Miss Elizabeth.
I will not relate all the particulars, but I fear that, were you
present, you would sweetly take me to task on my supreme lack
of social grace. My instructors in philosophy at university, on
the other hand, would be quite proud of my performance. As
you well know, Charles has often borne the brunt of my logic
and suffers me, in his good-natured way, to tear his ill-
considered opinions to pieces with no untoward effects on our
friendship. But in this instance, he had an unexpected
champion, the aforementioned Miss Elizabeth Bennet, who
entered the lists armed with the shield Sensibility, against
which the lance Logic is ever seen as a scurrilous, unworthy
weapon. Nevertheless, burnishing Logic with confidence, I
sallied forth, only to have it shatter into the veriest splinter
against that unanswerable defense. Now, I must discover a

*means of reinstating myself into Miss Elizabeth's good graces.
A simple matter for most of my sex, but a Gordian knot in my
own case. I fear she regards me at this moment as an
unfeeling, prosy fellow and has just dismissed me with the
recommendation that I "had much better finish [my] letter."
This advice I have taken, as even Logic agrees to its wisdom.*

*I will finish with information that Charles has well
established himself here among the local gentry and is quite
pleased with his circumstance. Netherfield Hall is a snug little
property that will respond well to his first, halting steps as a
landowner. The society is, in my opinion, quite savage; but I
am being persuaded that within it delight may be found.
Charles, of course, is half in love already with a local beauty.
Miss Bingley and Mrs. Hurst find nothing charming and,
when they are not pining for Town, drop broad hints on how
very agreeable they would find Pemberley.*

*A ball is to be held at Netherfield in the near future, alas!
Beyond that, neither I nor they have formed plans. I do foresee
a trip to London soon on business matters but am undecided
as to whether I will return to Hertfordshire or remain in Town
until I join you for Christmastide.*

*My dear sister, allow me to say again how heartened I am
that all is well with you. I will not remind you of your studies,
for I know well your diligence and already swell with pride at
your accomplishments.*

*May God keep you, Sweetling, for you are the true treasure
of Pemberley, as well as of my heart.*

I remain your obedient servant,
Fitzwilliam Darcy

Darcy sanded and blotted his letter, folded it into precise thirds,
and peered into the interior of the desk for a stick of sealing wax.
Locating one in the far reaches of a cluttered drawer, he lit it, al-

lowing a few drops to descend upon the letter's edge and, deftly withdrawing his seal from his waistcoat pocket, secured his letter to his sister. This pleasant duty discharged, he leaned back in the chair and contemplated his situation, absently tapping the letter in his hand into the palm of the other.

Miss Elizabeth occupied a settee only feet away, engrossed once more in the needlework she had briefly abandoned during their lively sortie earlier. She presented to him a picture of the earnest needlewoman, her full lower lip caught between dainty white teeth, as she brought needle to cloth with practiced ease. An inexplicable surge of contentment coursed through him as his gaze lingered on her concentrated aspect and the elegant way she plied her needle, her smallest finger crooked just so. This pleasurable sensation slipped rapidly into dismay as he considered the current state of their acquaintance. Sighing to himself, he rose and placed the letter into the silver servier from whence posts were collected.

How could he regain her good opinion, if he ever had it? Should he compliment her needlework? Unprofitable ruse! She would merely say her thanks and they would again be *point non-plus*. He was looking about the room, desperate for inspiration, when his eyes alighted upon the pianoforte tucked into a corner. *Perfect! . . . if she will consent.*

"Miss Bingley, Miss Elizabeth," he began a trifle awkwardly, "would you condescend to indulge us with music this evening?" Miss Bingley's languid features brightened at the invitation, and she rose with grace and alacrity. So eager was she to satisfy his request that she had nearly gained the pianoforte before remembering that he had also addressed Elizabeth. Politeness required that, as hostess, she offer her guest the first opportunity to entertain. She turned back to the room slowly and with a brittle smile invited Elizabeth to precede her.

To Darcy's disappointment, Elizabeth firmly declined the offer, but she did put away her embroidery. This he wished to interpret as an indication that she would oblige him when Miss Bingley had done. As Elizabeth drifted toward the instrument, Darcy could not prevent his eyes from following her, each step and rustle of her gown commanding his full attention. Miss Bingley began her first selection. A desire to engage Elizabeth in some manner warred with Darcy's repugnance at playing the fool, as fool he would certainly appear in any attempt, on his part, to embark on a flirtation. *A flirtation?* The thought shocked him as much by its novelty as by its revelatory nature. A flush crept up his neck even as Elizabeth's eyes made brief contact with his. Hooding them, he dropped his gaze to his hands, only to discover that he was twisting his ring furiously.

Miss Bingley came to the end of the mellow Italian love song she had chosen and received the appreciation of the room with grace but little apparent satisfaction. It was likely, Darcy suddenly realized as he joined in the applause, that she had chosen the song with hopes its words would direct his attention to herself. The smile on her lips clashed with the glitter in her eyes, telling him that his lapse instead into a brown study had been duly noted.

She turned her attention to Elizabeth. "Songs of love can be so tedious when one does not know the language," she drawled in malice-edged condescension. "Do *you* not find this so, Miss Eliza?"

Elizabeth paused in her exploration of the music books lying on the pianoforte. "Oh, Miss Bingley, that is too unfortunate! Especially as you played them so beautifully. Please, permit me to translate them for you!"

Darcy almost choked as comprehension of the neat turn that her insinuation had been given flooded Miss Bingley's face. "I did not mean . . . that is . . . that will not be necessary," she sputtered. In silent fury she snatched her music sheets from their resting place and embarked on a loud and lively Scotch air.

The mischievous dimple Darcy had so admired at Sir William's made an all too brief appearance. Its effect was, however, in no wise diminished by its lack of longevity. He rose from his chair with no consciousness of having done so and, before he had fully regained command of himself, was at her side. "Do not you feel a great inclination, Miss Bennet, to seize such an opportunity of dancing a reel?" The words tumbled out, surprising himself as much as anyone in the room.

Idiot! he castigated himself. *Dance a reel! What are you about?* Darcy knew her well enough now to be forewarned by the smile that played across her features. He had not, however, anticipated her silence. He repeated his question. It sounded even more ridiculous the second time, but to retreat now was unthinkable.

"Oh! I heard you before," Elizabeth assured him, "but I could not immediately determine what to say in reply." Her chin tilted up dangerously as she paused. Darcy once again felt the air between them electrify and promptly forgave himself his awkward address. He schooled his face ruthlessly against the effects of the thousands of charges flying betwixt them. "You wanted me, I know, to say yes, that you might have the pleasure of despising my taste," Elizabeth challenged, "but I always delight in overthrowing those kinds of schemes, and cheating a person of their premeditated contempt. I have, therefore, made up my mind to tell you, that I do not want to dance a reel at all; and now"—she fixed him with an imperious look—"despise me if you dare."

Magnificent! It was the only thought Darcy could lay hold of as he watched the flow of wit and emotion mingle with the charm of her pleasingly formed person. She did not yet interpret him aright, but if such delight as this followed, what did it signify? He placed his hand on his chest, as if acknowledging a hit direct, and solemnly bowed.

"Indeed, madam," he replied as he straightened, his face softened by the wry smile that lit it, "I do *not* dare." He bowed again and left her side. With a murmur of apology to the others, he left the room as well and sent for his man. Relief for his disordered thoughts and heightened senses was, he knew, to be found only in activity out-of-doors. Once changed, he would take his hound out for a run and discipline his own mind by engaging it in the dog's further training.

Some minutes later he left his chambers, pulling on his gloves as he made for the stairs and almost ran down them. Once outdoors, though, he slowed and sauntered toward the pens that hugged one side of the stables. *Bewitching minx!* he mused, unable to banish her from his thoughts. *With your impudent manners and lively mind! Yet so sweetly faithful to your sister—nursing her through the consequences of her own mother's folly.* The image of that lady came, then, forcefully to his mind. A moment's contemplation of the woman's vulgarity and avarice served to steady him, somewhat, in his fascination with her daughter.

He reached the hound's pen and swiftly released the latch but did not open the gate until the animal within, beside himself with joy at his master's appearance, displayed a proper decorum. Trafalgar quieted himself sufficiently to be granted his freedom, although his true opinion of the moment was betrayed by the rhythmic twitches of his tail. Darcy opened the gate, and the hound shot out, racing in a wide circle around him before loping up to throw himself at his feet. Darcy stooped down and fondled the dog's ears. He was rewarded with a quick, surreptitious lick across his chin.

"I swear to you, old man," he addressed his adoring suppliant, "she is so out of the common way that if it were not for the inferiority of her connections, your master should be in *some* danger." The hound's muscles suddenly bunched. "Trafalgar!" Darcy warned and tried to rise. "*Down!*" he shouted, but with an exultant bark the hound leapt up and toppled him over onto his back into the dirt.

CHAPTER 7

Dueling in Earnest

$\mathcal{B}$y the time Darcy had finished making himself present-able after Trafalgar's exuberant and unrepentant faux pas, there was little opportunity before dinner to inspect the package that had arrived for him during his valet's ministrations. He was fairly certain what it contained, and the anticipation of what lay between the pages of the two slim volumes made his hands fairly itch. Tear-ing open the paper wrapper, he held the handsome morocco-bound books up to the light from the window.

Yes, just as he had hoped! *The Siege of Badajoz: A Chronological Narrative of Wellesley's Great Challenge*, the title of the first volume glinted back at him in shiny gold leaf. The second, with equal glit-ter, proclaimed, *Triumph at Fuentes de Oñoro: Impressions of a Gentleman-Soldier.* He had placed his order for these immediately upon the rumor of their publication being conveyed to him by the owner of his favorite bookshop, who being well acquainted with his tastes and interests, kept him apprised of all new works. Like the rest of England, Darcy had followed Wellesley's campaigns in the newspapers as the reports came back from Spain over the sum-mer, but these volumes were the first complete accounts to be published after the events and by an anonymous author reputed to be one of the great man's own general staff. Darcy had been eagerly awaiting them for months. Determinedly tucking them under his arm, he walked through his chamber doorway as Fletcher opened it, resolving to decline any distractions that might be offered him after dinner.

Fortunately, dinner was a quiet affair that evening, the only excitement occurring when Miss Elizabeth announced that her sister would take her first steps out of her sickbed and join them in the drawing room later in the evening. Miss Bingley was all delight at the news and, calling a footman, adjured him to see that the sofa in that room was drawn closer to the hearth, "so dear Jane may not suffer the slightest draft or chill."

"And how shall we entertain her, I wonder?" she asked, turning to Darcy. "A game of whist or loo, perhaps?"

Darcy set his fork down and reached for his wineglass. "Perhaps, but that question is better answered by Miss Elizabeth, who knows her sister's pleasures and strength. I, for one, do not wish to play this evening. Bingley," he addressed his friend. "The narratives of the summer campaigns have arrived at last." He motioned to a small table beside the door.

"Indeed, Darcy! May I?" At Darcy's nod, Bingley retrieved them and settled back into his chair. Knowing well his friend's care of his books, he wiped his hands on his napkin, gently opened the first volume, and lightly turned the pages. "Outstanding!" he breathed, coming to an engraving that depicted heroic British and Spanish forces arrayed against the ciudad. "The engravings alone are worth the price of the book! I do not wonder why cards hold no allure for you this evening. May I borrow these when you are done?"

Darcy's smile of assent turned to apprehension as Miss Bingley snatched the second volume before her brother could lay his hand upon it. "Mr. Darcy, will you not allow me to read this while you are enjoying the other? I could not bear to wait until Charles is finished; he reads so seldom, it will be a year before he is through.

And," she added demurely, "I think it a sacred duty to acquaint oneself with the true gallantry of our brave soldiers."

There was no alternative but to release the long-desired tome into her keeping, and Darcy did so with a clipped "Of course, Miss Bingley. A noble sentiment, indeed." He took a slow sip of wine, wincing as he watched her lay his book down among the crumbs and stains of the tablecloth, and made a mental note to send to London for another copy. This one would undoubtedly be returned to him looking as if it had been present at the battle it chronicled.

The ladies then excused themselves and left the gentlemen to their port. Bingley handed back the book he had been examining to Darcy as the servant set the tray of liquor and glasses down on the table near the three men. "Hurst?" Bingley handed his brother-in-law a well-filled glass and then poured two more of smaller volume for himself and Darcy. Their conversation was, on the whole, inconsequential, and Darcy longed for the time when they could adjourn to the drawing room, where he could peruse his book without appearing rude. Bingley, too, seemed anxious to end the male ritual as soon as possible, his eyes straying to the doors every other minute as if he could see through them. By mutual but unspoken consent, they both rose and sauntered to the drawing room, Hurst trailing behind.

The ladies of the house were gathered around Miss Bennet in a pretty show of concern and good cheer. Miss Elizabeth sat a little apart, ostensibly working at her embroidery but watching the tableau at the fireside with a tender amusement. Bingley was, of course, before him in offering his congratulations to Miss Bennet on her recovery. Darcy then extended his with a sincerity of expression that was accepted graciously by Miss Jane but seemed to give rise to a look of surprise in her sister. Puzzled by her reaction to his correct behavior, he almost forgot the book in his hand as he watched Elizabeth's face relax once again into those soft lines of the loving sister he had seen at first.

He turned away from her, found a chair next to a bright lamp, and opened the long-awaited account of the summer's dearly bought victory.

"Is your chair quite comfortable, Mr. Darcy?" Miss Bingley asked.

"Quite, madam. Thank you."

"And the lamp . . . it is bright enough?"

"Perfectly bright, Miss Bingley. Thank you."

"It is not smoking? You will get the headache if it smokes."

"No, it is not smoking." Darcy's words were all politeness as he manfully restrained the impulse to grind his teeth in irritation at Miss Bingley's persistent interruptions, but a delicate snort of suppressed amusement from Miss Elizabeth's direction indicated that his true feelings were apparent, at least to some. Miss Bingley, it seemed, did not notice, and after a few moments of blessed silence in perusal of the book she had been so mad to read, she tossed it aside, expounding as she did in his direction on her fondness of reading and an evening so spent.

Darcy declined to respond to her gambit. Instead, he took a tighter grip on his book and sank lower into his chair in what was likely a vain hope of escaping further overtures. Cautiously, he peered over *Badajoz*'s cover and saw that, miraculously, Miss Bingley had turned her attention to her brother. With relief, he plunged back into the forward positions outside the Spanish city. It was so quiet he could hear the majestic ticking of the clock against the wall opposite him.

"Miss Eliza Bennet"—the syllables rolled penetratingly off Miss Bingley's tongue in the fashion employed by members of the ton to be heard in a crowded room—"let me persuade you to follow my example, and take a turn about the room. I assure you it is very refreshing after sitting so long in one attitude."

Darcy's head came up out of his book in some surprise at this invitation, and when he saw Miss Bingley cast Elizabeth a look of appeal, his curiosity overcame his caution. Unconsciously, he closed his book.

"Mr. Darcy, will you not join us, sir?" Miss Bingley invited as she encircled Elizabeth's arm with her own. Darcy wondered what Elizabeth made of Caroline's sudden, effusive attention. He wondered, also, what he was meant to make of it. *Better to remain an observer,* he decided as he lay aside the book and stretched out his legs, crossing them at the ankles. A decidedly mischievous notion then came into his head. *If I am not to be left to my book in peace . . .*

"Thank you, Miss Bingley, but I had rather remain where I am. I can imagine only two reasons for your choosing to walk up and down the room together, in either of which my joining you would certainly interfere."

Elizabeth's eyebrows rose at his statement, and Darcy's lips twitched in pleasure as she struggled not to indulge her wonder at his words. Miss Bingley had no such qualms. "Mr. Darcy! What can you mean? I am dying to know your meaning!" She tugged lightly at her companion's arm. "Miss Eliza, can you at all understand what he means?"

"Not at all," she answered airily, having admirably mastered her curiosity. "But depend upon it, he means to be severe on us." She looked at him with a mocking eye. "Our surest way of disappointing him will be to ask nothing about it." Darcy returned her setdown with a roguish glint in an eye.

"Oh, that will not do, Miss Eliza!" Miss Bingley tittered. "A true lady never disappoints a gentleman. And a gentleman," she addressed Darcy, "never disappoints a lady, especially in such an intriguing manner. Come, tell us what you mean."

"I have not the smallest objection to explaining them," Darcy protested. "You either choose this method of passing the evening because you are in each other's confidence, and have secret affairs to discuss"—he paused and templed his fingers before fixing Elizabeth with his regard—"or because you are conscious that your figures appear to the greatest advantage in walking." Elizabeth's reaction to his bold assertion was all he could have wished. Her eyes widened, and a blush spread over her face and shoulders. "If the first," he continued nonchalantly, "I should be completely in your way; and if the second"—he paused again delicately, allowing her time to recall his second reason—"I can admire you much better as I sit by the fire." Feeling a bit wicked, Darcy briefly considered that he had perhaps overstepped the bounds of a countrified sense of propriety. But true to his initial expectations, the lady rallied and treated him to a classically governesque purse of her lips that contrasted wonderfully with the fire in her eyes. All in all, he was rather pleased with his foray into the unfamiliar realm of flirtation.

"Oh, shocking! I never heard anything so abominable," cried Miss Bingley, livening to his rare exhibition. "How shall we punish him for such a speech?"

"Tease him," Elizabeth responded decisively, her chin lifting. "Laugh at him. Intimate as you are, you must know how it is to be done."

Laugh at me? Her words caused a frisson of pique to travel a crackling path down Darcy's spine, and the humor he had found in their exchange evaporated. The amusement left his face, replaced by a taut wariness.

"Tease calmness of temper and presence of mind!" exclaimed Miss Bingley. "No, no; I feel he may defy us there." The disbelief on Elizabeth's face said plainly she would not be satisfied. Although his eyes never left her face, Darcy shifted uneasily in his chair, wondering what form her offensive would take.

"Mr. Darcy is not to be laughed at! That is an uncommon advantage." Her eyes pierced him. "Uncommon I hope it will continue, for it would be a great loss to *me* to have many such acquaintance." She turned to Miss Bingley. "I dearly love a laugh."

All inclination for their former banter deserted him in her bald attempt to reduce him once again to an object of ridicule. Darcy's manner reverted to those forms that had served him in the past. The cool, practiced logician replaced the drawing room beau, and he swiftly marshaled his defenses and line of attack.

"Miss Bingley has given me credit for more than can be. The

wisest and the best of men—nay, the wisest and best of their actions—may be rendered ridiculous by a person whose first object
in life is a joke."

"Certainly," Elizabeth agreed coolly, "there are such people, but
I hope I am not one of *them*. I hope I never ridicule what is wise or
good. Follies and nonsense, whims and inconsistencies, do divert
me, I own, and I laugh at them whenever I can. But these, I suppose, are precisely what you are without."

Darcy knew he was checked. Who could claim to behave always
in the most wise and circumspect manner? *Checked . . . but not
mated yet!*

"Perhaps that is not possible for anyone." He gave her the point
but then fixed upon her steadily. "But it has been the study of my
life to avoid those weaknesses which often expose a strong understanding to ridicule."

"Such as vanity and pride," she drolly suggested.

So, we are returned to the assembly in Meryton! Darcy seized upon
her ulterior motivation, too tempted by the prospect of victory to
heed the small voice that warned of battles won but wars lost.

"Yes, vanity is a weakness indeed. But pride—where there is a
real superiority of mind—pride will be always under good regu-
lation."

She turned away at his words, whether in defeat or anger he
could not tell. *Confound it, man; you have been too harsh!* He bit
his lip and tried to discover from the attitude of her shoulders
what she was thinking, but with no success.

"Your examination of Mr. Darcy is over, I presume," Miss Bingley queried. "Pray what is the result?" She cast Darcy a commiserating grimace.

"I am perfectly convinced by it that Mr. Darcy has no defects."
Elizabeth rounded on him. "He owns it himself without disguise."

Down, but not defeated! Darcy shook his head, not sure
whether to be amused or affronted by this new attack. "No, I have
made no such pretension," he replied evenly. Deciding to try an-

other tack, he continued in a voice subdued in its sincerity, "I have faults enough, but they are not, I hope, of understanding. My temper I dare not vouch for. It is, I believe, too little yielding, certainly too little for the convenience of the world. It would, perhaps, be called resentful. My good opinion once lost is lost forever."

"*That* is a failing, indeed!" cried Elizabeth. "You have chosen your fault well. Implacable resentment is a fault at which I cannot laugh." She put her hands out before him in a show of surrender. "You are safe from me."

Darcy stared at her, his lips compressed in indecision as to the best response to such a wild accusation, and concluded he could only continue to press his point home. "There is, I believe, in every disposition a tendency to some particular evil, a natural defect, which not even the best education can overcome."

"And *your* defect is a propensity to hate everybody." Elizabeth countered him smugly. The accusation was so absurd that Darcy could not help but smile at the frustration that must have given it voice. However, he vowed that he would leave the field, if not in triumph, at least in good order. Let her be served her own medicine! He rose from his chair and, smiling down into her flushed, defiant countenance, replied quietly, "And yours, madam, is willfully to misunderstand them." He offered her a respectful bow, reached for his book, and bid the room good night.

Once back in his chambers, he shrugged off his coat and threw it onto one of the chairs. His waistcoat and neckcloth soon followed, forming a negligent heap. Fletcher's discreet knock caused him to whirl about, but Darcy declined his assistance, setting him free for the remainder of the evening but with orders to have his riding gear at the ready by seven the next morning. Running a hand distractedly through his hair, he sat down on the bed and set about removing his boots. That finished, he lay back and stretched his frame, working his muscles from the tips of his fingers down to his toes until the tension of the evening faded. He pulled himself up then and strode over to the window, looking out into the night.

A more forward, opinionated little baggage I defy anyone to find! Such cheek and impertinence! So ready to do battle on the slightest pretense. He paused a moment, his conscience demanding an examination of his mental outburst for bias. Darcy heaved a reluctant sigh. Ready to do battle with himself, to be sure. It was only he who seemed to call forth this rash barrage of penetrating wit. Perhaps he even encouraged it in some way, for she was certainly most amiable and genuine in her tenderness with those she loved. *Her face . . . when she looked on those others . . . such warm affection . . .*

Why, then, do you continue to attend to her? his inner voice interrupted in demand. Darcy left the window and threw himself onto the bed. Suddenly, before thought could mitigate its power, the answer thrummed through his whole body. *Because she is both—mind and heart—and what you have always desired.* For some time it was impossible to ignore the thrill and terror of his confession, but he had been prepared from birth for his station in life and what was due his family. As he turned onto his side and grasped a pillow firmly against his cheek, the resolution was already forming that, for both of their sakes, no sign of admiration should escape him from henceforth. The rapid thudding of his heart finally quieted, but try as he might, sleep eluded him until the early watches of morning.

Despite his lack of sleep, Darcy awoke at his habitual six o'clock. He made no move to rise at the sound of the clock but lay entangled in the dreams of a restless night and watched the earliest feeble rays of the sun push through the stark tree branches. His first desire was to wander back into the dream, but he felt a strange tightness take hold of his chest on the attempt. The resolutions of the evening then thrust themselves to the fore, banishing the wistful sweetness that yet lingered, and convinced him to delay no longer in rising. Better to seek the distracting power of a punishing gallop before the mists of the morning were burnt away. *Wiser still*

to avoid her entirely today, he instructed himself as he threw back the counterpane and rose, pulling off his nightshirt and ringing for Fletcher.

A steaming copper kettle of water carried by a kitchen lad heralded his valet's arrival. Darcy sat down and closed his eyes as Fletcher arranged his tools and began stropping the razor's blade in sweeping strokes. The rhythmic slap and scrape nearly put Darcy back to sleep, but he came suddenly awake when the warm blade made its first pass, causing Fletcher to nick him.

"Mr. Darcy, sir! If you would be so kind as not to move. I will need to apply sticking plaster, and we know how you dislike that." Darcy grunted at him and winced as the plaster was applied. "There now, sir. All should be well before the ladies must be faced."

"The only one who will see me this morning will be Nelson, and I doubt he will be shocked," he retorted, causing Fletcher to chuckle softly. A knock on the door forestalled the valet's ministrations. Stepping over to open it, he admitted another lad carrying a covered tray.

"I took the liberty of ordering you breakfast, Mr. Darcy. Just a little something before your ride, sir." Darcy nodded his approval, and the tray was placed on a table and a chair brought up. Fletcher dismissed the boy with all the imperiousness of his position and swiftly finished shaving his master, leaving him warm towels with which to complete his morning ablutions.

In short order, Darcy finished and presented himself in his dressing room, where Fletcher carefully outfitted him for his morning ride. Darcy donned the clothes mechanically, his mind curiously hazy. Murmuring his thanks, he returned to his chamber and lifted the lid from the breakfast tray. The strong aroma of coffee and a perfectly prepared bit of beef gently roused him out of his torpor, and after a few bites, he began to feel more himself. The chamber clock chimed seven; Darcy rose, picking up his gloves, hat, and crop, and quietly went out to meet the morning.

Stationed at the bottom of the carriage stairs, Nelson shook his head, stepping forward, then back, and generally intimidating the Netherfield grooms. His ears pricked at the opening of the door, and he swung his great head toward the sound. Upon beholding his master, he made a great show of stamping a hoof perilously close to the groom's foot and gave an indignant snort, sending trails of vapor into the cold morning air.

"G'morning, sir," the groom panted, making no attempt to disguise the relief on his face. "He's a bit high in the instep this morning, sir."

"So it would appear! He's been giving you trouble again?" Darcy frowned into Nelson's face, but the animal merely shrugged off the reprimand, tossed his head, and sent another flume of breath into the air. "You *do* look the veritable dragon this morning, old man." He took the reins and, declining a leg up from the beleaguered groom, vaulted into the saddle. Nelson took advantage of the lull in control as Darcy attended to the stirrups to execute a jolting dance, reminding his rider that, in the world of horseflesh, he was just as well connected as Darcy. "Oh, so that is how it is! So puffed up in your own conceit that you disdain to practice the manners of a gentleman." Darcy gathered the reins and drew them back until contact with Nelson's mouth was firmly established and then nodded at the groom to let go his head.

The horse's excitement as Darcy allowed him to break into a stiff-legged trot was palpable, confirming his rider's suspicion that this morning's outing would be a test of wills. Strangely, the prospect was not unwelcome. The rigors of such an exercise would surely distract or perhaps banish entirely the constriction that still hovered under his heart. "Evidently, we both need the blue devils ridden out of us!" Darcy whispered. Nelson's ears flicked back at his voice, and his snort assured his master of his complete agreement.

Darcy signaled the advance to a canter as they approached the fence that girdled the wide field east of the hall and set his jaw as he felt Nelson gather speed for the fence. In a matter of moments, it loomed before them, wavering in the morning mists. They thundered forward; the entire world was become only those sounds of pounding hooves and the creaking leather, and the brutal fact of the fence before them. Suddenly, the fence disappeared as Nelson's forelegs came up. His back arched, and in a silence outside of time, he carried his rider over the fence. He landed with a jolt that forced a grunt from his great lungs, but his hindquarters were already gathered for the long gallop across the field. Impulsively, Darcy gave him his head, man and beast throwing caution to the wind, flying as if chased by the Devil's own hounds.

Horse and rider returned several hours later, thoroughly exhausted but in complete charity with each other. Darcy slid his tired frame from Nelson's back and pulled the reins over the animal's head as the stable boys hurried over to guide their fearsome charge back to his stall. Mellowed by the exercise, Nelson allowed them to approach, eschewing his usual show of temper toward underlings and confining himself to giving his master a shove and a demanding whicker. Laughing wearily, Darcy reached into his pocket and extracted some sugar lumps, then waved them before Nelson's attentive face. Too tired to put up with such foolishness for long, the horse dove straight into Darcy's chest, requiring his treat. Grunting under the force of the blow, Darcy opened his hand and Nelson neatly lipped the lumps. Darcy rubbed at his chest as his horse crunched on the sugar and then, with a last firm pat, handed the reins over to the waiting lads. But before he would move, Nelson nosed gently over his master's chest and face and, by way of apology, blew lightly into his ear.

"Accepted! Unprincipled brute! Now off with you, and mind, you be civil to those lads." With feigned meekness, Nelson followed his young keepers into the stable yard, and Darcy turned to the hall. He was very late for breakfast now and, he noted with grim satisfaction, very dirty. It would be impossible to appear at table for quite another hour, long past a reasonable time for them to wait for him. Spying Stevenson in the hall, he commissioned him to deliver his regrets to his hosts and then headed for the soothing tub of hot water Fletcher would soon have ready for him.

He was no more than halfway up the stairs when a door below opened.

". . . very kind, Mr. Bingley, but it must be so. She will be quite well by then, and we have trespassed on your hospitality long enough." Elizabeth's clear voice drifted up to him.

"Trespassed, Miss Elizabeth! I hope you will not think of it so, for we do not. I would not have Miss Bennet's health imperiled for the world, certainly not for some mistaken notion of overstaying your welcome. We are, after all, neighbors, and must . . . uh . . . care for each other as we would ourselves."

Darcy heard Elizabeth's delightful laugh in her reply that "you have not *quoted* Scripture precisely, Mr. Bingley, but with your *application* of last Sunday's sermon, I can find no fault. Such diligent attention makes one all anticipation what will be the result of tomorrow's." Darcy pressed his fingers to his mouth, smothering the chuckle that threatened to escape and reveal his presence. When the danger was over, his hand dropped but unconsciously began to rub again at his chest, the tightness once more afflicting him.

"Then you are determined to leave tomorrow?" Darcy recognized the wheedle in Bingley's voice, a sign that his persuasive powers had reached an end.

"Oh, fie, Mr. Bingley! You would cause me to feel a complete ingrate, but you must know I am immune to such machinations. You forget that I have three younger sisters who regularly employ similar tones. I am well versed, sir, in resisting wheedles."

Bingley's rueful laugh echoed in the hall. "You know me too well already, Miss Elizabeth."

"Too well to believe that you do not know how sincerely you are thanked and how gratefully you are regarded by your Bennet neighbors," she replied softly. "Truly, you have been most kind to my beloved Jane and to me." She paused for a moment, then added, "Now, I must go up to Jane, and if she continues well, we will *both* be down later this morning. Mr. Bingley."

As stealthily as possible, Darcy leapt up the remaining steps and, with quick strides, rounded the corner to the passage that led to his suite of rooms. Once through the door, he closed it carefully, making no sound, and let out the breath he'd been holding. *She leaves tomorrow then.* His eyes swept the chamber as if in search of something, he knew not what. Then, with a groan, he pulled the bell rope, sat down heavily in the large wingback chair, and worked at the buttons on his coat. *A godsend, really. She has been here long enough!* The buttons loosened, he attacked his neckcloth, pulling fiercely at the ends and yanking at the knots. *And you like her more than you should . . .* He paused in his struggle with the yard of linen and let his hands drop. *Like her! Poor fool, you cannot even be honest with yourself!* He rose and paced the length of his chamber, opened the dressing room door, and, finding no activity within, marched back to the bell rope and pulled at it again. He had no more than flung himself back into the chair when Fletcher opened the dressing room door.

"Mr. Darcy, your—"

"Time and more that you should have made an appearance! Is my bath ready, or must I carry the water up myself?" he bellowed at his valet. The look on Fletcher's face smote Darcy to the core, and for a space of a few breaths, master and servant beheld each other in frozen silence.

"Fletcher, would you be so kind as to forgive me my lamentable manners and totally unjust words? You have served me well and faithfully these seven years and do not deserve my bad temper." The valet's shoulders relaxed ever so slightly, and he bowed his glad compliance. "Good man," Darcy responded gratefully, and got up from the chair. He walked past the valet into the dressing room, where the first buckets of hot water were being lowered into the bath. Fletcher reached over and carefully pulled his master's coat off his shoulders and down his arms. The offending neckcloth was gently removed. Darcy sat down while a kitchen lad worked on his boots and his valet arranged his kit.

"That will do nicely, Fletcher. Give me, say, twenty minutes."

"Very good, sir. Nothing else I can get for you, sir?" Darcy shook his head wearily. "I *did* hear a bit of news, sir."

"Indeed? And what is your 'bit of news,' Fletcher?"

"The Misses Bennet will depart for their home tomorrow after Sunday services." Fletcher opened the servants' door to the dressing room. "But perhaps you already have heard." Darcy looked up sharply at his valet, but Fletcher was already safely on the other side of the door.

The walls of Badajoz yet stood after a day of incessant artillery bombardment, and the command to withdraw had just been dispatched to the company commanders when Darcy heard the library door click open. He had come downstairs to find the public rooms empty of both the Bingleys and their guests. "Taking the air up at the folly, sir" had been a footman's answer to his query of their whereabouts. So, with the house wonderfully serene, he had taken his book to the library and settled in for an hour of "following the drum" until his host returned.

The door was directly behind him, so at the sound he called over his shoulder, "Charles, this is indeed incredible! You must let me read it to—" A flash of yellow sprigged muslin at the corner of his eye immediately informed him that it was not Bingley with whom he shared the room. Darcy looked up to see a vision of loveliness before him, the sunlight glancing through the library window causing her gown to glow softly and highlight the auburn of her hair. He swallowed hard. *Steady on . . . not the slightest sign!*

"Miss Elizabeth," he said tonelessly as he rose from his chair. His perfunctory bow was answered with a curtsy its equal.

"Mr. Darcy, pray do not let me disturb you."

"Madam." Darcy bowed again and resumed his seat. Fumbling awkwardly, he opened his book to the passage he had been about to offer Bingley and stared hard at the page, all his senses on edge until she should either find her book and sit down or, please Heaven, quit the room. He forced himself to look no farther than his paragraph, but the soft tread of her slippers, the rustle of her gown, and the faint scent of lavender teased his resolve and kept him more aware than he wished of where she was in the room.

Finally, she chose a book. Darcy willed himself not to look up but instead, with slow deliberation, turned the page. The print danced before his eyes, forcing him to blink several times and draw the book closer. She floated past him then, her skirts brushing his shoes, and sat in the chair to his right, separated from him only by a small table that supported a brass lamp. Silence now reigned in the room, punctuated only by the sound of pages being turned and an occasional sigh from the recesses of the chair on his right.

Darcy commanded his body to relax into his chair, and when a sufficient obedience had been achieved, he returned his attention to his book, only to find that not a word from the previous page had registered in his brain. Annoyed with himself, he turned back to read it again. A delicate yawn followed by more distracting sighs arrested him in midpage, and it was some moments before he could recall himself to his study. His whole being was alive to her every action, requiring every ounce of his will to appear indifferent to her presence. He could quit the library, of course, take his book to any one of innumerable places, but an irascible stubbornness forbade him to retreat from this, his habitual refuge from the world, and surrender it into *her* keeping! He fixed his eyes on the top of the page again and forced himself to pay strict attention to each word. *There, now!* He turned the well-thumbed leaf.

Elizabeth rose from the chair and replaced her book on the shelf, but to Darcy's agitation, rather than leaving, she commenced to search for another one. The agonies caused him by her first search repeated themselves with no less intensity. He was seriously considering retreat as his best option when a knock on the door startled both of them.

"Enter," Darcy voiced hoarsely.

"Excuse me, sir . . . madam. Miss Elizabeth, ma'am. Miss Bennet has awakened and is asking for you," Stevenson quietly informed her.

"Oh! Thank you, Stevenson. I shall be right up," she responded, and, turning to Darcy, swept him a careless curtsy and hurried out of the room.

With the click of the heavy oak door once more reverberating through the room, Darcy let his book drop to his lap and closed his eyes, his fingers working strongly on the bridge between them. *This is intolerable!* Finding no relief for his jangled sensibilities, he sprang from the chair and proceeded to pace the length of the fine Aubusson carpet Bingley had laid down the day before.

Thank God she leaves tomorrow, before I am turned into the most pitiable mooncalf who ever pined for a lady's favor! And for what do I daily become more the fool? She has caused a rift between Bingley and myself, set Miss Bingley's tongue like a cat among the chickens, found fault with all I say, insulted me to my face, and while being thoroughly indifferent to my presence, cuts up my *peace entirely!* His right shoe made contact with something as he paced, sending it skittering across the floor. He looked down to see *Badajoz* flying toward the shelves.

"No!" he shouted uselessly as it came to rest with a thump against the wall. Darcy strode over and picked up the prized volume, turning it over and over. No damage that a little oil would not set right. As he rubbed the leather cover against his trousers, he noticed a volume on the shelf before him that was not quite in line with its neighbors. Tucking his own book under his arm, he reached over to nudge it back but then stopped, recognizing it as the book Elizabeth had been sighing over. His hand fell to the shelf, his fingers tapping on it as he looked at the book's spine. *What had she been reading?* His animus was quickly overpowered by his accursed fascination with her. *What kind of book does she enjoy?* He stood there in indecision, arguing against an invasion of her privacy on the one hand and for the satisfaction of his compelling curiosity on the other.

It is sure to be mere drivel, he assured himself finally, and with a seeming will of its own, his hand closed swiftly on the book, drew it out, and flipped it open to the title page. The title, *Paradise Lost,* stared back into his astonished face. His eyes scanned down the page. "Being the work of John Milton." Further examination revealed a bookmark composed of several embroidery threads marking the place where she had last read. Darcy turned there briefly. Then, closing the book carefully, he slowly replaced it on the shelf, his mind awhirl with questions as he examined the brightly colored threads lying in the palm of his hand.

Milton, of all poets, and *Paradise Lost* of all the dreary man's works! *What is she about, reading such ponderous verse nearly a century and a half old? It is certainly not fashionable today. Good heavens, no one reads Milton!* No sooner had that last thought been silently uttered than a chill shook Darcy's frame, and he remembered clearly the last time he had seen Milton's work. *Paradise Regained,* bound in lovingly worn calfskin, had held an honored place among the books on the table beside his father's bed during the last months of his life. Darcy's brow furrowed darkly as a fierce stab of pain shook him at the remembrance of those days. He brought the hand cradling Elizabeth's bookmark up to his chest and pressed it there, willing the pain away.

Voices and the sound of boots in the hall alerted Darcy that Bingley and his party had returned from the folly. Pocketing the threads, he quickly moved away from the bookshelf, his composure, or something like, reasserting itself, and was nearly to the library door when it opened to reveal Bingley's flushed countenance.

"Darcy, at last! You have managed to elude us all morning, sir, and I simply won't have you skulking about the library on a day such as today. We have visited the folly—a marvelous structure, by the by—and find ourselves in sore need of sustenance. I've ordered some refreshments in the conservatory so Miss Bennet may enjoy some of the sunshine, and I insist that you join us," Bingley said. Darcy bowed his compliance. Bingley paused and then in an apologetic tone continued, "Ah, Darcy, good fellow, I know this is dashed impertinent of me, but would it be possible to, well . . . could you refrain from wrangling with Miss Bennet's sister today? You may have heard they will be leaving tomorrow. I would not wish her to be overset."

"Wrangle with Miss Elizabeth! My dear Charles, I do *not* 'wrangle' with her or with anyone!"

"Debate, then. Darcy"—he paused and looked at his friend beseechingly—"I am exceedingly sorry that you and Miss Elizabeth do not get on, but—"

"Have no fear, Bingley. I believe I know how to behave in company," Darcy cut him off, unable to quell an impulse to sarcasm. Bingley colored at his tone, causing Darcy to condemn his hasty words for an unprecedented second time in one day.

"Charles, I beg that you will overlook my graceless words and deplorable manners. I have not felt myself lately, a disagreeable sensation, I assure you, and have been so impolitic as to cause others to feel the effects of it. For the embarrassment this has caused you, I am heartily sorry."

"Embarrassment . . . caused *me*?" Bingley sputtered. He threw back his head and laughed in his friend's puzzled face. "Darcy, when I think of the situations from which you have rescued me, due entirely to my own stupidity! Well, I despaired of ever making it up to you. Paying me back in the same coin is *not* what I would have expected, and the installment is minute compared with my great balance." He paused and swept Darcy a regal bow. "It is forgotten, sir, with pleasure. Now come along and rejoin the human race. We are really not such a bad lot, after all."

Darcy smiled broadly in the face of such easy good nature and

thanked God that He had provided him such a friend. Setting his
book down on the desk, he followed Bingley out the door.

Although his words to Bingley had warranted his ability to
conduct himself in company as a gentleman, Darcy did not view
the gathering in the conservatory with equanimity. That any topic
remotely interesting or entertaining enough to distract him from
his awareness of Elizabeth would arise in the conversation was
highly doubtful. Hurst, he dismissed immediately. Bingley would
be dancing attendance upon Miss Jane Bennet. Miss Bingley, abet-
ted by her sister, would in turn fawn upon him or attempt to confound the lady she so clearly regarded as her rival. The only hope
of any lively discourse was centered in the very person to whom
the danger of his paying attention was beyond calculation. If he
was to be successful in crushing any suggestion that Elizabeth Bennet held the slightest material influence over his felicity, his behavior toward her now would either confirm or deny it.

The ladies and Hurst were before them, engaged in desultory
admiration of the specimens of flora that still boasted blossoms.
As Darcy anticipated, Bingley broke from him and strode over to
the Bennet sisters, exclaiming as he did on how well Jane Bennet
was looking. A delicate smile teased her lips at his salutation, and
she serenely nodded her acceptance of the offer of his arm for her
support. Her sister happily relinquished the lady's arm into
Bingley's keeping and stepped away from them with a gracious-
ness that Darcy would have liked to admire but resolutely denied
to himself. Instead, he turned away from the gathering and examined the room.

Netherfield's conservatory was a small one and stood in need
of the services of an expert gardener, but the suggestion of wild-
ness given by its unkempt appearance lent it some piquancy. Evidently, a previous inhabitant had indulged in a passion for the
exotica of the plant kingdom, for rather than the staid groupings
of most gardens under glass, this one pulsed with the energy of
rampant, twining vines and lush foliage. The moist, earthy scent of

the air reminded him of his own extensive gardens and the pleasures of the conservatory at Pemberley.

The appearance of servants laden with the tea tray and dishes
of sweets and cakes drew the company to the wrought-iron table
in the center of the room. The last to accept his cup, Bingley
paused at Darcy's side and motioned with a quirk of his chin to
the vacant seats next to Elizabeth and her sister. Even as he silently
declined the invitation, Darcy could not prevent or deny the bit-
tersweet pull on his senses the opportunity presented. Determinedly, he took up a position somewhat apart from the others,
from which he could safely bide his time.

As it was, the conversation was consumed with the ball that
Bingley had promised. Since the others were well aware of his
aversion to the scheme, Darcy's opinions were not solicited, even
by Miss Bingley, and he was left to his silent contemplation. Relieved that he would not have to take part in a conversation
fraught with traps that would militate against his plan, Darcy
breathed in the tangy scents of earth and vegetation. Suddenly
there swept over him an acute longing. *Pemberley!* For a few moments he forgot all around him, his mind's eye roving hungrily
over the geography of his beloved home.

The conservatory had been a favorite place of his when he was a
child and youth. There, until her death, his mother had reigned as a
benevolent tyrant, taking personal care of her roses and coaxing the
exotic slips imported for her by her husband to thrive and blossom.
Among the family and household, it had never been "the Conservatory," for early in his marriage his father had one day gaily dubbed
his wife's efforts there "an Eden." And Eden it had remained. As his
own death approached, his father had insisted upon being carried
down to Eden each day for a few hours of the companionship and
solace of his late wife's flowers. Often Darcy would join him there
after a harrowing day wrestling with the responsibilities his sire's
weakening health had thrust upon him. Sometimes they would talk
of the past, sometimes of the difficult days ahead, but more com-

monly they would sit in a shared silence deeper than words. For three years following his father's passing, during which all his energy and thought had centered on Pemberley and the completion of his father's designs for it, Eden had been a painful reminder of his loss, and he had rarely set foot into it until Georgiana one day expressed a desire for "a little garden." Together they had chosen a space in Eden to be cleared for her use, and he had become a regular visitor there again, now to praise his sister's efforts.

Darcy reached out and fingered the blossom of an unknown vine, then gently tucked its drooping head back into the greenery, that its interior glories might better be seen. The sound of a soft step behind him caused him to drop his hand quickly and turn, blocking his handiwork from view. Elizabeth approached him slowly, a look of puzzlement on her face, and then, rather than stopping, she moved past him to examine his rearrangement of the flower.

"A lovely flower, Mr. Darcy, and now displayed to advantage. But do you not think that the admiration it will attract will be detrimental to its character?"

Darcy looked down into her teasing eyes but would not be drawn into battle. "Do you garden, Miss Elizabeth?"

"Since girlhood. A little plot, but it gives me pleasure. And do you, sir, garden?"

"An ardent admirer only."

"So I see." She nodded toward the flower, then stopped and cast up at him a searching glance. Caught by the question in her eyes, he could not look away. He bit at his lower lip. Could another meaning for his words have occurred to her?

"Or rather, a perfectionist in this, as in all things?" she dared him. Darcy merely smiled and offered her a bow, experiencing an indecent gratification with the dissatisfaction his reticence had caused to be mirrored in her face. Leaving her to puzzle through his meaning, he moved past her to remind Bingley of their engagement in the billiards room.

After he and Bingley had exhausted the lure of the billiard

table, Darcy kept himself employed in one activity or another for the rest of the day. He read; he played several rubbers of whist with Bingley's sisters and Hurst. At dinner he spoke only to Bingley and Hurst on the subject of a day of shooting. Afterward, he wrote letters to any relation or friend he could think of who might reasonably be expecting communication from him. Finally, the evening drew to a close and he could in good conscience retreat to his rooms. Closing the door, he rang for Fletcher and congratulated himself on keeping to his purpose, but on wearily slumping down into a chair, he found that the effort had fatigued him all out of proportion to its intended effect.

Do not think about it, he adjured himself, closing his eyes and yawning. *You are much too tired to parse it all out.* He stretched his legs and settled back into the chair to await the arrival of his valet.

"Ahem.

"Mr. Darcy, sir.

"Ahem!"

Darcy's eyes opened slowly, but upon resting them on Fletcher, he sat up with a jolt. "Fletcher! I must have fallen asleep!"

"Yes, sir. You were quite caught in Hypnos's thrall. Do you require anything more than the usual tonight, sir?"

"No, no." Darcy shook his head and yawned. "I just wish to continue what I started here in this chair and as soon as it may be possible."

"Certainly, sir. May I inquire as to which coat and waistcoat you wish readied for Services tomorrow?" Fletcher asked as he swiftly divested his master of coat and cravat. Darcy sighed; the energy needed to wrap his mind around his valet's question seemed unavailable to him.

"Perhaps the green, sir, with the gold and gray striped waistcoat?"

Darcy managed a wry grin as he looked down at Fletcher. "Yes, I suppose. Rather grand for a little country church, though, wouldn't you say?"

"Grand, sir? Memorable, certainly, sir, but grand? No sir,"

Fletcher assured him as he set about preparing his master's night-clothes.

Darcy peered narrowly at his valet. "Memorable, eh? And why should I want to style myself in a 'memorable' fashion tomorrow?"

The regard Fletcher turned to him at his question was a portrait of professionalism piqued. "Mr. Darcy, sir! I have a reputation to maintain!"

"In Hertfordshire?"

"In whatevershire you happen to be, sir. It is my duty, sir, to see you turned out in a manner in keeping with your station and the occasion." Fletcher continued with his preparations, investing them with an increased dignity.

"And services at a country church require a 'memorable' turnout?" Darcy probed, his suspicions aroused by Fletcher's protestations.

"Pardon me, sir, but I was under the apprehension that the Lord was equally present at a 'country church' as he is in London at Saint ———'s."

"Humph," Darcy snorted. "I am not entirely convinced that your sincerity in this is as good as your theology, but I am too fatigued to discuss it further. The green it shall be."

"And the gold and gray waistcoat, sir?"

"The gold and gray," Darcy acquiesced. "Although why I should appear 'memorable' tomorrow I still do not fathom."

"Very good, sir. Good night, Mr. Darcy." The smile on Fletcher's face as he left gave Darcy pause, but the previous night's lack of sleep, the morning's brutal ride, and the joyless struggle with his attraction to Elizabeth Bennet had taken their toll. In a matter of moments, he was deep in a dreamless slumber.

CHAPTER 8

His Own Worst Enemy

*D*arcy adjusted his neckcloth to a less constricting degree of tightness than his valet had deemed necessary and glanced at himself in the mirror as Fletcher gave a last flick of his brush across the shoulders of his green coat.

"There now, sir." Fletcher circled him with a critical eye. He stopped at the waistcoat and, with a sure thumb, pressed anew the crease of the lapel, then nodded his head in satisfaction.

"I have your approval, then?" Darcy queried in some exasperation with the inordinate amount of attention Fletcher was giving to preparations for a simple morning's services at Meryton Church.

"You will do, sir."

"Do! Fletcher, you have not gone totty-headed on me, I trust? I warned you when I engaged your services that I was not desirous of playing the coxcomb."

"Certainly not, sir!" Fletcher drew up in pained effrontery. "Nor would I allow it were anyone to convince you to make the attempt. It is *not* your style, sir."

"On that, at least, we are agreed!" Darcy reached for his gloves as Fletcher opened the chamber door, his master's hat in hand.

"A pleasant Lord's Day morning to you, sir." He bowed and handed Darcy his beaver and prayer book. Darcy's nod as he left was of that slow, thoughtful sort designed to remind Fletcher who was the master. In no confusion as to its meaning, the valet cast his eyes downward with an appropriate degree of servility and swiftly closed the door with a firm click.

Shaking his head in bemusement at his valet's inexplicable behavior, Darcy descended the stairs to the main hall. Seeing no one yet gathered for what should have been an imminent departure, he withdrew his pocket watch to see if he had mistaken the time. His own timepiece matched the one adorning his chamber and the clock in the hall. Frowning, he replaced it and started toward the breakfast room, only to be recalled by the sound of voices from the hall above. Turning on his heel, he retraced his steps, rounded the corner newel post of the staircase, and looked up, prepared to deliver a sharp request for haste.

"Elizabeth!" Her name escaped his lips as only a whisper, but she seemed to have heard, for her eyes rose from watching her footing as she descended the stairs to meet and return his appreciative stare. She was dressed charmingly in a cream-colored gown picked out with delicate white embroidery, over which she wore a curry-hued spencer trimmed in green. The colors suited her admirably, Darcy noted, and suffused her complexion with a warm glow. She appeared hesitant, looking at him with a curiously wide-eyed expression. Without considering, Darcy took one step toward her, then another and, when he came aside her, stopped and looked down into her confused countenance.

"Miss Elizabeth," he murmured, and bowed, careful of the narrow stair. "Permit me?" He offered her his arm and indicated the remaining steps.

"Mr. Darcy . . . thank you, sir." Her voice wavered as she took his arm and hastily looked about the hall. "My sister is just behind me . . . The others are coming."

"I hope that is so, or we shall be very late," Darcy managed in a low, steady voice despite the inner tremors he was experiencing at the slight pressure her hand exerted on his arm. It looked so well there; the soft cream and curry seemed to melt right into his coat sleeve. Almost as if . . .

No, no, Fletcher couldn't have known! His suspicion reawakened, Darcy looked up from his arm to the profile of the woman at his side and then back up the stairs behind them, half-expecting to see his valet lurking in the shadows of the upper hall. Instead, he beheld the rest of their party about to join them.

Resplendent in a violet gown and purple pelisse with a matching bonnet trimmed with sweeping gray feathers, Miss Bingley began her descent. "Mr. Darcy! Louisa and Hurst are just now coming, but Charles and Miss Bennet are here, as you see . . ." Her voice trailed off as she drew closer, and a look of puzzlement wrinkled her brow as she beheld Darcy.

"Miss Bingley?" he prompted at her loss of words. Seemingly confounded into silence, she let her eyes travel from himself to Elizabeth as the others joined them in the hall.

"Miss Elizabeth." Bingley approached them, smiling. "You must allow me to say how in looks you are this morning, both you and Darcy, actually. You could not be more complementary if it had been planned."

Darcy flushed uncomfortably, although whether the greater part was caused by Bingley's ingenuous observation or the suspicion of his valet's connivance, he was not sure.

"An interesting coincidence merely, Charles." Miss Bingley's voice came bitingly to life. "But not so great as to cause further remark."

"Coincidence!" Bingley hooted as he escorted Miss Jane Bennet to the door. "I'd lay good odds that—" The thunderous frown Darcy turned on him almost caused him to swallow his tongue. "Lay good odds that it is, as you say, all the merest chance. Is everyone here? Right! We must not be late for church," he finished hurriedly, and, putting on his hat, ushered the ladies out the door.

Darcy chose to ride with the Hursts and leave the entertaining of the unattached ladies in Bingley's capable hands. He was certainly in too great an ill humor to receive Miss Bingley's speculations or countenance her incivility to Elizabeth. The somnolent atmosphere Hurts so ably projected was just what he needed to gather his wits and emotions together under tight rein. To further discourage his traveling companions from entering into pointless chatter, Darcy opened his prayer book at random and bent his mind to preparing for the morning.

> *O, God, who by Thy Spirit dost lead men to desire*
> *Thy perfection, to seek for truth and to rejoice in beauty:*
> *Illuminate and inspire us, we beseech Thee . . .*

Rejoice in beauty. Darcy looked unseeing out the carriage window, the countryside obscured by a pair of fine eyes and a beguiling smile that warmed him considerably in the silent and chill autumn morning. *To rejoice in her beauty . . . Would I wish that intimate right?* He sighed to himself and addressed the text again. *Inspire us . . .* He sank back then into the cushions under the troubling conviction that he was suffering from a surfeit of inspiration rather than its lack. How strange that, after having spent the last two years reacquainting himself with the pleasures of London Society and surrounded by the most handsome, refined, and eligible young women in England, he should find the beauty and inspiration that set his pulse racing and disordered his composure in an obscure corner of Hertfordshire.

> *. . . that in whatsoever is true and pure and lovely,*
> *Thy name may be hallowed and Thy kingdom come on earth;*
> *through Jesus Christ our Lord. Amen.*

Darcy gently closed the book. *True . . . pure . . . lovely.* In all honesty, what better prerequisites were there for the woman one spent one's life with? His memory harkened back to Miss Bingley's long list of talents for the truly accomplished woman and his added requirement that she be well read. Would the embodiment of that list offer a better surety of his future happiness than a woman who was true, pure, and lovely?

The carriage slowed as the driver turned the team in to the churchyard and then brought them to a stop at the walk to the main door. Darcy waited for Hurst to descend and hand down his wife before he moved to the door himself. He grimly noted that Miss Bingley lingered behind the others in hopes, no doubt, of sitting by him in the pew. Duty bound, he offered her his arm, which she accepted with a proprietary air that was directed at Elizabeth primarily but included all of Meryton in general. As Darcy escorted her to the church door, he discovered a theretofore unrealized artistic sensibility that was quite pained by the clash of Miss Bingley's purple with his own green, and the question flashed through his mind whether Fletcher had had, in some devious way, a hand in this as well.

About to follow Miss Bingley through the door, Darcy stopped short as Elizabeth met him going out, a wry smile of apology on her lips. As he sat down on the end of the pew, he leaned forward and turned a questioning brow down the line at Bingley, who mouthed back "shawl" and shrugged his shoulders. The choirmaster then rose and signaled his boys to begin the processional. The dozen-member choir began their solemn pace up the aisle, followed by the vicar and his young assistant. A few heartbeats after they passed him, Darcy felt a swoosh of warm air and looked down to find Elizabeth standing beside him, a heavy woolen shawl in her arms.

"Please, sir, if you would be so kind? Pass this to Jane," she whispered breathlessly. Darcy took the shawl and passed it on to Miss Bingley, discreetly observing Elizabeth out of the corner of his eye as she watched it make its way down the pew. He knew the exact moment Miss Bennet received her shawl by the tender smile that illuminated her sister's face and felt his own begin to answer it when the choir ended its hymn and the vicar called them to prayer.

The familiar words of the invocation flowed over Darcy, their currents witnessing to him of a higher order of majesty that rarely failed to compel his attention, although Miss Bingley's whispered complaints of the cold and the length of the prayer were formidable obstacles. The "Amen" was sounded, echoed thankfully by several in their party, and the first hymn announced. It was one not known to Darcy, so he elected to listen rather than pick his way through it. That his tutor would be the lady whose song had so enchanted him the week previous was further inducement to hold his peace. He was not disappointed; Elizabeth's voice swelled in sure tones, with feeling and a grace that moved him deeply. At the last verse he joined his baritone to her soprano much to the giggling delight of a pair of very young ladies in front of them. As they resumed their seats, Darcy suffered their backward glances only once before treating them to a brow lifted in freezing censure, which served only to send them again into paroxysms of silliness. To his further indignation, Elizabeth seemed unable to resist joining, quickly clasping a gloved hand over her mouth and peeping up mischievously at him. Darcy petulantly ignored her and sternly directed his attention to the vicar.

Sunday's confession was assigned. Darcy murmured the lines from memory without undue contemplation, the phrases concerning disobedience and ingratitude being, he believed, of little application. When the sin of pride was added to the catalog, Elizabeth stirred beside him and delicately but distinctly cleared her throat, giving him, he was persuaded, perfect justification for laying emphasis on the following transgression, of *willfulness,* in a manner she could not mistake.

When the second hymn was announced, they were at *point nonplus,* and Darcy steeled himself against the effects of her voice on his clearly traitorous senses. This one he knew quite well. Turning slightly in Miss Bingley's direction, he succeeded in avoiding Elizabeth's amused eyes, but with the unfortunate effect of giving the other lady renewed claim on his attention. It was a poor scheme withal. As Elizabeth's voice still filled up his senses, he now had Miss Bingley's comments and compliments to deal with as well.

"Prepare ye the way of the Lord," the Reverend Mr. Stanley grandly intoned the Scripture. "Make straight in the desert a highway for our God." Darcy drew out his prayer book and swiftly turned the pages to those passages.

"Tch!" Darcy looked down at the sound into Elizabeth's rueful countenance as she bit her lower lip in consternation at her empty hands. Hesitating only a moment, he gallantly nudged the left side of his prayer book into her hand and bent his head to accommodate her view of it.

"Almighty God, give us grace . . . ," they read together. Bent as he was over the passage, Darcy's every breath set the curls at Elizabeth's ears and temple to dancing, distracting him mightily from the page they shared. ". . . that we may cast away the works of darkness, and put upon us the armor of light . . ." With great effort of will, he set himself to concentrate on the text and was able to finish without his mind wandering into perilous byways. Beside him, Elizabeth settled back into the hard pew, unconsciously searching for a comfortable position from which to apprehend the Reverend Mr. Stanley's sermon. Darcy's attempt to do likewise was a dismal failure. Neatly sandwiched as he was between two ladies, he dared not let any part of his person rest too near theirs, so he was reduced to sitting absolutely erect in a manner horribly reminiscent of the schoolroom. There was nothing for it, so resigned to his lot, he crossed his arms closely over his chest and trained his gaze on the vicar's face.

Providentially, Mr. Stanley was a vigorous sermonizer, catching Darcy's interest well enough to allow him to disregard, for the most part, the discomfort of his constricted limbs and his tense awareness of the maddening female on his left. However, when the service concluded and the last hymn was sung, he was more than ready to rise and seek in the outdoors an opportunity to work the stiffness out of his back and the lady out of his mind. "Mr. Darcy" came two voices, one from either side of him.

"Miss Bingley, Miss Elizabeth?" He waited, curious to see who would defer to whom for his attention.

"Please, Miss Bingley, you were before me." Elizabeth curtsied and moved away to link her arm with that of Squire Justin, assuring him as she did so of her sister's full recovery to health. Unreasonably disappointed, Darcy turned to Miss Bingley and asked how he could be of service. Smiling triumphantly, she took his arm, giving Darcy no choice but to escort her down the crowded aisle.

"No foot warmers, Mr. Darcy, in *this* weather! It is not to be believed! Next week, I promise you, I shall order the bricks from the carriage to be brought in, warmers or no."

"As you will, Miss Bingley," he replied, distracted by a flurry of movement in the section of pews reserved for servants.

"Perhaps Charles should demand the sexton do something about it. How *can* one be expected to attend to the vicar while turning to ice?"

"Hmm," Darcy replied, only half-listening. Mildly curious, he searched through the crowd of servants until he found the locus of the disturbance and then was shocked to see at its center his own valet.

"What the d——!"

"Mr. Darcy!" exclaimed Miss Bingley. "Whatever can be the matter?" Receiving no response, she followed Darcy's rigid stare into the face of his valet, who with a hand resting protectively on the arm of a young woman, returned his regard with a flustered hauteur the equal of his own. Behind them stood a rather tall, solid-looking footman possessed of a glower that could likely kindle a blaze at twenty paces.

"Is that not your valet?" Miss Bingley demanded. Darcy choked out an affirmative, his jaw clenching and unclenching dangerously. Caught between two dangers, Fletcher dropped his eyes in deference to his master, whose look in reply promised a future reckoning. The footman, seeing himself caught out in his loutish behavior by a gentleman, backed away from Fletcher and the girl, and exited the church in the opposite direction.

Darcy resumed his way down the aisle, Miss Bingley, now silent, on his arm. "Your valet . . . he has been with you long?" she inquired finally.

"Quite," Darcy replied stiffly.

"He serves you well? No freaks of distemper or problems with color?"

"Certainly not! At least . . ." Darcy paused, considering what he had just witnessed. "He is usually completely reliable. I wonder what could be your interest in my valet, madam?"

"Oh, merely idle curiosity, sir. But tell me, have you ever known him to mistake green for gray?"

After handing Miss Bingley into the carriage outside Meryton Church, Darcy went to Hurst's conveyance and returned to Netherfield as he had come. The ladies were mounting the stairs to their rooms by the time he laid aside his hat and gloves and shrugged off his greatcoat in Netherfield's entrance hall. Talk of the Bennet sisters' imminent return to Longbourn drifted down upon him as he paused and, with concern, observed the wistful way Bingley gazed after them.

"If you cared to offer me something warm to drink, old man, I daresay I would agree to it," Darcy proposed carefully.

Bingley came back to himself and, with an apologetic shake of his head, replied that of course he would order something up immediately. Would chocolate be agreeable?

"Excellent! In the library? You must hear the account I read yesterday of the breaching of the walls of Badajoz." Bingley weakly smiled his assent and wandered off to request the desired refreshments while Darcy headed for the library, eager to be absent from any public room that might attract Bingley's sisters or, more particularly, their departing guests. His prolonged nearness to Elizabeth in church had unsettled him and certainly thwarted his plan to stay aloof from her until her departure. This little time remaining, he knew, must be put to good use. His best course lay in safeguarding himself from any contact with her until propriety demanded his presence. If his plan required Bingley's distraction from the eldest Miss Bennet, so much the better.

They spent a companionable hour "taking" Badajoz from the comfort of chairs set before the library's hearth. The author's suspenseful narrative, coupled with Darcy's talent for infusing the account with a sense of immediacy and heroism, quite captured Bingley's attention. Looking up from his text, Darcy was pleased to see his friend's countenance gradually change from that of polite interest to eager anticipation so that, by the time Stevenson apprised them that the Misses Bennet were about to take their leave, he congratulated himself upon detecting in Bingley a momentary disappointment for the interruption.

Accompanying his friend to the front hall, Darcy was careful to remain in the background and kept his gaze traveling indifferently among the participants in their farewells. Miss Bingley's relief at the ladies' departure was almost palpable, her sister's scarcely less so. Hurst had wandered out of the hall as soon as was decently possible, leaving Bingley alone to express a sincere sense of loss for the ladies' company. Coming forward at last, Darcy bowed briefly to Miss Jane Bennet and wished her a pleasant journey home and continuing good health. He then turned to her sister with similar words at the ready but was almost startled out of his studied gravity by the intense examination he met in her eyes.

"Miss Elizabeth?" he questioned.

"Mr. Darcy," she responded in a voice that necessitated he take a step closer to hear her better. "Mr. Darcy, I assure you that I have no desire to intrude into your domestic affairs or embroil you in local matters." She paused in obvious discomfort but, gathering herself, plunged on. "I fear that you will find this an intolerable sort of imposition, but please allow me to acquaint you with the great service your man performed this morning for little Annie Garlick."

"Mr. Fletcher is quite aware of the behavior I expect of those in my employ," he replied haughtily, yet curious about her interest in the incident.

"Oh, I am so pleased to hear it, Mr. Darcy!" was her disjunctive rejoinder.

She has done it again! he thought, not knowing whether to smile or frown at her. *Now what, exactly, does she mean me to have said?*

"How is that, Miss Elizabeth?"

"Why, knowing that he had your complete support and your high expectations to bolster him, he did what none in the servant class was willing to do, nor any of the local gentlemen were pleased to do."

Darcy decided against obtuseness. "The hulking footman," he supplied.

"Yes"—she smiled up at him—"he has been pressing poor Annie in a most inappropriate manner. Your man was a knight in shining armor to her."

The impression of Fletcher, so clad and accoutred, presented itself for Darcy's inspection and threatened to send him into a state of amusement he had rarely enjoyed at a lady's instigation. He masked his laughter by clearing his throat. "Hmm, a knight! Well, I shall keep your words in mind when next I speak to him." He bowed with slow grace before her. "Good day."

"Mr. Darcy." She curtsied and was gone.

⊰❦⊱

Later, when Fletcher quietly entered his master's rooms to prepare him for dinner, Darcy greeted his arrival with far more interest than he imagined the man desired. "Fletcher, I wish to speak to you about this morning," he began.

"Yes, sir, one moment, sir," the valet replied and disappeared into the dressing room. Darcy paused, quirking an eyebrow in surprise. When Fletcher did not reappear after a few moments, Darcy started toward the dressing room door, only to collide with the man, causing him to drop the black evening breeches in his arms. As Darcy quick-stepped, Fletcher swooped down to retrieve them, only to catch them under his master's boot, nearly tripping him as he tugged. The sound of ripping fabric rent the air, causing both men to cease their movements. "Mr. Darcy, sir. Your breeches!" Fletcher cried. The horror-stricken look on Fletcher's face contrasted so ironically with the heroic image conjured earlier by Elizabeth's words that Darcy's lips began to twitch. Soon a grin pulled at the corners of his mouth; then unalloyed mirth followed hot on its heels as Fletcher displayed the ruined breeches and regarded him in confusion. At this juncture, Darcy could only collapse into a nearby chair and press a hand to his eyes in an attempt to recover himself.

"Mr. Darcy? Sir?" Fletcher's voice held a note of concern as Darcy continued to try to choke down the laughter that threatened every time he looked at his valet or the breeches.

"Mr. Fletcher," he finally managed, "I remember distinctly that I had something of import to discuss with you, but on my life, I cannot recall what it was. You probably know better than I what I should be saying to you at this moment; so if you would be so kind, consider it said! And do not grieve over the breeches, man!"

"Yes, sir. Certainly . . . I shall find another pair immediately. Thank you, sir!" Fletcher stammered and was as good as his word.

In a record twenty minutes Darcy was ready to leave his chambers. As the valet began picking up his discarded clothing, Darcy paused for some moments. The plottings of last evening, crowned by the scene at church, required at least a show of displeasure on his part. Though for the former he had no real proof and for the latter . . . Well, the man had garnered praise from a considerable quarter. Pulling out his watch, Darcy fiddled with the stem and checked its time against the chamber clock. Finally, he replaced it in his waistcoat pocket. "Fletcher, a moment."

"Mr. Darcy." Fletcher's demeanor told Darcy he had regained a measure of his usual aplomb.

"I mentioned a matter of importance, you may recall?" Fletcher stilled his movements and looked apprehensively at his master. "I do not know why or how, but it must not be repeated. Do I make myself clear?"

Fletcher nodded.

"Miss Bingley very ably communicated her annoyance, and I do not wish to entertain it again."

"Miss Bingley, sir? What has Annie done to Miss Bingley?" Fletcher's puzzlement matched Darcy's.

"Annie and Miss Bingley? Why, nothing!" Darcy replied.

"Then you are not displeased about Annie, sir? Truly, what else could a Christian do but defend the little innocent against that great—"

"I speak not of the young woman, Fletcher, but of Miss Bingley! Although I cannot be pleased to see someone so intimately in my employ involved in such an altercation."

"Mr. Darcy, I swear on my life that I *never* altercated with Miss Bingley," Fletcher averred in horror.

"No, no, not Miss Bingley." Darcy was close to despairing of making himself understood. "Fletcher, listen . . ." The chamber clock struck eight, which meant he should be downstairs that very moment. "I am convinced you understand my meaning," he pronounced in frustration, "and I expect your entire compliance."

"Of course, sir." Fletcher bowed. Darcy nodded, incompletely satisfied but at a loss as to how to obtain that satisfaction or now even identify what exactly would. With another nod to Fletcher, he hurried down to the dining room.

The pleasurable quietness of Sunday passed into an unexpected tedium on Monday. Bingley's interest in the intricacies of estate management waxed low and was ill-compensated by the brightening of Miss Bingley's manner now her uninvited guests were gone. Several of the local worthies and their ladies came to dinner, but none brought the sparkle to which Darcy had become accustomed. Therefore, the following day, when Bingley suggested a ride into Meryton ending in a visit to Longbourn, "to inquire after Miss Bennet's health for politeness's sake," he was disposed to agree with an alacrity that surprised his friend.

The four miles to Meryton by way of winding country lanes gave both men ample time to fill their lungs with the bracing air of a fine autumn day. Catching their masters' sense of an escape well made, their restive mounts matched it, employing all their cunning toward making the outing an eventful one. In this they were encouraged by their masters' laughter and affectionately derisive oaths as to their origins until the village itself was in sight; where perforce, gentlemanly manners on the parts of all were once more assumed. As they swung onto the main thoroughfare, Bingley pulled his horse to a stop and all but stood in his stirrups, displaying an eagerness for the scene before them that mystified as well as amused his companion.

"What is it, Bingley? What do you see?" Darcy called to him as he, himself, began to search the street.

"Don't you see them, Darcy? The Bennet family, or rather the ladies at least, and some other gentlemen. Over on the left, near the linener's." Thus directed, Darcy found them, grouped round by several officers and two other gentlemen, one of whom appeared to be garbed in parson's black.

"How fortunate! Now we need not press on to Longbourn nor, come to that, even stop to make your inquiries in the street. Miss Bennet is here and in obvious good health; therefore, we—"

Bingley's glare was all Darcy had hoped for. He set his heels to Nelson's sides and grinned as he shouted over his shoulder, "Gudgeon! Are you coming?"

As soon as Bingley caught him up, Darcy slowed to a sedate pace and approached the group. None in the party had yet noticed them, the ladies' view being blocked by the unknown gentlemen. A flutter of anticipation welled unbidden in Darcy's chest as first Miss Jane Bennet and then Miss Elizabeth became aware of their arrival.

"Miss Bennet and, yes, all your sisters! How delightful to meet you!" Bingley greeted as he brought his mount to a halt.

"Mr. Bingley! How do you do, sir?" replied several of the younger girls, flushed with all the agreeable attention they were receiving.

"Sirs, we have just been forming a new acquaintance as we introduce our newly come cousin to Meryton," Elizabeth explained over the giggles of her siblings. "May I present our cousin Mr. Collins, from Kent?" Aware that the black-clad gentleman had turned, Darcy briefly rested his eyes upon him and nodded. The walk into Meryton had done marvelous things to Miss Elizabeth's downy cheeks, and the pleasure in her eyes, though not, he knew, for himself, was still wonderful to behold. He tore his eyes from her as she embarked upon her second introduction and essayed to attend to it.

That gentleman had not turned during the previous introduction but had maintained an attitude which kept his face averted from the horseman. It passed quickly through Darcy's mind that his figure seemed familiar. *It cannot be . . . !*

". . . introduce Mr. Wickham, who has just joined Colonel Forster's company." Elizabeth beamed as the gentleman, in one fluid motion, turned and bowed.

Darcy froze in shock and anger. His face drained of all color save for his eyes, which flashed darkly at the new officer. Immediately sensing his master's turmoil, Nelson began backing away and threw his head in growing agitation. Darcy's movements were practiced as he brought the animal under control, but his focus continued to drill into Wickham's reddening countenance. Unable to hold against Darcy's furious scrutiny, Wickham flinched but smoothly disguised his reaction with a touch of his hat by way of a salute. With lips clasped in an unrelenting, grim line, Darcy returned the salutation with the merest veneer of civility and turned to Bingley, his mind and emotions in utter chaos.

Mercifully, Bingley continued his pleasantries with the ladies and gentlemen only a few minutes more before bidding the group adieu. To Darcy, the interview was interminable. He sat stiffly in his saddle, hardly knowing where to look, his mind reeling.

How can it be? Joined the regiment? Why? How? Questions and suspicions flowed thick and fast. *Why here? Did he know I would be in Hertfordshire . . . follow me? His object, what can be his object?* As he reached down and pretended to adjust a stirrup, a wave of nauseating fear shook him to his core. *Georgiana! My God, has he done something to Georgiana and come to throw it in my face!* Darcy could not prevent the tremors of rage and fear that coursed through his body any more than he could forbid the sun to rise. His hands shook, the street seemed to tilt crazily, and all his being cried out to leap upon the devil whose discomposure of moments ago was now replaced with an air of modesty and congeniality.

"Miss Bennet, Miss Elizabeth"—Bingley's voice broke through Darcy's turmoil—"please extend my compliments to Mr. and Mrs. Bennet. Mr. Collins, Mr.—Excuse me, *Lieutenant* Wickham. Your servant, sirs." Bingley swept his beaver from his brow and, nodding once more to the ladies, nudged his mount into a turn back to the street. Recalled to his manners, Darcy did likewise, glimpsing as he did a questioning frown upon Elizabeth's face.

How this must appear to her! he thought regretfully as he followed Bingley out of Meryton. Familiar with Miss Elizabeth Bennet's turn of mind, he guessed that she was examining the incident with dangerous zeal. *What will she make of it? Will Wickham offer to enlighten her? No! No, doing so would expose him, and that he surely cannot afford,* Darcy thought bitterly. *What does a lieutenancy cost? No, he can afford little, to have thrown in his lot with the army! But what of Georgiana?* His mind revolved back upon his fears for his sister. Had Wickham attempted to contact her, impose upon her in some way while her brother had been absent?

Bingley's tone-deaf whistling of a popular love ballad warred with the tumult of Darcy's emotions and emerged the victor. "You have my attention, Bingley," he snapped, resolving as he did so to send an immediate express to his sister. "Cease and desist, I beg you!"

"You do not like the ballad, Darcy? It is all the rage, you know." Bingley smiled imperturbably back at him.

Darcy lifted an imperious brow. "A ballad, you say? I rather feared that you were summoning the local cattle and expect to be inundated by your four-footed admirers at any moment."

"Darcy! You exaggerate!" Bingley's charge was met with a snort in a denial of any such tendency. "Well, I have never laid claim to musical talents, at least not in your hearing, but surely a man can be excused for holding forth when under the inspiration of such loveliness as I have just beheld." Darcy misdoubted that he actually heard Bingley heave a lovelorn sigh. "How fortunate to have met them in the village! We might have missed them entirely."

"Yes, that is so," Darcy replied quietly as the fortuitous nature of the encounter broke upon him. He might have first come upon Wickham at a social function in the neighborhood. Forster's officers seemed to be always about. It was very likely Wickham would be invited along with his fellows to round out a dinner party or liven an assembly. In such restricted society as was to be found in Hertfordshire, they would be continually in each other's company! Darcy ground his teeth. "Intolerable!"

"What did you say?" Bingley brought his horse up short and turned to stare at his companion.

Darcy stared back uncomprehendingly, then realized that he must have spoken aloud the conclusion of his thoughts. "Charles, I must in all seriousness ask of you a great favor."

Bingley's eyes widened at the solemnity of his tone. "Anything within my power, Darcy, anything."

A brief, reluctant smile creased Darcy's face at Bingley's ready agreement; then he took a deep breath. "I ask that you make it clear to Colonel Forster that his newest officer is not welcome at your ball next week." The surprise and doubt on Bingley's face caused him to hurry on. "I am fully aware of the position in which this places you and can only offer my deepest apologies for doing so. An explanation I cannot give, save to tell you that my acquaintance with Lieutenant Wickham is of long standing, his father, before his death, having been steward to mine, and that he has repaid my family's generosity in a monstrous fashion which will forever stand between us."

"Good heavens, Darcy! Can Forster know he has acquired such a scoundrel for an officer?"

"Doubtless he will in time. Wickham has never failed to reveal his true colors eventually, but his manner is so plausible, his ability to insinuate himself so uncanny, that the damage he means to inflict is done before his victim knows it." Bingley's gathered brows and shocked silence told Darcy that his purpose was answered. "You must, of course, do as you see fit concerning Wickham in all other respects. It is only for this ball that I ask your indulgence in fixing your guest list. If you must include him or suffer his company at a public function, do not think of me. I shall not be missed, I am convinced." He looked aside, remembering the frown on Elizabeth's face.

"Not be missed? Rubbish! The man shall not cross my threshold, I promise you."

"Thank you," Darcy replied simply, but his words seemed to cause Bingley an unwarranted degree of pleasure. "Bingley?"

"Oh, nothing! It is just so seldom that I can do *you* a real service that your occasions to thank *me* are very rare."

Darcy almost smiled. "Perhaps I should allow you more opportunity, then, as it pleases you so."

"Perhaps you should!" agreed Bingley, enough sincerity behind his laughing reply to give Darcy something else to think upon as they directed their horses down Netherfield's drive.

The leaden feelings of apprehension that had plagued Darcy upon discovering Wickham in the shire were little relieved by Bingley's assurances that "the man" would never be admitted to Netherfield. His past relations with Wickham militated against such complacency; he dared not rest until he had confirmed to himself that Georgiana was not, indeed, involved in some way with the man's appearance in Hertfordshire. Therefore, immediately after dinner that evening, Darcy excused himself from the entertainments Miss Bingley had planned and withdrew to the writing desk in the drawing room. Drawing out a sheet of paper and finding the quill well pared, he dipped it into the inkwell and put it to paper.

19 November 1811
Netherfield Hall
Meryton
Hertfordshire

Dearest Georgiana,

He paused then, and found himself at a complete loss. *What shall I say? How shall I begin what can only bring her pain?* He set the quill into its stand, sank against the delicately carved back of the chair, and stared unseeing at the all but blank page before him. *Consider, man! Would you not have heard from Georgiana or her companion if anything were amiss? You excuse your temper, plead apprehension on her behalf; but truly, do you do well to seek your own peace of mind at the expense of Georgiana's, and it so hard and lately won?* Darcy closed his eyes, his fingers working at the tension that seemed to have made a home in his temples since the afternoon's encounter. *How should I proceed? If ever I were in want of advice . . .* His gaze traveled to his companions.

Miss Bingley and Mrs. Hurst were deep in the pages of *Le Beau Monde,* while Hurst read aloud to them titillating bits of London gossip from a lately delivered newspaper. Bingley was trying his best to ignore their bursts of scandalized laughter and concentrate on *Badajoz,* his interest having been caught since their reading of it the day before. In this effort he was ill-fated, having been forced to look up repeatedly as Hurst now insisted upon regaling him every few minutes with the results of last week's races and boxing matches. Darcy sighed heavily and turned back to his letter. There was no help to be garnered from that quarter, to be sure.

A rap at the door and the entrance of Stevenson, silver tray in hand, brought all activity to a halt. The tray, supporting a single letter, passed under breathless scrutiny until it was presented to Darcy. Recognizing the hand that wrote its direction, he swiftly took possession of the post and secured it in his coat pocket.

"A letter, Mr. Darcy?" Miss Bingley's query betrayed the power of a rampant curiosity.

"A letter, yes, Miss Bingley." Darcy rose and bowed to his hostess and host. "If you will excuse me. No, don't get up, I beg you," he tossed to Bingley, who had begun to struggle out of his chair. In a few long strides he was out of the room and into the hall to the library. Shutting the door of that welcome sanctuary firmly behind him, he went to the hearth, stirred up the coals to a soft glow, and dropped into one of the chairs drawn close to catch the feeble warmth. With fumbling, nerveless fingers, he lit a nearby lamp and withdrew the letter from his pocket.

It lay there in his hands, and on his life, he could not find the will to loosen the seal. Turning it over several times, he read its direction again: "Mr. Fitzwilliam Darcy, Netherfield Hall, Meryton, Hertfordshire," in the unmistakable hand of his beloved sister. What should he find within? *Dearest sister, are you destroyed?* In an agony of dread, Darcy leaned forward, took a deep, trembling breath, and quickly broke the seal.

> *15 November 1811*
> *Pemberley Manor*
> *Lambton*
> *Derbyshire*

Dear Brother,

> *Your letter of the 11th was of such a tender and amusing nature that I have placed it among my keepsakes to treasure always, as I do your care and affection for such a troublesome sister as myself. Your noble, generous determination to shoulder the responsibility for all that occurred last summer*

leaves me much affected. I would not presume to contest you,
but you must allow me, dear Brother, to bear that which truly
falls to my account. You must know that the contrition it
called for was needful, indeed, instrumental, in my recovery,
not unlike the painful impasse between you and Father which
you mentioned. (Yes, I do indeed remember your strokes and
the sorrow of our father, although the frights that prompted
them have long been forgotten!) I would not have you dwell
upon it more. It is done, confessed, and forgiven. I am free of
it, save as a lesson learned, and desire that you regard it no
longer. I assure you, Mrs. Annesley and I are too much
engaged to do so!

Too much engaged . . . regard it no longer. Darcy's eyes scanned the
paragraph again, fearful he had missed something. *Not have you*
dwell upon it . . . free . . . a lesson learned. He collapsed into the comfort of the chair, his eyes closed, pressing the letter against his lips.
The throbbing at his temple quieted as relief spread sweetly through
his body. *Wickham has not troubled her further.* Evidently, his appearance here had nothing whatever to do with Georgiana. Darcy
savored the alleviation of his fears for little more than a moment before turning once more to the questions of why Wickham was in
Hertfordshire and how he would manage him. They seemed fated to
meet commonly if he prolonged his stay at Netherfield.

"*If* I prolong my stay," Darcy murmured to himself. No one
would question his leaving for London. There was always the excuse of unexpected business. He was committed to remain for the
ball, but after? Unbidden, a pair of utterly bewitching eyes set
above a lovely, dimpled smile recalled themselves to his remembrance. Should he regret leaving? He looked down at the unfinished letter in his hand and lifted it again to the light.

Please extend my compliments to Miss Bingley. She is all
politeness to ascribe "perfection" to my small talents. I hope I

am sensible to the exactness of her taste and can only be honored that she holds my efforts in such esteem. To your friend Mr. Bingley, please forward my congratulations on his acquisition of a pleasing situation. With you to guide him, his efforts cannot but be successful.

Now, dear Brother, with the remainder of your letter I am more than a little astonished. I cannot think how anyone could deem you, who have been the most considerate and kind of brothers to me, an "unfeeling, prosy fellow." Miss Elizabeth Bennet must be an Unusual Female indeed to have defended against your argumentation, dismissed you in such a manner, and taken you into dislike. Perhaps she is one who holds to first impressions, and your acquaintance, in her estimation, did not begin well? That it was a lapse in social grace which occasioned this discord between you I cannot believe. I hope that this letter finds you reestablished in her good opinion, as I cannot bear that someone should so misjudge your character, so dear you are to me!

I close with a fervent wish to see you and pray that God may keep you until you join us for Christmas. There is so much I would say, so much I have learned, but it must wait until I behold your dear face. As you honored me as Pemberley's "treasure," so I remind you that you are its heart. Return soon!

Your loving sister,
Georgiana Darcy

Darcy's eyes lingered over the elegant signature, and then, slowly, he folded the letter along its creases and tucked it securely into his coat's inner pocket. *Georgiana, my dear girl!* he mused, templing his fingers and resting his chin upon them as he stared into the glowing coals of the hearth. He tried to imagine her as she wrote, so astute in her perception and advice to him, but he could not picture it. Such a creature was in complete opposition to the one he had placed in Mrs. Annesley's keeping only five months before!

He laughed softly then at her disbelief that all the world did not see him as she did, complimented by her complete faith in his ability to retrieve his standing in Elizabeth Bennet's skeptical eye. How close she had come to the mark! Indeed, their acquaintance could hardly have begun less favorably!

As ridiculous as he knew it to be, his sister's confidence in him caused a glimmer of optimism to rise from the morass of irresolution he'd fallen into these several days past. A determination to correct Elizabeth's estimation seized him. He ticked off the circumstances in his favor: Wickham would not be present, there would be a week's worth of absence from which to garner topics of conversation, the general conviviality a ball afforded, the distraction provided by a large number of people, and finally, the surprise of his partiality and condescension.

His original motive for writing relieved, he rose with new energy from his hearthside reverie and returned to the society of his hosts and the penning of his letter. Later, over glasses of brandy and sherry, he merely smiled when Miss Bingley observed that she had rarely seen anyone so amused by the composition of a letter to his family.

CHAPTER 9

The Illustration of His Character

A lingering inclement weather descended upon the county, enveloping the land in a chill mist that often resolved itself into rain. Miss Bingley decried its tiresome arrival, looking upon its unwelcome stay as a daily personal affront. Her brother regarded it with some trepidation, fearful of its effect on attendance at the ball, but Darcy's satisfaction with their enforced isolation mystified his companions. The days before the ball passed as he and Bingley worked on plans for the improvement of Netherfield and, when the weather allowed, on their expertise out in the game fields. Several evenings were spent abroad at influential houses in the shire, and a few afternoons were devoted to discovering the reliability of tales concerning legendary local breeding stock. As he intended, to all outward appearances Darcy seemed unconcerned with the approaching ball. But in truth, he was preparing for it assiduously.

His strategy was elegant in its simplicity: pique Elizabeth's curiosity by his absence from all venues of intercourse with her and then, at the ball, make her the unmistakable object of his attention. The surprise and confusion engendered by such action would, he hoped, allow him to claim her hand for at least one set, during which he would offer a well-crafted apology for his lamentable manners at their first meeting. He trusted in Miss Elizabeth Bennet's unpredictable wit to inspire their conversation from there on. Surprise . . . the complete suddenness and partiality of his address! Darcy smiled to himself as he imagined her flustering prettily. She would be fairly caught and without resources. *Then, Miss Elizabeth Bennet, we shall begin again.*

Therefore, when invited to accompany the Bingleys on their call upon the Bennets to issue the invitation to the much-anticipated ball, he solemnly declined and instead occupied himself in correspondence with his man of business, then spent a profitable hour or so with Trafalgar out in the fields. He carefully avoided anyplace where he might meet Elizabeth Bennet, his only glimpse of her before the ball occurring at Meryton Church on Sunday, and even then, no more passed between them than an acknowledging nod on his part, matched by its cool reception on hers.

It was now Tuesday morning, the Day itself. Darcy gave a last tug at his coat as Fletcher, carefully cradling his dancing pumps, returned from a search for the appropriate vintage of champagne with which to give them a faultless shine. Earlier, Fletcher had sent to Erewile House, Darcy's London home, for his best black coat and breeches, which now hung at the ready. The valet had scoured the local establishments for an acceptably snowy pair of stockings but, in the end, had been forced to send to London for these as well. Darcy noted that his shirt was starched and pressed, a supply of neckcloths was in similar condition, and his watch, links, emerald stickpin, and fobs lay on the dresser, gleaming as richly as the smile of satisfaction on Fletcher's face as he emerged from the dressing room, pumps in hand.

"There, sir." His valet waved the shoes before him for his inspection. "Polished up as nice as if I'd found the '98 instead of having to use the '02." Darcy nodded, his mind occupied with the intricate niceties of the apology he was still attempting to compose.

"Ahem." Fletcher cleared his throat and waited for his employer's eyes to alight upon him. "Mr. Darcy . . . about your waistcoat for this evening," he ventured carefully.

Darcy shot him a suspicious frown. "Yes, what about my waistcoat? It is the black silk made to match the breeches, is it not?"

"Yes, sir, but I was thinking . . ." Fletcher paused as Darcy's eyes narrowed further, and then he finished hurriedly, "the emerald green and gold shot silk."

"Fletcher!"

"Merely a suggestion, sir. Nothing more. The plain black it shall be." The valet put the pumps down beside the chair on which the suit was carefully laid. "Although"—he sighed—"why you should wish to disappear into the woodwork, overshadowed by flashy young men in their vulgar dress uniforms, I cannot pretend to know."

"I do not intend to 'disappear into the woodwork' tonight, Fletcher!"

"Just so, sir."

"Meaning what?"

"As you say, sir, you do not *intend* to become invisible tonight."

"But you believe that in the plain black waistcoat, and in spite of my intentions, I will?" Darcy challenged.

"Mr. Darcy," Fletcher replied patiently, drawing from his wealth of sartorial experience, "I am convinced that you are noticed in whatever place you grace with your attendance. But I have observed, sir, that a room filled with red coats tends to distract certain persons, primarily the female portion of the race. The ladies, God bless them, seem to require something upon which to focus."

Dubious at first, Darcy pondered the idea as Fletcher retrieved the debated waistcoat from the packing box from London. A small voice in the back of his mind expressed amazement that he was even considering such nonsense, but when Fletcher rejoined him, he found his own attention caught by the soft glitter of the emerald and gold threads, which created a rich paisley pattern on the black silk background. *Perhaps . . . it could not hurt!*

"As you wish, Fletcher. Take the plain one away and leave that."
Darcy knew that he had better leave before Fletcher talked him into
something he would regret. "Be ready for me at seven o'clock," he
ordered briskly.

"Very good, sir."

Darcy found that, once again, he was leaving his rooms mis-
trusting the bland expression on the valet's face and wondered
whatever had become of his biddable man. He had certainly begun
to behave in a most peculiar manner.

As he entered the breakfast room, Darcy found Bingley just sitting down and quizzed him on such an early appearance as he
poured his coffee. "Oh, the anticipation of the ball, I suppose," Bingley replied. "I have hosted small, private parties in Town, of course,
but this!" He waved his own cup in an arc before gulping half of it
down. "This is a fence quite beyond my height. I could hardly sleep
last night for wondering whether I had forgotten something or
whether what I had remembered was properly done."

"Miss Bingley is satisfied with your efforts, no doubt."

"On the contrary, Miss Bingley is satisfied with little about this
entire affair. Her serenity, I beg to inform you, sir, is for your pleasure alone. If it were not for the enjoyment I expect in a certain
lady's company, I would not have wished to embark on this interminable odyssey at all!"

"Come, come, Bingley. It is expected that a man of your position and in possession of a country house will host such occasions
yearly and"—he added at Bingley's grimace—"various smaller social gatherings throughout the year. It is so at Pemberley and
Erewile House; you know that."

"Everything runs so smoothly there; I am sure you are not
troubled in the least! Everything here is at sixes and sevens
and . . . and this food is cold! Where are the servants?" Bingley
threw down his napkin and made to rise.

"Bingley! Be easy, sir." Darcy put a restraining hand on his arm.
"A gentleman does not berate his servants, and you are quite in dan-

ger of breaching that wise maxim." Darcy met the distinctly mulish expression that Bingley turned upon him with an arched brow.

"Oh, blast it all; I know you are right, Darcy." Bingley collapsed back into his chair. "I will behave myself, so you may pack away that imperious look and help me deal with this infernal ball." He ran his hands through his hair in frustration and then flashed Darcy the ingenuous grin his friend knew so well. "At least one thing has turned out well, quite providential in fact."

"Pray tell me your one thing, Charles, so we may rejoice together." Darcy laughed.

"That fellow you wished not to see. Wickham."

"Yes?" Darcy's jaw flexed unconsciously.

"Went to see Colonel Forster about him but met Mr. Denny before I could speak to him. Good thing, that. Denny desired me to tell Caroline the number of officers who would be able to accept the invitation, and he mentioned Wickham specifically."

"Mentioned him how, Bingley?"

"Won't be coming! Cannot come. He suddenly recollected some affairs in London he must attend to and left yesterday. Not expected to return for several days. So," Bingley ended triumphantly, "you need have no concern about him."

A theretofore unrealized tenseness in Darcy's chest began to uncoil as he nodded in agreement with Bingley's happy assessment. He chose to interpret it as relief that Bingley had not been required to make Wickham's exclusion from the ball embarrassingly official. But quick upon its heels, the evening and all its possibilities opened up before him, and the smile that played irrepressibly upon his features he allowed Bingley to read as he wished.

"Apology be hanged!" The bar of soap hit the foot of the bath with a sharp *whack* and sank with ne'er a whimper to the bottom as Darcy leaned back against the copper head, frustration writ large upon his features. "Give me a syllogism to solve, a Greek epic to translate, or an unruly horse to school, but *do not* require of me an infernal pretty speech!" The exact wording of this essential apology had plagued him the entire day. Each time he thought he might have it, it died a quick, ignominious death in his imagined delivery.

Darcy groaned as the chamber clock informed him that time was running forward. His lack of talent in matters of address had been problematic in the past, but now it was become ruinous to something he highly desired. He must get it right; everything hinged upon it! Reaching for the bell, he rang for Fletcher and hunched forward as the valet emptied a pitcher of water over his head. A warmed towel was pressed into his hand, and with it he wiped the water and soap out of his eyes. Rising into his dressing gown, he stepped out of the bath and over to more warmed towels to complete drying before Fletcher returned with his small clothes and the shaving kit.

"Miss Bennet, you must allow . . . must excuse . . . My dear Miss Elizabeth, you may recall our first meeting—*no, I would rather you didn't recall it, precisely*—I beg to be permitted to—*no, not beg*—Miss Eliza, pray forgive . . .

"Arrrrrgh! Forgive me for behaving like a perfect ass." Darcy threw the towel across the room, nearly hitting the returning Fletcher.

"Certainly, sir. Say no more, sir," Fletcher said.

Darcy eyed the man dangerously for a moment, a sharp retort nearly bridging his lips before his valet's unruffled mien brought home to him the humor of it. He could not laugh, the problem was too imminent, but he *could* step back from the precipice of ill temper he was perilously close to plunging down.

"I was not addressing you, Fletcher," he growled in a much subdued tone as he turned to divest himself of the damp dressing gown. "Although I do apologize for the towel. I was not shying it at you apurpose."

Fletcher passed Darcy his small clothes and then shook out the fine linen shirt, ready to slip it up his arms. "It is I, Mr. Darcy, who must apologize for my levity. It was inexcusable, sir, and I will take steps—"

"No, no Fletcher, it is quite all right. I stood in need of just such a diversion. Notwithstanding"—he paused and caught Fletcher's eye in the mirror before him—"such displays should be indulged in judiciously."

"Yes, sir." Fletcher bent over his task of unrolling the silk stockings and, in a carefully preserved silence, handed them to his master. They were soon followed by the black silk garters. The entire process of dressing became a blur to Darcy, his mind fixed upon his ill-preparedness for his coming meeting with Elizabeth Bennet and his dislike of large social gatherings. In point of fact, his stomach was already beginning to knot, and a chill moisture was forming at his brow. *What shall I say to her?* he silently asked his reflection in the mirror as he buttoned his collar.

Fletcher hovered quietly about him, assisting him with this and that, all the while evidencing a hesitant, sympathetic concern that only served to heighten his disquiet. For a few insane moments, Darcy was sorely tempted to unburden himself. To lay the problem before another and ask for advice seemed sweet relief. But, of course, he could not. Not since his sire had died had he entrusted his cares to anyone in even the smallest detail. *No, it was a ridiculous notion!*

He made no pretense of trying to tie his neckcloth and motioned Fletcher to the task. With deft movements, the valet knotted an exquisite fall and, after placing the emerald stickpin in its snowy folds, retrieved the shimmering waistcoat, holding it out for Darcy to shoulder. As he rose from the chair, their eyes met. Fletcher opened his mouth, almost speaking but, at the look of firm refusal in Darcy's face, resumed his place. In silence, he slipped the waistcoat up over Darcy's shoulders and then picked up the coat.

"Your coat, sir."

"Thank you, Fletcher," Darcy acknowledged quietly. He finished the last button on the waistcoat and then eased into the black evening coat. The valet tugged at the lapels, straightening the seams, and checked the fall of the tails. "How does it look, then?"

"Excellent, sir. Were you making an appearance at Court, none could find fault."

"No one, Fletcher?" He snorted, then added under his breath, "You are wrong there, my good man. There *is* one, I fear."

"The lady doth protest too much, methinks."

"What?" Darcy rounded on him, startled by the valet's audacity.

"Shakespeare, sir. *Hamlet.*"

"I *know* it is *Hamlet,* but what do you mean by it?"

"Mean, sir? Why nothing, Mr. Darcy. One of many memorable lines from the play, don't you agree?" Fletcher bent over and began collecting the discarded items from his master's bath. "Although *Hamlet* is not my favorite play, sir."

Darcy had a distinct premonition that he should not pursue where his valet teased him to follow, but he could not seem to help it. "And that would be . . . ?"

Fletcher paused in his task and looked at him intently. "*The Comedy of Errors,* Mr. Darcy, *The Comedy of Errors.*"

The sound of tuning instruments and the rushing of servants broke upon Darcy immediately when Fletcher opened the chamber door. He took a step toward the portal but then stopped and looked back to his desk in indecision.

"Mr. Darcy?" the valet inquired.

"A moment, Fletcher." Darcy walked over to his desk and opened the drawer for his personal correspondence, extracting a folded sheet, which he opened and began to read. A slight smile graced his features as he refolded the letter and slipped it into his inside coat pocket. Patting his breast at the letter's resting place, he stepped determinedly to the door. "Good evening, then, Fletcher. I will ring for you around two, I expect."

"Very good, sir. My best wishes for the evening, Mr. Darcy."

Darcy nodded his reception of his valet's regard and turned to the steps. The musicians now fell silent, and Darcy, pausing at the top of the stairs, could almost feel the entirety of Netherfield draw in its breath, straining for the signal to begin. The sound of an approaching carriage broke the stillness, and as servants scrambled to receive the first of the guests, the musicians struck their notes. Taking a deep, steadying breath, Darcy pulled on his gloves as he slowly descended the stairs and slipped into the glittering swirl of Hertfordshire society. The ball, it seemed, was begun.

The music had been playing a full three-quarters of an hour, and still they had not come. Darcy pulled at his gloves again, smoothing them over his hands as he nodded in response to several greetings cast his way. The lateness of the Bennet family surprised him, for if he had been a wagering man, he would have laid odds that Mrs. Bennet would be among the first to arrive at a ball given virtually at the behest of her daughters. As it was, he had filled his time doing his duty by Bingley, but he took care to do so circumspectly, skirting the fringes of the ever-burgeoning company as he tensely awaited Elizabeth Bennet's arrival.

Not all the guests were unwelcome, of course. Darcy's greeting of Colonel Forster and several of his senior officers was returned politely if not with actual warmth. If there was any lack of that, it was well supplied by Squire Justin, whose response to Darcy's salutation was marked by an intimate litany of sly but affectionate observations of his neighbors and punctuated with infectious chortles of laughter. Darcy did not succeed in avoiding Mrs. Long and her hopeful niece and was saved from being forced to give them a setdown only by the timely intervention of the vicar and his lady.

Excusing himself with gratitude for their rescue, Darcy retreated to the window overlooking the drive and peered into the night. *Could something have happened?* He lifted his chin and tugged discreetly at the knot of his neckcloth. *If she does not come soon* . . . A carriage swung into view, its lanterns bobbing madly as the horses were pulled to a stop at the torches that lit the foot of the stairs. The stable lads sprang forward and grabbed the harness of the leader while an underfootman opened the carriage door and flipped down its folding steps. Darcy leaned closer to the window, squinting against the flickering of the torches. *She has come!*

He backed away from the window and plunged into the crowded room, making his way toward the hall and its receiving line of the Bingleys and Hursts. His progress was not fortunate. By the time he had gained the door, Elizabeth and her family had already been handed down the line and had dispersed into a gathering that continued to swell. He turned back, hoping to discover her in the gallery to the ballroom. His progress again was slow, and he was silently cursing the success of Bingley's little country ball when he saw her.

She was talking to one of the officers as they made their way to the ballroom before him. He could not see her face, but her form was unmistakable to him. Her hair was caught up with delicate ribbons entwined with the daintiest of flowers, leaving three delightful curls to swing enticingly about her neck. He quickened his steps, only to be blocked by some callow youths who, looking distinctly uncomfortable in their dress uniforms, stopped and gawked about them as if they had never been in polite society before. Darcy maneuvered around them, determined to reach Elizabeth before she was once again swallowed up in the crowd. She had not gone far. She was, in fact, only a few yards away, apparently listening to the officer, a Mr. Denny, most earnestly.

The young officers he had overtaken pushed past him, all now holding the hands of females whom Darcy was able to identify as Elizabeth's younger sisters. They encircled her and Denny and, one of them pulling on that officer, bore him away to the ballroom. Elizabeth turned, waving them off with a wistful smile. As she did, Darcy finally saw her complete. The sight utterly ravished him. It was, suddenly, painful to breathe. The roaring of the blood through his veins caused the world about him to go silent.

> *Part of my soul, I seek thee and thee claim*
> *My other half . . .*

Where had he read that? He mused as he stood unmoving, mesmerized by the vision before him. *"Part of my soul . . ."* He commanded his limbs to move. He took a step toward those marvelous eyes alight with so much life. *"I seek thee . . ."* Another step and he thought their eyes met, but it could not have been, for she was turning away. *"My soul . . ."*

"Miss Elizabeth!" Darcy called in a voice that was at once low and carrying. She had heard him, for she stopped, and after the briefest hesitation, she turned back.

"Mr. Darcy." Elizabeth made him her curtsy as he did her his bow, but the countenance she then raised to him was nothing like that which had filled his senses only moments before. The coolness he found in the tilt of her chin contrasted bewilderingly with the snap in her eyes. Miss Bennet was not best pleased, that was certain; but the cause eluded him, as did all of the little speeches he had composed in the hope of gaining her favor. In confusion, Darcy retreated to a safe inquiry after her health.

"I am quite well, sir."

"And your sister Miss Bennet has suffered no relapse?"

"I am happy to say that Jane enjoys as good a health as myself, Mr. Darcy."

"Ah, I am glad of it." Darcy fell silent, the contemplation of her charming features rendering his mental faculties nigh useless. One of her delicate brows lifted at his lack of further words.

"My sister's joy in this evening, then, will be complete." She curtsied again. "Mr. Darcy," she said, and left him standing in the gallery. Her cool abruptness surprised him, but the pleasure of watching her figure as she walked away was compensation enough for the present. He lightly brushed the front of his coat, listening for the rustle of paper.

Milton! The source of the phrases came to him in a rush. *The book she had been reading in the library!* He smiled to himself as he sauntered toward the ballroom. Adam's paean upon first seeing Eve. How fitting! He entered the ballroom and stationed himself where he could obtain the best view of the dancing. Elizabeth was to one side, already deep in conversation with her friend Miss Lucas. *"To have thee by my side . . ."* A sigh escaped him as he shifted his weight and clasped his gloved hands behind his back. *How fitting. How very true!*

The musicians struck a chord announcing that the dancing was to begin. Bingley, Darcy observed, had already claimed the hand of Miss Bennet and was even now escorting her to the head of the line, a singular honor that would escape no one. Caroline Bingley followed on the arm of Sir William, her sister and brother-in-law in her wake. He slanted a glance at Elizabeth, who was still engaged with Miss Lucas, only to have his view of her obscured by a gentleman of vague familiarity and decidedly odd parts. Darcy frowned to himself as the man bowed over Elizabeth's hand and the lady cast her friend a helpless look. They took their place in the set, and Darcy circled round to satisfy himself as to the man's identity.

Ah yes. Her cousin from Kent . . . the clergyman. He laughed quietly to himself at the pursed lips and set chin of his fair tormentor as she struggled to acquiesce gracefully in standing up with her cousin. The music began, and in only seconds Darcy had to look away to prevent it from causing him to break into an unseemly display of mirth. The man truly was no dancer! Darcy's less admirable self drew his eyes back to Elizabeth's misery. At the next turn in the dance, the man went in the wrong direction, then compounded the confusion he had created by profuse apologies where only his attention to the steps was wanted. He next very nearly bowled over a large, stately dame when, head down, he launched prematurely into the weaving of the hey, causing Elizabeth to hiss him instructions while she flushed crimson in mortification. Then, possessing himself of her hands, he wheeled her about with such enthusiasm that Darcy almost feared for her safety and that of those about them.

It can only be his clerical garb, he surmised as he watched in amused fascination, *that keeps the indulgent smiles upon the faces of the others in the set.* All, that was, save Elizabeth. Her face offered no such charity to her cousin. Humiliation suffused her being, and when Darcy unwittingly caught her eye in a turn, the force of it rocked him. His responding impulse to go to her aid was so strong that only his doubt of her welcome of his intervention prevented his taking more than one step in her direction. That step was subtly redirected, and Darcy strolled down the line of dancers, feigning a nonchalance that he rather wished he truly did feel. The emotions Elizabeth Bennet had stirred within him this night were unfamiliar and supremely unsettling in their power. Distance was called for.

He reached the other end of the room and turned round just in time to witness another faux pas of Elizabeth's absurd relative. The dance ended, he abandoned his partner and proceeded to present his apologies to the other members of the set, leaving her without escort off the floor. The look she directed to his back would have singed his clerical collar to a ring of ash were it possible. *And you would deserve it, stupid man!*

Darcy considered his plan of surprising her into accepting his hand and despite his uncertainty, still found it, the most likely to answer his objective, but not yet. He would only draw her fire. Let her recover from the clergyman. Then . . . One of Forster's lieutenants brushed past him and advanced upon Elizabeth with determined strides. Darcy waited long enough to watch her accept him for the next dance before beginning a search for Bingley amid the swirling gowns, polished brass, and competing waistcoats.

"I believe you may safely rate your ball a success, Bingley," he told him, upon finding his friend between dances. "Mayhap too successful!"

"Too successful? A *crush* is what you really mean." Bingley laughed back at him. "To be honest, I could do with a few less officers who seem to have nothing better to do than dance attendance upon women with whom I wish to converse!"

"Women? Bingley." Darcy swept a speaking glance about them. "From the look of it, you are well supplied with any number of women who would gladly—"

"Woman, Darcy! Confound you; do not pretend to misunderstand me!"

"Bingley, I understand too well." Darcy dropped his voice. "You opened the ball with her and danced the entire set together. Anything more will be remarked upon to such a degree that the whole shire will expect to hear the banns announced on Sunday."

"Well, at least I have danced—and I expect to do quite a bit more—while you have done nothing but stalk about being civil or stare at Elizabeth Bennet." Bingley paused to nod and smile a return of a greeting from a newcomer. "And do not poker up at me, for it won't wash. I know you too well, my friend."

"Slings and arrows, Bingley, slings and arrows quite misflung. I do, indeed, mean to dance this evening, when the time is right."

"When the time . . . Darcy!"

"Ask me no questions—"

"And you'll tell me no lies." Bingley shook his head despairingly. "When *will* the time be right? At the twelfth stroke of midnight? What are you planning, Darcy?"

"A surprise attack, Bingley, and more I will not divulge." Darcy moved off before his host pried too closely into his plans. The music was almost ended for the country dance that separated the sets, and he would need to reach Elizabeth before another red coat whisked her off. A shiver of apprehension traveled down his spine as Darcy remembered his valet's fears and predictions for the evening, and he looked briefly at the waistcoat Fletcher had pressed upon him. *Well, we shall see, shall we not, my man.*

When he reached her, Elizabeth was once again engaged with

Miss Lucas and not aware of his approach. At Miss Lucas's discreet "ahem," Elizabeth whirled about, almost into his chest.

"Miss Bennet." He bowed quickly and, barely waiting for her curtsy, pressed an advantage that was all he could have wished for. "Would you do me the honor of standing up with me for the next set?"

Elizabeth's mouth opened and then shut, her discomposure satisfyingly evident in her every aspect. She stared at him, then looked to her friend. Darcy waited patiently.

"I did not . . . that is, I was going . . . sitting . . ." She looked up into his eyes. He lifted an inquiring brow. "Yes," she assented in a tight, little voice. Darcy bowed his appreciation and strode away, savoring the wonderful confusion of her mind and the impending realization of all his planning. Just before attaining his former post at the edge of the floor, he chanced a backward glance, and with it all satisfaction fled. She was clearly agitated. In growing apprehension, Darcy watched her from under hooded eyes as she spoke furiously to Miss Lucas, a high flush on her face, her eyes darting about the room. The sight continued to baffle him as he approached to claim her hand for their set, driving his weeklong anticipation of pleasure to the edges of his consciousness. He bowed stiffly; she curtsied. He extended his hand; she placed hers in it but would not look him in the face. Any ease he had ever felt in her company deserted him as he led her to their places.

The murmur of surprise that swept the room as they faced each other, while expected under the circumstances, only served to impress upon him what a fool he was making of himself over a woman who was, even now, regarding him with indifference. He had imagined her flustered; he had imagined her piqued. But in all his imaginings she had quickly and prettily turned into an engaging partner. The creature before him exhibited no such dulcet inclinations. What had happened to the lovely, beguiling Eve?

Darcy favored Elizabeth with the most formal of bows, bending deeply. As he rose, he trained his eyes past her left cheek, but not before flicking over her a surreptitious glance. "*To have thee by my side . . .*" He stifled the thought. There was not a hint of pliancy from the stone maiden before him. *Come, fool, complete your folly!* he growled to himself, feeling the familiar coldness grip his chest. They joined hands and turned, facing the near end of the ballroom. Her tension, communicated to him through their conjoined fingers, increased perceptibly as they stepped forward into the pattern of the dance. Though he dared not look, Darcy could sense that she was peeping up at him. With what object, he could not guess and, until he knew something of her mind, decided that silence was his best course. Whatever solace he might derive from her company would, it appeared, be found only in the heady touch, release, and cradling of her gloved fingers. It must needs suffice.

Elizabeth's hand stirred slightly in his grasp. "This choice of dance must seem rather out of fashion to one accustomed to St. James's, Mr. Darcy." In equal parts encouraged and alerted by her sudden bid for conversation, he looked down upon his partner. Whatever had caused her complaint of him she now seemed willing to overlook, but knowing her as he did, he was not confident of her true intent.

"As I told Sir William, I do not dance at St. James's and, therefore, do not know what is considered *dernier cri*," he replied cautiously. "The choice is well enough, in my opinion." The pattern separated them for a few moments, but the respite afforded Darcy no inspiration. He rejoined her in silence.

"It is *your* turn to say something now, Mr. Darcy," she advised him pertly. "*I* talked about the dance, and *you* ought to make some kind of remark on the size of the room, or the number of couples."

Darcy peered down into her face with relief. Here, now, was the Elizabeth he knew. "Miss Bennet, pray instruct me! Whatever you wish me to say shall, on my honor, be said."

Elizabeth acknowledged the gallantry of his remark with a curl of her lips into a reluctant little smile. "Very well; that reply will do for the present." Darcy braved her devastating eyes until the last second as she circled him in the figure. When she reappeared on his other side, it was she who looked him a challenge. "Perhaps, by and by, I may observe that private balls are much pleasanter than public ones." He reached for her hand as they both turned again to face the end of the room. "But *now* we may be silent." The tension in her fingers was abated; they rested more easily now in his palm.

Darcy fully realized her condescension to silence was, in truth, a command to him to pick up the threads of the conversation. "Do you talk by rule, then, while you are dancing?" he countered, indulgence in her little conceit being, surely, the safest response.

Her brows arched at that, and Darcy thought he detected a glint in her eyes that belied the return of severity to her lips. "Sometimes." His instructress paused as Darcy circled her. "One must speak a little, you know." This time it was her hand that sought the clasp of the next figure. "It would look odd to be entirely silent for half an hour together." She regarded him as if considering a point of logic. "And yet, for the advantage of *some,* conversation ought to be so arranged, as that they may have the trouble of saying as little as possible."

There was the sting of half-truth in that one! "Are you consulting your own feelings in the present case," he parried, smoothly if not with grace, "or do you imagine that you are gratifying mine?" The sharp little intake of breath by his partner told him the sally had found its mark, but a response was rendered impossible as the pattern separated them once more.

"Both," she replied, to his complete surprise, when they were joined again. His astonishment was to increase. "For I have always seen a great similarity in the turn of our minds. We are each of an unsocial, taciturn disposition, unwilling to speak, unless we expect to say something that will amaze the whole room, and be handed down to posterity with all the éclat of a proverb."

Darcy could not tell whether she was trying to provoke him to laughter or to ire. Again, he parried and feinted. "This is no very striking resemblance of your own character, I am sure." He offered her the requisite demibow of the pattern, then waited, motionless, as she circled him. "How near it may be to *mine,* I cannot pretend to say. *You* think it a faithful portrait undoubtedly."

She returned to her place and took his outstretched hand. "I must not decide on my own performance."

But I must decide upon it! Darcy thought to himself as they went down the dance, silent now by mutual consent. *How strangely she behaves! Why?* He glanced at her repeatedly as they worked their way through the figures, looking for some indication of her temper. *Does she, in truth, think me such a curmudgeon? Or does she give offense merely for amusement?* The more he considered her comportment toward him, the more he found his irritation growing. *Is this, then, your vengeance for Meryton! Tit for tat!*

With some acrimony, he moved toward his partner to regain her hand from the gentleman on his right, causing the paper in his breast pocket to rustle gently. Georgiana's letter! All but forgotten, its contents now forcefully recommended themselves to his conscience, and for the sake of his sister's regard for him, Darcy resolved to try once more to bridge the torrent of Elizabeth's ill-use of him.

"Miss Bennet," he began when she was secure in his possession for the next figure, "Bingley and I were on our way to Longbourn when we had the felicity of meeting you in the village last week. Do you and your sisters very often walk to Meryton?"

"Indeed, sir, we do." She looked up at him closely. "When you met us there the other day, we had just been forming a new acquaintance."

Wickham! The anger he had felt upon seeing that face on the streets of Meryton returned in full measure: the insolence of his bow, the smirk on his lips, the knowing look in his eyes! Darcy's jaws clamped tightly, and he looked fixedly ahead for some moments, unwilling to betray his disconcertment. At length, when sufficiently in command of himself to venture a response, he looked down into her countenance.

"Mr. Wickham is blessed with such happy manners as may ensure his *making* friends—whether he may be equally capable of *retaining* them, is less certain."

"He has been so unlucky as to lose *your* friendship," she answered him heatedly, "and in a manner he is likely to suffer from all his life."

Darcy's mind reeled at her charge. Unlucky to lose his friendship! What could he possibly have to say for his infamous conduct? What monstrous falsehood was he peddling? Helpless to stop the roiling anger that again smote him, Darcy could give her no reply. The rest of their dance might have been conducted in silence if Sir William had not intruded on their separate reveries with fulsome admiration of their dancing.

"It is evident that you belong to the first circles, Mr. Darcy," he complimented. "Allow me to say, however, that your fair partner does not disgrace you, and that I must hope to have this pleasure often repeated, especially when a certain desirable event, my dear Miss Eliza, shall take place." Darcy followed Sir William's nod and found himself apprehending Bingley and Miss Bennet dancing together once again. His eyes narrowed in displeasure at Bingley's complete disregard of his warning. "I appeal to Mr. Darcy—but let me not interrupt you, sir. You will not thank me for detaining you from the bewitching converse of that young lady whose bright eyes are also upbraiding me."

At the mention of his partner's eyes, Darcy recovered himself and turned to her, determined to take back the ground he had lost at Wickham's hand, whatever the lies the blackguard had propounded. Perhaps, with prodding, Elizabeth would reveal them. He opened himself to attack. "Sir William's interruption has made me forget what we were talking of," he confessed with a tight smile.

"I do not think we were speaking at all. Sir William could not have interrupted any two people in the room who had less to say for themselves," she returned dismissively. "We have tried two or three subjects already without success, and what we are to talk of next I cannot imagine."

She declines to continue the subject. What now? He cast about for some promising topic upon which to engage her attention toward himself and away from Wickham.

"Part of my soul, I seek thee . . ."

"What think you of books?" he asked quickly, smiling at the memory of the shared library that day.

"Books—oh! No. I am sure we never read the same, or not with the same feelings."

He almost laughed outright at her hasty denial. "I am sorry you think so; but if that be the case, there can at least be no want of subject. We may compare our different opinions," he pressed her.

"No—I cannot talk of books in a ballroom," she insisted shakily. "My head is always full of something else."

"The *present* always occupies you in such scenes—does it?" He allowed the doubt to seep into his voice.

"Yes, always," she affirmed, her attention distracted by some thoughts of her own. And then, suddenly, "I remember hearing you once say, Mr. Darcy, that you hardly ever forgave, that your resentment once created was unappeasable. You are very cautious, I suppose, as to its *being created.*"

What is this? Darcy's suspicion was immediately alerted. A reply was required if he was to discover her meaning.

"I am," he avowed firmly.

"And never allow yourself to be blinded by prejudice?" she pursued.

"I hope not." His alarm at the direction of her questions increased.

"It is particularly incumbent on those who never change their opinion, to be secure of judging properly at first." Elizabeth's look as she parted from him to salute the lady to her left was piercing. Darcy stiffened, sensing a trap, but of what nature and to what end he was at a complete loss. Of only one thing was he sure: Wickham was in this. In some way, this was his doing.

"May I ask to what these questions tend?" he demanded icily when they were again hand in hand.

"Merely to the illustration of *your* character," she said with a small, forced laugh. "I am trying to make it out." They broke, presented their demibows, and joined hands again, moving around each other in a complete circle.

"And what is your success?" Darcy inquired, tight-lipped.

"I do not get on at all." She shook her head and tried to disarm him with a smile. "I hear such different accounts of you as puzzle me exceedingly."

Definitely Wickham!

"I can readily believe that reports may vary greatly with respect to me," he responded, summoning all his reserve to quell the tumult of emotions that threatened his composure, "and I could wish, Miss Bennet, that you were not to sketch my character at the present moment, as there is reason to fear that the performance would reflect no credit on either."

Her color was high as he turned to her and took her fingers into his grasp. Whether this was from anger at his words or the embarrassment she should have felt for her own, Darcy could not discern. To his amazement, she persisted.

"But if I do not take your likeness now, I may never have another opportunity."

Did she seriously think he would bandy about his character on a ballroom floor? Darcy's willingness to indulge her questioning ended abruptly. Determined to have this avenue of conversation closed, he turned to her a countenance of deep hauteur and replied in freezing tones, "I would by no means suspend any pleasure of yours, Miss Bennet."

There could be no doubt that his manner had finally abashed her. She missed the next move in the figure, nearly tripping over the demitrain of her dress. Darcy moved quickly to rescue her from a certain fall. Elizabeth moved away from his clasp as quickly as possible, murmuring a disjointed thanks.

"It is my pleasure to be of service, Miss Bennet," he told her quietly. She said no more, and they finished the set in silence and in silence parted after Darcy escorted her to a group of her friends. He could not prevent his gaze from searching her out after he took up a position across the room. She had left her friends and seemed engaged in a minute examination of one of the bouquets of flowers that graced the area. Her pensive air communicated itself to him clearly, and he wondered, with growing sympathy, what Wickham had told her that was robbing her of peace.

More devilry to lay to his account, the wretch! What tales can he be spreading to cause her to so trespass the bounds of propriety? And Forster! This could explain his coolness tonight when I greeted him. Wickham! Not here, yet here all the same. An evil imp, come between me and . . . He stopped this line of thought. *Come to cut up my peace!*

Darcy suddenly felt the need for some fresh air and solitude. With a last glance at Elizabeth, he turned, made his way through the gay line of dancers, and sought the first egress to the outside. The chill air hit his face and, as he anticipated, began to clear his head. The threads of emerald and gold in his waistcoat shimmered and blinked, catching Darcy's eye as he paced the veranda in the light of an unforgiving moon. He snorted as he remembered Fletcher's admonishment that his problem with "the lady" was no more than a comedy of errors.

If this be comedy, Fletcher, your tragedy I could not bear. He stopped and looked up at Lady Moon. *I am not angry with her. She is not blameworthy, she is . . .* It was the cold, surely, that caused him to shiver. *My other half?* Darcy shook his head and, wrapping his arms about him, clapped his hands against his sides and stamped his feet. *Your foolishness seems to have followed you out-of-doors. So, why are you out here freezing? You can be just as much a fool warm as cold.*

CHAPTER 10

Beyond the Pale

"*M*r. Darcy, you are not going out-of-doors!" Darcy looked over his shoulder as he shut the door and beheld the amused face of Caroline Bingley. "Shame on you, sir," she continued in playful dismay, "to leave me alone to entertain the barbarians—and within my very gates! Most unhandsomely done!"

Darcy laughed lightly and offered her his arm. "You are too late, Miss Bingley. I am just returned from a quest for fresh air. I will say in my defense that it is doubtful my absence has occasioned the display of any untoward behavior on the part of your guests. All seems well," he added as he looked about them. "In any event, you may certainly command the services of your brother should you need reinforcements."

At his assurances, Miss Bingley's look changed to one of distress. "Charles! He would be of no use at all, provoking man!" At Darcy's quizzical look, she hastened to elaborate, "It is *his* behavior that has suffered most in your absence. Such thoughtlessness as he so plainly displays in paying exclusive court to Miss Bennet cannot long be ignored by the other guests." She lifted her hand in a helpless gesture. "Mr. Darcy, what is to be done? If his friends do not counsel him, I fear he will commit a grave error—one that may well shut the doors of Society against him."

"He is still by her side, then?" Darcy's face grew somber.

"Oh, yes"—Miss Bingley sniffed—"he may as well be leashed. Truly, Mr. Darcy, people are beginning to talk! Only just now, that insufferable Sir William was hinting to me that my duties as Netherfield's mistress would soon burden me no longer. If he could say such a thing to me, he has said as much to others. Of that you may be sure." She paused and, laying her hand on Darcy's arm, looked beseechingly up into his face. "Charles will listen to you. You have ever been his *good* friend."

"I will speak to your brother, Miss Bingley. That is all I can promise." Darcy looked past her to the doorway of the ballroom, and she followed his gaze, but he saw no more than the ridiculous clergyman who had accompanied the Bennets that evening.

"Your guidance is all I could wish for Charles. He is, indeed, fortunate in his friends." She gave Darcy's arm a discreet pat. "On another subject entirely, did I not see a letter from your aunt, Lady Catherine De Bourgh, arrive today? The lady requires you at Rosings for Christmas, no doubt?"

"The letter was from Lady Catherine," Darcy admitted as he led her back into the ballroom, "but my aunt knows better than to command me to Rosings for Christmas. Visits are, of a necessity, always undertaken in the spring and, if possible, in the company of my cousin Colonel Fitzwilliam. My cousin Anne, Lady Catherine's daughter, is of a delicate constitution and is especially discomfited in winter," he explained.

"Then, will we have the felicity of your company in London for the holidays as well as the Season?"

"Again, no, Miss Bingley. After my affairs in London are concluded next week, I am for Pemberley and Christmas with my sister." He shrugged. "My father and his before him always spent Christmas at Pemberley. Our people expect it, and it has become a tradition of the Darcys that, under my father's rule, was anticipated for weeks. It is now five years since his death, and it is time for Georgiana and I to revive that custom. I believe she would little enjoy Christmas in London, away from all the pleasant memories of seasons past."

"Such an indulgent brother!" Miss Bingley teased.

"Perhaps," Darcy considered, "but Georgiana is deserving of any pleasure it is in my power to supply."

"I am certain she is," she quickly agreed. "Will she return with you to London for the Season this year?"

"I believe her still too young for a Season, Miss Bingley, but I intend to persuade her to come to Town for some of the winter at least." A fluttering at his elbow intruded on Darcy's notice, and he turned to witness Elizabeth's unfortunate relation rising from a deep bow. *What importunity is this!* Darcy nodded curtly to him, momentarily fascinated by the man's ill-bred presumption.

"Mr. Darcy," the gentleman began without preamble, "please allow me to pay my respects, sir, after first hastening to assure you that my neglect was due entirely to a complete ignorance of the connection between yourself and my most noble patroness, Lady Catherine De Bourgh. For you must know that your gracious and most beneficent relation has entrusted this humble servant with the care of her people by bestowing upon me the living at Hunsford parish. That I should meet here, in this place, with that wonderful lady's nephew was beyond my power of imagining; therefore, I did not look for it and must extend to you my deepest apologies for not making myself known to you immediately, sir." He finished breathlessly and bobbed another bow.

"You are too fastidious, sir," Darcy replied with cool civility. "I am sure you do Lady Catherine much service—"

"In that, Mr. Darcy," Mr. Collins interrupted, "I hope I find my meat and drink. Lady Catherine De Bourgh is a woman of such perspicacity and strength of mind that she can be nothing but greatly valued by all her relations. As her nephew, you must be anxious to know how she goes on, and I am in the happy possession of such recent knowledge of Her Ladyship that it allows me to assure you of her continued good health."

The man is in every way a fool, Darcy decided, his civility tried beyond the bounds of courtesy. He looked past his aunt's parson to find Bingley, but he was not to be seen in the ballroom. *Bingley, do not tell me you are taking her into supper as well!* He groaned silently. He had to find him! But it appeared that the obsequious rambling of the man before him would continue indefinitely unless forcefully brought to a halt. At Collins's next pause for breath, Darcy quickly inclined his head and, without a word, moved away in the direction of the supper room, determined to bring his friend to his senses.

The room set aside for the serving of supper overflowed with guests. Darcy slowed, then halted just inside the door, reluctance to becoming shoulder-to-shoulder intimate with all of Hertford-shire almost dissuading him from his search. He peered about the room, his height advantageous to his purpose, and located his quarry. Miss Bingley had not exaggerated the matter. There sat Charles, Miss Jane Bennet still at his side, surrounded at table by a goodly number of his guests, blithely disregarding all the strictures that would relieve him of the necessity of declaring himself to Miss Bennet's father in the morning.

Idiot! Darcy despaired silently. *What in the name of Heaven are you doing? How can I help you now?* There were no means of discreetly attracting Bingley's notice. He could push through the throng, but what to say when he had gained Bingley's side, entangled as he was with guests? *A servant! Yes, a servant could be sent to summon him away!* But what should he say to Bingley in such a necessarily short interview that would serve the purpose? Rather, he was more likely to arouse Charles's unfortunate mulish streak, and Heaven knew what would come of that! No other plausible solutions were forthcoming, leaving Darcy in an uneasy quandary. There appeared to be nothing for it but to wait until Bingley was separated from his company.

With this unsatisfactory course adopted, the delicious smells of the banquet table began to play upon Darcy's senses. Grateful to be occupied with no more momentous a decision than what he would prefer to eat, he drifted over to the board and availed himself of a plate of choice viands and a glass of wine. He then turned to the task of finding his name card among the settings that crowded the long tables. His gaze swept up and back the rows of tables, searching for the empty seat that would indicate his reservation. *There!* Darcy espied the card across the near table, but as he made for it, his attention was arrested by the bob and sway of flower-adorned curls. He looked again at the name card and then across from it, meeting Elizabeth's startled, wary eyes. It flashed into his mind that this seating had been done apurpose, and not by Miss Bingley. He glanced over at his friend. Charles? Whoever had arranged it, it could not be undone. With a tingling of apprehension, he set his plate down and quietly took his seat opposite Elizabeth.

". . . it will be soon, of that you may be assured, Lady Lucas. I do not hold with long engagements, and I do not believe I deceive myself that Mr. Bingley does either. Only look at them, and you will see that he is most impatient to settle the matter."

The complacent purr in the woman's voice put Darcy strongly in mind of his first impression of Mrs. Fanny Bennet. She sat opposite him but two at table, as plump and indifferent to his presence as an old tabby cat whose esurient eye was wholly focused on a particularly toothsome mouse. He had always detested cats, their selective attention to authority and their propensity to amuse themselves with the harassment of their food hardly recommending their kind to Darcy's disciplined view of life. Mrs. Bennet, on the first evening of their acquaintance, had struck him in much the same manner.

"Such a charming young man, and so rich! A fitting match for my beautiful Jane in every way. And when one considers that Netherfield is but three miles from Longbourn! Well . . . as a mother yourself, Lady Lucas, you can appreciate the advantages immediately."

Darcy flinched at the appalling vulgarity of Mrs. Bennet's discussion of her expectations of Bingley as son-in-law. He picked up his knife and fork and, hardly knowing what he was doing, began to rend apart his meat.

"You may well imagine what a comfort it is to me to witness daily the fond regard Mr. Bingley's sisters shower upon Jane. It is certain that they must desire the connection. And why not? The Bennet name, while not noble, is not unknown among the great of Britain."

The bit of ham he had swallowed threatening to choke him, Darcy quickly grasped his wineglass and eased its passage with a generous imbibing. *Insupportable!* Steely contempt iced his countenance. Was the woman mad or merely adept at self-delusion? He flicked a glance across the table to Elizabeth and immediately felt the heat of her blushes upon his own cheeks. Her eyes were looking everywhere but in his direction, her lower lip caught in agitation. Darcy looked back down into his wineglass and swirled the remaining contents.

"Moreover, it is such a promising thing for the younger girls, and a great relief for myself. You wonder at my saying this? Why, to be sure . . . Jane's marrying so greatly cannot help but throw her sisters in the way of other rich men."

"Mama, please!" Elizabeth's plea registered in his hearing, but Darcy's indignation for his friend, and not a little for himself, discounted it.

". . . and that being so, it will be so pleasant to be able to consign them to the care of their sister. Then I will no longer be obliged to go into company more than I like."

"Mama, do lower your voice, I beg you!" There was real desperation in Elizabeth's voice, and when he heard it, Darcy's contempt made room for anger at the woman on behalf of her daughter's plight.

"Lizzy, do not interrupt me so. Excuse me, Lady Lucas, where was I? Oh, yes! I was just about to assure you that, in my own good fortune, I am not unconcerned with the disposition of your own dutiful girls. I am sure that you will, in no time at all, be in the same happy situation as myself."

Darcy observed Elizabeth turn once again to her mother, vexation and shame alive on her face, accentuated by an overbrightness in her eyes. She hissed something in an inaudible tone. He guessed it was something about himself. His conjecture was not long in being confirmed.

"What is Mr. Darcy to me, pray, that I should be afraid of him?" Mrs. Bennet's rhetoric stung him like a slap in the face. "I am sure we owe him no such particular civility as to be obliged to say nothing *he* may not like to hear."

Darcy took a slow sip of his wine and set the glass down with deliberation. *Never* had he been witness to such a monumental display of impropriety in polite society. Further, to be its object was so astounding, so distasteful, that it rendered him speechless. Mrs. Bennet rattled on, oblivious to the looks of discomfort directed at her by both her daughter and Lady Lucas. To his relief, Darcy saw that no one looked at him except Elizabeth, whose misery at her mother's behavior flushed her face and shoulders with shame. An unguarded wish to relieve her in some way tempered his disgust but did nothing toward changing his new-formed, implacable resolve that there was nothing under Heaven that would stop him from preventing a misalliance between Bingley and this family. He picked up his fork and, without tasting a bite, bent his attention to consuming the food on his plate, all the while considering strategy for his forthcoming campaign.

What remained of the evening Darcy passed in careful scrutiny of the Bennet family. His first object was to make a determination of the extent of his friend's infatuation and of Miss Bennet's affections. Fully cognizant of Charles's tendency to enthusiasm, Darcy could not conclude with certainty whether Bingley was truly "in love" or had only succumbed to the allure of a pretty face and gentle manners. Miss Bennet was another matter. Under Darcy's close observation, she appeared to receive Bingley's attentions with becoming grace and modesty, but the joyful intensity of Bingley's intercourse was not mirrored in her own face or deportment. She seemed pleased by him, to be sure, but untouched; and Darcy could detect no more in her manner than a proper acknowledgment of the honor his friend did her by his singular regard. No, he decided, she had not the look of true attachment about her. If Charles believed so, he deluded himself.

The supper over, entertainment was requested with a general cry from the gentlemen for song from the ladies. Darcy leaned back into his chair, experiencing in equal parts hope and fear that Elizabeth would answer the call. A glance told him that she was in no state to perform. Her eyes were downcast in a study of her gloves, her lips almost bloodless as they pressed close. Only when a general wave of movement from among the younger ladies resolved itself into the figure of another Bennet daughter did she look up.

"Oh dear . . . Mary Bennet." Darcy heard a whisper come from behind him, which was then answered by a soft groan. "Screw up your courage now, lads" came an admonition from a lieutenant down the table to his fellows nearby. "Survive this and the Frenchies' battle cries won't bother you a bit."

Darcy shot an alarmed glance at Elizabeth lest she have heard the ill-mannered comments that floated on the tide of general expectations. Her eyes were closed in what looked like pain. Her lips moved, but no sound issued forth. Polite applause recalled his attention to the performance at hand, and he turned, preparing himself for whatever might come.

The longer Miss Mary Bennet sang, the more grave his manner grew. In contrast to her elder sister, this Bennet female had a voice remarkable only for a weakness that she attempted to mask with affected movements suited more to the stage than to a private supper. Neither her inability to sustain the melody nor the ridicule her performance excited deterred her, for she needed but a modicum of applause at her finish to encourage the selection of another song.

Such eagerness to make a spectacle of a lack of talent and modesty was no less distasteful to Darcy than it was incomprehensible. Had no one thought to restrain such immodest tendencies in the girl? Her mother he discounted immediately, but what of her father? Mr. Bennet was reputed to be a peculiar sort of man, who but for the silent salute at Squire Justin's, had remained largely unknown to him. *He* obviously exerts little influence upon his wife. Darcy grimaced to himself. *Does that disregard extend to his daughters as well?* He discreetly searched the room and discovered the gentleman in question making his way to the front. A very masculine sense of relief at the sight of a father taking command of his family gave him pause, and Darcy allowed himself a glimpse at Elizabeth, hoping to discern a lessening of her anxiety.

"That will do extremely well, child," he heard Mr. Bennet admonish his daughter. "You have delighted us long enough. Let the other young ladies have time to exhibit." Stunned by the baldness of Mr. Bennet's words, Darcy could not believe what his ears told him. But the truth of it was testified by the fresh wash of pink that rushed over Elizabeth's face. He quickly trained his eyes on the floor. *Such withering remarks to address to one's own flesh! And in public, no less!* Darcy's embarrassment at merely playing witness to such an exchange was nearly as acute as his opprobrium at its display.

"If I were so fortunate as to be able to sing, I should have great pleasure, I am sure, in obliging the company with an air." The vaguely familiar voice stirred Darcy out of his reverie. He looked up to behold his aunt's fawning vicar. "I do not mean, however, to assert that we can be justified in devoting too much of our time to music, for there are certainly other things to be attended to . . ."

Are we now to have a sermon in the midst of a ball! The disbelief under which Darcy labored verged upon the fantastic. He received the clergyman's glances toward him with a growing dread.

". . . as comfortable as possible. And I do not think it of light

importance that a clergyman should have attentive and conciliatory manners towards everyone, especially towards those to whom
he owes his preferment."

Do not do it, man! Do not address to me . . .

"I cannot acquit him of that duty," Mr. Collins continued, and
then, with an ingratiating smile, he turned to Darcy. "Nor could I
think well of the man who should omit an occasion of testifying his
respect towards anybody connected with the family." To Darcy's
horror, the room lapsed into complete silence as the vicar bowed
deeply to him. Fortunately, the man looked for no response but
took his seat. After a few moments the room concluded that there
would be no acknowledgment of the strange clergyman's speech
and turned to other entertainment.

Darcy allowed himself to breathe again and motioned to a servant to refill his wineglass. Grasping it in fingers cold with outrage,
he rose and walked swiftly into the meager shadow of the hearth's
great mantel. He took a generous sip from his glass and then
turned to observe Bingley's guests. His original assessment had
been all too correct! Fuming, he took another gulp. Country society and its idea of manners fell appallingly wide of the mark. Ever
since his entrance into its provincial precincts, he had been insulted, presumed upon, or toadied to by its chief inhabitants. The
rules of good society were unknown, young women were allowed
to run wild, and at any moment one could be subjected to stupen-
dous indecorum, even at a ball!

Darcy's narrowed gaze traveled over the crowd until he found
Bingley in a far corner, his head bent close in private conversation
with Miss Bennet while the ball swung crazily out of control. *No!*
Darcy shook his head. For Charles's own sake, it must be stopped!
Despite her mother's assertions, Miss Bennet had no claims beyond being the daughter of a gentleman, no connections that
would benefit his friend, and little dowry to add to his income or
property to increase his estate. Rather, she would bring to him an
impossibly vulgar mother-in-law, four—no, three—unremarkable

sisters he would be expected to foist upon Society, a caustic recluse for a father-in-law, and untold numbers of relations in the professional class. It was a script that presaged disaster. Darcy knew the extent of his influence with his friend, and this might well test its limits, but he must, *he must,* disengage him from this ruinous course.

He downed the last of his wine and, with gathered purpose, placed the glass on the nearest table, prepared to set the wheels in motion when sounds of rustling paper interrupted his thoughts and sent them rushing back to the hopes with which he had begun the evening. What had he wanted to come from this night? Merely Elizabeth Bennet's good opinion? Darcy stepped back into the shadows. She was still at her chair, listening respectfully to a lady whose talents hers far eclipsed. Her color was still somewhat high, but it became her. The singing ceased, and the supper room began to empty in favor of more dancing. Elizabeth arose with the others and made her way to her friend Miss Lucas.

Her respect. He had wanted her respect, her friendship—an oasis of wit and grace in a desert of provincial dullness. He wanted the aliveness he felt in her presence, which flowed through him like fine wine. He wanted those marvelous eyes turned upon him with something deeper than amusement or rivalry. Elizabeth and Miss Lucas drifted out of the room; Darcy's eyes followed them, a pang forming deep within his chest. The letter in his breast pocket crinkled again as he unwittingly brushed the spot. There would be no winning of Miss Elizabeth Bennet's good opinion now. What he meant to do, what he *must* do, for Charles's sake, would secure her animosity irrevocably.

"Caroline, I beg you not to require my opinion or assistance on anything further tonight." Bingley addressed his sister after the door closed on the departing Bennet family. "The entire evening was splendid, my dear." He paused in his compliment as the hall clock struck the half hour. "Is it really two-thirty? Good heavens! Darcy, if we are to be off tomorrow, I must find my bed immediately." Bingley stopped at the foot of the staircase, unsuccessfully suppressed a yawn, then beamed disarmingly at his sister. "Truly, Caroline, you are to be congratulated. They will be talking of this night for weeks to come. Well done, and good night to you all!" he called to the nearby servants, who yet worked to restore the now empty public rooms to order. "Darcy"—he nodded to his friend—"you will have to help yourself to the brandy tonight. I shan't be able."

"To bed, Charles. Should I require it, I know where it is. Tell your man to have you ready by noon or I'll come for you myself," Darcy threatened lightly.

"On that dire note, I bid you all a good night"—Bingley shuddered—"except for Darcy, who I hope tosses and turns the night through."

Darcy grimaced in response to his jest and wondered how accurately Bingley's wish for him would be fulfilled. That sleep would elude him tonight he did not doubt. The task ahead lay uneasily upon his mind.

"Louisa, you and Mr. Hurst must not wait for me. I have a small duty left to me still this evening." Miss Bingley smiled wearily to her sister. Darcy saw that Mrs. Hurst appeared too fatigued to question the propriety of her sister staying downstairs with only himself for company, and for once, he was glad of it. His design for separating Bingley from Miss Bennet required a confederate, and in Miss Bingley he knew he would find a most willing one.

"Mr. Darcy." Miss Bingley turned to him as soon as the Hursts had mounted the stairs. "Charles is still in her toils! I looked for you to speak to him!"

"I am most sorry to disappoint you, Miss Bingley. There was no opportunity that would have answered. I could not very well take him by the collar and shake him like an errant puppy." Darcy looked down upon her coldly. "And you know how he would take a lecture on *this* subject, even from me."

"He will listen to nothing but praise of Miss Bennet."

"Precisely," Darcy replied sharply. "But if you are able to follow my instructions, I think we may yet save him from committing a disastrous error."

"Anything, Mr. Darcy. Anything within my power."

Darcy's blood ran cold at her words, so like those Charles had pledged to him only a few days before. What was he doing? Such duplicity as he contemplated was entirely repugnant to his character. He forcefully quelled the wave of unease that rose in his vitals, reminding himself of the fatal nature of his friend's inclinations.

"Mr. Darcy, what do you want me to do?" Miss Bingley pressed him.

"Wait a few days until after we have left for London. Then dismiss the servants, close up the house, and follow us to Town. But do not let Charles know that you have arrived. When I am satisfied that my plans have borne fruit, I will send you a note. Only then should you make him aware of your arrival. You need only affirm to your brother what I have told him, but in the lightest of tones. *Do not bedevil him!* Can you do this, Miss Bingley?"

"Y-y-yes, it shall be as you say, Mr. Darcy." Miss Bingley shivered at the intensity of his manner.

"Very well, Miss Bingley. Then I, too, bid you good night." He bowed and turned abruptly for the stairs, but paused at the first to fix her once more with his imperious eye. "One more thing. You should send round a letter to Miss Bennet. Tell her that Charles will, in all likelihood, stay in Town and that you have gone to join him. Tell her that none of you will be back to Netherfield before Christmas. Indeed, that you may never return. Say all that is polite, but make the material point very clear. Charles will not be coming back! Do you understand?"

"Yes, sir." Miss Bingley nodded quickly, her eyes wide. Darcy bowed to her again and continued on his way to his chambers. It was now hard on three in the morning, and each step to his rooms testified to how profoundly exhausted the tensions and emotions of this night had rendered him. The knob of his chamber door turned even as he reached for it, the door quietly swinging open to reveal a gravely silent Fletcher against the illumination of a single candle at the bedstead.

"Mr. Darcy, sir."

"Fletcher." He sighed as he sat down. "I did not think a country ball would end so late."

"Do not concern yourself, sir. I have put the intervening time to good use and packed up *all* your belongings, sir," the valet replied as he pulled the emerald stickpin from Darcy's neckcloth and began to unravel the knot. As he unbuttoned the controversial waistcoat, Darcy peered curiously at the head bent in service.

"*All* my belongings?"

"Yes, sir . . . and sent notice to the stable to crate Master Trafalgar for Pemberley. Will you wish to ride Master Nelson on your journey, or shall he be sent down as well, sir?" Fletcher dropped to his knee and carefully removed Darcy's dancing pumps.

"Send Nelson to Pemberley. Fletcher, you *knew* I would not be returning?"

His valet looked askance at him. "Of course, Mr. Darcy. Do you still wish to depart at noon, sir?"

Darcy regarded his valet uneasily. "Perhaps you should tell me!"

"Oh, no, sir. That would be quite beforehand of me and worthy of dismissal, although I have heard that Lord ——— is very dependent upon the judgment of *his* man, who accompanies him, I believe, even to the gaming table."

"So I have heard as well," Darcy replied slowly. "Then I shall rephrase it. What time would you suggest, Fletcher?"

"Noon is the latest acceptable time, sir, as that will bring you to Erewile House somewhat late but not excessively so. It also recommends itself by being the earliest possible time that Mr. Bingley's man may contrive to have him ready. May I remove your coat now, sir?"

Darcy struggled out of his chair, shrugged off the coat and, as

Fletcher reached for it, the waistcoat as well. He was certain he heard the man sigh as he laid them both across an upholstered stool. Darcy watched him from under hooded eyes as he unbuttoned his cuffs and those at his throat.

"Noon it shall remain. You cannot be *sorry* to leave Hertfordshire, Fletcher?"

The valet did not answer immediately as he poured out hot water from the copper kettle kept warm by the fire into the basin on the washstand, but his countenance turned wistful.

"Sorry, sir? London has its pleasures, and Pemberley is the fairest spot on God's green earth. Hertfordshire? Hertfordshire, I have found, has its own treasures, sir; and what man is not loath to leave behind a treasure?"

"What man indeed?" whispered Darcy, visions of his first sight of Elizabeth that evening arising before his eyes: the comely form, the impudent curls, her flashing eyes, and, later, her troubled brow, chastened voice, and anguished gaze. Darcy closed his eyes wearily.

"Mr. Darcy?"

"The man who knows his duty and, against all natural inclination, performs it. That man, Fletcher, will in the end know no regret."

"As you say, sir." Fletcher's face betrayed no reaction to Darcy's assertion as he motioned to the basin and the bedclothes lying across the counterpane. "Is there anything more you require tonight, sir?"

"No, no, that will be all. I have kept you up long enough. If I am not stirring by ten, please rouse me."

Fletcher gathered up the discarded evening clothes and, bowing in acknowledgment of his dismissal, retreated to the dressing room door. "Mr. Darcy, sir." He paused at the threshold. Darcy finished pulling his shirt over his head and looked at him inquiringly. "There is some brandy on the table next to the fire should you desire it. Good night, sir."

Darcy looked over at the table as the door quietly clicked shut. He had not intended to partake at this late hour, but the idea now held an appeal. Perhaps it would still the competing voices in his head long enough to allow him to fall asleep. He poured himself a tumbler but left it on the table in indecision while he finished his ablutions and assumed his bedclothes. It stood there still when he had done, shining invitingly in the firelight. His hand closed around it, and with a quick motion, he downed half the glass. The liquid fire burned satisfactorily on its way down, its false warmth flooding his body within moments.

His duty! Yes, he knew his duty quite well—and the consequences of neglecting it. Georgiana had only just been rescued from his one instance of neglect of his duty. He would not fail Charles similarly. Not for all the "treasures" of Hertfordshire.

Darcy quickly downed the rest of the glass before her face could arise before him again and set it down on the tray. He walked over to the bed and pulled back the sheets, still warm from the heating pan, and slid between them, arranging his limbs in a position most likely to encourage sleep. He blew out the candle. Darkness enfolded him as the effects of brandy drunk too fast made themselves felt. A pair of fine eyes looked down upon him in confusion and sorrow, and Darcy turned in to his pillow to avoid them.

"Dear God," he whispered into the depths of the night, "I pray I do right!"

CHAPTER 11

Certain Evils

$\mathcal{W}$ith Fletcher's help, Bingley's man had his master ready to leave at precisely noon. By twelve forty-five they had left Meryton behind them and were bowling along down tolerably good road at a ground-eating pace in Bingley's carriage. Although he was dressed and breakfasted, Bingley's only contribution to the first hour or so of their journey had consisted of gentle snorts and snores. The sway and dip of the well-sprung equipage had been encouragement enough for Darcy to doze as well, as against all reason he had awakened at his usual early hour from a very troubled night. It was not until they made their stop at a coaching inn for a change of horses that Darcy put the first movement of his campaign in motion.

"Bingley! Charles, do wake up." Darcy leaned over and, firmly gripping his friend's shoulder, gave him an ungentle shake. "We are changing horses, and I, for one, need to stretch my limbs a bit. A pint would not be unwelcome, either. Shall we sample the local brew?" He cocked a brow at the muffled groans that issued from the folds of Bingley's neckcloth. "Perhaps some coffee would answer better. Come, sir; up and out!"

Bingley opened one eye and, seeing the inflexible face before him, gave a great sigh and roused himself enough to stumble down the carriage steps. Darcy grabbed his arm and, laughing, propelled him toward the inn's wide doorway. His query "A room, innkeeper?" was quickly answered, and a buxom daughter of the house curtsied them into a comfortable private dining room with a window that commanded the yard. An order for something hot and stimulating was given as Bingley slumped down into a worn but respectable couch.

"How *can* you be so infernally awake, Darcy?" Bingley yawned, squinting up at his companion's profile against the sun streaming in through the window. "You were later than I to bed and up hours before me, I'll wager, if your Fletcher had anything to do with it. That man is a positive martinet! He had my poor Kandle in such a quake he could barely hold my razor steady. I had to shave myself this morning, or he would have presented you with my corpse rather than — Don't laugh, I swear to you, I'm not exaggerating!"

"Corpse, indeed! Bingley, you do nothing *but* exaggerate, or worse, allow your imagination to run away with you."

"Now that is doing it a bit too brown, Darcy." Bingley frowned, mildly affronted. "But if I am to be so accused, tell me, sir, how one is worse than the other so I may decide whether I am insulted or amused." Bingley straightened his waistcoat and tugged at his coat. "Harumpf." He cleared his throat sonorously and, picking up a spoon, solemnly tapped it on the table. "You may proceed."

"The man who exaggerates is perfectly aware that he does so," Darcy began as he leaned carelessly against the window frame, his arms crossed upon his chest, "and does not expect anyone to take his protestations to heart. He may come to employ it habitually, but he is still in possession of the truth of the matter and, if pressed, will admit it. But the man in thrall to his imagination has relinquished the command of his faculties to an illusion and will hold to it despite all facts to the contrary. Further, he will demand the rest of the world's credulity in the matter and regard any who refuse as enemies or oppressors or—"

A knock on the door interrupted his discourse. The innkeeper's daughter entered and deposited a steaming tray of mugs and covered dishes. Bingley's study of the spoon in his hand prevented him from seeing the cheery smile of the maid as she dipped a curtsy in his direction and quietly closed the door on her way out.

"—Or at the least, a very dull fellow indeed," Darcy concluded lightly. He crossed to the table and began lifting covers to examine what had been brought for their repast. "Charles, are you not hungry? This looks passable." He held out a plate. "Charles?"

Bingley looked up at the sound of his name and, shooting Darcy a quick, wry grin, relieved him of the plate and joined him over the tray. "I believe I shall choose to be amused, particularly *because* you are such a 'dull fellow.'"

"Just so," Darcy replied before they fell upon the plain but honest offerings.

After a brisk walk about its environs, they were glad upon their return to the inn to find the coach ready for them. Heated bricks inserted, they clambered inside. Bingley gave the command; the horses leaned into their harnesses, and the two fell back against the squabs. When the horses achieved an even gait, Darcy leaned over and opened his traveling bag, withdrawing *Fuentes d'Oñoro* from its hold, and settled in closer to the window.

"Oh, you wish to read?" Bingley's voice held a note of disappointment.

"Yes, if you would not mind. There is no more than an hour of light left, and I promise to put it away before the lamps must be lighted. Would you like *Badajoz*? It is right here in my bag." Bingley shrugged his acceptance, and Darcy handed him the volume, little worse for the wear of Miss Bingley's perusal and its careen across the library floor. It was plain that Bingley wished to continue their discussion from the inn, but Darcy kept resolutely to his plan. Leaning back again into the light, he fingered the ends of the embroidery threads that held his place before sliding one finger into the slight breach and opening the book. The colorful threads lay nestled in the crevice of the binding, an intricately feminine knot gathering them at the top. With one eye on his friend, he quickly secreted the token into his coat pocket and then devoted himself to his book, not returning the mark to a new resting place until the shadows made it impossible to read any longer. As he put it away, Bingley returned the other and remarked that they were almost to London. "Do you join me for dinner at Grenier's?"

"Your invitation is appreciated, Bingley, but I must remain at home. I have a full schedule of appointments to attend to tomorrow. What say you to dinner at Erewile House tomorrow evening?"

" 'Capital!' as Sir William Lucas would say." Bingley chuckled briefly and then sobered. "Darcy, I'm thinking of making an offer on Netherfield."

"An offer? That is rather premature, don't you think?"

"I thought you approved of Netherfield."

"Yes, it is well enough"—Darcy measured out his words—"but I would not advise you to purchase it, at least not yet. This was but your first taste of country living. You found it agreeable. But I find it incumbent upon me to remind you, your sisters did not."

"Oh, Caroline!" Bingley replied disparagingly. "Only something as grand as Pemberley would satisfy her, and even if I were to fall into such an estate, we both know that I am not ready for it. Netherfield is perfect!"

"Perhaps. Still, I should not call it wise to be hasty in this. You hold a contract to rent for a year? Take that year. Hertfordshire is not the only bit of country in England."

The carriage slowed as they approached the Highgate Toll. The busy tollgate's noise being inimical to further conversation, Darcy leaned back into the shadows and covertly watched his friend. Bingley's brow was creased in a rare furrow that bespoke a mind suddenly cast into uncertainty. As the carriage rolled toward Mayfair, though, he appeared to shake free from his disquiet.

"I hope that you will not have to spend all your time in business affairs before you leave for Derbyshire."

"Not all my time, no. There is the pleasant duty of searching out Christmas gifts for Georgiana. I should look in at my club as well."

"Certainly, but what of enjoyable things like . . . a play or a look in at St. Martin's. Belcher is to display against Cribb, I have heard, and after deal with a newcomer, a fellow from Belgium. Blerét, I think." He did not give over at Darcy's shrug. "L'Catalani is to perform at Lady Melbourne's; surely you will be finished with your accounts by then?"

"You are singularly well informed, Charles," Darcy replied dryly, his voice edged with a sudden, inexplicable irritation. "Pray, leave your recommendations with Hinchcliffe, and I shall endeavor to oblige you as often as I can."

"Your secretary! Oh, I would not dare. I don't believe he entirely approves of me, Darcy."

"Has Hinchcliffe been impertinent to you? I am sorry for it."

"Do not apologize." Bingley smiled at his friend's perturbation. "I know how invaluable he is to you. Both he and your Fletcher are quite well regarded, you know. I have, in fact, overheard any number of gentlemen of our acquaintance lament their inability to entice one or the other of them away from your employ. Such complete loyalty!"

Darcy winced guiltily at the appellation and looked away to the window. The carriage turned into Grosvenor Square and came to a gentle stop in front of Erewile House. "Besides, it is likely a great honor to be snubbed by him. Further, if he should ever discover it is I who peached on him, Hinchcliffe will deny me the services of the nephew he has been training. So say nothing, I beg you."

Grunting in agreement to Bingley's request, Darcy began arranging his traveling bag to be brought into the house. The carriage door was pulled open by a footman. Behind him, holding high a lamp, was Erewile House's venerable butler, a look of relief warring with deference.

"Mr. Darcy, sir. So good to have you safely home."

"Thank you, Witcher," he returned as he descended from the carriage, "but you should not be out here in the cold, my good man."

"Thank you, sir, but Mrs. Witcher was just that certain the weather would turn before you arrived that only my personal assurance of your safety will do."

"I desire, then, that you go and inform her so, directly. The footman can handle what is needed." Darcy turned back to the carriage door. "Bingley, I will not keep you from your dinner. Eight tomorrow evening?"

"Eight it shall be."

Darcy nodded curtly at his reply, and the footman shut the carriage door. He mounted the steps as Bingley's carriage pulled away, in seconds gaining the warm, welcoming hall of his London home.

"Pardon me, sir, but Mr. Fletcher wishes to know if you require a bath to be drawn before dining." Witcher stepped up behind him to help with the divesting of coat, hat, and gloves. "Monsieur Jules begs leave to inform you that dinner can be served within the hour if you so desire, and a nice hot toddy is on its way to the library at this very moment."

Ah, yes, it is good to be home, Darcy thought wearily. "You may tell Fletcher that a bath is highly desired. Dinner in an hour and a half would please me immeasurably."

"Very good, sir. And the toddy, sir?"

"I am on my way to the library. Thank you, Witcher."

"Mr. Darcy." Witcher bowed as his master started up the stairs to his sanctuary. Upon entering, Darcy found a fire blazing cheerily in the hearth and the promised hot drink on a tray at the side of his favorite chair. A quick look at his desk's burnished top revealed his appointment book and correspondence neatly arranged and precisely annotated in Hinchcliffe's clear hand. His books were already unpacked and lying in wait of his attention on the shelf reserved for his current reading.

Everything was as it should be. Sighing to himself, he strode over to the jug of hot liquor. He poured a comforting amount into the mug on the tray and blew out the candle before settling down into the hearthside chair and propping up his heels on the footstool before it. He took a long draw on his drink and, closing his eyes, leaned back. He tried mightily to think of nothing but the hot, sweet liquid sliding down his throat and the pleasurable sensations of once again being home, among his own people and possessions. But the vision of Bingley's troubled face in response to his purposeful remarks would not be dismissed.

Bingley! He groaned aloud and, sitting up, leaned forward to stare into the fire. *It is all to good purpose,* he told himself for the thousandth time, *and it is of no matter how the whole affair makes you feel.* As he took another draw from the mug, his eyes strayed about the room and fell upon the book he had been reading in the carriage. Remembering what lay inside its pages, he quickly turned away. Surely Fletcher was ready for him by now! He set the mug down upon the tray and strode out the library door.

The next morning found Darcy awaking from the first night of true repose he had experienced in some time. Almost before the bell pull had stopped swaying, Fletcher appeared and, with quiet expertise, prepared him for a day devoted to his business affairs. Breakfast and the perusal of the morning's newspaper, Darcy noted, had been blessedly devoid of Miss Bingley's chattering interruptions, and when both were finished, he looked up to be informed that his secretary awaited his pleasure in the library.

"Mr. Darcy, sir." Hinchcliffe rose from his chair set directly across the wide desk from Darcy's own.

"Hinchcliffe"—Darcy acknowledged his slight bow—"it appears we have quite a day ahead of us. Did you receive the instructions concerning the disposition of the charitable funds for this year?" He sat down opposite his secretary, who then resumed his own seat.

"Yes, sir." He drew Darcy's letter out of the leather case in his lap and lay it on the desk for his master's approval. Each recipient of Darcy's yearly largesse was noted and checked off in Hinchcliffe's neat script. "Expressions of gratitude for your interest arrive daily, sir." He withdrew more letters from the case and laid them beside Darcy's. Darcy swept up the letters and glanced through them before pushing them back across the desk.

"Very good, Hinchcliffe." An almost imperceptible nod of the head was the sum of his secretary's response to his words. Its curt nature and Darcy's unconcern over such procacious behavior in a servant would have surprised many of his acquaintances. Of course, they could not know that Hinchcliffe had been his father's secretary, engaged into his service since Darcy had been a lad of twelve.

Their first meeting had not been an auspicious one. Elated to be home on a short holiday from Eton, Darcy had run into Erewile House straight out of the carriage, through the entry hall, and right into a tall, black-clad form just coming into the hall. When the last bit of paper had finally drifted to the floor, he'd found himself lying across the legs of a stern-eyed man of about thirty years. The fall had knocked the man's wig askew at a comical angle in such a marked contrast to the granite set of his jaw that Darcy had been unable to prevent a sign of the humor of their situation from escaping him. That had lasted only until the strange servant untangled his limbs and rose to his full height. To Darcy's twelve-year-old amazement, the man had seemed a giant and one with a darkling eye focused wholly upon himself.

"Master Darcy, I believe," the giant had rumbled.

"Yes, sir," he had responded in a much subdued voice, sure that he had been unlucky enough to have tumbled over an unknown schoolmaster engaged to keep him at his studies during the holiday.

"I am your father's new secretary, Mr. Hinchcliffe," the giant had continued, his diction precise and his voice stentorian. "You, sir, are awaited in the library. You will pardon me if I do not announce you, as I have an unexpected task to complete. I suggest you bestir yourself before your father comes in search of you." Fixing him with a final, stern look, Hinchcliffe had turned and begun retrieving the papers that littered the hall while Darcy walked quickly up the steps and slipped inside the library door to safety.

For years Hinchcliffe had been a rigid fixture among the servants whom Darcy had learnt to appreciate only when he had come home from university to find his beloved father's health in an alarming state. During those two harrowing years before his death, Hinchcliffe had tutored Darcy on all his father's business interests and concerns, and he could conceive of no other more suited to be his own secretary than the man who knew the Darcy interests so intimately and had kept them so faithfully and so well. He did not look for warmth from Hinchcliffe, nor did he expect deference. It was enough for Darcy to be certain that he had merited the respect and loyalty of a man who had known of all his concerns since boyhood and, further, tendered him the services of a true master at his craft.

"Mr. Darcy, sir, there is one thing more I must bring to your notice." Hinchcliffe withdrew yet another letter from his case and, carefully opening it, laid it on the desk. "I received this from Miss Darcy a few days ago. Shall I do as she has requested, sir?"

Darcy took up the letter and read it softly aloud:

> *21 November 1811*
> *Pemberley House*
> *Lambton*
> *Derbyshire*

> *Mr. Hinchcliffe,*
> *If you please, make out a check from my Charity Funds in*
> *the amount of twenty pounds to be given over to the Society*
> *for Returning Young Women to Their Friends in the Country,*

the address follows, and see that a check for one hundred
pounds per annum is made over to them hereafter.

Sincerely,
Miss Georgiana Darcy

Eyebrows arched high in surprise, Darcy looked over the top of the letter at his secretary. "The Society for Returning Young Women! Hinchcliffe, are you acquainted with this society?"

"I was not, sir, previous to Miss Darcy's letter. I have made inquiries, and it is a legitimate society with connections to Clapham, sir. Very respectable board of directors, subscribers are from the best families and even a few peers. Nothing objectionable, sir."

"Hmm," Darcy replied, staring at the letter thoughtfully. "That may be so, but I object to my sister knowing of such women . . . such evils," he amended. *And further, that she did not consult first with me! Why did she not?* He frowned.

"Shall I comply with Miss Darcy's directions, Mr. Darcy?" Hinchcliffe's voice rumbled quietly.

"Yes," he answered slowly, drawing out his assent to the request. "Make over the twenty-pound bequest, but do not send the hundred until you have heard from me on it. I would speak to Miss Darcy first."

"Very good, sir. Your first appointment is with the manager of the warehouse that handles the imported goods from your shipping interests. Shall I show him in?"

Darcy nodded, and the day began in earnest with a series of meetings and negotiations. Bargains were struck and funds withdrawn or invested in quick succession, with only a short pause in the late afternoon for a cold collation and glass of ale. This had been pressed upon him most insistently by his watchful housekeeper, Mrs. Witcher. When the door had closed behind the last man in his appointment book, the clock was very near to striking six.

"A most productive day." He sighed, closing the account books and sitting back in his desk chair. Hinchcliffe leaned across the desk, pulling the accounts into a neat pile and then taking them in a stack to the safebox hidden behind a set of weighty tomes on a bookshelf.

"Yes, sir," replied the secretary as he took a small key attached with a chain to his waistcoat, locked the safebox, and replaced the books. "Will that be all, Mr. Darcy?"

"Yes, that is all! Go and get some dinner; I have worked you unmercifully." As Hinchcliffe bowed slightly and turned to go, Darcy had a sudden thought. "Hinchcliffe, how is your nephew coming along? The one you are training. Is he looking for a position?"

"Your interest is most kind, Mr. Darcy. The young man is coming along nicely, sir, but I would not say he is ready as yet to look for a situation. Another half year will tell."

"I dine tonight with Mr. Bingley, who is quite interested in acquiring your nephew's services. A better master would be hard to find."

"Mr. Bingley, sir?" Hinchcliffe paused and then continued. "Ah, yes, I recall him now, sir. Fortune through trade, Yorkshire family, I believe." He sniffed delicately.

"Correct on every count, and my *particular* friend," Darcy emphasized. "I would consider it a great favor, when your nephew is ready, if he would give serious thought to entering into Mr. Bingley's employ."

"He would deem it an honor to oblige you, Mr. Darcy. Good evening, sir."

As the door closed on his still formidable secretary, Darcy struggled out of his coat and, laying it across his desk, walked over to the hearth, stretching his back muscles as he went. Bingley was likely right about Hinchcliffe snubbing him, he thought, as he reached for the decanter and poured out a glass. He shook his head and then took a sip from the heavy cut-glass tumbler, letting the liquid roll down his throat. *At least you have done him a good turn in this that he will appreciate immediately. Not like the other. That will take some time.*

The clock struck the half hour. Darcy threw back the last of the contents of his glass and set it down on the tray. Bingley would be there in an hour or so, and he had been confined to the house the entire day. He needed some exercise; a brisk walk about the square would be just the thing. Slipping his coat on, he rang for his great-coat and hat. Witcher appeared with them, and with a caution that he would be back in twenty minutes and desired Fletcher to be ready for him, Darcy ran down the stairs and set off at an invigo-rating pace.

"Now then, Darcy, are you finished with work so Jack may play, or is he to continue to be a dull boy?" Bingley accepted the glass of deep red wine his friend offered and sat in his customary chair at the dining table in one of the smaller parlors of Erewile House. As the servants moved quietly about, uncovering dishes and serving them, Darcy lifted his glass in a toast.

"To a swift and successful conclusion of Jack's obligations, so his friends will not languish in boredom."

"Hear, hear." Bingley laughed and downed a portion of the fine burgundy. "Truly, are you free from your account books and solic-itors? It has been well over a week!"

"Not yet, and before you ask, I have had little opportunity to look at any cards, so I have not decided on anything. Except . . ." He paused, slowly twirling the stem of the wineglass.

"Yes . . . except?"

"You mentioned the diva L'Catalani, and I find myself sorely tempted to attend Lady Melbourne's soiree."

"Tempted, you say! Do you mean to go? I should like to go, but only if you are. That set is a bit above my touch." Bingley began to tuck into the delicious meal before him.

Darcy snorted. "That set! Do not let their titles and airs fool you, Bingley. They hide a dangerous, deceptive lot that you would do well to stay clear of. Intrigue and ambition are their creed, and woe to the man or woman who becomes entangled in their plots."

"Rather a dark view, Darcy! But I daresay I am too much of a nobody to attract their attention and could chance a venture into the lion's den without much harm being done. And to hear L'Catalani!" he entreated. "Darcy, we *must* attend!"

A shadow of hesitation passed over Darcy's features as he regarded his friend, but in the face of such earnestness, he could not but agree. "So be it, Bingley; we shall go. But be forewarned and keep your head. I shall call for you at nine tomorrow evening."

"Marvelous, Darcy." Both then fell to their dinners, Bingley interspersing sporting news and men's club gossip between mouthfuls of stuffed capon, chartreuse, and veal d'olive. When the two had done justice to Monsignor Jules's artistry, they repaired to the library for a glass of port, which Bingley accepted from Darcy with a deep sigh.

"Charles?"

"It has been two weeks, you know."

"Two weeks?"

"Yes, two weeks since the ball. Two weeks since I last saw Miss Bennet. It seems an age! Wasn't she lovely? I could scarce keep from her side." Bingley's attention seemed to waver from his surroundings.

"Yes, well, that was obvious to anyone with eyes, old man." Darcy paused and, gathering his powers, asked disinterestedly, "Would you say that she feels the same?"

Bingley shook himself slightly and turned in puzzlement to his friend. "Yes, of course. Why would you ask?"

"On what, exactly, do you base your opinion? Did she confess herself to you?"

"No, no, of course not!" Bingley put his glass down, stepped away, and then returned to pick it up again. "What a thing to suggest, Darcy! Miss Bennet is a lady, gently bred. She would never—"

"She looked at you, then, in such a way that left no need for words of love, of attachment?" he pressed.

Bingley's mouth opened in protest. "I remind you again, Miss Bennet is a gentlewoman. It would be entirely inappropriate."

"Then tell me, Charles." He closed in, allowing his friend no opportunity to stray from the point. "On what grounds do you believe she holds you in greater regard than other men of her close acquaintance? You admit she has not spoken of love, nor given you glances full of tender meaning. What then?"

"A man just knows," Bingley sputtered.

Darcy shrugged skeptically.

"You believe me to be exaggerating the thing, but I swear to you, I am not! Not this time."

"Ah, yes. 'Not this time,'" Darcy returned softly. Bingley stared into his glass while Darcy, forcefully maintaining an air of nonchalance, sat down and sipped at his port. As the silence between them stretched on, he glanced at Charles now and again, attempting to gauge his thoughts. The repeated flex of his jaw bespoke deep agitation.

"You believe me to be imagining it, the warmth of her regard?" Bingley's question seemed more a statement than an inquiry.

"Charles," he returned in a conciliatory tone, "you must be the judge of that. I only wish to caution you, warn you away from an alliance that would bring you more pain than satisfaction. The difficulties of Miss Bennet's family and connections are many, yet these may be borne if you are absolutely convinced of her devotion. But if marriage were contracted with only want of advancement in Society on the lady's part . . ." He left the rest unspoken.

Bingley gulped down the remaining contents of his glass. "Yes, well, no more need be said. Nine tomorrow evening, then?" He rose from his chair and, to Darcy's surprise, sketched him a bow. "I think I will make an early night of it, Darcy. I have some appointments of my own in the morning. I imagine I should dress to the nines for Lady Melbourne's?"

"Yes, but with restraint. Brummell will, undoubtedly, be there, and it would be better not to attract his opinion at all than to suffer his wit. You must go then?"

"Regretfully, yes. Oh, do not get up!" he hastened to add as Darcy made to rise. "I can make my way to the door."

"Nonsense." Darcy left his chair and summoned a footman. "Mr. Bingley's things, please." He turned back to his friend. "Charles, I have spoken to Hinchcliffe."

"Not about his behavior toward me! Darcy!"

"No, no . . . about his nephew. He shall be ready to apply to you in a few months or so; I have Hinchcliffe's assurance on it." They had reached the hall and Witcher, who stood with Bingley's hat, coat, and gloves at the ready.

"Thank you, Darcy." Bingley managed a smile that, though small, devastated Darcy with its sincerity. "I appreciate your advocacy in this immensely. You have ever been my good friend."

Darcy did not wait for the great front door to click shut before he turned and sought again the sanctuary of his library. He nearly threw himself into his chair and sat motionless as a servant scurried in to stoke the fire on the hearth.

"*You have ever been my good friend.*" He closed his eyes, his jaw clenching. *Are not the wounds of a friend blessed?* He directed his question heavenward. Better a moment's pain than a lifetime of disgust and regret because that friend did nothing!

A sudden need to *do* something, anything, gripped him. Darcy sprang to his feet. Striding over to the sword case, he tore off his coat, waistcoat, and neckcloth, and threw them on a chair. Swiftly unlatching the case, he examined the collection and, reaching in, selected a perfectly balanced rapier. Taking a lamp from his desk, he continued his pace out of his library and into the hall. *Where to go?* Hesitating only briefly, he struck out for the ballroom. He encountered no servants on his way and slipped into the great room without a sound. Setting the lamp upon a Sheraton console hugging the wall, he moved out onto the floor, executing wide, slashing figures as he went. The muscles in his shoulder protested a month's disuse in the exercise, but he ignored them and continued the regimen until they loosened and he was sure of his blade's balance and reach. Then, bringing the blade upright to his lips, he assumed the *en garde,* holding his body in the curiously taut yet easy pose of the experienced swordsman.

He lunged. An imaginary opponent parried his move. He lunged again. This time his thrust was parried, and he faced a lightning riposte. Darcy brought the rapier up and blocked the attack, then twisted his wrist, using his blade to set his opponent off balance. It did not succeed. Block . . . block again, thrust. He laughed. *That had shaken him!* Darcy lunged as the other backed a step, then two.

The flame of the lamp glinted again and again off his sword as Darcy worked through the classic forms of advance and retreat. Back and forth across the dark floor he chased, harried, and otherwise engaged his imaginary foe until beads of moisture stood out on his forehead and his sword arm decried the weight of his blade. With a final, sweeping arc, he brought it up in salute and, bowing, honored the empty darkness that had opposed him.

His sides aching, Darcy caught up the lamp and, slipping silently down the hall, brought it and the rapier back to the library. He returned the sword to its case and retrieved his discarded clothing. Tired as he was, he knew he was not yet ready to succumb to sleep. *His book!* He would read until sleep demanded his surrender. From where he stood, he could see *Fuentes d'Oñoro* standing at attention and, next to it, his father's long-ago gift to him, Whitefield's sermons. Reaching across to the shelves, he pulled out *Fuentes d'Oñoro* and, tucking it under his arm, blew out the lamp and made his way to his bedchamber.

CHAPTER 12

All That Glitters . . .

With his accustomed precision, Darcy placed his signature on the last document of business he expected to encounter before leaving London for Christmas and Pemberley and handed it back to Hinchcliffe to sand and seal. At last, he was free from the tedious aspects of his return to Town and could give his attention to more pleasurable activities! Although, he acknowledged to himself as he closed up his ledgers and books, this evening's soiree at the home of Lord and Lady Melbourne in Whitehall would not answer all his ideas of pleasure. Only the much-heralded appearance of L'Catalani could have enticed him to accept one of Lady Melbourne's invitations, for in general he followed his advice to Bingley and avoided her set as much as was possible.

It was not only that lady's encouragement of the prince regent's eccentricities that caused Darcy to maintain a distant attitude. The intrigue and rumors of irregularities within the walls of Melbourne House reached back over thirty years, to the birth of the viscount's heir, and continued into the present in scandalized *on-dits* concerning the conduct of that heir's new wife. Darcy had been present at the marriage of the Honorable William Lamb to Lady Caroline

Ponsonby on one of his rare visits to Town during his father's illness. Lamb he had regarded as a good sort, levelheaded in his pursuit of a political career and of a more serious cast than his antecedents might lead his constituents to expect. But his marriage to Lady Caroline, already celebrated for her unconventional flights of behavior, was, to Darcy's thinking, ill-advised. In this he had been proved a sage, and Darcy considered, as he nodded his permission to Hinchcliffe's request to lock up the books, which lady might be the more likely to stage a scene at the soiree, the temperamental diva or the highly strung Lady Caroline.

"Another good day's work, Hinchcliffe," Darcy complimented his secretary. "You have overseen everything admirably. I could never have accomplished so much without your attention beforehand."

"It is my pleasure, sir," the somber man replied with a slight inclination of his gaze. "Has the date of your departure for Pemberley been settled, sir? I should like to begin the arrangements."

"Tuesday the 17th, I should think, if I can see Lawrence on Monday. Have I received a reply to my inquiry?"

"It arrived this afternoon, Mr. Darcy." Hinchcliffe opened the ever-present leather case, extracted a rather crumpled, paint-stained note, and read, " 'Mr. Thomas Lawrence will be pleased to entertain Mr. Fitzwilliam Darcy at half past two of the clock on Monday, the 16th of December at his residence, Cavendish Square.' Shall I send a confirmation, sir?"

"Yes, do so. If my interview goes well and he agrees, he shall paint Miss Darcy when she comes to London with me in January." He smiled into Hinchcliffe's surprised countenance. "Indeed, I have every confidence that I will be able to convince her to return with me. Not a Season, of course—she is too young—but there will be quiet gatherings enough and operas and plays and"—he paused, then added quietly—"and it will be good to have her among us, will it not?"

"It will, indeed, Mr. Darcy." The softened look that passed

briefly over Hinchcliffe's face confirmed what Darcy had known for years. He may have had a secure hold upon his secretary's loyalty, but it was his sister, born the year he came into their service, who held Hinchcliffe's devotion.

The library clock struck four, and as if on cue, Witcher opened the door, but not with the expected announcement of tea. "Mr. Darcy, sir, Lord Dyfed Brougham to see—"

"Yes, yes, I'm here to see you, Fitz; and I know you are home. Don't try to brush me off with any Banbury tales, 'cause I'm on to 'um!" The elegant but imposing figure of Lord Brougham filled the doorway and then sidled past the butler. "Good show, Witcher, but Fitz'll see me, won't you, old man?" He rounded on Darcy with a confident grin.

"Dy, have you nothing better to do than rattle my servants?" Darcy shook his head at his old university friend.

"Nothing else whatsoever! Except, perhaps, to plague you!" Lord Brougham stretched out his hand and gripped Darcy's in a hearty shake. "Where have you been this last month? I came to Town to find your knocker down, and all Witcher would tell me was that 'Mr. Darcy is visiting in the country.' I offered him a pony if he would say where, but Mr. Witcher here"—Lord Brougham tossed his chin toward the butler—"would mumble not a word."

"Let that teach you not to try to bribe loyal family servants," Darcy shot back at him with a laugh.

"Well, all those years at University didn't teach me anything, so I doubt me this will. Hopeless case, don't you know!" Brougham dropped carelessly into one of the hearthside chairs and looked around him. "I've caught you at the books, have I, Fitz?"

"No, in point of fact, we just finished; and I was expecting tea—"

"Tea! Now there's an idea!" He sat up with a bound. "Let's you and I toddle over to the club. I daresay you haven't looked in at Boodle's since you returned from . . . Now just where were you?"

"Hertfordshire."

"Lord, you don't say! Hertfordshire!" Brougham mused distractedly. "Whatever for, Fitz?"

"I'll tell you when we get to the club." Darcy turned to his butler, who well acquainted with Lord Brougham's high spirits, was smiling discreetly behind his hand. "My things, Witcher, if you please. It appears I will be taking tea at Boodle's."

The two men clattered down the front steps of Erewile House and into Lord Brougham's curricle, which in minutes conveyed them, under his expert whip, to the hushed hallowedness of Boodle's. The club's imperious doorman ushered them inside, where various footmen rushed quietly to relieve them of their greatcoats, hats, and gloves.

Facing his friend across the black-and-white mosaic floor of Italian marble, Darcy cocked a brow. "Where to, Dy?"

"Someplace where we can talk privately and not scandalize the older members. Corner of the dining room, I should think." Brougham winked in response to the veil of reserve with which Darcy immediately cloaked his face. "Oh, nothing so very bad as that, Fitz! Unless you've been kicking your heels up in—where was that? Herefordshire?"

"Hertfordshire, as you well know," he replied dampeningly.

"Oho! We do have some ground to cover, I see." Brougham started toward one of the gleaming wooden passageways that arched over stairs leading from the entry hall to the club's upper floors.

Perhaps this was not wise. Darcy's eyes narrowed on his friend's back as he followed him up to the dining room. He knew very well that Dy's dilettante façade hid a keen mind, which despite his protestations, was as capable of designing a bridge as of composing a sonnet. They had vigorously competed with each other at University, and Darcy remembered, if his friend did not, the multitude of prizes Dy had won at Cambridge. All the while, he recalled uneasily, giving their tutors fits.

In the intervening seven years, Dy had managed, with a studied elegance and frivolous manner, to make Society forget about them as well and account him no more than a charming fribble. Darcy had often wondered why the charade, but Dy had smoothly deflected all his attempts at satisfying himself on the question. How or why his friend had determined to conduct his life in such a fashion remained an untouched subject between them, but as it did not corrupt the firmness of their long friendship, Darcy had chosen early on to leave the question unanswered. But his forbearance in pressing Dy upon his idle existence was, he had found, not always reciprocated. *If I am not extremely careful,* he cautioned himself, *Dy will discover from my own lips what I wish most to conceal.*

They entered the spacious dining room, and Brougham immediately commandeered the coziest table. "Here, just the ticket, Fitz." He pulled out a chair for Darcy and then sat down at the one that offered the best view of the entire room. "Let us get our tea ordered, and then you can tell me all about your expedition to the country." As the waiters discharged dish upon dish of what Boodle's considered a suitable tea for its gentleman members, Darcy and Dy entertained each other with the commonplaces and ribbings that long friendship allowed. When they were finally left to themselves, Dy sobered somewhat and grew more candid as he caught his friend up on the economic rumors and political speculations that truly mattered to men in Darcy's position.

"What an amazing fount of information you are," Darcy commented dryly as Brougham finally paused for a long draw on his tea. "One could almost suppose it a passion."

"Oh, nothing so fatiguing! One hears things, you know. Assemblies, routs, hunts, gaming hells . . . all the same, nothing but chatter. I just happen to have a devilishly retentive mind." He cast Darcy a soulful look and sighed. "Merely one more curse I must bear."

"And what are the others, pray?" Darcy laughed outright at Dy's bid for sympathy. "A very considerable fortune, a fine person, and—"

"Please, desist! You are embarrassing me! Which is particularly annoying as it was I who intended to embarrass you. Now, tell me about Hertfordshire," Brougham demanded.

"Are you sure you do not mean Herefordshire?" Darcy threw back at him while scrambling for his dropped guard.

"No, I am sure you said Hertfordshire. Come, come; tell Papa what you did. Confession, you know . . . good for the soul and all that." Brougham looked at him intently.

Darcy found himself twisting the napkin in his lap. Dy's face was all sincerity, touched with a wry humor that warmly invited his confidence. The idea of enlisting his old friend's help seemed, at first, entirely incredible. But as they sat in silence, sipping at their tea, it slowly took on the appearance of reason. He would not tell him all, of course. Nothing about . . . well, nothing but what Dy needed to know to help him with Bingley.

"You know my friend Charles Bingley?"

Brougham nodded his head. "Young chap from up north with more ready than sense. You have done him more than a few good turns from the look of him lately."

"He took a year's lease on a small property in Hertfordshire and got himself entangled with a young woman from a most unsuitable family." Darcy wove his tale, careful to leave unmentioned his own fall into a tender fascination. "So," he concluded, "as the man has turned quite intractable on the subject and will not listen to reason, I am engaged in a game of subterfuge. Planting doubts, that sort of thing. I find it is exceedingly uncomfortable."

"I would imagine so! Not your game at all, Fitz. Do you think he suspects anything?"

"No, I do not believe so. At least, I doubt it. He trusts me implicitly, you see." Darcy flushed and fell to examining his ruby-crowned ring.

"Likely you are right that he does not suspect. 'The heart that is conscious of its own integrity is ever slow to credit another's treachery.' Ah, sorry, Fitz!" Brougham apologized at Darcy's pained expression. "Did not mean it the way it sounded. Well, you *do* have a serpent by the tail! What is your next move?"

"We are to attend Lady Melbourne's soiree tonight."

"The divine Catalani! Fitz, you are in luck. I myself have sent my acceptance to this soiree. How can I assist with the enchanted Mr. Bingley?"

"Help introduce him to new enchantments. You know how awkward I am at these things, Dy. But wait," Darcy responded quickly to the knowing look on Brougham's face, "by that I mean proper young ladies. If you introduce him to any of Lady Caroline's intimates, I'll call you out, just see if I don't!"

Brougham threw up his hands in mock horror. "Heaven forbid, Fitz. But just where, at a soiree hosted by Lady M, do you propose I find these 'proper young ladies'?"

"I should not think it much of a challenge to one 'cursed with such a retentive mind'!" Darcy quoted back to him. The apparent reasonableness of taking Dy into his confidence was beginning to fade.

"Yes," Brougham drawled, "there is that. I shall do my best, my friend. Now, do we go together or shall I 'happen' to meet you there?"

"We shall meet you there, but I won't pretend it is not planned. I shall tell Charles that we've arranged to meet at, say, half past nine near the card room."

"Done and done! Nothing like a bit of intrigue to liven up the evening. Can I drop you at Erewile House?"

The two rose from table and sauntered through the various rooms of the club, pausing now and then to exchange a word with one or the other's acquaintances, but in general making their way to the front door. Brougham's curricle was called for, and the horses pointed toward Grosvenor Square.

"You haven't told me about Georgiana," Brougham accused Darcy. "Lord, she must be quite a young lady by now."

"Yes . . . yes, she is. I intend to bring her back with me to Town in January."

"Not for a Season! She cannot be that grown!"

"On that we agree! No, I only wish to allow her some of the delights of Town. She so enjoys music and has cultivated a very fine taste."

"And you wax eloquent whenever you speak of her." Brougham's face took on a distant look. "I envy you, Fitz. I envied you even when Georgiana was a troublesome little moppet who innocently spoiled our plans for fun. Remember that summer I spent at Pemberley after our first year at Cambridge?"

"How could I forget? It was you who found her! The sight of her in your lap as you rode into the courtyard I shall never forget."

Brougham's sigh was so quiet that Darcy almost missed it. "Fitz, now I have a confession to make. It was I who hid the blasted doll she was looking for. If I had not found her—" He stopped abruptly. "Well, I did, and that, as they say, is that. And here we are!" He brought the matched bays to a neat stop and leaned over to unlatch Darcy's door. "Lady M's card room at half past nine. I'll be the one with the posy in his buttonhole." He saluted Darcy with his whip. "Au revoir!"

Darcy stood in the gathering dusk, frowning after the curricle until it turned the corner and disappeared from sight. Then, shaking his head slowly, he mounted the steps to Erewile House.

"Mr. Darcy, sir!" The bedchamber door had barely shut behind him when Fletcher, in a fine agitation, nearly sprang upon him from behind it.

"Great heavens, Fletcher!" expostulated Darcy, more than a little startled. "I have not rung for you yet."

"No time for ringing, Mr. Darcy. We must begin! Your bath will be ready momentarily. Shall we decide on your attire for the evening? Did you have anything in mind?" Darcy surveyed his chamber, noting with amused alarm that most every item of evening attire he owned was draped or stacked here and there. A pile of freshly starched cravats lay docilely beside his jewel case. His several pairs of evening shoes were polished to perfection. It all had the look, he thought, as his gaze returned to his valet, of a military campaign.

"I believe you have been seriously misinformed, Fletcher. It is only a soiree, not a summons to Carlton House."

"Indeed, sir"—Fletcher sniffed—"if it were only Carlton House! But it is, rather, Melbourne House, a much more refined address, sir."

"Umph" was all Darcy replied as he started toward the dressing room, Fletcher in his wake. His valet's ministrations during his disrobing and bathing were performed with the utmost professionalism and speed. A whispered command to a kitchen lad here or a low-pitched inquiry to himself there, and Darcy found that he was bathed, wrapped in a dressing gown, and in his shaving chair in amazingly short order.

As Fletcher expertly tested the edge of his blade, Darcy settled back into the chair. The routine nature of shaving—Fletcher always executed the strokes in the same order and manner—ever allowed him a few precious moments of reflection. This evening there was much to reflect upon . . . too much, if he permitted his mind to wander where it would. Dy's sudden appearance had the mark of Providence. Brougham was much more capable of guiding Charles through the labyrinthine intricacies of a gathering of Society's flowers than he could ever be. Aside from a true appreciation for the acclaimed diva, his only interest in the soiree was as an opportunity to distract Charles from his infatuation in Hertfordshire. The attention of the young ladies to a new, rich face appearing among them would be, for Charles, heady wine indeed. That, in addition to the doubts Darcy had planted in the other quarter, would, he hoped, channel Bingley's wavering convictions into proper courses. Tomorrow, he would send a note to Miss Bingley, and if she could restrain her disparagement of Hertfordshire and do as he had instructed, Charles would be safely out of danger, and he could go home to Pemberley.

"There, sir. Your towel, sir." Fletcher dropped a soft Turkish towel into his hand and, turning to the tray of toiletries, selected a bottle. "The sandalwood, I should think, sir." Darcy nodded and received a daub of the scent mixed with alcohol into his palm.

"Have you decided on your attire, Mr. Darcy?"

Darcy pulled himself out of the comfort of the chair and looked into Fletcher's face, animated for the first time since their return to London. "No, I have not given it any thought, whereas you have given it a great deal, if the condition of my bedchamber be the judge! What do you suggest, Fletcher, keeping in mind that the Beau himself will be in attendance and the regent, too, most likely?" He strolled back into his bedchamber and again surveyed the troops.

"Restrained elegance, Mr. Darcy. And as you, sir, have more claim to that than certain celebrated fellows—"

"I have no wish to compete with Mr. Brummell," Darcy clarified as he removed his dressing gown. "I mentioned him only in warning and do not wish to occasion any undue notice on anyone's part."

"I perfectly understand, sir. No *undue* notice." Fletcher paused and fingered the fine white lawn of the shirt he had chosen for his master. "I think the dark blue with the black silk waistcoat. The one embroidered with sapphirine threads, like the green you wore at Netherfield."

Darcy swiveled round. "No! Something else." Fletcher held up the waistcoat against the blue, almost black superfine coat and breeches. "Oh," he breathed. "Blue." His voice fell to a mumble. "Yes, that will do."

"Yes, sir." The valet held out the shirt and slipped it up his arms. Fletcher's enthusiasm increased with each article of clothing Darcy assumed, a marked contrast with his demeanor since returning to London. Evidently, his valet also had interests residing in Hertfordshire, and Darcy was vaguely sorry for it. What a disaster that trip had become! He looked down as Fletcher finished buttoning the waistcoat and went to select a neckcloth. Yes, it was very like the one he had worn at Netherfield. Was it only two weeks ago? The metallic threads alternately glittered and dulled as he moved before the dressing mirror. How hopeful he had been of a good result from the evening.

Fletcher returned, and Darcy sat down, lifting his chin to allow the valet room to practice his artistry. While his man folded and knotted, his mind involuntarily slipped back to that evening, to those few moments he had possessed himself of her hand and they had moved together in harmony rather than opposition. The flow of her gown around her, the flowers entwined in her hair.

> *. . . so lovely fair*
> *That what seemed fair in all the world seemed now*
> *Mean, or in her summed up, in her contained*
> *And in her looks, which from that time infused*
> *Sweetness into my heart, unfelt before,*
> *And into all things from her air inspired*
> *The spirit of love and amorous delight.*

With a start, Darcy recalled his thoughts from the unprofitable path in which they had strayed and, shaking himself, received a pained adjuration from Fletcher: "Please, sir, do not move just yet." The lines were ones he had found marked by the embroidery threads that he had stolen from the Milton in Netherfield's library. *An idiotish fancy,* he told himself as he turned from his valet, but the self-excoriation did not stop him from retrieving the threads from the book at his bedside. As he gently wound them about his finger and then poked them down into his breast pocket, the words they had lain against, not unlike the woman they brought to mind, caught and held him.

A knock at the door announced the welcome distraction of a tray from Monsieur Jules. The covers were lifted by another lad from the kitchen to reveal a savory fortification against supper at Melbourne House not being served until midnight.

"Here, sir." Fletcher came into the bedchamber. "Save for your fob and coat, you are ready." Darcy examined the valet's efforts in the mirror with a critical eye. Fletcher's face appeared alongside his reflection. "Should anyone ask"—he beamed with sartorial pride—"it is the Roquet. My own creation," he added diffidently.

"Roquet? 'To strike out of the game?' And who am I to strike out with this?" Darcy indicated the constriction that encircled his neck in an untold number of knots and folds.

"Whomever you wish, Mr. Darcy." Fletcher bowed to his employer's raised eyebrow, then took the napkin from the tray and shook it out. "Sir?"

Darcy sat down to his repast, his brow furrowed in speculation upon his valet, who returned his regard with an imperturbable aplomb. "A case of *Measure for Measure,* Fletcher?" he asked finally, as he took the napkin.

The ghost of a smirk passed over the valet's face. "Quite so, sir. Quite so."

Leaning to look out the window of his carriage, Darcy watched as his groomsman jumped down from the box and bounded down Jermyn Street to Grenier's, armed with a note advising Bingley that he had arrived and to wait until the carriage had pulled up to the hotel's door. Satisfied, he settled back into the squabs, pulling his evening cloak and the carriage rug closer. The ride to Melbourne House would be of no moment, he thought as he waited in the deep shadows of a cold late autumn's evening; but the wait for the long line of carriages attempting to discharge their passengers and then the receiving line within could take up well over an hour, even two. Not that he was anxious to arrive at his destination. *Thank Heaven, Dy will be there!* Someone of sense and decency with whom to converse and to provide an excuse for not attending to every Lady This or Miss That and her mama!

The carriage rocked slightly as the door was pulled open and

Bingley's muffled form climbed in. "Charles!" Darcy exclaimed. "Did you not receive my note?"

A slip of paper was waved before his nose. "Yes, and here it is! The line in front of Grenier's is frightful tonight. Every man and his uncle is going out or coming in, and you would be waiting until your bricks were stone cold. Much easier for me to come to you and, with your groomsman along, little danger. Yes, I've heard!" Bingley cut off Darcy's remonstrance. "Horrible business down in Wapping. In all the papers!" He sat back into the seat opposite, unwrapping a thick scarf from around his chin. "Is it true the regent has forbidden anyone to be received at Carlton House after eight?"

Darcy nodded as the carriage pulled away from the curb and his driver began the tedious negotiation of the streets to Whitehall. "Forbidden it to strangers. The door will not be refused to His Majesty's intimates, of course, as none of them are, as yet, sus- pected of mass murder," he added dryly.

Bingley's answering laugh evidenced a nervous tremor. "Darcy, this soiree. It seemed like a great go yesterday, but the more I thought about it today . . ." His voice trailed off, and he fell to studying his gloves.

"You shall do very well, Charles," Darcy assured him. "I have never seen you do aught but land on your feet, no matter where you are. Your talent for entering into whatever society you find yourself is truly remarkable. Incomprehensible, but remarkable."

Bingley chuckled again nervously. "Well, tonight shall be the test. I almost wish it were Caroline making this venture rather than myself. She would revel in it!"

Darcy grimaced in the dark. "I find your presence much more agreeable. Which reminds me, besides the ornaments of society you will meet tonight, I wish to introduce you to an old friend of mine, Lord Dyfed Brougham. We were at Cambridge together; he ran tame at Pemberley for a summer or more."

"Brougham, you say? I do not believe I have met him or his family."

"Unlikely. Brougham is his parents' only surviving child, and they were older when he was born. The old earl passed away before I had met him our first year at University. Brougham himself is rather a will-o'-the-wisp; one never knows when he may appear. But," Darcy advised, "he is just the man to guide you through tonight's gauntlet. Follow his lead, and you are sure to come out with your skin whole."

"And what shall you be doing?"

"I hope to have an opportunity actually to hear L'Catalani! The last time I attended a performance, the noise from the gallery was so appalling, even her great voice could not be heard. Aside from that, I plan to spend the majority of the evening avoiding danger as best as I am able."

"Danger! You make it all sound so sinister, Darcy. I fear you do not anticipate enjoying yourself in the least. I hope I am not interfering with your pleasure in the evening!"

"Of course not, don't be a gudgeon!" Darcy shifted uneasily. "I have never enjoyed large gatherings, as you well know, and have little patience with the intrigues that so delight the *haut ton*." He leaned forward. "But do not allow that to spoil your evening. Stay close to Brougham, and you will certainly enjoy yourself. Just take care not to be drawn into anything which might require me to act as your second."

"I almost believe you are serious!"

The carriage swayed to a stop at the corner before Whitehall, joining the line of others awaiting their turn to pull up to the torchlit stairs and shivering footmen of Melbourne House. Darcy knocked on the roof with his stick, and in moments his groom appeared at the door.

"Mr. Darcy, sir."

"Harry, I think we shall walk from here. Did Mr. Witcher give you anything?"

"Yes, sir." Harry grinned and patted his coat pocket, which jingled impressively. "Me an' James be well supplied fer an evenin' at the Bull 'n' Boar. Thank 'e, sir," he replied as he reached inside the carriage door to let down the steps.

"Good man, Harry." Darcy climbed down, Bingley close behind him. "Be available by two. I hope to make an early evening of it, unless Mr. Bingley will not be pulled away."

"Aye, sir. Two o'clock it is, an' a good evenin' to ya, Mr. Darcy."

The two men turned and walked hurriedly down the street, which was already crowded with gawkers and hawkers of every description. Darcy's grip tightened on his heavily crowned walking stick. He pulled himself up to every inch of his tall frame, projecting an air of uncompromising purpose as he strode through the throng, Bingley at his heels. In short order they gained the line of torches illuminating the walks on either side of Melbourne House and, upon presenting their cards to the footman, were immediately escorted up the steps and inside the doorway past guests who had arrived before them.

Bingley turned a questioning brow upon him as a servant hurried to relieve them of their hats and cloaks, but Darcy would only shrug in answer. It had always been thus, this deferential treatment, and it would be difficult to explain to Bingley, newcomer that he was, that it was merely part and parcel of the game Society loved so well to play. Although, Darcy acknowledged to himself as he turned to the butler and extended his card again, he had not entirely expected such marked distinction here at Melbourne. He had rarely mixed with this set, despite the many opportunities and invitations to do so, and knew he was regarded by the majority as stiff-rumped in his adherence to principle and decorum. But his name and fortune outweighed all these defects tonight, it seemed. It remained to observe who Lady Melbourne's other guests might be. Then, perhaps, he could make a determination on the manner of his reception.

He stepped to the arched doorway that led into the public rooms and waited for the Melbournes' butler to announce him and then Bingley. A quick survey confirmed that they were all here, the peers and politicians, the literati and the artists, the men whose hour was upon them and those whose hour was nearly past. Peeresses and very rich misses hung lightly on their arms, their brilliancy of gown contrasting with the Brummellian starkness of the gentlemen, their eyes darting here and there in the quest to see and be seen. Music swelled from the ballroom beyond. The mingled sounds of voices and music were deafening.

Darcy turned back to Bingley and smiled wryly into the overawed expression on his friend's face. Of course it would be daunting to a young man as unaffected as Charles! Darcy experienced a pang of uncertainty as to the wisdom of his plan, but it was much too late for reconsideration. The butler was, even now, announcing them.

Lady Melbourne broke from a group and advanced upon them with a smile long praised for its warmth if not for its sincerity. "Mr. Darcy, how absolutely delightful!" She extended her elegantly gloved hand, which he took smoothly and bowed. "Sefton," she called over her shoulder. "See, he has come, though you vowed he would not!" Lord Sefton sketched Darcy a curt, apologetic bow.

"Your servant, Darcy," the founder of the Four-in-Hand Club drawled. "Just trying to prevent the lady from suffering a disappointment. 'Sides, you never *do* come, leastways not till now."

"Hush, Sefton, you shall make him think we do nothing but gossip, and that is not *entirely* true." Lady Melbourne flashed her famous dark eyes up at Darcy and smiled. "We find any number of ways to amuse ourselves, Mr. Darcy, and many of them are here tonight for the enjoying." She took his arm, at the same moment noticing Bingley, who had been standing mute behind him. "Oh, pray excuse me, sir! A friend of yours, Mr. Darcy?"

"Indeed. May I have the honor of introducing him to Your Ladyship?" At her curious nod, Darcy made the introduction. To his relief, Charles appeared to have roused himself from his wonder at the surroundings to the point that he was able to receive the lady's hand with creditable grace.

"Mr. Bingley, you must take every opportunity to enjoy your-self tonight. There is dancing in the ballroom, cards in several rooms off the hall . . ." She paused. Darcy could see her quickly summing up Charles and assigning him a position among her ranks of acquaintants. *Where will she place him?* he wondered, which was followed by the more pertinent question, *And where, tonight, does she place me?* "But if your tastes run, as do your friend's, to the philosophical and political, my son Lamb is enter-taining the more scholarly of our guests in the Blue Room. Now, where may I introduce you?"

"Lady Melbourne, you are very kind." Bingley bowed again to his hostess, then looked uncertainly at Darcy. "I hardly know where to begin . . ."

"Then allow me to choose for you, Mr. Bingley." She turned and, after appraising those near her, gracefully lifted her fan and motioned to a young woman who immediately excused herself from her distinguished companion and came to her. "My dear Miss Cecil, allow me to introduce to you Mr. Bingley, a particular friend of our Mr. Darcy. Mr. Bingley, Miss Cecil, grandniece to the marquess of Salisbury, Hertfordshire." Darcy watched as Bingley made his bow, wishing the young woman were better known to him. She curtsied prettily to his friend and to him, but there was a haughtiness in her air he could not like, although she was a very well-looking woman.

"Miss Cecil"—Bingley's open smile set about working its usual charm—"should you like to dance or—"

"Of course she wishes to dance, Mr. Bingley; do you not, my dear?" Lady Melbourne smiled archly at Miss Cecil, who, quickly exchanging a glance with Her Ladyship, nodded her agreement and took Bingley's proffered arm.

"Then dance we shall, Miss Cecil, if you will be so kind as to show me the way. Darcy," he tossed over his shoulder to his friend, "you shall have to do without me. Good luck! Lady Melbourne." He bowed and was soon lost in the crowd of guests, leaving Darcy with no doubt that he had been expertly outmaneuvered and wondering where, in Heaven's name, Dy had gotten himself.

"There, Darcy, your young friend is well engaged." Lady Melbourne lightly rapped his arm with her fan. "Now you need no longer play nurse to the charming puppy and may amuse yourself with no encumbrance." She looked up at him, then, from under lowered lashes. "And what *does* amuse you, Darcy? Sefton was quite right; you never *do* come. Yet you are here! I wonder what could be the reason."

"The reason, dear lady, is as plain as a pikestaff," a voice intoned from behind her. Darcy's left brow shot up as a splendid figure in the glossiest of black frock coats and the snowiest of starched linen came to stand before them. A circle of onlookers immediately formed while the man proceeded to favor Darcy with a minute scrutiny, one hand held behind his back as the other cupped his chin, the index finger tapping his cheek.

"And that reason is—" Lady Melbourne began but was cut off with a swiftly upraised palm.

"Hisssst, I must have *quiet*, madam!"

Her Ladyship rolled her eyes at Darcy in apology, but his attention was wholly upon his examiner, whom he watched with narrowed hauteur. The silence demanded by Society's unchallenged arbiter of Fashion spread outward, catching the notice of more and more of the other guests. Darcy drew himself up even straighter, determined not to reveal his distaste for this display to the man's insolent gaze or deliver the setdown that hovered on his tongue, either of which he knew would be a deadly error. Even the prince submitted to the man's exquisite taste.

"Hmm," the man commented as he looked at Darcy from one side, then the other. Then, suddenly, "What!" and he stepped closer, peering through a gold-handled quizzing glass, which had dangled from a fob at his waistcoat. "Ah, yes, I see!" Heaving a great sigh, the man retreated a pace and finally looked into Darcy's face. "What is it called?"

Darcy's lips twitched briefly at the resignation in the man's voice, but he retained his stony aspect, replying indifferently, "The Roquet."

The other's brows rose at that. "Rather a bold name, wouldn't you say? Fletcher?"

Darcy inclined his head slightly. "Fletcher."

"Come now, Brummell, do not keep us all in suspense." Dy's welcome voice reached Darcy, who turned to see him shoulder his way to where they stood. "More than a few guineas are put down on this. What is the verdict, man?"

The entire room gasped in astonishment as the Beau offered Darcy a deep obeisance. "Let it be known: the Roquet is a masterpiece, worthy of the highest acclaim, and in the face of such genius, I hereby place my own creation, the Sphinx, in honorable retirement."

"Surely, Brummell, you do not mean to say that Mr. Darcy has come merely to issue challenge to your cravat!" Lady Melbourne's protest was almost lost in the general shouts at the Beau's astonishing concession and the totting up of guineas lost or won by it.

"But that is precisely what I mean, ma'am." Brummell lazily turned his quizzing glass upon her. "Although I could not attach the term *merely* to such a matter. I am quite cast down, Your Ladyship, *quite* cast down. My one consolation is that I have been bested by a true artist. Do observe, ma'am, the foldings here and the knot thus—"

"Brummell, if you wish to conduct a lesson, I will gladly put a room at your disposal, but Mr. Darcy—"

The Beau turned and surprised Darcy with a wink only he could see, saying, "Heavens no, Your Ladyship! If I spilled all I knew, who would pay me the least attention thereafter?" He bowed to them both, intoned "Your servant, Darcy," and sauntered away, only to stop suddenly before a gentleman and in a few moments declaim, "My dear fellow, you call *that* a waistcoat?"

Lady Melbourne laughed lightly and drew Darcy's arm to her

once again. "I had not thought you a rival of Brummell's, Darcy. How is it that I have not heard of this before? And who is Fletcher?"

"*Rival* I most certainly am not, Your Ladyship," he answered forcefully. The appreciative look that she returned him on this declaration caused a flush to begin creeping up his collar.

She looked away, as if determining a route through the crowded room. "And Fletcher?" The smile she turned back upon him was one of polite interest only.

"My valet, ma'am."

"Yes, of course." She indicated a direction, and Darcy could not but escort her. Out of nowhere, Dy fell in beside them.

"Lady Melbourne, please allow me to say what a shocking crush you have accomplished tonight! It but lacks the regent's presence to be the biggest 'do' since the fete at Carlton House."

"Brougham, you exaggerate obscenely, but I forgive you for it. I hope you will not be disappointed when I tell you that dear Prinny will not be coming tonight, and further that I have resisted furnishing my guests with a fish-stocked stream down the length of my table."

Brougham's face fell dramatically. "Ma'am, I had not heard! But this news is most distressing. Darcy, did you hear? The prince is not to come—"

"Darcy," the lady interrupted, turning her attention back to him, "were you at the fete at Carlton House? I do not recall you there, but in such a confusion one can easily miss even one's greatest friends."

"No, ma'am, I was not in London at the time."

"Not in London! I distinctly remember you accompanying me to the Grand Review only days before," Dy said, looking at him curiously over the top of Lady Melbourne's headdress.

"I was in Ramsgate . . . visiting my sister, my lord." Darcy returned him a hard stare, hoping to discourage further discussion.

"Visiting your sister, Darcy, instead of attending the prince's fete!" Lady Melbourne looked up at him closely. "What an uncommonly attentive brother you are! But that is your reputation, sir. You are attentive to all your concerns, as was your dear father before you."

Darcy bowed his head in acknowledgment of her compliment. "That is high praise indeed, my lady."

"I wonder, sir, are you attentive as well to the broader concerns?"

Chill fingers of warning played down Darcy's back and were only heightened by the slight narrowing of Dy's eyes above the lady's head. "Broader concerns, ma'am?"

"Concerns that lay beyond the charming borders of Pemberley, beyond even Derbyshire."

"I hope I am a good and loyal subject of the king, my lady," Darcy hedged. He looked again to his friend, but Dy only shrugged and appeared exceedingly bored.

"As are we all, Darcy," Lady Melbourne replied smoothly. "But the tiller is not in His Majesty's hands alone, and at times, the course of the ship of state must be amended, different stars followed, to bring it safely to port." She stopped their progress through the guest-thronged hall and indicated a door that opened from it. "Let me introduce you to some of those whose broad concerns encompass all our smaller ones."

The door cracked open upon Lady Melbourne's soft knock, and while she conducted a whispered exchange with the servant who stood within, Darcy cocked a brow at Dy in indication that *now* would be an excellent time to bring his vaunted social acumen to bear and forestall their proceeding any further into Her Ladyship's toils. But as his friend was unaccountably absorbed in a study of the lace at his cuff and returned him no answer, there appeared to be nothing for it. So, frowning in irritation, Darcy reluctantly crossed the threshold into the room when it opened for them.

The handsome salon into which they were admitted was not overly crowded, but it was decidedly masculine in its occupation;

not a single female was present save their hostess. Lady Melbourne smiled at Darcy reassuringly as she held out her hand to a gentleman who was nodding to the servant she had sent. The man's eyes narrowed as he observed them at the door, but he moved quickly enough to Her Ladyship's side. "Lady Melbourne," he greeted her tersely with a tight smile and short bow.

"Lamb," the lady addressed her son, her smile wide but somewhat brittle, "are you acquainted with Mr. Fitzwilliam Darcy, Derbyshire?"

The Honorable William Lamb allowed himself another tight smile. "Yes, ma'am, although not so well as I should like. Your servant, sir." He bowed to Darcy. Darcy returned the courtesy, shocked that he had not recognized the man. The years since he had attended Lamb's marriage ceremony had not, evidently, been kind ones, leaving a man Darcy knew to be his senior by only four years looking much worn.

"I am certain you know Lord Brougham," Lady Melbourne continued, "as he is always here, there, and about."

"Yes, of course, Your Ladyship. It was that shooting party of Grenville's the last time, wasn't it, Lamb?"

"I believe you are right, Brougham. Caught nothing but a cold that day, but marvelous geography, as I remember." Lamb's features relaxed somewhat at the memory but cooled again before he turned pointedly to his parent, saying, "Madam, you must not neglect the rest of your guests. I shall take these two in hand."

The flash of fire in her eyes was unmistakable. "Then I shall leave you to it!" Lady Melbourne curtsied, and in a swirl of skirts left them.

"A formidable lady," Dy murmured as they watched her leave.

"Indeed!" Lamb returned with feeling. "But now, gentlemen, I must ask you a question: Did you seek us out"—his hand swept the room—"or were you press-ganged by Her Ladyship?" Dy chuckled at the allusion but made no answer, leaving Darcy to smooth their way.

"Lady Melbourne is not a woman I should wish to gainsay."
Darcy hesitated, then added wryly, "Even were I given the opportunity."

A genuine smile then spread across Lamb's features. He offered his hand to Darcy. "Well said, sir, and quite politic of you! Perhaps you are in the right place after all! But, in truth, you have come tonight to hear the diva my mother has promised, not to argue politics; is that not so?"

Darcy took his hand in a firm grasp. "You have it, sir, although I am not uninterested in the 'broader concerns' as Her Ladyship described them. Rather, I believe we should find ourselves on opposite sides of the room on many issues."

"The Darcys were ever a Tory lot," Lamb groused in jest. I suppose there is no hope of you throwing for Canning against Castlereagh? I thought not!" he concluded at Darcy's polite grimace. "And I know far better than to solicit Brougham here, who has as much interest in politics as does a fence post." Dy's answering bow elegantly acknowledged Lamb's perspicacity in the matter. "Ah well, it is all one with the events of the day. You have heard that our illustrious regent will not appear tonight?"

"Lady Melbourne said as much," Darcy replied. "The duties of state have commanded his attention, no doubt."

"No, actually it was the demands of His Highness's tailors that commanded his attention! After he summoned his ministers upon a matter of 'vital concern' and kept them waiting upon his arrival for the entire day, a note was sent round to the effect that his tailors had delayed him and that now his mama was in want of him; and they should all go home! So tonight he takes his aches and pains and imagined maladies to be soothed at Windsor." Lamb looked at Darcy keenly. "I suppose you can guess that I am not in charity with His Highness at the moment, I nor anyone else in this room." Lamb paused as Darcy cast his gaze over the occupants of the salon. The mood was decidedly rancorous. Angry words often broke through the hum of strident voices as Britain's Whig aristocracy and politicians gnashed their teeth over the regent's latest ill treatment of his avowed friends and supporters.

"It was not well done of His Highness, certainly," Darcy agreed. "Although I cannot be unhappy with the result of his negligence. What shall you do now?"

"We have not totally consigned ourselves to returning to the wilderness as yet! We have had our forty years and more of wandering under His Highness's father and rather thought that, with the son, we had finally arrived at the Promised Land. But the blasted Jericho walls refuse to fall down! Canning is determined to continue storming them, though, and deny Castlereagh and Perceval. I shall, of course, support him."

A discreet cough reminded both men that Lord Brougham was a party to their conversation. "Oh, pardon me, Lamb! Didn't mean to interrupt! Just a thought, though. Trumpets!"

"Trumpets?" Lamb looked uncomprehendingly at him and then to Darcy.

"Trumpets," repeated Brougham firmly.

"Brougham," Lamb growled impatiently, "what are you playing at?"

"Didn't *storm* Jericho to bring the walls down, now did they? Blew trumpets and shouted, as I recall." Brougham looked down modestly, examining his perfectly pared fingernails. "P'rhaps you fellows ought to look into it."

"A theologian is among us!" Lamb shook his head derisively. "I never would have guessed you for a parson, Brougham, any more than a politician." He looked then at a group whose disappointment in the day's events was threatening to spill over acceptable bounds. "Although your point is taken, and I shall endeavor to be more accurate with my metaphors. Gentlemen"—he gestured toward his discordant guests—"I must leave you to your own devices and take charge of the room before Bloody Revolution is declared. Then the Tories *would* have our carcasses! Darcy . . . Brougham."

As Lamb walked away in the direction of the thundering voices, Darcy turned to his friend. "Great lot of help you were!" he muttered in disgust.

"Don't be an ass, Fitz. I got rid of him for you; did I not?" Gone was the vacant-eyed fribble of moments before, and in his place Darcy beheld a man with an edge of steel to his voice. "All we need do now is walk out the door."

"Dy, what is this?" he demanded sharply.

"A very interesting evening, I would say, and not over yet!" The smile Dy cast upon Darcy was broad and guileless, giving him to doubt his previous impression. "But we have left your friend Mr. Bingley unsupervised quite long enough, I should think." Dy strolled to the door, turning back to Darcy as the servant opened it. "Oughtn't we go find him?"

"Bingley!" Conscience-stricken, Darcy advanced to the threshold, and together the two hurried down the corridor and across the hall, and shouldered their way up to the crowd-thronged archway leading to the ballroom. All that could be seen of the great room beyond were the blazing candles held aloft in glittering chandeliers of cut glass festooned with twinings of holly, ivy, and gold cord in honor of the approaching season. The music of the ensemble within gave Darcy pause; it was not the staid and stately measures that usually denoted a *ton* ball, nor the tunes of popular country dances. Rather, the music held a distinct rhythm based on three that Darcy found pleasing to the ear.

With Dy close behind, he politely made his way through the onlookers crowding the door. Achieving the last ring of spectators before the floor, Darcy made a final plea to be let through and, lifting his head to begin his search for Bingley, was brought to a standstill. Wide-eyed, he turned to his friend.

"What is it, Fitz?" Dy asked, and then followed Darcy's stare as it returned to the ballroom floor. "Hah!" he laughed. "I had heard rumors but did not credit them. Well, one should never doubt a scandalous story if Lady Caroline is at its center. It is called the waltz, Fitz."

"It's indecent!" Darcy expostulated in fascinated disgust.

"That may be, but it will, no doubt, become all the rage."

"Rage or no—" A wave of opprobrious gasps mixed with appreciative cheers and lewd laughter interrupted his declaration. The music stopped, leaving the couples on the floor in apprehension and all eyes straining for the source of the excitement. A private entrance to the room lay open to Darcy's left, and from its secrecy he saw emerge the tawny-crowned person of Lady Caroline Lamb on the arm of a gentleman quite unknown to him. From where he stood he could see only her face, her delicate chin raised high, her eyes glittering in amusement and daring. As she and her companion made their way through the throng, it parted before them, and Darcy noted more than a few faces of both ladies and gentlemen color and turn away from the procession.

Suddenly, an older woman sank in a faint, the gentlemen nearest to her crying out in dismay. Several young ladies followed her example, and soon the floor was littered here and there with insensible females being coaxed back to consciousness by alarmed young men who, nonetheless, craned their necks to catch another glimpse of the source of the uproar. More than a few women were being propelled from the room by insistent husbands or fathers amid shouts for carriages and cloaks.

"What the devil is going on?" Darcy demanded of the chaos around him. Dy tugged at his sleeve and solemnly pointed back down the room to where Lady Caroline and her swain had finally broken free from her mother-in-law's guests. Darcy's jaw dropped in disbelief while his own face flooded crimson. "Great God in Heaven, she's . . . she's . . . Her clothes!"

"Yes . . . what little there are of them," interposed Dy in a lowered voice. "I believe the effect is achieved by sprinkling the sheerest of gowns with water."

The music was beginning again, and several giggling couples had joined Lady Caroline and her escort on the floor when a high-pitched wail from behind them caused Darcy and Dy to whirl about just in time to be pushed out of the way by a stately-looking woman who strode to the fore, shrieking all the while in a flood of Italian.

"L'Catalani," whispered Dy, "and she is *most* displeased." Darcy's Italian was somewhat neglected, but he understood enough to recognize the tenor of the lady's complaint. Comparisons of Lady Caroline with certain Covent Garden strumpets and the depth of the insult her appearance in such dishabille had offered to the diva were thoroughly explored before the Melbourne footmen arrived to escort the lady to her carriage. On her way she passed the rigid figure of the lady's husband, to whom she gave a most pitying look before exclaiming, "The English! Bah!" and hurried out the door.

One glance at Lamb's face was all Darcy could stomach, and as the man walked determinedly toward his wife, Darcy grabbed Dy's arm. "Bingley must be found immediately, and then do what you will, for we are leaving."

"A very sensible notion." Dy had to shout to be heard above the din. "How can I be of service?"

"My coachman and groom are waiting at the Bull 'n' Boar. Find them and tell them to ready my carriage immediately. Bingley and I will meet you at the corner."

Dy nodded crisply and plunged into the stream of guests struggling to depart. Darcy turned back to his search and, aided by his height, became quickly convinced that Bingley was not in the ballroom. He made, then, for the supper room, pushing his way through without apology until he finally stood before its open doors and peered in.

"Bingley!" Charles looked up at his name being bellowed across the room and, with an expression of undisguised relief, excused himself from Miss Cecil and hurried to Darcy.

"Where have you been, Darcy? I've been trying to entertain

Miss Cecil for nigh onto an hour, ever since they started that new dancing, which, I hope you will not take this amiss, is not quite the thing, if you get my meaning."

"Charles, we must leave, now!" Darcy interrupted. "Something extremely untoward has—is— We're going!" he commanded in exasperation. Charles gave him a startled look but offered no resistance. Making a hurried bow to Miss Cecil, he followed Darcy into the hall and to the steps, where after issuing an imperious command, Darcy was able to obtain their hats and cloaks. They barely waited for the doorman to perform his duty before Darcy had them stepping out into the frigid night air.

"What in Heaven's name happened?" Bingley demanded, slapping his hands against his sides as they made their way down the sidewalk. "Why are so many leaving, Darcy?"

"Because not everyone has taken leave of their senses!" was all the answer Darcy was willing to offer. The evening had been, in truth, an unmitigated disaster. How had such a simple plan gone so very wrong? A shout caused the two men to look to the street, where they beheld Darcy's carriage pulling smartly up to the curb. Harry leapt down and opened the door. The vehicle's noble occupant leaned out, filling the doorway.

"Brougham's Hackney Service! Can I take you two gentlemen anywhere?"

"Brougham . . . Bingley. Bingley . . . Lord Dyfed Brougham. Now move aside, Dy!" Darcy followed Bingley into the carriage and then turned to his groom. "Harry, let's go home."

CHAPTER 13

The Wounds of a Friend

"Mr. Darcy!" a much surprised Witcher exclaimed as he opened the great front door of Erewile House to admit his master and two companions several hours in advance of when he had been expected.

"Brandy in the library, if you please, Witcher." Darcy flung his cloak and other accoutrements into the hands of the downstairs footman and motioned his friends to do the same. "And direct whatever kitchen staff is about to see what may be had to eat."

"Nothing for me, Darcy," Bingley broke in. "Had enough of those dashed biscuits to founder a horse while I was entertaining Miss Cecil. Or trying to," he added in an undertone.

"Well enough! Gentlemen, if you please?" Darcy indicated the stairs to the library and then led the way. Once inside, his friends disposed themselves in the comfortable chairs to await the ordered trays. A thoughtful silence pervaded the air as Darcy leaned down and stoked up the fire in the hearth.

"Here now," Bingley's straining curiosity broke the quiet. "Will someone tell me what happened that turned the soiree out into the street? My lord"—he turned to Brougham—"I apply to you, sir, as Darcy will not breathe a word of it."

Brougham looked over to their host, his brows peaked in question. "He's bound to read it in the scandal sheets tomorrow, Fitz."

"True, but it is to be hoped we got out in time."

"In time for what? What scandal is this?" Bingley looked back and forth between them. "I demand to know!"

"In time, my dear Mr. Bingley, to avoid having your initials printed in the newspaper as a participant in the bacchanalia we just left," Brougham dryly informed him. "For you, sir, I have every hope, but for Fitz . . . Well"—he sighed dramatically—"it is unlikely *he* will escape mention. Not after having brought Brummell to his knees! Oho, I think not!"

Darcy met Dy's snicker with a thunderous frown, but at the last bit his countenance dropped. "Brummell! I had forgotten! The blasted cravat!" He fell into a chair and nursed his temples.

"*Darcy* bested the Beau?" Bingley sat up straight and peered at both men, trying to detect if they were playing him a joke.

"Win, place, and show! Unmanned the trumpery fellow to the point that he retired the Sphinx! By the by, Fitz, when do you give Fletcher the news?" Darcy's searing glare and Bingley's guarded disbelief encouraged Brougham into further displays of mirth, which were curbed only by a knock on the library door.

"Enter!" Darcy growled, and in moments several trays of food wafted their way through the door and onto tables. He rose and poured a round as the servants quietly left, and handed the glasses to the others. "I would propose a toast, if I could think of one," he muttered, "but at the moment—"

"To friendship," Brougham interrupted him in a quiet but firm voice. Darcy studied him for several heartbeats; the regard Brougham returned him was both steady and warm. Under such an onslaught, it was not long before a grin reluctantly tugged at the corners of his mouth.

"To friendship, then!" he responded, and held out his glass. Brougham brought his up, and Bingley eagerly joined his to them both, vowing the same. Tossing back the contents with a laugh, the three fell upon the viands supplied by Darcy's staff and then settled back into the comfortable depths of cushions before the hearth.

While Dy regaled Bingley with an account of the events of the evening far more humorous than he recalled experiencing, Darcy watched Charles closely. It had not gone at all well. In point of fact, it had well nigh been a disaster, and he could not help but wince at the thought of what the morning papers would bring. As Charles was alternately amused and astounded by Brougham's narrative, Darcy sensed an underlying wistfulness in his friend's demeanor. When he answered Dy's questions concerning Miss Cecil, Darcy's unease was confirmed as Charles tentatively compared the lady unfavorably with one he had but lately met in Hertfordshire.

"Hertfordshire! Darcy told me. Will you offer?"

"Dy!" Darcy warned.

"On the estate. Make an offer on the estate." Brougham made a face at him, then turned his attention back to Bingley.

"I had been considering it," Bingley replied, oblivious to the exchange, "and had almost made up my mind. But now I am not sure. Darcy advises me to take more time and look about."

"That is, in general, excellent advice; but there may be other considerations."

"Yes," Bingley agreed, rather too quickly for Darcy's peace. "I thought there might be, but Darcy . . . Well; I could be mistaken."

"I see . . ." Brougham let the thought dangle. "Quite right to be sure of your ground before charging your fences. Did I tell you about Samson, Fitz?" Brougham leaned back into his chair. "Lost him at Melton, the old sod!"

"No!" Darcy responded feelingly to the regret in his friend's voice. At Bingley's question, he explained, "Brougham's favorite horse, and gotten by the same sire as my Nelson. What happened, Dy?"

"Stupid accident, really. I have been over Melton any number of times, know it like the back of my hand; save that this year one of the local landowners took his fields out of the run. I arrived too late to have a look at the new fields and, for certain 'considerations,' which I shall not name, rashly joined the fray." He paused to sip at his brandy and looked solemnly across to Bingley. "There was a hedge, you see, tallest I have ever tried and, unknown to me, a ditch on the other side like to reach China. Samson took the hedge like a hero, but the ditch caught us both by surprise. We went down hard, but Samson took the brunt of it, allowing me to roll away with only a twisted ankle and a bruised shoulder. I had always laughed at the formality of Melton: the pistol and shot in the saddlebag and all that. But I tell you now, that day I was glad of it. To condemn him to hours of such pain while I dragged myself off to find a farmer . . . and all because of my folly—" Brougham stopped abruptly and looked down into the amber liquid in his glass before taking a swallow. "Be sure of your ground, my friends, be damn sure."

The crackle of the fire in the hearth was all that disturbed the silence for a few moments after Brougham's adjuration. From under lowered eyelids, Darcy observed Bingley's response to Dy's story and was gratified to see the thoughtful turn of his manner. He glanced then over at Brougham, nodding his head in thanks for his help.

Dy gave him an almost imperceptible shrug of his shoulders accompanied by a quick, tight smile and then rose to his feet. "Gentlemen, I must bid you good night. This has been a very eventful, not to mention *revealing*, evening. I think it safe to say we saw more of some people than we bargained for." Groans interrupted him, but he persisted. "And were *exposed*"—more groans— "to some new experiences." As Bingley chuckled over his puns, Brougham offered him his hand. "Mr. Bingley, a pleasure, sir!"

"The pleasure is entirely mine, Lord Brougham!" Bingley clasped his hand and bowed over it, utterly pleased to have been granted entree into His Lordship's interest.

"Fitz"—Brougham turned to Darcy—"I doubt I will see you again before you leave for Pemberley. You *will* give my love to Georgiana?"

"Have no fear!"

"Good! Send me a note when you return to Town, or I shall have to try to bribe Witcher again, much good will it do me. Oh! Give Fletcher my very best regards and congratulations. Would it puff him up too much if I sent him a token of my esteem? The expression on Brummell's face was one I shall meditate upon with glee for days to come."

"I am tempted to put him into your hands entirely! Charles"— Darcy turned to him—"excuse me a moment while I accompany Brougham to the door." At Bingley's nod, Darcy ushered his friend out into the hall, pausing only to assure himself of the click of the library door. With a jerk of his head, he led Brougham down the hall to the steps.

"Dy"—he laid a hand on Brougham's arm—"my sincere condolences on Samson; he was a magnificent animal."

"Yes, he was, was he not?" Brougham sighed as they descended the stairs. "As I said, 'a hero'! It could have been *me* with the broken neck. Any chance of Nelson getting his like?"

"I shall look into it, I promise you." Darcy glanced about and, seeing no servants, continued, "But I really wished to detain you in order to thank you. Your story has given Bingley pause, I think."

"Do you really?" They reached the front hall, where Witcher and the footman on duty hurried forth with His Lordship's outer apparel. "Interesting, that!"

"Why? What do you mean?"

Brougham slipped on his cloak and placed his beaver jauntily atop his head. "Because the story was for *your* benefit! There is more to Hertfordshire than you have told me, old friend. I know you wish to do Bingley a service in this affair, and he may well be in need of it, but 'ware yourself, Fitz. Make sure of your ground and doubly sure of the nature of your interest." Brougham clapped him roughly on his shoulder. "Good night, then, and Happy Christmas! Witcher"—he turned a broad smile upon the old man—"my compliments to your lovely wife, and a Happy Christmas to you as well."

"Thank you, Your Lordship, and a Happy Christmas to you, sir!"

As Witcher closed the door upon Brougham, Darcy climbed the stairs back to the library, distracted by Dy's parting remark.

"Darcy." Bingley's sudden appearance from the shadows at the top of the stairs sent Darcy's thoughts skittering. "It is getting rather late. I believe I shall take myself off as well." Darcy turned, and they both descended the stairs. "What an evening!"

"Agreed, and one I intend never to repeat!" Darcy rejoined. "I shall take my chances at Drury Lane to hear L'Catalani in the future."

"Oh, that's right, we never *did* hear the diva! But really, Darcy, I have never seen such opulence and elegance in my life! Everything was in the height of fashion and taste. Although there were more than a few whom I would not hesitate to call 'high in the instep,' many were quite amiable. And Brummell, Darcy! To think *you* cast him in the shade!"

"Yes, well, the less said about that, the better I will like it."

"As Lord Brougham said, there is not much likelihood of that! He is a great gun, is he not? Such condescension." They reached the bottom, and Bingley took his things from the footman. "Great pity about his horse. Makes one think, does it not?"

Darcy looked steadily into Bingley's now sober countenance. "Making sure of your ground before you take the fence?"

"Yes . . . quite." Bingley took a deep breath. "I begin to see the wisdom in your counsel. I was rushing my fences, not sure of the ground, and disregarding the warnings of a friend," he confessed. "I must think about Miss Bennet rationally, as you have advised me."

Darcy ruthlessly suppressed his elation at Bingley's words. "That is all I could wish for, Charles," he responded quietly. "Proper reflection on the matter will, I am certain, yield a satisfactory answer." Although the smile Bingley returned him was weak and wistfulness had returned to shadow his eyes, Darcy allowed himself to hope that his campaign was nearing a triumphant conclusion. If Miss Bingley could add to his counsel a suitably disinterested testimony corroborating Miss Bennet's indifference, the matter would be resolved, he was sure of it. A note must be sent immediately.

"Good night then, Darcy. Dinner at Grenier's on Sunday?"

"Make it Monday after I beard Lawrence in his den, and I shall be there."

"Lawrence!"

"Yes, I intend him to paint Georgiana when I bring her back with me after Christmas. The next morning, I hope, will see me set out for Pemberley."

"Then it must be Monday! Good night, again, Darcy. Mr. Witcher."

Darcy waited until Bingley had climbed into the hack summoned for him and the driver urged his horse forward before turning from the door.

"Will that be all, Mr. Darcy?" Witcher asked, recalling him from his bemusement.

"Yes, Witcher. Dismiss the staff to their rest and have breakfast ready at ten, I think."

"Very good, sir. Shall I ring Fletcher?"

"Yes, do so! And Witcher"—he stopped the butler as he reached for the bell pull—"I shall have a note ready to send round early in the morning. No answer is desired."

"Yes, sir." Witcher pulled on the rope, and Darcy once again mounted the stairs to discharge two last duties. The first was a note to Miss Bingley; the second would be a confrontation with his now celebrated valet. When Darcy finally gained his chambers, it was to find his nightclothes neatly laid out upon his bed, hot and cold ewers of water standing at the ready, and his toiletries lying in neat ranks upon the washstand. Gone was every stitch of the clothing that had been marshaled for his inspection earlier that evening. Unappeased by Fletcher's meticulous industry, Darcy closed the chamber door with decided force and strode quickly to the center of the room, his hands clasped behind his back, summoning a grave look upon his face. The dressing room door sprang open almost before he had settled his features.

"Mr. D—"

"Fletcher, I wish to have a word with you!"

At Darcy's tone, Fletcher's eyes at first went wide and then quickly lowered. "Yes, Mr. Darcy, sir."

"I distinctly recall warning you that I had no wish to compete with Mr. Brummell nor to occasion any undue notice on anyone's part." His indignation rekindled, Darcy warmed to his subject. "I believe those were my exact instructions, were they not?"

"Yes, sir, Mr. Darcy."

"Mr. Fletcher, you have failed me, then, on both counts."

Fletcher's head came up, expressions from guilt to uncertainty and on to caution passing over his features in quick succession. "In truth, sir?"

"In excruciating truth, Fletcher! You have made me the 'glass of fashion and the mold of form,' and I do *not* thank you for it! As it happens, I should have liked to have passed unnoticed at Melbourne House this evening; but, thanks to this blasted cravat, there was no chance of that. I find myself now in a most disagreeable position." He began pacing the room. " '*Measure for Measure,*' you said. Little did I realize that you meant Brummell! Were you aware that he knows you by name, man?"

"I had heard rumors . . ." Fletcher's face blanched white, in guilt or surprise, Darcy could not tell.

"Rumors! I wonder you are not in direct communication! They were laying bets, Fletcher, bets!" Darcy stopped only a pace away from his valet, whose eyes had once more returned to the floor. "I will not have it, Fletcher, I absolutely will not have it! If you desire to valet a fashion card, you have my leave to find one who delights in preening before Society. But if you will continue in my employ, you will content yourself with my simpler requirements." He turned away, sat down on his dressing chair, and growled, "Now untie this infernal thing."

"Yes, Mr. Darcy." Fletcher approached him carefully and with expert fingers began disassembling the intricate article. "Mr. Darcy?" he asked after working out the knot.

"Yes, Fletcher?"

"If I may, sir . . . Exactly *how* grievously did I fail you tonight, sir?"

Darcy looked at him measuredly. Anxiety and pride waged undisguised war on a countenance that was usually closed to him. Fletcher's excellent control was in near shambles, and given his intimate relationship with the man, Darcy had to consider the reason why. That he had succeeded in intimidating Fletcher he dismissed out of hand. No, the answer was not to be found in his anxiety; therefore, he must look to the man's pride. He cleared his throat. "The Sphinx is retired."

Fletcher's hands trembled. "*That* grievously, sir!" He, too, cleared his throat. "Please allow me to offer my most humble apologies and beg you would not 'think too precisely on the event.'" The offending neckcloth lay now in a limp heap on the dressing table.

"Humph," Darcy snorted, and looked askance at his valet. He had guessed aright; Fletcher had succumbed to the siren call of his art, and by bringing the celebrated arbiter of fashion to heel, he had unquestionably achieved the pinnacle of his profession. A wave of understanding and sympathy for Fletcher's pride in his art swept through Darcy, but it was soon tempered by the remembrance that the success had been won on *his* unsuspecting and unwilling person. Fletcher appeared truly chastened, and the inconvenience of securing in a new valet . . . He shook his head. The man had been with him since he finished University, and he could not imagine instructing a new one in all those preferences that Fletcher comprehended so well. Firmness seemed to be what was called for and, perhaps, an olive branch.

"I suppose 'things without all remedy should be without regard. What's done is done,' but, Fletcher, do not serve me this kind of trick again. 'More matter and less art.' Do you understand?"

"Yes, sir." The relief in Fletcher's voice and mien was palpable.

"Do not imagine that I am entirely mollified," Darcy continued as he rose for Fletcher to help him out of his frock coat. "Until some fellow trumps your Roquet, I will be forced to suffer any number of fools wanting to know how it is done. Thank Heaven I leave for Pemberley soon."

" 'The quality of mercy is not str——' " the valet began, quoting the Bard with sincerity.

"Yes, well, I beg you will not allow this triumph of yours and its attendant notoriety to interfere with your duties or those of the rest of this household."

"No, sir," replied his valet. The sapphirine waistcoat was eased from Darcy's shoulders, and as he turned to watch Fletcher's careful folding of his clothes in preparation to quit the room, it was plain that the man's equanimity had been overbalanced this night. The entire month had been far too unsettling for both of them.

"Fletcher," Darcy called as his valet moved toward the door, "Lord Brougham desired me to extend his congratulations."

"He did, sir! Lord Brougham is most kind."

"He wished you to know that the expression on Brummell's face as he surveyed his defeat at your hands will entertain him for days to come. And Fletcher," he ended, "my guarded congratulations as well."

"Thank you, Mr. Darcy!" Fletcher bowed deeply.

They bade each other a good night, and Darcy turned to readying for bed, devoutly praying that his task of dissuading Bingley was near an end and that nothing would stand in the way of a speedy withdrawal to Pemberley. Both of them might there recoup their balance. Everything would return to the way it had been.

Darcy shook out the pages of the *Morning Post* and methodically refolded the paper before finishing a last piece of buttered toast and draining his cup of morning coffee. The news he had missed while in Hertfordshire was shocking and disturbing, the latest incidents of public disturbance chasing the reports of the scandal at Melbourne House off the front pages of the *Post* and making him all the more eager to complete his business and quit London for Pemberley as soon as possible. He consulted his pocket watch; it still lacked three-quarters of an hour before his business agent was due in the library. Not, Darcy sighed as he returned the watch to his pocket, that there were not more personal reasons than alarm at the rioting of weavers in the Midlands to cause his disquiet with his situation in London.

He pushed back his chair and, rising, walked over to the window overlooking the greensward of Grosvenor Square, now blanketed with snow. The trees of the park were dark sentinels against the whiteness, save for the upper branches, whose thready fingers were delicately encased in ice that sparkled in the midmorning sun. Darcy took a deep breath and let it out slowly, covering one of the window's chill panes with vapor that hardened to frost on the pane, so cold was the day. He ran his finger up through the ice, drawing a tiny Punch against the starry backdrop of frost. How many years had it been since he had drawn frost pictures for Georgiana? Ten? Every bit of ten, he was certain.

He curled his fingers into a fist and with its side obliterated the clown and the stars as he finished his review of his campaign thus far. No, the necessities that bound him to London chafed sorely, but no matter in what manner he examined the problem, he was fairly caught between his promises to Miss Bingley and his own concern over his friend. He was obliged to see it to a conclusion.

The meeting with his business agent proved blessedly short, and Darcy found himself free to indulge in the one activity in his short visit to Town that he had anticipated with pleasure: the selection of Christmas gifts for his sister. As the heavily swathed James and Harry argued up on the box over the best route to Piccadilly given the early morning's snowfall, Darcy turned his attention to the coming season and all its attendant responsibilities. Both Mr. Witcher in London and Mr. Reynolds at Pemberley had received funds for gifts for the staff under their respective rules. Hinchcliffe would countenance for himself nothing more personal than a holiday purse each year, which, Darcy suspected, he had by now parlayed into quite a nest egg. Fletcher's Christmas gift had always been the same as well: transportation to his family's home in Nottingham for a week and a tidy sum to lighten the hearts and ease the lives of his aging parents. Quite a tidy sum this year, if the weight of Dy's tribute to Fletcher's genius, which had arrived this morning, was any indicator. Darcy snorted to himself as the carriage pulled to a stop at Hatchards. Harry had the door open and the steps down almost immediately.

"It be a cold 'un today, Mr. Darcy, sir." He shivered despite his coat and muffler.

"Indeed, Harry! Tell James to keep the horses moving, and you may come with me."

"Thank 'e, sir. James!" Harry went over to the box to give the instructions and hurried back to follow Darcy into the establishment. The bell on the door rang merrily as they entered, bringing Mr. Hatchard's eyes up from his counter.

"Mr. Darcy, so good to see you, sir!" He advanced upon them. Darcy nodded Harry's dismissal to the servants' waiting room before returning the greeting. "And how have you enjoyed the volumes sent to you in Hertfordshire? I trust they arrived satisfactorily?"

"Yes, you are most obliging, Hatchard. Anything more in that line?"

"No, sir, not even a whisper. Wellesley's in winter quarters in Portugal, you know. Perhaps, between parties and balls, someone may find the time to scribble a few lines. I look for a number of manuscripts to arrive in the spring and will certainly keep you apprised."

"Very good! I am looking for something for Miss Darcy today. Do you have any suggestions?"

"Miss Darcy! Ah, there is so much, despite what Mr. Walter Scott may think." Mr. Hatchard led him over to an alcove furnished with a table and chairs. In a few moments a stack of volumes were set before him. Darcy paged through the selections, his nose wrinkling over most, if not giving them a frown, in statement of review. Settling on Miss Porter's *The Scottish Chiefs* and Miss Edgeworth's latest volume of *Tales from Fashionable Life*, he set them on the counter to be wrapped and sauntered down an aisle to browse.

"Darcy! I say, Darcy, what good fortune!" Darcy looked up from the shelf he was perusing to see "Poodle" Byng coming toward him, his trademark canine companion trotting in his wake.

And now it begins. Darcy cast a beseeching glance toward Heaven.

"Darcy, old man, what *was* that knot you was wearin' at Melbourne's last night? Dashed complicated thing. Had the Beau in a snit for the rest of the evening. Bit off poor Skeffington's head over his waistcoat, don't you know." Poodle's genial smile transformed into one of unwarranted intimacy as he continued. "S'fellow told me it was called the Roquefort, but I told 'im I didn't believe it. 'It ain't the Roquefort,' says I. 'Roquefort's a cheese, you muttonhead.' It was Vasingstoke said it; everyone knows he was kicked in the brainbox by his pony when he was first breeched. 'Roquefort's a cheese,' says I, 'and I'll lay anybody here a monkey that Darcy'd never wear a cheese round his neck,' didn't I, Pompey?" He addressed his dog, who yipped obligingly. In firm conviction, they both turned expectant eyes upon Darcy.

"No, Byng, you are quite right. It is the Roquet. And don't," he continued hurriedly, "I beg you, ask me for instructions. It is my valet's creation. Only he can tie the thing."

"The Roquet! Aha, just wait till I tell Vasingstoke. 'Strike 'im out of the game,' is it? Well, no small wonder Brummell was in such high dudgeon! But a hint only, my good fellow, is all I ask. No wish to compete, mind you; just tweak Brummell's nose a bit."

Darcy reached behind him and grabbed a book from the shelf. "Please accept my apologies and assurances that I cannot satisfy your request, Byng. I was paying no attention when Fletcher tied it and cannot begin to hint you upon the proper course. You must excuse me and will understand that I cannot keep my cattle waiting outside any longer in this weather and must take this"—he brought forward the volume—"to Hatchard." He nodded him a bow, stepped around the dog, who followed his movements with a growl, and walked quickly to the counter.

"Will that be all, Mr. Darcy?" Hatchard's eyebrows then went up in surprise as Darcy laid his subterfuge atop the other books he had chosen. "The new edition of *Practical View*! I was not aware you had interests in that area!"

"What? Oh . . . just wrap it with the rest, if you please, and ring for Harry."

In seconds Harry was at the counter and accepting the package Hatchard had carefully wrapped. Darcy followed him out the door, unwilling to wait inside until the carriage was brought and risk further importunities from Byng and his canine confidante.

Down the street, near St. James's, Darcy popped in at Hoby's to be measured for a new pair of boots. There he was forced to fend off more Roquet admirers. He then directed his driver to Leicester Square and Madame LaCoure's Silkwares Shoppe. With the modiste's guidance, he chose three lengths of silk and two of muslin, promising to return with his sister to select the appropriate laces and ribbons. Then, it was on to DeWachter's in Clerkenwell, the jeweler patronized by the Darcys for several generations, where he chose a modest but perfectly matched pearl choker and bracelet and accepted Mr. DeWachter's congratulations on his "triumph" with as much grace as he could. His last stop was the printing establishment from which Georgiana ordered her music. Sweeping up whatever new offerings there were of composers they both admired, Darcy allowed himself and his final packages to be tucked into the carriage.

"Mr. Darcy, sir?" Harry queried as he arranged the parcels and shook out the carriage robe.

"Yes, Harry?"

"What be this 'ere Roquet, sir?"

Darcy sighed heavily. "Fletcher's new way of tying a neckcloth. Why do you ask, Harry?"

"Oh, sir, I've 'ad two gentlemen offer me a golden boy each if I was to smuggle 'em into yer dressing room to see it." Harry shook his head. "Beggin' yer pardon, sir, but the Quality be a strange lot sometimes."

Darcy closed his eyes. "Truer words were never spoken. Let's go home, Harry."

❧❦❧

Upon his return from his shopping expedition, Darcy was met by Hinchcliffe with several piles of lately delivered cards and invitations entreating his attendance at a staggering number of routs, breakfasts, pugilistic exhibitions, discreet clubs, political meetings, and theatrical performances. Darcy eyed them with dismay and then threw the lot on his desk.

"Shall I send replies in the usual fashion, sir?" Hinchcliffe leaned over and neatly scooped them onto a silver tray.

"Yes. Regrets to any unknown to you beneath a baronet, sincere regrets to any above, and send the rest in to me. As it is, even should you begin immediately, I fear you will be up most of the night." Hinchcliffe inclined his head in silent agreement and departed for his office.

At the click of the door, a sudden restlessness seized Darcy, propelling him aimlessly about his library. It lacked an hour or more until supper, and although he had planned to dine alone that

evening, a perverse wish for some easy companionship gripped
him. After the New Year, when he returned to Town with Georgiana, evenings such as this could be pleasantly occupied with the
sharing of books and music with his sister. But even as he contemplated these future pleasures, he discovered, to his chagrin, that the
prospect did not entirely answer. A gaping, unnamed discontent
whose existence he had never suspected arose before him and now
threatened to rob him of his satisfaction and complacency.

His pacing brought him to a bookshelf, and with hopes that
the discipline involved in following the course of a battle would restore his thoughts to order, he plucked *Fuentes de Oñoro* from its
place and dropped into a chair by the fire. Stretching out his legs
to the hearth, he slid his finger along the pages and opened the
book to the place held for him by the embroidery threads. As he
bent to read, the words blurred in his vision, cast into incompre-
hensibility by the glint of the firelight on the knotted strands of
silk that lay across his page. Elizabeth! How he had resisted every
thought of her! His breath quickened as a flood of memories overpowered his mind: Elizabeth at the door of Netherfield, hesitant
but determined; on the stair, tired but faithful in the care of her
sister; in the drawing room, with arched brow challenging his
character; at the pianoforte, unconscious of the grace she brought
to her song; at the ball, Milton's Eve, sparkling of eye, suffused
with Edenic loveliness.

She would have laughed at Brummell's pompous distress over
a mere cravat. She would not, he was certain, have been overawed
by Lady Melbourne or fainted at Lady Caroline's scandalous display. He could almost see her in the next chair, smiling at him with
that expression which, he had begun to learn, portended something delightful. His vague discontent sharpened at the thought.
Uncertainty, delight, longing—they all had crept into his experience unaware, and alone in his home, he suddenly felt their effects
most acutely. His fingers closed around the threads. What had Dy
cautioned him? To know his ground, yes, but the other? To be

doubly sure of the nature of his interest in Bingley's affairs. How much of his interest was directed solely toward Bingley's good? Was it nearer to the truth that separating Charles from Miss Jane Bennet was his surest defense against the confliction raised by his own heedless attraction to her sister?

Darcy sat forward, his elbows on his knees, the strands cradled in his palm, and stared hard into the glowing embers. He wished his friend the greatest felicity in marriage, to be sure. At least as great as was reasonable to expect in unions of like fortune and class. His own future married state he barely thought upon except in terms of avoidance. His estates and businesses were well managed and prosperous, making a marriage of interest unnecessary and giving him the freedom to pick when and where he chose in hope of some degree of happiness. There were often times in the night that he wished for the comforts of marriage, and occasionally a face and figure had tugged at his vitals. But the reality of spending his life with and entrusting his people to one of the frail minds and hardened natures behind the pretty faces that recommended themselves to him in those dark, silent hours had always succeeded in convincing him of the folly of trading his happiness for his comfort. He knew that both were possible; he had seen it in the lives of his parents before his mother's death and in the faraway smile that would sometimes steal across his father's face after. But now . . . ?

He held up the strands to the firelight, allowing the currents of air from the hearth to lift and stir the gossamer threads, weaving, then unweaving them in twists of color. *Like your thought of her,* he admitted to himself, *weaving and unweaving. You busily unweave your connections to her by dissuading Bingley and yet reweave them when alone with your undisciplined thoughts and stolen tokens.*

A knock at the door caused Darcy to start. Quickly he laid the threads once more in the book and snapped it shut. "Enter."

Hinchcliffe took a step inside. "Mr. Darcy, there is a note here without direction and in a hand I do not know. It is addressed in a rather cryptic fashion. I though you would wish to see it immedi-ately." So saying, he advanced and held out a cream-colored mis-sive with no decoration or hint as to its sender.

"Thank you, Hinchcliffe." Darcy took the note and, nodding his dismissal, waited until his secretary had departed before open-ing the sheet to the lamplight.

> *Sir,*
>
> *Your instructions are received and will be followed precisely. I have sent to B, who, as you can guess, was quite surprised at my arrival and received word he will quit his rooms tomorrow for Aldford Street. I rely on you, sir, for his deliverance, knowing how well that reliance is placed.*
>
> *C.*

Darcy crumpled the note and threw it into the fire. "The answer to all your ambitions," he jeered aloud at himself. "To be Caroline Bingley's 'reliance' and her brother's 'deliverer'! Good God, man, what office shall be next? Archbishop, surely!" He slumped back into his chair, only to be brought up again by a second knock at the door.

"Yes, what is it!" he shouted.

The door opened by the hand of a very young servant girl, who with wide blue eyes and a small voice, announced, "You . . . Your d-dinner, s-s-sir." She bobbed a wobbly curtsy, her blond curls dancing, and then fled.

Darcy stared in dismay through the open doorway framing the retreating figure. "You are becoming a regular Bluebeard, frighten-ing servant girls . . ."

"Is there aught amiss, Mr. Darcy?" It took but a moment for Witcher to appear at the door.

"No, Witcher"—he sighed—"nothing is amiss but my humor."

"Maddie did nothing untoward then, sir?"

"Maddie?"

"My granddaughter, Mr. Darcy. She came to announce dinner, sir. First time abovestairs, sir." Witcher puffed a little with grandfatherly pride. Darcy's spirits sank another notch.

"Your granddaughter!" He went over to his desk and, opening a drawer, fished out a shilling. "Here, for your granddaughter, to celebrate the success of her first day abovestairs." Beaming, Witcher accepted the largesse with a promise to bestow it upon the girl later that evening.

"Your dinner is ready, Mr. Darcy. Jules has prepared a lovely repast of your favorites that awaits your attention. Shall I have it served?"

"Yes, please. I will be there directly." When Witcher had left him, Darcy retrieved his book and placed it carefully back on the shelf, stroking the ends of the silken tangle as he did so. For a moment he paused and allowed her face to arise before him. Shaking his head gently at the vision, he let his hand fall to his side. "No, you must leave," he whispered, "for I am his deliverer." With heavy deliberation, he turned his back to her and, crossing the library and entering the hall, closed the library door quietly behind him.

ACKNOWLEDGMENTS

Many expressions of gratitude are due to a great number of people who have encouraged me along the way to publication of this book. The first go to my friends and fellow writers at Crown Hill Writers' Guild, Susan Kaye Blackwell and Laura Louise Lyons, whose support, advice, and "bracing admonitions" broke more than one instance of writer's block. The next goes to my husband, Michael, my "Sword-brother" in the battle to write Darcy's story in a manner faithful to both Austen and the man we both knew Darcy to be. Third, a great debt of gratitude goes to Margaret Coleman, whose beautiful covers on the Wytherngate Press edition of the series had no small part in their success. Many, many thanks are due to Lloyd Jassin for his excellent representation and promotion. Last, warm and grateful thanks to all those readers at Austenesque, the Republic of Pemberley, the Derbyshire Writer's Guild, and Firthness for their constant encouragement and enthusiasm for this project.

Bless you all!

AN ASSEMBLY SUCH AS THIS

SUMMARY

In this, the first book of her *Fitzwilliam Darcy, Gentleman* trilogy, Pamela Aidan reintroduces us to Jane Austen's Mr. Darcy— through his own eyes. We meet Darcy during his visit to Hertford- shire to see his friend Charles Bingley at his estate, Netherfield Park. There he struggles to maintain "proper reserve" in the face of crude country manners, surprising country misses, and Caroline Bingley's country plots! Revealing to us Darcy's growing fascina- tion with Elizabeth Bennet, the book culminates with the disas- trous ball at Netherfield—where he and Elizabeth quarrel—and his subsequent return to London with the express intention of for- getting Elizabeth and keeping Charles from ever returning to Hertfordshire.

DISCUSSION POINTS

1. Darcy notes with pleasure that he's assuming the same role of educator to Charles Bingley as his father once assumed for him. What does this insight tell you about Darcy and his rela- tionship with the Bingleys?

2. Charles Bingley is often found expressing his gratitude to Darcy for his assistance, advice, and various acts of goodwill. But Darcy cuts him off every time. Why do you think he does this?

3. At the Assembly that opens the novel, Darcy claims that only the Bingley and Hurst sisters are worth dancing with or talking to. Why, then, does he take such joy in rebuffing Caroline's advances?

4. Darcy often notes with disdain the "ambitions" of the various women he encounters at functions, both in Hertfordshire and London. Compare his two worst nightmares—Caroline Bingley and Mrs. Bennet, or "the tabby" as Darcy calls her.

5. At Squire Justin's, Darcy first begins to wax poetic to himself about Elizabeth. He compares her eyes to fine French brandy, notes her fingers as "delicately formed," her brow as "lovely," and is otherwise enchanted by her. What is at war within Darcy? Why is he so resistant where Charles leaps forward with abandon?

6. When Darcy finally confesses to himself his feelings for Elizabeth, he checks himself by remembering "he had been well prepared from birth for his station in life and what was due his family." What do you think he means by this?

7. After Darcy and Caroline compile an outrageous list of accomplishments that the perfect woman must possess, he muses, "Would the embodiment of that list offer a better surety of his future happiness than a woman who was true, pure, and lovely?" What do you think?

8. Fletcher and Darcy butt heads several times over the course of the novel. Do you sympathize with Fletcher, given his attempts to surreptitiously help his master find happiness? Or is he overstepping his bounds as a valet, selfishly attempting to reach "the pinnacle of his profession" through Darcy?

9. How do you feel about the ending of this first part of the trilogy? Darcy is introspective and aware of his dubious motives in keeping Bingley away from Hertfordshire, yet at novel's end he is still continuing with them. Why?

10. What other Jane Austen novels would you like to see Aidan's take on? If you were to write a spin-off, which novel or series would you choose and why?

11. In the original *Pride and Prejudice*, Darcy's standoffishness is often attributed to his high social standing, as if snobbery were a part of being a gentleman. Now that you've been given a glimpse into what might have been going through Darcy's head, what do you think of this opinion of him?

12. Do Austen's characters, as portrayed by Aidan, live up to your expectations? How are they similar to their counterparts in *Pride and Prejudice*? How are they different?

ENHANCE YOUR BOOK CLUB EXPERIENCE

1. Don your Regency best (the nicest gown in your closet will do—and don't forget a bonnet!), whip out your finest china, and host your next Book Club meeting over tea and sweets that even Darcy wouldn't pass up.

2. Call your local Chamber of Commerce, Tourism Board, or check out the Historical Museums' Guide for Historical Museums in the United States (http://www.censusfinder.com/guide_to_historical_museums.htm) and the National Register of Historic Places (http://www.cr.nps.gov/places.htm) to find a grand estate open to the public in your region. Have the members of your Club meet there for a tour through the high life. Can't you just imagine the ladies strolling down that carpeted marble staircase?

3. Spend some time browsing the Internet checking out the many Austen fansites, such as The Republic of Pemberley (http://www.pemberley.com), Misjudgments (http://www.dreamcreations.net/pride/), and http://www.visitprideandprejudice.com.

Q&A with Pamela Aidan

An Assembly Such as This *is your first novel. Have you ever written fiction before the* **Fitzwilliam Darcy, Gentleman** *trilogy?*
No, the trilogy is my first venture into fiction or extended writing of any kind beyond college papers.

What inspired you to begin writing fanfiction for **Pride and Prejudice?**
Pride and Prejudice has been my favorite literary novel since high school, one that I returned to again and again, but I believe the credit for turning me into a writer belongs to the BBC/A&E version produced in 1995 and the director and actors who created the first truly faithful rendition ever attempted. It was a marvelous, inspiring interpretation. Further, it was Colin Firth's performance that really opened up my eyes. Darcy is so sketchy in Austen and very unlikable, but Firth's acting brought to the fore intriguing suggestions of who Darcy might really be. Darcy's side of the story suddenly begged to be explored. I had hoped someone would take up the challenge, but it seemed that if I wanted his side of the story, I'd have to write it myself! Believe me, it was with great fear and trembling—I have immense respect for Austen—and a certain amazement at my own audacity that I began this "traipsing after Jane!"

Besides leading to independent spin-off novels, what role do you think fanfiction plays in the world of books and publishing?
Fanfiction can revive interest in the original novels from which they are derived, bringing them back into public awareness after decades or a century or more of neglect. It breathes new life into older stories and reintroduces the great characters of literature. The part fanfiction has to play is that by appropriating riveting characters and plot outline, people, who may never have thought to try to write, learn the craft from an author they admire.

How do you think working as a librarian influenced your work as an author?

My work as a librarian gave me a tools with which to evaluate my writing and the perspective to step away from the author role into the critic's role.

Even though the Regency is long ago and far away, there is much in this novel for readers to connect to, especially the universal humanity of its characters. Which character do you most identify with?

I suppose that the character I most identify with would have to be Darcy himself, not that I see myself as Darcy or having his problems. In the course of writing the trilogy, he became as well-known to me as my own sons. In a way, I felt like Darcy's mother, intensely interested in his well-being and ultimate happiness—that he, in fact, "turns out well."

What, in your opinion, made Mr. Darcy the perfect choice for the novel's main character?

Darcy was the perfect choice because he wins Austen's most beloved and admired character by achieving a near complete reversal in his outlook and behavior that is never disclosed. It takes more than fascination or infatuation to effect such a deep-seated change that would cause a man to succor his worst enemy with no hope of appreciation or reward.

Many female readers love Jane Austen because of her witty, strong female characters. Why do you think your readers respond to Austen's (and your) male characters so well?

Austen's females don't compromise their characters or their sense of what is right in the face of pressure or to attract a man and are admired for it by her male characters. Austen's heroes actively pursue this kind of woman, women who are worthy of their respect, and they win them at the price of changing and growing. Although there might be some initial resistance or blindness to this necessity, they eventually do it and gladly in a way that affirms both their own self-worth as well as the supreme worth of their object. There's a hunger among modern women—and it seems to be international—to be seen as such a treasure worth winning at any price.

Jane Austen is often celebrated as one of the original "women's fiction" writers. Which Austen novel is your favorite, and why?
Pride and Prejudice is my favorite because the characters' strengths and flaws are so well-matched. The manner of discovery and resolution of those flaws leads the reader to know that Darcy and Elizabeth's marriage will be one of equals not only in wit and intelligence, but in humility, grace, and love. They will do very well!

We hear that you owe your marital happiness to Jane Austen. How did you meet your husband?
I was living in Georgia and halfway through the online writing of the second book in my trilogy, *Duty and Desire,* I received my first fan letter from a man. I had received many letters of appreciation, but this was the first from someone who communicated appreciation *and* criticism in a very thoughtful, insightful manner. He lived in Idaho and his fascination with Austen had begun just before the A&E movie came out when one of his daughters strongly suggested he read *Pride and Prejudice.* He did and then eagerly devoured her remaining books and fell in love with the movie. He then began to search the Internet for more about Austen, discovered my work at The Republic of Pemberley, and wrote of his pleasure in my story. I wrote back thanking him for his male perspective, especially as I was presuming to write from a man's point of view. His next communication to me was written *as* Darcy! What a shock to open up an e-mail from my own character commending me on the job I was doing creating his life! We continued to correspond about the story (Michael writing as himself) and then eventually on a personal level for almost four years be-

fore we ever met. A year after we met, I moved from Georgia to Idaho and we were married. We share so many things and are extremely happy with each other! Women have asked me where to find a Darcy; I tell them he's already taken!

What can readers expect to see from you next?

Many readers have begged for more about Darcy and Elizabeth, of course, but they have demanded more about the characters which I have created as well. It is my intent to explore Lord Dyfed Brougham's mysterious life and his intentions toward Georgiana Darcy in the midst of the changes brought by the end of the Napoleonic Wars and its effect on the entire Darcy family.

Journey back to the world of
Pride and Prejudice in
Pamela Aidan's next novel in the

Fitzwilliam Darcy,
GENTLEMAN
series,
Duty and Desire

coming from Touchstone in
October 2006

Natural Frailty

". . . through him who liveth and reigneth with thee and the Holy Ghost, now and ever. Amen."

Darcy recited the collect for the first Sunday in Advent, his prayer book closed upon his thumb as he stood alone in his family's pew at St——'s. The morning had dawned reluctantly, appearing determined to shroud its rising with a fog drawn up from the snow-covered earth. It seeped, cold and pitiless, into the bones of man and beast, and seemed to cling to the very stones of the sanctuary. Darcy shivered. He had almost forgone the services, his temper unimproved by the passage of the night, but habit had pulled him out of bed, and knowing his staff had arisen early in the expectation of his attendance, he had dressed, broken his fast, and departed.

His dark green frock coat buttoned high against the chill, Darcy surveyed the richly appointed hall, its architecture and furnishings encouraging his eye to travel upward to the soaring ribs of the ceiling and the grandeur of the colored light that fell from the great windows. His gaze falling, he noted with little surprise that, although this day marked the first Sunday of that season of joy, the church was not overfull. It rarely was. Few of the families whose names graced sumptuous gifts of panel, stained glass, or plate deigned to grace the repository of their munificence with their actual presence. That, however, had not been the Darcy family's practice. And although he stood alone, in his mind's eye Darcy could well imagine his forebears in sober reflection in the pew beside him.

The first Scripture reading of the morning was announced, and Darcy opened his book to the selection for the day.

"Owe no man anything, but to love one another: for he that loveth another hath fulfilled the law . . ."

The click of boot heels and rattle of a sword in its sheath echoed in the vastness behind him, distracting Darcy from the text. In the next moment, he was forcefully nudged down the pew by a scarlet-clad shoulder.

"Good Lord, it is wretched weather! Thought you might stay home this morning. Need to speak to you," Colonel Richard Fitzwilliam whispered loudly into his cousin's ear.

"Quiet!" Darcy whispered back tersely, half amused, half annoyed at Fitzwilliam's characteristic irreverence. He skewered a corner of his book into his cousin's arm until he surrendered and reached for it. "Here . . . read!"

". . . if there be any other commandment, it is briefly comprehended in this saying, namely, Thou shalt love thy neighbor as thyself . . ."

"Ouch! Fitz. Is that bloody 'loving thy neighbor'?" Fitzwilliam looked at him reproachfully as he rubbed his arm.

"Richard, your language!" Darcy murmured back. "Just read . . . here." He pointed to the place, and Fitzwilliam bent his head to the text, a large grin on his face.

". . . let us therefore cast off the works of darkness, and let us put on the armor of light. Let us walk honestly, as in the day; not in rioting and drunkenness . . ."

"That leaves out the Army," Fitzwilliam quipped out of the side of his mouth. "Navy, too."

". . . not in chambering and wantonness . . ."

"Down goes the peerage."

"Richard!" Darcy breathed menacingly.

". . . not in strife and envying. But put ye on the Lord Jesus Christ, and make not provision for the flesh, to fulfill the lusts thereof."

"Finished off the entire ton with that one." Fitzwilliam glanced over his shoulder. "But none of *them* are about, so here endeth the lesson."

Darcy rolled his eyes and then stepped heavily on his cousin's booted foot, for which encouragement to piety he was rewarded with an elbow in his side. They sat down, Darcy putting space between himself and Fitzwilliam. Another grin flickered across the Colonel's face as the two turned their attention to the Reverend Doctor's sermon upon the Gospel of St. Matthew, Chapter 21.

By the time the good Doctor came to the multitudes of Jerusalem spreading their garments and branches in the way, Fitzwilliam had leaned back and, with crossed arms, fallen into a pose that could well be mistaken for a nap. Darcy shifted his position, placing his boots closer to the foot warmers, and assayed to attend to the sermon, which had departed from the text and now drifted into the realm of philosophical discourse. It was rather the same sort of plea to the rational mind and self-interested morality that he had heard expounded innumerable times before. The "infirmity of the nature of man" was lamented, and the "occasional failings and sudden surprises" of the petty transgressions he was heir to lightly touched upon and softly laid at the feet of the "natural frailty" that resided in the human breast.

Natural frailty! Darcy stirred at the familiar expression and looked down at the tips of his boots, his lips compressed in an unforgiving line as he tested the appellative against his own experience at the hands of a certain other. The exercise produced unwelcome implications. Was he tamely to accept "frailty" as the explanation— nay, the excuse—for behavior as invidious as that which George

Wickham had visited upon his sister, Georgiana, and himself? Was he expected to pity Wickham for his weakness, succor him? Resentment, as bitter as it was cold, reawakened in his chest, and the Reverend Doctor was attended to with a more critical ear.

"In such times," intoned the minister, "we must lay hold of the unqualified mercy of the Supreme Being, who will, in nowise, hold us to an account so strict as to end in our disappointment, but who offers us now in Christ the cordial of a moderated, rational requisition of Divine justice. If sincerity has been your watchword and the performance of your duty has been your creed, then with justified complacency you may rest upon the evidence of your lives."

Evidence! What complacency could Wickham's "evidence" afford him? *Surely, he is beyond any claim to mercy!* Darcy's umbrage protested, a niggling unease attacking the edges of his certainty. He leaned back and crossed his arms over his chest, mirroring in knife-edged attention what his cousin did in slumber.

"And, if exempt at least from any gross vice," the Doctor continued, "or if sometimes accidentally betrayed into it, on its never having been indulged habitually, you may congratulate yourself on your inoffensiveness to your Creator and society in general. Or if not even so"—the Doctor delicately cleared his throat—"yet on the balance being in your favor or, on the whole, not much against you, when your good and bad actions are fairly weighed, and due allowance is made for human frailty, you may with assurance consider your portion of humanity's contract with the Almighty fulfilled and the rewards of blessedness secured."

Darcy stared at the pulpit, his mind and body forcibly communicating afresh to him the odium of Wickham's deeds, and his reanimated rage forged new links in the chain of his soul-deep resentment. Would Wickham escape even the bar of eternal justice? "On the balance . . . not much against . . . fairly weighed . . . due allowance!" Wickham himself could hardly have pled his case with more eloquence and sympathetic appeal! Darcy's jaw tightened—a dangerous, darkling eye the only relief from a chilling, stony countenance.

The Reverend Doctor continued. "To that end, 'Know thyself,' as the philosopher says, and in prudence of mind, conduct yourselves according to the advice of St. James as to useful good works and, certainly, in the performance of your duty. But always, my dear congregation, *moderately,* as befits a rational being. Thus endeth the lesson. Amen." The Doctor closed his Bible upon his notes, but Darcy could not so easily shut up his roiling anger and indignation. His whole being demanded action, but he could neither move to relieve it nor guess what course would satisfy its demands.

The choir stood to sing the recessional, the rustle of their unison movements and the triumphal chords of the organ rousing Fitzwilliam from his inattention. He sat up straight and blinked, owl-like, at his cousin. "Did I miss anything?" He yawned as they came to their feet.

"It was much the same as always," Darcy replied, averting his face from his cousin, who would need but a glance to know something was amiss. Taking advantage of Fitzwilliam's ritualistic endeavors to shake loose from the effects of slumber, Darcy slowly retrieved his hat and book. A diversion was required. With a studied carelessness, he turned to his cousin. "Save for when His Grace, the Duke of Cumberland, ran down the aisle, confessing to the murder of his valet."

"Cumberland!" Fitzwilliam's eyes sprang open, and he swiveled halfway round before catching himself and turning on Darcy. "Cumberland indeed! Badly done, Fitz, taking advantage of a poor soldier worn out in the service of—"

"In the service of the ladies of London, shielding them from the terrors of a moment of boredom!" Darcy snorted. "Yes, you have my unalloyed sympathy, Richard."

Fitzwilliam laughed and stepped into the aisle. "Shall you mind me stretching out my boots under your dinner table today, Fitz? His Lordship and the rest of the family left for Matlock last week, and I am sore in need of a quiet meal away from the soldiery. I think I'm getting too old for kicking up continually." He sighed. "Settled and quiet would, I believe, answer all my ideas of happiness. In truth, it is beginning to appear highly attractive."

"'Settled and quiet' was exactly what you were during the greater part of services this morning, but"—Darcy smiled tightly as his cousin protested his perception of the matter—"I'll not berate you upon that score."

"As you said, 'it was much the same as always.'"

"Yes, quite so," Darcy drawled. "Rather, tell me the name of the 'highly attractive' lady with whom you aspire to be settled and quiet."

"Now, Fitz, did I mention a lady?" The heightened color around Fitzwilliam's stock belied the carelessness of his question.

"Richard, there has *always* been a lady." They had, by now, reached the church door, and with more reserve than usual, Darcy nodded to the Reverend Doctor. As they stepped out from the doorway, Darcy's groom, Harry, who had been watching for them, motioned for the carriage, which smartly rolled forward to the curb.

"This is the most deuced awful weather." Fitzwilliam shivered as he waited for Harry to open the door. "I hope we are not in for an entire winter of it. Glad the pater and mater left for home when they did." He climbed in behind Darcy and hurriedly spread a carriage robe over his legs. "By the by, Fitz"—he squinted across at his cousin as the carriage pulled away—"is that the knot that cut Brummell off at the knees? Show your poor cousin how it is done, there's a good fellow. The Roquefort is it?"

"The Roquet, Richard," Darcy ground back at him. "Not you as well!"

❧

"Fitz? Fitz, I do not believe you have heard a thing I have said!" Colonel Fitzwilliam put down his glass of after-dinner port and joined his cousin's vigil at his library window. "And it was rather witty, if I must say so myself."

"You are wrong, Richard, on both counts," Darcy replied drily, his face still set toward the panes.

"On *both* counts?" Fitzwilliam leaned in against the window's frame for a better look at his cousin's face.

Darcy turned to him, his lips pursed in a condescending smile. "I heard *every* word you said, and it was *not* witty. Amusing? Perhaps, but not anything that would pass for wit." He lifted his own glass and finished off the contents as he awaited Fitzwilliam's counter to his thrust.

"Well, I shall be glad, then, to be considered 'amusing' according to your exacting taste, Cousin." Fitzwilliam paused and cocked a knowing brow at him. "But you must admit that you were not devoting your whole attention to me and have not acted yourself today. Anything you care to tell me?"

Darcy glanced uneasily at his cousin, silently cursing his acute powers of observation. He had never been able to hide anything from Richard for long; his cousin knew him far too well. Perhaps the time had come to speak his concerns. Taking a deep breath, Darcy turned back to the warm haven of his library. "I have had several letters from Georgiana in the last month."

"Georgiana!" Fitzwilliam's teasing smile faded into concern. "There has been no change, then?"

"On the contrary!" Darcy plunged on to the heart of the matter. "There has been a very marked change, and although I welcome it most gratefully, I do not entirely comprehend it."

Fitzwilliam straightened. "A *marked* change, you say? In what way?"

"She has left off her melancholy and begs forgiveness for troubling us all with it. I am instructed—yes, *instructed*," Darcy repeated at the disbelieving look Fitzwilliam returned him, "to regard the whole matter no longer, as *she* does not, save as a lesson learned." Fitzwilliam uttered an exclamation. "And that is not all! She writes that she has started visiting our tenants as Mother did."

"Is it possible?" Fitzwilliam shook his head. "The last time we were together, she could not as much as look at me or speak above a whisper."

"There is yet more! Her last letter was most warmly phrased, and if you may be persuaded to believe it, Richard, she offered *me* advice on a matter about which I had written her." Darcy walked over to his desk while Fitzwilliam pondered his words in stunned silence. He opened a drawer, withdrew a sheet, and held it out to his cousin. "Then, when I had returned to London, Hinchcliffe showed me this."

"The Society for Returning Young Women to Their Friends in the Country . . . one hundred pounds per annum," Fitzwilliam read. "Fitz, are you playing me a joke, because it's a damned poor one."

"I am not joking, I assure you." Darcy retrieved the letter and faced his cousin squarely. "What do you make of it, Richard?"

Fitzwilliam cast about for his port and, finding it, threw back what remained. "I don't know. It appears incredible!" He looked at Darcy intently. "You said her letter was 'warmly phrased.' She sounded *happy*, then?"

"Happy?" Darcy rolled the word about in his mind, then shook his head. "I would not describe it so. Contented? Matured?" He looked to his cousin in an uncomfortable loss for words. "In any event, I will join her at Pemberley in a few days' time, and I intend to keep her by me." He paused. "I bring her back to Town with me in January."

"If she has improved as you believe . . ." Fitzwilliam allowed his sentence to dangle as he stared into his empty glass, his brow knit.

"Do you go to Matlock for Christmas, or must you remain in Town? You could then see for yourself and advise me, for I would value your opinion, Richard." Darcy's steady look into his cousin's eyes underscored his words.

Fitzwilliam nodded, acknowledging both the import and the singularity of Darcy's request. "I am granted a week's leave and had not yet decided where to spend it. His Lordship will be much pleased to see me at Matlock, and Her Ladyship will, of course, be cast into transports that all her family are home. Shall you host the family for a week as in Christmas past?"

Darcy nodded, and after replacing the letter in his desk, he poured his cousin and himself more of the port. He tipped the glass to his lips after saluting him, letting the pleasant burn slide down his throat as he closed his eyes. There was more he wished Richard's views upon, but how to begin?

"I have seen Wickham." Darcy's quiet announcement broke the silence like the crack of a rifle shot.

"Wickham! He would not dare!" Fitzwilliam fairly exploded.

"No, we met quite by accident while I was accompanying Bingley in Hertfordshire. Apparently, he has come upon enough money to purchase a lieutenancy and has joined a militia stationed in Meryton."

"A militia! Wickham? He must be at the end of his resources, or hiding from pressing obligations, to do so. Wickham a soldier! I wish, by God, I had him under *my* command!"

Fitzwilliam paced the length of the room, then turned and demanded, "Did you speak with his commanding officer? Tell him what a villain he's acquired?"

"How could I?" Darcy remonstrated in response to Fitzwilliam's glower. "I would be called upon to furnish proof that neither I— *nor you*—can ever give." Darcy held Fitzwilliam's blazing eyes with his own until the latter's shoulders slumped in acknowledgment. Darcy indicated the armchairs by the hearth, and both sat down heavily, their faces turned away each from the other in private, frustrated thought. For several long minutes the only sound in the room was a wind blasting against the windowpanes.

"Richard, how do you account for Wickham?"

Fitzwilliam raised a blank face. "Account for him?"

"Explain him." Darcy bit his lower lip, then let out the breath he was holding and expanded on a question that had plagued him for over a decade. "He received more than he could have dreamt of from my father and was put in the way of advancing well beyond his origins. Yet he squandered it all, even as it was given, and repaid all my father's solicitude with the attempted seduction of his daughter." He paused, took another swallow of the port, then continued in a lowered voice, "Would you call it a 'natural frailty'?"

"Natural frailty! He's a blackguard, and there is the beginning and end of it!" Fitzwilliam roared. He stopped then and mastered himself before continuing in a more subdued tone. "And so he was from the start, as you have cause to remember. I may be only a year older than you, but I saw him playing his hand against you even when we were children."

"My father never saw it." Darcy swirled the liquid in his glass.

"Humph," Fitzwilliam snorted. "As to that, I am not entirely convinced. Your father was an unusually perceptive man. I cannot help but think he had Wickham's measure, although why he did not act, I cannot say. But in one thing he *was* deceived. I do not believe he could ever have conceived of Wickham's harming Georgiana. Nor could any of us! We knew him to be a sneak, thief, liar, and profligate, but"—Fitzwilliam pounded the arm of his chair—"even we, who suffered his tricks, could not guess the depths of his viciousness!"

"Perhaps he only fell into it accidentally. The pressures of his debts . . . time against him . . ." Darcy recalled the morning's sermon.

"Accidentally fell into it! Fitz, it was a cold-blooded, carefully planned campaign! Probably was about it for months!"

"But, Richard." Darcy faced his cousin directly, his countenance awash with confliction. "Human frailty cannot be so summarily dismissed. I make no claims to be immune from its effects, and you, surely, do not, as you appeal to it regularly! We all hope that, given its consideration, the balance will weigh out in our favor for our attention to duty and to charity."

Fitzwilliam cocked his head to one side and looked deeply into his cousin's eyes. "That is true, Fitz," he replied slowly, "and I am no theologian . . . or philosopher, for that matter. That is rather your line than mine. But if you are asking me whether we are to excuse Wickham's behavior to Georgiana because he could not help himself or if, in the end, his scale will be tipped to the good, I beg leave to tell you, Cousin, you may go to the Devil! For, barring sudden and immediate sainthood, the creature's a rogue of the deepest dye and will remain so. Even the Army can't change that!"

A knock at the door prevented Darcy from addressing his cousin's position. He called permission, and Witcher entered, carrying a silver tray on which lay a folded note.

"Sir, this just came, and the boy was told to wait for a reply."

"Thank you, Witcher," Darcy replied, plucking up the note. "If you would wait a moment, I shall pen a reply directly." The seal broken, he unfolded the sheet and immediately recognized his friend Charles Bingley's scrawling hand.

> *Darcy,*
> *It is the strangest thing, but Caroline has removed to Town and shut up Netherfield, saying she cannot be happy in Hertfordshire! And intends to stay in London for Christmas—Louisa and Hurst as well. Needless to say, I have removed myself from Grenier's and am now comfortably at home. (As comfortably as may be, in all events.) Therefore, please present yourself in Aldford Street for dinner on Monday evening, as I will be quite absent from the hotel. That is, unless you would rather dine at the hotel. Please advise me!*
>
> > *Your servant,*
> > *Bingley*

Darcy looked up at Fitzwilliam. "It is from Bingley. He desires my advice on whether we should dine at his home or elsewhere." He rose from the chair and went to his desk.

"Thunder an' turf, can't the puppy decide even where he will eat without your help?"

"It would appear not." Darcy chuckled mirthlessly. "But I cannot fault him at present as I have been the instrument of his misdoubt." He reached for his pen, inspected the point, and dipped it into the inkwell.

"You have been encouraging him to depend upon you far too much, Fitz," Fitzwilliam warned him.

"That is the irony of it." Darcy wrote his reply that Aldford Street was acceptable. Bingley's sister Caroline would, he knew, be quite incensed with him if he avoided her at this juncture. "Until a few weeks ago, I was pushing him out from under my wings. But something arose in Hertfordshire that proved beyond his powers, and I am forced to play mother hen once more. Here, Witcher." Darcy sanded and folded the note, then placed it on the tray. "Now, let us leave the subject!"

"I am yours to command, Cousin!" Fitzwilliam sketched him a bow. "What do you say to a few racks of billiards before I must report back to the Guards? And perhaps," he added slyly, "we might agree to a little wager on the results?"

"Shot your bolt already this month, Cousin?"

"Blame it on the ladies, Fitz. What's a poor man to do? Natural frailty, don't you know!"

A few racks of billiards later, Darcy found his purse a bit lighter and his cousin's smile correspondingly broader. Although, for Richard's benefit, he made a show of chagrin at his losses, he was in nowise displeased to part with the guineas that would see Fitzwilliam comfortably through to the end of the quarter. Darcy knew his cousin to be generous to a fault with the men—boys, really—under his command, particularly those who were younger sons, as he was. The Colonel looked after them rather like a mother hen himself, making sure they wrote home, rescuing them from scrapes, and roughly cozening them into creditable specimens of His Majesty's Guard. But such shifts required expenditures that his quarterly allowance could not always cover without curtailing Fitzwilliam's own varied activities. Applying to His

Lordship for additional funds was not a course his cousin desired to pursue on a regular basis. Therefore, Darcy unfailingly made his box available to his cousin for interests that they shared, such as the theater and opera, and for those they did not, the occasional wager on the roll of a ball or turn of a card provided what was lacking. This arrangement was never acknowledged by either, of course, but was understood, the funds needed being generously lost on the one hand and graciously received on the other.

"Well, old man, I shall display some unwonted mercy and take myself off to the Guard before I win Pemberley from you." Fitzwilliam stretched out his shoulder muscles before reaching for his regimentals. He slid the guineas into an inner pocket and shrugged into the scarlet.

Darcy feigned a grimace. "So you keep saying, but the day has not yet come, nor will it, Cousin." He picked up his own coat and led the way out to the stairs, Fitzwilliam behind him. "You will come, then, Christmas week?" he asked.

"Depend upon it," Fitzwilliam replied as they descended the stairs. "You have me confounded with this news of Georgiana, and even did I not share guardianship of her, I should be concerned on the basis of our close relationship alone. Besides, it has been too long since we have shared Christmas! Her Ladyship will be in high gig to have me home *and* spend Christmas at Pemberley again." They reached the hall, and Fitzwilliam turned a serious mien upon his host. "She has been concerned about you, Fitz, about both of you, really. This invitation will, I am sure, ease her mind."

"My aunt's solicitude is appreciated," Darcy assured his cousin, "and I confess I have been negligent in my correspondence with her of late. That will be remedied. I shall write her tonight!"

"Then I'll leave you to it. Do me a kindness and tell her that you saw me today and that we dined together, et cetera, et cetera." A sudden thought seized him. "And don't fail to mention I was in church, there's a good fellow! She will be glad to hear from you, of course, but doubly glad to know her scapegrace of a son spent a sober Sunday. I would write her myself, but she will *believe* you."

Witcher opened the door at his master's nod, and the cousins gripped each other's hands in a firm, familiar manner. "I shall so write, Richard," Darcy promised solemnly but then laughed. "Although retrieving your character to my aunt seems rather a lost cause at this late date." At Fitzwilliam's answering crow, he added mischievously, "Perhaps if you made attendance a habit . . ."

"Ho, no! Thank you, Cousin. Just write your little bit, and all will be well. Good-bye, then, until Christmas! Witcher!" Fitzwilliam nodded at the old butler and, pulling his cloak tight, ran down the steps of Erewile House and into the hack summoned for him while Darcy turned back to the stairs and the not unpleasant task of writing his aunt Fitzwilliam.

The sun had long surrendered in its battle against the clouds and fog. Vacating the field to his sister moon, he had already retired to observe what she could make of it when Darcy committed the final syllables of his letter to paper. As he sanded and blotted the missive, he noticed the darkness with regret. Now not only the weather but also the light was against any notion of a brisk turn about the square to work out the cramped sinews of his limbs and the perturbation of his mind. He laid the letter on the silver servier for Hinchcliffe to post in the morning and arose from his desk with a groan.

"Wickham!" Darcy went to the window and, leaning one arm against the frame, peered out into the night. The square before him was unnaturally silent, the sound of any passing horse or carriage being muffled by the pervasive fog. The morning's sermon had caught him off his guard and unsettled what had previously been a fixed disposition of mind. The sensation was most disagreeable, and his attempt to reason it out with Richard had proved utterly useless. The question still remained: How *did* one account for Wickham and men like him? Further, was he prepared to believe that Wickham was in little worse a position in the eyes of Eternity than himself?

Richard had not understood, thinking Darcy wished to find excuse for Wickham's actions. But the truth was that Darcy's hot resentment of the man rose because he seemed to be intimately involved in Elizabeth Bennet's poor opinion of Darcy.

Darcy straightened, walked back to his desk, and blew out the lamp upon it. Standing motionless in the dark library, he wearily reviewed the morrow's duties. In the morning he must clear his desk of any remaining items of business. Then, at half past two, present himself in Cavendish Square and commission Thomas Lawrence to paint Georgiana's portrait on their return to Town. Last, he was expected at Aldford Street for dinner with Bingley and his sister.

He closed his eyes, and another groan escaped him. Bingley! If all went well, *that* coil, at least, would be cleared. He prayed that Caroline Bingley had followed his directions precisely and restricted herself to disinterested affirmations of the doubts he had planted in her brother's mind. If she had tried to bully him into giving up Miss Jane Bennet, Darcy knew that all his own subtleties of suggestion would have been for naught and he would be confronting a Bingley with heels dug in and head lowered in mulish obstinacy.

The thought chilled him. He had not considered failure. If, against his family and friend, Bingley insisted upon Miss Bennet . . . Would he cut the connection or stand by Bingley? Stand by him, surely! But at what cost? Perhaps very little. It well might be that Bingley the married man would no longer be interested in the attractions of Town and, as relations between the wed and their bachelor fellows did tend to thin . . . Darcy shook his head. No, Bingley would remain Bingley. Although his company at some events might fail, Darcy could not doubt his continued warm regard. And that would mean . . .

"Elizabeth." He had not meant to think of Miss Bennet's sister, let alone to say her name aloud, but it echoed in the darkness of the room and fell softly against his ear. Darcy gripped the edge of his desk with painful force and commanded himself not to be a fool. "She dislikes you, idiot! That should provide proof enough against being in her company." Before he could berate himself further, the door suddenly swung open, and the blaze of a lamp held aloft caused Darcy to blink and cover his eyes.

"Mr. Darcy!" The lamp was lowered and set on a hall table. "Your pardon, sir. I heard a sound, and as the library was dark, we could not think what it could be." When his eyes had finally adjusted, Darcy was able to discern his butler in the doorway with one of the sturdier footmen behind him armed with a kitchen faggot. "With that business in Wapping, sir. All those poor souls murdered in their beds."

Darcy looked askance at his staff. "It is quite all right, Witcher. Understandable, I suppose, but we *are* a goodly distance from Wapping!"

"Yes, sir." Witcher bowed his head. "I guess it is the fog, sir. Has everyone a bit nervous not knowing what is behind or afore you. Just the kind of weather for mischief." He motioned the footman away to his post and then bowed to Darcy. "Your pardon, again, sir. Shall I leave you this lamp?"

"No, you may take it with you. Good night, Witcher."

"And to you, Mr. Darcy." Darcy waited until the elderly servant had descended the stairs to the servants' floor before starting up them to his bedchamber. Sleep would be his only escape from the piercing uncertainties of this day. "'To sleep' but, dear God, not 'to dream,' I beg you," he murmured.

Watch for the next two delightful installments of the

Fitzwilliam Darcy,

G E N T L E M A N

trilogy.

Coming in October 2006

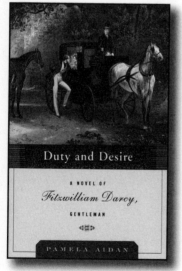

0-7432-9136-0

Coming in May 2007

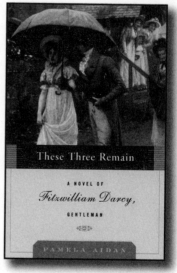

0-7432-9137-9

Available wherever books are sold or at www.simonsays.com.